P9-CQN-419

THE CELEBRATION

Center Point
Large Print

Also by Wanda E. Brunstetter and available from Center Point Large Print:

The Lopsided Christmas Cake
The Seekers
The Farmers' Market Mishap
The Blessing

The Celebration

Wanda E. Brunstetter

Center Point Large Print
Thorndike, Maine

This Center Point Large Print edition
is published in the year 2018 by arrangement with
Barbour Publishing, Inc.

The text of this Large Print edition is unabridged.
In other aspects, this book may vary
from the original edition.
Printed in the United States of America
on permanent paper.
Set in 16-point Times New Roman type.

ISBN: 978-1-68324-712-8

Library of Congress Cataloging-in-Publication Data

Names: Brunstetter, Wanda E., author.
Title: The celebration / Wanda E. Brunstetter.
Description: Center Point large print edition. | Thorndike, Maine :
    Center Point Large Print, 2018. | Series: Amish cooking class |
    Includes bibliographical references and index.
Identifiers: LCCN 2017058585 | ISBN 9781683247128
    (hardcover : alk. paper)
Subjects: LCSH: Amish—Fiction. | Amish cooking—Fiction. |
    Large type books. | GSAFD: Christian fiction.
Classification: LCC PS3602.R864 C45 2018 | DDC 813/.6—dc23
LC record available at https://lccn.loc.gov/2017058585

Dedication

To my son, Richard Jr.,
and my daughter, Lorine.
When you two were born,
it was cause for celebration!

*The LORD hath heard my supplication;
the LORD will receive my prayer.*
PSALM 6:9

Prologue

Walnut Creek, Ohio

Heidi Troyer sat on the back porch, watching Marsha and Randy play in the yard. It was hard to believe the children had been living with her and Lyle for the past four months. The time had gone so quickly since their arrival a few days before Christmas.

While not completely adjusted to her surroundings, Marsha had finally begun to speak, but usually only when spoken to. Randy was still moody at times, and occasionally didn't want to cooperate. Heidi continued to look for ways to get through to the children and make them feel loved and a part of this family.

Of course, they aren't really our children, Heidi thought with regret. *They were placed in our foster care and are still grieving the deaths of their parents.*

Breathing deeply, Heidi enjoyed the warmth of an April breeze. Spring was a rejuvenating time of year, especially with the sound of the children's laughter. She chuckled as she watched Randy and Marsha blow cottony seeds from a dandelion. Heidi remembered how she and her siblings had done the same thing when they were children.

She leaned her head against the back of the wicker chair and closed her eyes. *Lord, please give me the grace to accept things if it becomes necessary for Marsha and Randy to leave our home. And give Lyle and me the wisdom to know how to help these precious children adjust to life without their parents.*

"Are you all right?" Lyle asked as he touched her shoulder.

Her eyes snapped open. "*Jah*. I was praying— asking God for wisdom to know how to help the children adjust to their new life."

He took a seat in the chair beside her. "It's only been a few months, and the *kinner* are doing better than when they first came here."

"You're right, but only with us. When other people are around, Marsha doesn't say a word, and Randy sometimes responds negatively." Heidi released a lingering sigh. "After church last Sunday, they both stayed close to me and didn't interact with the other children. I would think by now that they'd be more comfortable around other kinner."

Lyle pulled his fingers through the ends of his thick beard. "Say, I have an idea. You might think it's a crazy notion, but it would be something to think about at least."

Her interest piqued; Heidi placed her hand on his arm. "What is it, Lyle? I'm open to any suggestions that could help Randy's attitude and bring Marsha out of her shell."

"I was thinking you could teach another cooking class."

Heidi's brows furrowed. "How would that help?"

Lyle glanced toward Randy and Marsha, who were kneeling on the grass, petting one of the barn cats. "What if this time, you held the class for children instead of adults? Randy and Marsha would be included, of course. It would give them a chance to interact with other children and, at the same time, do something fun."

Heidi cupped her chin in the palm of her hands. "Hmm . . . That is something to ponder. Of course, Marsha's too young to learn how to cook, but she could watch and maybe take part by stirring things, cracking eggs, or doing some simpler tasks that might be involved in the recipes I choose." She reached over and clasped his hand. "*Danki*, Lyle. It's an interesting idea, and I'll give it some thought."

Chapter 1

Dover, Ohio

Darren Keller poured himself a cup of coffee and headed for the living room to relax for the evening. As a full-time fireman, he had days less demanding. The men would do chores around the fire station and keep up with maintaining the trucks. Then there were days like today: unusually long and full of action. In addition to responding to three house fires, his fire department had been called out to a seven-car pileup on the interstate, involving a propane truck. Several people had been injured, and there'd been a huge fire to put out. Thankfully, no one was killed.

Darren liked his job, but it could be stressful. When his wife, Caroline, died from a brain tumor two years ago, he'd been tempted to find another job. Darren had struggled with whether it was fair to his son, Jeremy, to be raised by a single parent who might not always be there for him. There was always the possibility of being injured. Worse yet, he could be killed during the dangerous situations firemen often face. After having a heated debate with himself and seeking out a friend's counsel, he decided to stick with the job he knew and loved, remembering to take every precaution. He felt thankful for his parents' promise that, if something should happen to him, they would take care of Jeremy.

Brushing his thick, curly hair off his forehead, Darren leaned back in the easy chair and closed his eyes. An image of his beautiful wife came to mind. Darren could almost hear her sweet voice reminding him of the importance of his job. Caroline had always supported his choice to be a fireman, and he felt sure she would approve of him continuing in the profession. He couldn't count the many times his wife had said she was proud of him for the heroic deeds he considered to be normal. Even the smallest of acts, Caroline believed, were valiant, and many times she referred to Darren as a "gallant knight in shining armor." Courageous or not, it was his instinct to help and protect.

I miss you, Caroline. Jeremy misses you too. I'm doing the best I can to set a good example and teach him all he needs to know. But he needs a mom—someone to show him the softer side of life.

Hearing the *clomp, clomp* of feet racing through the hall, Darren opened his eyes. Stocking footed, Jeremy slid into the room, in hot pursuit of his dog, Bacon. The reddish dachshund zipped behind Darren's chair, and when Jeremy charged after, he slipped and fell.

"You okay?" Darren grabbed the arms of his chair, prepared to get up.

"Yeah." Jeremy blinked, and his cheeks flushed a bright pink. "Guess I shoulda been wearin' my shoes."

"Glad you're okay." Hoping to make light of the situation, Darren pointed to the floor. "Hope the floor's okay too."

With a groan, and an eye roll, Jeremy clambered to his feet. "That stupid mutt never comes when I call him."

Darren shook his head. "Now don't blame Bacon, and he's not a stupid mutt. The little fella's still a pup, and you shouldn't have been running through the house."

Rubbing his elbow, Jeremy dropped his brown-eyed gaze to the floor. "Sorry, Dad."

Darren clapped his hands. "Come here, Bacon. There's no need for you to hide."

Looking sheepish, as he crawled on his belly, the dog came out from behind the chair.

Darren reached down and rubbed Bacon's silky ears. He'd given the dog to Jeremy for his birthday last month, hoping it would not only offer the boy companionship, but teach him responsibility.

"Hey, Dad, are there any of those cookies left that Mrs. Larsen brought us last week?" Jeremy leaned close to Darren's chair. Corine Larsen was a sweet grandmotherly woman who looked after Jeremy when Darren was at work.

"Nope. I put the last of 'em in your lunch box when you left for school this morning."

Jeremy frowned. "Would ya buy some more cookies?"

"I could, but it might be fun if you learned how to bake them yourself."

Jeremy tipped his head. "Are you gonna teach me?"

Darren reached for the newspaper lying on the side table beside his chair. "No, but I saw an ad earlier about a woman who lives in Walnut Creek. Starting next month, she'll be teaching a cooking class for kids every other Saturday for six weeks. Since you'll be getting out of school for the summer next week, a cooking class might be fun. What do you think?"

"No way! There'd probably be a bunch of girls there." Jeremy folded his arms. "I think it's a bad idea, Dad."

"I don't. In fact, I'm going to call the number listed and get more details."

Berlin, Ohio

Miranda Cooper stared at her reflection in the full-length bedroom mirror. Her straight, shoulder-length auburn hair lacked body. She should probably try a different style, or maybe get a perm to fluff it up. But why bother with that? Miranda wasn't trying to impress anyone—

least of all her husband, Trent, who'd moved out of their house a month ago, because she asked him to.

"Well, it doesn't matter." She plumped her tresses. "He's not here to notice anymore. If only he hadn't . . ."

Miranda's six-year-old son bolted into her room through the open door. "Who ya talkin' to, Mommy?"

"No one, Kevin. Well, actually, I was talking to myself."

He stared up at her with a curious expression. "What were you sayin' to yourself?"

"Nothing important." Miranda ruffled the boy's sandy brown hair, then smoothed it down over his ears. She kept the sides long enough to cover her son's ears, which sometimes made him the brunt of other children's teasing. Kids could be cruel. It wasn't Kevin's fault his ears stuck out. His older sister, Debbie, was protective and usually stood up for him. With two years between them, they'd always gotten along well.

Kevin flopped down on her bed, and Miranda tickled his bare toes. "Where's your sister?"

"In her room, fixin' her ponytail." Kevin sat up. "Hey, can we get a trampoline for the backyard? Aaron's parents bought him one last week."

"That might be a question you can ask your dad, but maybe you should wait and see if the fun of it wears off for your friend. I've noticed a lot

15

of trampolines in people's backyards, but rarely see anyone playing on them." Miranda sat beside Kevin. "For now, when you go over to Aaron's house, you can enjoy his."

"Okay, Mommy." Kevin jumped up and ran out of the room.

"Don't forget to pick up your clothes!" Miranda shook her head. Getting Kevin to pick up after himself was like reminding her husband to visit the kids more often.

I wish there was something fun for Debbie and Kevin to do this summer. Miranda twirled her fingers around a strand of her hair. *Maybe I should sign them up for the cooking class I read about in the paper this morning. I think they might enjoy doing it together.*

Canton, Ohio

Denise McGuire sank to the edge of her bed, covering her face with her hands. If ever there was a time she felt like giving up her career as a Realtor, it was now. The events of today had been stressful. Her first appointment had been scheduled for nine o'clock this morning, but thanks to her daughter having a hissy fit during breakfast, Miranda had been forty minutes late. When she finally got to her office, the people had left. Not a good way to start the day—especially with prospective clients.

On top of that, by the time she dropped Kassidy off at her school, Miranda had developed a headache. Who wouldn't get a headache when they'd been listening to their eleven-year-old daughter carry on from the moment she'd taken a seat at the breakfast table until she'd gotten out of Denise's luxury sedan in the school parking lot? Kassidy's tirade had been about something so stupid—wanting to get her hair dyed dark brown like her mother's, because she hated her own red hair. No matter what Denise said to discourage her daughter, Kassidy was relentless—shouting and screaming that she wasn't loved and wished she had different parents. Before he'd left for work, Denise's husband, Greg, had tried to reason with their daughter, but he'd gotten nowhere. Greg had a way of knowing when to bolt, leaving Denise to deal with their daughter. Once Kassidy made her mind up about something, there was no rationalizing with her.

Maybe it's my fault, because I'm so busy with my job and other obligations. I need to find something we can both do together this summer, when Kassidy's out of school. Denise rubbed her forehead. *But when would I have the time? My schedule is erratic, and many people look for houses during the summer.* Normally, sales increased once the weather turned warm, which also meant Denise's income increased.

She rose from the bed and moved over to

stand by the window. The sun had already set, and shadows lay across their expansive backyard. Greg was at a meeting with some other lawyers from his firm and would no doubt get home late this evening. "Even if he was here," she murmured, "he probably wouldn't want to discuss the situation with Kassidy."

These days, with Greg's busy law practice, he was rarely at home. When he was, he wanted to relax and be left alone. Denise could relate, as she needed some downtime too. But she always made a little time each day to connect with their daughter, although sometimes she wondered why. Dealing with Kassidy's negative attitude was draining. It seemed there was no pleasing the girl.

Denise leaned her forehead against the window, hoping the cool glass might ease her pounding head. She stood up straight, as a thought popped into her head. After showing another client a home at noon, she had stopped for a bite to eat in Sugarcreek. When Denise left the restaurant, she'd seen a flyer on a bulletin board near the door, advertising cooking classes for children. At the time, she hadn't paid much attention to it, but wished now she'd had the presence of mind to write down the information.

I think I'll go back to that restaurant tomorrow and see what I can find out about the cooking classes. The activity with other children might be good for Kassidy. Denise couldn't count all the times she'd tried teaching her daughter to cook a few simple things. Maybe someone who wasn't related would have better luck.

Chapter 2

Millersburg, Ohio

"It's time for bed, Becky," Ellen Blackburn called from the kitchen, where she sat with a cup of herbal tea. She'd put a cherry pie in the oven after talking on the phone with her friend Barb. While Ellen waited for the pie to bake, she jotted a few things down on her grocery list. The store where she frequently shopped had good prices on fresh fruits and vegetables this week, and she wanted to make sure the fridge was restocked with healthy items.

Ellen was careful about food choices, not only for herself, but also for her ten-year-old daughter. She wanted to be a good role model and start Becky out young, teaching her good eating habits. Ellen believed if people ate healthy food, nine times out of ten, they would stay healthy throughout their life. Every so often, though, like this evening, Ellen got in the mood to bake something on the sweeter side.

Hearing voices from the other room, Ellen shouted once more: "Becky, please turn off the TV."

But again, her daughter did not respond.

Setting her cup on the table and pushing her chair aside, Ellen rose to her feet. *Is Becky so engrossed in the program she's watching that she doesn't hear me?*

When Ellen entered the living room, she was surprised to discover that even though the television was still on, Becky was asleep on the couch.

She pointed the remote toward the TV and turned it off, then bent down and gently shook her daughter's shoulder. "Wake up, sweetie. It's time for bed."

Becky's eyelids fluttered, then closed again.

Ellen stroked her daughter's olive-tone face. "Wake up, sleepyhead. You need to brush your teeth and go to bed."

Yawning, Becky sat up and swung her legs over the couch. "I missed the rest of my show, Mom. I wanted to see how it ended."

"I'm sure it'll be back as a rerun soon."

"Yeah, and since school will be out for the summer soon, I can watch all my favorite programs."

Ellen shook her head. "Sorry, honey, but you're not going to spend the whole summer watching TV. There are lots of other things you can do."

"Like what?"

"I'm thinking about signing you up for a children's cooking class." Ellen pointed to the newspaper lying on the coffee table. "I read about one, and I believe you would enjoy it."

Becky squinted her hazel-green eyes, the way she always did when she was thinking. "Would it be just me and the teacher, or would other kids be there too?"

"I doubt it would only be you. I'm sure other children would take part in the class."

"I don't wanna do it then."

Ellen sighed. Sometimes Becky's shyness got in the way of her making new friends. It was something she needed to work through. Learning how to cook with other children might be exactly what her daughter needed.

"We'll talk about this later. Right now, you need to get your teeth brushed."

"Okay, Mom."

Ellen watched her daughter skip down the hallway toward the bathroom. Then a smoky aroma reached her nostrils.

"Oh no!" Ellen ran toward the kitchen. "Bet I forgot to turn the oven temperature down. Maybe I'm the one who needs cooking lessons."

Walnut Creek

"I'm not tired. I don't wanna go to bed." Randy sat on the living-room floor with his arms folded, staring up at Heidi defiantly. His blue eyes held her steady gaze.

This wasn't the first time the boy had challenged Heidi's authority. Just when she felt they were gaining some ground, Randy exuded stubbornness.

In a firmer tone, Heidi said, "Please do as I say and help your sister pick up the toys."

Randy continued to sit, holding his lips in a straight line. Marsha sat beside her brother, seemingly oblivious to the conflict going on. Her blond ponytail bobbed as she rocked back and forth, holding her baby doll.

With a sigh of exasperation, Heidi turned to look at Lyle. He sat on the sofa reading the latest edition of *The Connection* magazine.

Lyle set the magazine aside and rose to his feet. Then he marched across the room, bent down, and looked directly at Randy. "Okay, little buddy, let's go brush your teeth, and then I'll tuck you into bed."

Without a word of argument, the boy gathered his toys, put them in the wicker basket across the room, and padded down the hall.

Heidi pursed her lips. *Now why couldn't Randy have done that for me?* Although pleased because the child obeyed Lyle, it frustrated Heidi that he hadn't listened to her. *Do I need to take a firmer hand or try to be more patient?*

At times like this, Heidi wondered if she had what it took to be a good parent. *Of course,* she reminded herself, *if I had been given the opportunity to raise a child from infancy, things might be different.*

For a brief moment, her thoughts went to the baby she and her husband had almost adopted—until Kendra Perkins changed her mind and decided to keep her infant daughter. Well, that was in the past, and she needed to move on.

Remembering that Marsha still sat on the floor, holding her doll, Heidi knelt next to the child. "It's time for bed, Marsha." She held out her hand.

The little girl looked up at her and blinked several times. Then, with a quick nod, she took Heidi's hand and stood.

Heidi smiled and hugged the child, relieved that Marsha hadn't put up a fuss. This was progress. Often, when Randy became stubborn, his sister did too.

Heidi led Marsha down the hall and into the room that would have been their baby's nursery, had they been able to adopt. Since Marsha sometimes woke up crying during the night, Heidi wanted her to sleep in a room close to the bedroom she shared with Lyle. When the children arrived last December, Lyle had set up two small beds in the nursery so Marsha and her brother could be together. But a few months later, Randy decided he wanted to sleep in one of the upstairs bedrooms. The little guy tried to be so independent and brave, but at times Heidi found him crying. She tried to offer comfort, but Randy always pulled away. He seemed more comfortable with Lyle. Heidi assumed the boy had been close to his father and related better to a man.

"Let's put your doll on the bed so we can take off your dress and put your nightgown on." Heidi spoke softly to Marsha, and she felt grateful when the little girl did what she asked.

Once Marsha was in her nightgown, Heidi led her down the hall to the bathroom so she could wash her face and brush her teeth. After the task was done, they returned to the bedroom.

Before Heidi pulled back the covers, she handed Marsha her doll, and then helped the child into bed. Leaning over, she placed a gentle kiss on the little girl's forehead. "Sleep well, little one."

Marsha's eyelids fluttered, then closed. In no time at all, she was asleep.

Seeing a need for the Amish-style dress the child had worn today to be washed, Heidi picked it up and quietly left the room. She'd begun dressing Randy and Marsha in Plain clothes soon after they'd come to live with them. She and Lyle were also teaching the children some Pennsylvania Dutch words. Since Marsha and Randy would be staying with them, perhaps indefinitely, it only made sense to introduce them to Amish customs, as well as their traditional language. Someday, if the children desired it, they might join the Amish faith.

After Heidi put Marsha's dress in the laundry basket, she returned to the living room, where she found Lyle sitting on the sofa reading *The Connection* again.

"Marsha's in bed sleeping. How'd things go with Randy?" she asked, taking a seat beside him.

He placed the magazine in his lap, turning to look at her. "I don't know if he's asleep or not, but at least the little guy is in bed."

"I'm beginning to wonder if he will ever respond as positively to me as he does to you." Heidi sighed. "I think Randy resents me for some reason."

Lyle shook his head. "It's not you he resents, Heidi. Randy is still trying to come to terms with his parents' death, and I suspect he might be angry at them for leaving him and his sister. If there's anything he resents, it's having to live with strangers."

She bit down on her bottom lip. "Do you think he doesn't care for wearing Amish clothes or being asked to learn our language?"

"I don't know. Randy is hard to figure out, but I've never heard him say anything negative about wearing Amish clothes or learning our Pennsylvania Dutch words." Lyle clasped Heidi's hand, squeezing it gently. "We need to be patient and keep showing the children how much we care about them. Eventually they'll come around."

Heidi slowly nodded. "I hope and pray you're right. When Gail Saunders, the social worker, comes around again to see how things are going, I wouldn't want her to think Randy and Marsha don't like it here." Tears welled in her eyes. "I want them to continue living with us, Lyle."

"So do I. We need to remember that if it's the Lord's will for the children to remain in our care, things will work out for everyone."

Chapter 3

Since I don't have an auction to preside over today, why don't you leave the kinner home with me while you visit your friend Loretta this morning?" Lyle asked as he and Heidi sat at the kitchen table having a second cup of coffee after breakfast.

She blew on the steaming brew. "I appreciate your willingness, but it'll be good for Marsha and Randy to interact with Loretta's children. They need to make some friends; don't you agree?"

"Very true, but you're with the children all day, so I thought you might enjoy some time to yourself."

"If I was going shopping for groceries, I would prefer to go alone. But since Loretta mentioned that her kinner would enjoy spending time with Randy and Marsha, it's best I take them along. Sure wouldn't want to disappoint Conner and Abby."

"All right then, I'll spend the day catching up on a few things around here." Lyle placed his coffee mug in the sink. "Since it's so nice out this first day of June, would you like me to hitch your horse to the open buggy?"

"That'd be nice." Heidi joined him at the sink, running water in both cups to prevent any coffee stains.

"Guess I'll head outside now." Lyle kissed Heidi. "I'll let you know when your horse and buggy are ready to go."

"Danki." She tenderly squeezed her husband's hand before he went out the back door.

Dear Lord, she prayed silently, *I've thanked You many times for this, but again, I'm grateful for Your blessings, including my marriage to such a thoughtful, loving man.*

As Heidi guided her horse down the road toward the Millers' place, she thought about Loretta and how she had joined the Amish church and married Lyle's friend Eli. What a blessing it had been to attend their wedding last spring. Plus, it was nice having Loretta and her two children living closer, since they'd moved into Eli's house. Heidi and Lyle had also attended the wedding of her former student Charlene this spring. Weddings and births were always time for celebration.

Heidi redirected her thoughts when she heard Randy whisper something to Marsha from the back seat of the buggy. She strained to hear what he said but couldn't make out the words.

"Look at the baby *kieh* in the field over there," Heidi called to the children.

"What's a kieh?" Randy questioned.

"It's the Amish word for *cows*." She glanced over her shoulder. "Do you remember the word for baby?"

"*Boppli*."

"That's right. And more than one boppli would be *bopplin*."

"Boppli kieh," Randy said.

Heidi nodded. "You're *schmaert*, Randy."

"You think I'm smart?"

"Yes, I do. You're a bright boy, and you catch on fast to the new words you've been taught."

"My sister's schmaert too," Randy asserted. "But she don't talk much. Not since Mommy and Daddy died."

Heidi's heart went out to the boy. "You're right, Randy. Marsha is smart." She glanced over her shoulder again and smiled at Marsha. "You're a schmaert little *maedel*."

"What's a maedel?" Randy asked.

"Maedel means girl. Marsha is a schmaert little maedel."

Marsha giggled and repeated what Heidi had said.

Hope welled in Heidi's chest. Marsha was talking a little more and beginning to learn some new Pennsylvania Dutch words.

"I'm glad you and the kinner could come visit us today." Loretta gestured out the kitchen window, where they could see her children and their two dogs playing with Randy and Marsha in the backyard. It was good to see them interacting and having a good time.

"The kinner seem to like both of your *hund.*" Heidi nodded toward the happy scene. "Marsha and Randy took a quick liking to our dog, Rusty, too."

Loretta smiled. "It's hard to believe we've had Donnelly over a year already. Eli's dog, Lady, and our Donnelly, get along well. Those two stick together like glue." She chuckled as the sound of laughter rippled through the open window like a pleasant breeze. "I have to admit, though, I wasn't too sure it was a good idea when Eli surprised us with Donnelly last year. He must have known what he was doing, however, because that pup quickly became one of the family."

"Isn't it amazing how our lives have changed in one short year?" Heidi looked toward Randy and Marsha, both squealing with glee as Donnelly lapped kisses on their faces and Lady sat patiently waiting her turn. "And now, because of our foster children, I'm going to teach a children's cooking class."

"Oh yes, that's right. When do you start the first class?" Loretta asked, handing Heidi a glass of lemonade.

"Two days from now." Heidi seated herself at the table. "I am hoping it won't be too big a challenge."

"You're a good teacher. I'm sure you'll do fine." Loretta took a seat across from Heidi. "I would have signed Abby and Conner up for your classes, but they'll be spending a few weeks with my parents this summer, and it will come right in the middle of your cooking classes."

Heidi smiled. "Well, maybe some other time, if I should ever decide to teach cooking to children again."

The sounds of the children's laughter and barking dogs grew silent. Loretta and Heidi jumped up at the same time and went to the window.

"Who's that man talking to the children?" Heidi asked.

"Oh, that's Sam Jones. He was my neighbor before the children and I moved here." Loretta shook her head. "The kids sure miss him, but he visits as often as he can."

Heidi watched as Sam made his way to the back door with the kids following close behind, and the wagging-tailed dogs trying to sniff the bag Sam carried.

"Did you sell your house in Sugarcreek yet?" Heidi asked.

"Jah. It was on the market only a week before a solid offer came in. The last time Sam visited, he told us he got some new neighbors who also have young children." Loretta picked up her glass and took a drink. "I'm sure Sam has them spoiled by now. He was the best neighbor and has the most amazing raspberry patch. I won't be surprised if he brings us some from his first picking. He's been like a grandfather to my kinner. And speaking of children . . . Will Randy and Marsha take part in the cooking classes?" Loretta asked.

Heidi nodded.

"Those two are fortunate to have you and Lyle as foster parents."

"We feel privileged we've been given the opportunity to care for them."

"Have you considered adopting the children?"

Heidi's tongue darted out to lick some sweet lemonade from her lips. "Perhaps if they do well in our care, we will be given the opportunity to become their legal parents."

"From what I can tell, they are already doing well." Loretta leaned forward, placing her hand on Heidi's arm. "I'll be praying for you and Lyle, as well as the kinner."

"Danki. If it's God's will for us to adopt Randy and Marsha, I'm confident things will work out."

Chapter 4

A re you ready for the big day?" Lyle asked when he entered the kitchen Saturday morning.

Heidi turned from the stove, where she'd been boiling a pan of eggs, and watched her husband wash his hands at the kitchen sink. "I believe so. My only concern is the age difference among those who'll be attending the class. Counting Marsha, the children range from three to eleven years old." She shook her head. "Some of the older ones may catch on quickly, while the younger children will likely have a shorter attention span and may be harder to teach."

After drying his hands, Lyle walked over to Heidi and gave her shoulders a gentle squeeze. "There you go again, worrying about something that may not happen. Remember how you fretted before your other two cooking classes started? And look how well those classes turned out. You made some lasting friendships too."

"You're right. I did."

Lyle turned, plucked a grape from the bowl of fruit on the counter, and popped it into his mouth. "You never know. The younger students might surprise you with their ability to follow directions. And maybe some of the older students will help the younger ones if they struggle or fall behind."

"I suppose." Heidi blew out a series of short breaths. "I'm also concerned about how well Randy and Marsha will interact with the other children."

"Isn't that the reason you decided to teach these classes—so they could be with other kinner?"

Wiggling her bare toes, Heidi nodded. "It doesn't mean things will work out the way I'd hoped."

Lyle glanced at the clock on the kitchen wall, then pulled another grape off its stem. "Here, eat one of these. They're sure good." He held the juicy morsel up to Heidi's mouth.

Heidi took the grape and ate it. Her husband was only trying to take her mind off her nerves, but it didn't help much.

She removed the kettle of eggs from the stove and was about to rinse them in cool water, when she heard Marsha's shrill cry from the living room.

"*Ach!* I hope she's not hurt." She hurried from the kitchen behind Lyle. Seeing Marsha on the living-room floor, Heidi rushed forward, stubbing her big toe on the leg of a chair. "Ouch!" *Guess that's what I get for not putting on my shoes this morning.*

Lyle looked at Heidi, his brows pulling in. "Are you okay?"

"I stubbed my toe, but I'll be fine."

They both went down on their knees beside Marsha. "What's wrong?" Heidi asked. "Why are you crying?"

With tears rolling down her cheeks, Marsha pointed at the scratch marks on her arm. Seeing a clump of gray fur on the floor beside the little girl, Heidi realized what had happened. One of the cats must have gotten into the house and scratched Marsha's arm. A crying child—a sore toe—she didn't need to deal with either of these right now, not with her first class starting soon.

Heidi looked at Lyle. "Would you please search for the cat while I put some antiseptic and a bandage on Marsha's arm?"

"Sure thing." Lyle rose to his feet. "Want me to see where Randy is too?"

"Jah, please do. We all need to be ready before my young students arrive for the cooking class." Heidi helped Marsha up and took her by the hand. Then she limped her way down the hall to the bathroom. Hopefully the rest of this day would go better.

Canton

"Are you ready to go, Kassidy?" Denise rapped on her daughter's bedroom door.

"Go where, Mom?"

"Remember I told you last night that I'd be taking you somewhere special this morning?"

"Yeah, I remember, but I don't feel like going anywhere today."

Denise grasped the doorknob and stepped into Kassidy's bedroom. She found her pajama-clad daughter sprawled out on the bed, doing something on her cell phone.

Denise's muscles tensed, and her chin jutted out. "I hope you're not texting anyone. And for heaven's sake, Kassidy, you're not even dressed. If you're not ready in the next fifteen minutes, we are going to be late."

Kassidy sat up, swinging her legs over the side of the bed. "Late for what?"

"I told you, it's a surprise."

"Are you and Dad taking me to get a new smartphone?" Kassidy held up her cell phone. "I hope so, 'cause this one's having some issues. Besides, it's outdated, and I'd like a better one. This phone is a piece of junk."

"Your dad's meeting a friend at the golf course this morning, and we'll talk about your phone later." Denise gestured to her daughter's closet. "Now please hurry and get dressed." She left the room before Kassidy could offer a retort.

Denise waited a few seconds, then tiptoed quietly back to the entrance of her daughter's bedroom. Peeking around the doorway, she saw

Kassidy throw her cell phone on the bed and stomp her way over to the closet. Then, as she went from hanger to hanger, trying to decide what to wear, Kassidy stiffened her shoulders and repeated her mother's words. "Now hurry and get dressed." She pulled one outfit out, throwing it on the bed, then reached for another. Kassidy didn't realize she had more clothes than some children got in a lifetime.

I hope I didn't make a mistake signing her up for cooking classes. Denise leaned away from Kassidy's door and rubbed her temples. *Did I make the right decision by not telling her about the cooking classes? Should I say something on the way to Walnut Creek, or wait until we get there and hope she's pleasantly surprised?*

Dover

"How come you don't have to work today?" Jeremy asked, looking at his dad from across the kitchen table.

Darren drank some coffee and set his mug on the table. "You're kidding, right?"

Jeremy tipped his head. "What do ya mean?"

"I told you earlier this week that I'd signed you up to take cooking classes. And last night I reminded you. How could you have forgotten so quickly?"

"I didn't forget. Just figured you'd probably get

Mrs. Larsen to take me 'cause you'd be working today."

"No, I made sure today would be free for me. I worked Monday through Friday so I could take today off." Darren took another swig of coffee. "Thought I'd drop you off at the home where the classes are being taught, then browse around some of the shops in the area until it's time to pick you up."

Jeremy's brows furrowed. "Sure wish you hadn't signed me up for this. I'm gonna feel stupid taking cooking classes with a bunch of girls."

"You don't know that. There could be other boys there too." Darren put his empty mug in the sink, reached into his pocket, and put a piece of chewing gum in his mouth. "You'd better go comb your hair so we can get going."

"Aw, Dad," Jeremy whined, "can't you at least stay with me during the class?"

"I'm sure none of the other parents are going to stay with their kids. Wouldn't you feel funny if I was the only one who did?" Darren tried to sound encouraging.

"Maybe. If I don't like the class, can I quit?"

"We'll see how it goes."

Millersburg

Ellen stood on the front porch, waiting for Becky to join her. Ever since she'd been reminded about the cooking class this morning, Becky had dragged her feet. It was out of the girl's comfort zone to interact with strangers. She'd made it clear that she didn't want to go. Ellen would not give in, however. She felt certain something as fun as taking cooking classes was what her daughter needed. Perhaps Becky would make some new friends there too.

A warm breeze came up, lifting Ellen's hair away from her face. The temperature had been rising the last few days. Summer was definitely on its way. She looked forward to taking days off from the hospital and being able to spend time with Becky. She'd arranged her work schedule so she could have every other Saturday off, which would allow her to attend the cooking classes with her daughter. Maybe after each class was over for the day, they could go out to lunch, do some shopping, or visit one of the parks in the area. Walnut Creek wasn't far from Millersburg and had a nice restaurant, as well as several gift shops to browse in.

Ellen watched the billowy white clouds overhead. Ever since she was a child she'd enjoyed studying the different shapes of the clouds, trying to imagine what her future held and always hoping she could someday be a nurse.

The screen door squeaked open and slammed shut, halting Ellen's musings. She turned and smiled at her daughter. "You ready to go, sweetie?"

Becky shrugged, dropping her gaze.

Ellen clasped her daughter's hand. "It'll be fun. You'll see."

Berlin

"Are you two ready? It's almost time to go," Miranda called to Debbie and Kevin as she stood in the hallway beneath the stairs.

"I'm coming, Mom." Debbie's ponytail bounced as she bounded down the stairs. "I can't wait to go to the cooking class."

Miranda smiled. At least one of her children looked forward to attending the class. In fact Debbie hadn't stopped talking about the class since Miranda signed her children up for it.

She wasn't sure about Kevin, though. But at least he hadn't said he didn't want to go. Debbie was always willing and eager to help Miranda in the kitchen, which was no doubt the reason she was excited to learn how to make some kid-friendly dishes.

Kevin plodded down the steps, wearing his favorite baseball hat—a gift from his dad last Christmas. *Too bad Trent doesn't spend more time with the kids instead of getting them gifts,* Miranda fumed. Even before they separated, he hadn't given Debbie and Kevin enough attention. But what was the use in thinking about that now? They needed to get going. It

41

wouldn't be good to be late for the first class.

"Let's go, kids." Miranda grabbed her purse and car keys and herded the children out the door.

After everyone buckled in, Miranda started the car. She'd no more than pulled out of the driveway when Debbie called from the back seat, "What do you think the teacher will show us how to make, Mom?"

"I don't know, honey, but I'm sure it'll be easy for you to make."

"How many other kids will be there?"

"I'm not sure about that either. You'll have to wait and see."

"I can't wait to tell my friend, Linda, about the cooking class." Debbie's tone bubbled with enthusiasm. "She'll probably wish she could take the class too."

"I hope there'll be some other boys there," Kevin said, sitting beside his sister.

Miranda nodded. She was glad her kids were open to the idea of taking the class, and hoped, for Kevin's sake, that he wasn't the only boy.

Chapter 5

Walnut Creek

As Darren drove his four-wheel drive SUV down the road, following the directions on his GPS, he couldn't help wondering what it would be like to live out here in the country. He spotted several Amish men working their fields and saw children running barefoot through the grass in their yards. Everything seemed peaceful here, at a much slower pace.

He rolled down his window and drew a deep breath. *Too bad Jeremy and I can't live in a place like this, instead of in town. Bet we'd both be a lot happier. I know I would.* With the stress of Darren's demanding job as a fireman, he was always eager to get home and unwind. *Of course,* he reasoned, *having a big yard and acreage to take care of might add more stress than relaxation.*

Darren glanced in the rearview mirror at Jeremy, sitting in the back seat with a scowl. He'd hoped by the time they got to Walnut Creek his son would have mellowed out a bit. So much for wishful thinking.

Darren still didn't plan to stay with his son for the whole time today. Instead of browsing some of the shops, he might stop in at the fire station in Berlin, since it was less than ten minutes from Walnut Creek. Darren had gotten to know a few fellow fire fighters from outside his station, both in Berlin and in Sugarcreek, since a lot of times several stations responded to the same fire. That was one of the things Darren enjoyed about being a fireman—the comradery between fellow fighters. The only time there might be a little competition was when they played a game of baseball. Even then, it was friendly competition, and afterward, they'd all meet at a restaurant to eat. Of course, the losing team had to pay for the winners' meals.

When Darren's vehicle approached a mailbox by the side of the road, showing the address he'd been looking for, he turned his vehicle up the driveway. Another car was parked near the house, and Darren watched as an attractive woman with blond hair got out, along with a young brunette girl who looked to be about Jeremy's age. The woman walked up the porch steps with an air of confidence and knocked on the door, while the girl stood beside her, head down and shoulders slumped. A few seconds later, the door opened, and mother and daughter, both wearing blue jeans and a T-shirt, stepped inside. Darren wondered if the woman planned to stay with her daughter.

He hadn't given it much thought until now, but maybe all the parents who brought their kids for the cooking class would stay—at least for today.

Jeremy groaned. "See, I told you, Dad. I'm the only boy signed up for the cooking class. Can't we forget about this and find something else to do today? I'm gonna feel stupid if I'm the only guy here today."

"You won't be the only guy." Darren thought things through a bit and changed his mind about leaving. It might be good to get to know some of the other kids' parents. "I'll be right here with you—at least for today's class, so let's get out of the car and head on in."

Jeremy opened the back door and got out, but he remained unmoving next to the SUV. Darren nudged his son and started walking across the grass toward the house. Dragging his feet, Jeremy trudged along beside him. Well, at least he hadn't gotten back in the car.

"Look Mommy, there's a horse over there in the field," Kevin pointed as they pulled into the driveway.

"Yes, honey, the Amish don't drive cars. They use a horse and buggy as their transportation." Miranda stopped the car midway up the driveway, putting the windows down so her kids could take a better look.

"They have cows too." Debbie's tone was

as enthusiastic as her brother's, and they both looked toward the barn where several cows milled around. "Do you think we can go see the animals after the class is done?"

"We'll see." Miranda took a whiff of the country air. While some people might find it offensive, to her it was calming.

"I didn't know there'd be animals here." Kevin giggled when a cat ran in front of their car. "I wonder what else they have in the barn."

"I don't know, but I hope we find out," Debbie responded. "Wouldn't it be fun if the Amish family took us for a ride with the horse and buggy sometime?"

Miranda smiled as her children laughed, watching one cat chase another into the barn. "Okay, you two. Let me find a place to park, and then we'll head inside." *Maybe this will be a positive experience for my Kevin and Debbie.*

"What are we doing out here in the middle of nowhere?" From the back seat, Kassidy tapped Denise's shoulder. "I don't see much of anything but farms and a bunch of horses and cows."

"Just relax and enjoy the ride. We're almost there."

"Almost where?"

"Here." Denise turned her car up a graveled driveway and parked it near two other vehicles. Then she turned in her seat to face Kassidy.

Kassidy huffed out a long breath. "What is this place? Looks like an old farmhouse to me."

"It is a farmhouse, and the Amish woman who lives here teaches cooking classes."

"If you're taking some cooking classes I don't see why you brought me along. I'm old enough to stay home for a few hours by myself, you know."

Denise clenched her jaw as she glanced back at Kassidy. Creases had formed across her daughter's forehead, and her eyebrows squished together.

"The classes aren't for me, Kassidy. Heidi Troyer will be teaching children how to cook, every other Saturday for six weeks."

"Huh?"

Denise pursed her lips. "I believe you heard what I said."

"So you signed me up to take cooking classes? Is that your big surprise?"

"Yes. It should be fun. I think you'll enjoy learning how to make some easy dishes."

"I'm not a child. I am almost twelve years old, so I don't need to know how to make easy dishes." Kassidy's lips moved rapidly. "And when will I be old enough to sit up front with you or just use a regular seatbelt? I'm tired of sitting in this safety seat."

Denise drew in some air and blew out a quick breath. "Just get out of the car, please."

Kassidy sat with her arms folded, unmoving.

That's just great. What am I going to do if I can't get her to go inside? Denise opened her door, then looked back at her daughter. "Please get out so we can go inside and meet Mrs. Troyer." She stepped out, went around to the other side of the vehicle, and stood by the back door. When the girl made no move to get out, Denise opened the door. "Kassidy, if you don't get out right now I'll take your cell phone."

Kassidy's eyes narrowed. "That's not fair."

"Neither is your stubborn refusal to get out of the car."

"Okay, okay." The girl's cheeks reddened as she unbuckled and slid out of the safety seat, then shut the car door. "I don't want to take a cooking class, Mom." She glanced around. "Especially not here in the middle of cow country."

"Don't be so melodramatic." Denise motioned to the two-story house. "Let's go knock on the door. I'm sure once you meet the Amish woman and some of the other students, you'll find you like it."

"I don't want to! This is stupid!"

Denise put her finger to her lips. "Keep your voice down. I will not stand for you throwing a temper tantrum out here in the yard."

"Fine, then let's go home." Kassidy's arms flailed in the open air. "You didn't even ask if I wanted to take these stupid classes."

Denise stood her ground. "We are not going

home, and you're not going to get your way this time. If you don't go inside with me, I'm taking your phone."

Another vehicle pulled in and parked. Denise watched as a woman with shoulder-length auburn hair got out, along with a young boy and a girl. She turned to face her daughter again. "See, Kassidy, there are other children here today, and they're both smiling. Let's go inside and see who else will be taking the class with you."

Kassidy took a few steps through the grass, then stopped, wrinkling her nose. "Oh, yuck! I stepped in doggie doo-doo, and now my one shoe is ruined!"

Denise glanced at the woman and her two children, all heading in their direction. "Kassidy, please keep your voice down. People are staring."

"I don't care." Kassidy lifted her foot, then hopped over to the porch stairs on the other foot. "How am I gonna get this horrible smell off my shoe?"

By this time, the woman and her children had also reached the porch. The boy pointed at Kassidy's foot and plugged his nose. "Phew! That sure stinks!"

Kassidy's nostrils flared, like a bull ready to charge. "Well, your ears stick out like bat wings." She put her thumbs in her ears and wiggled her fingers.

Horrified, Denise pointed at her daughter. "Apologize to the little boy this instant."

Kassidy shook her head, pulling off her sneaker. "He's the one who should apologize; he said I stink."

"Did not. Said *that* stinks." The boy pointed at Kassidy's shoe.

Denise grimaced. So much for hoping her surprise would be welcome. Not only did her daughter not want to take the cooking classes, but now she had a shoe covered in doggie-doo and she'd made an enemy out of one of the other students. *How much worse can it get?*

Just as the question entered her mind, Denise couldn't believe what her daughter was about to do. Still holding the shoe, Kassidy began scraping the bottom of it on the edge of the porch.

Mortified, Denise's mouth opened. "Kassidy McGuire—stop!"

Chapter 6

Denise held her throbbing temples. She could hardly believe what her daughter had done. Now, in addition to the telltale smelly smudges on Kassidy's shoe, a blob of doo-doo clung to the edge of the Amish woman's front porch.

Standing behind her son, and urging him forward, the boy's mother stepped up to Denise. "I'm sorry about Kevin's rude behavior." She nudged the boy's arm. "Tell the girl you're sorry for what you said."

He pushed his shoulders forward and mumbled, "Sorry."

Denise placed her hands on Kassidy's shoulders. "Now it's your turn to apologize for the hurtful remark you made about his ears."

"I don't want to." Kassidy folded her arms.

Denise's lips pressed together as she whispered, "Guess you're ready to give up your cell phone."

"No, I'm not." Kassidy's hands and arms went limp, as though in defeat. "Sorry for what I said." Her unconvincing tone sounded like a half-hearted apology, but at least it had been said.

Denise glanced at her watch. "It's time for the class to start and we are holding things up." She gestured to her daughter's shoe. "Leave it on the grass beneath the porch, and we'll deal with it, as well as the mess you made on the porch, after class. I'm sure Mrs. Troyer has something you can use to clean it all up."

Kassidy's face reddened as she flapped her hands. "Don't see why I have to do it. It's not my fault some stupid pooch made a mess in the grass. People ought to either keep their mutts locked up or at least, clean up after their dogs when they've done their business." She pointed to her other shoe. "And what should I do with this? I can't go inside with only one shoe on."

"Oh Kassidy, really? Just take it off and leave it here on the porch. No one is going to say anything. You can just wear your socks." Denise tapped her foot. "This discussion is over. It's time to go inside." She turned and knocked on the door.

A few seconds later, a pretty Amish woman with brilliant blue eyes and dark hair opened the door. "Welcome to my home. I'm Heidi Troyer. Please come inside." She gestured to Denise and Kassidy, and also to the other woman and her two children.

As they entered the house, Denise noticed Heidi wore a pair of flip-flops. When she looked closer, and saw Heidi's black and blue toe, Denise was tempted to ask what happened. However she didn't want to appear nosy or impolite. Especially since Heidi hadn't asked why Kassidy wasn't wearing her shoes. However, that didn't stop another boy, who looked to be close to Kassidy's age, from pointing to her feet and asking what happened to her shoes.

Kassidy wrinkled her nose. "Left 'em both outside 'cause I stepped in doggie doo-doo."

The boy snickered, until the man standing beside him said, "Don't be rude, Jeremy. You need to mind your own business."

"I'm sorry about that," Heidi apologized. "Our Brittany spaniel normally goes out in the field to do her business, but she must not have made it in time. I'll take care of cleaning your shoes after class."

Denise stepped forward. "Actually it's only one of her shoes, and there's a little more than what remains on the shoe to clean off. Thanks to my daughter's impulsiveness, most of it is now stuck to the edge of your porch. I am so sorry about that."

Heidi's brows pulled slightly inward, but then a faint smile formed on her lips. "It's okay. I'm sure we've all done that at least once in our life. We'll deal with it later. Now, if you children will follow me to the kitchen, you can introduce yourselves, and then we'll begin our first class."

Heidi was surprised when the children's parents joined them in the kitchen. She had expected they would drop their kids off and return for them when the class was over. She hadn't set out enough chairs for this many people and wondered how well the children would respond to her with their parents looking on. Surely, the adults didn't plan to accompany their children to every class. Hopefully they would only stay today, in order to help their kids become adjusted.

After they scrounged more chairs to put around the expansive kitchen table, Heidi introduced herself, as well as Randy and Marsha. Randy muttered a quick, "Hi," but Marsha hid behind Heidi, refusing to speak to anyone. This wasn't unusual, since she said very little. Heidi figured the little girl would not join in any of the conversation during today's cooking class.

"Your children are cute." The auburn-haired woman smiled. "Are they going to take part in the cooking class too?"

"Yes, they will. My husband, Lyle, and I are foster parents to Randy and Marsha." Quickly changing the subject, Heidi said, "Now, starting on my right, I'd like everyone to introduce themselves. Please tell a little about yourselves and why you decided to take my cooking classes."

The tall man with dark curly hair spoke first. "My name is Darren Keller, and I'm a single father." He gestured to the dark-haired boy beside him. "This is my son, Jeremy, and he's ten years old. I thought taking a cooking class would be something fun for him to do during his summer break." He nudged the boy. "Say hello, Jeremy."

"Uh, hi everyone." A dot of red erupted on Jeremy's cheeks.

Darren smiled at Heidi. "My son was worried he would be the only boy here today."

Heidi felt sorry for Darren's son. Would he have been more eager to speak if his father hadn't been here coaching him? She glanced at the brunette who sat next to Jeremy. "Would you and your daughter like to go next?"

The woman sat up straight, patting her perfect-looking hair in place. "My name is Denise McGuire, and this is my eleven-year-old daughter, Kassidy. I signed her up for the class so she could learn to cook, and also to give her something meaningful to do this summer."

Kassidy rolled her blue-green eyes. "I didn't even know my mom signed me up till I got here today, and I don't want to learn how to cook." The girl looked right at Heidi. "I can think of lots better things to do during summer break than spend time in the kitchen."

Heidi hadn't expected the girl to be so blunt. Maybe cooking classes for kids wasn't a good idea. She hadn't expected she'd be dealing with a problem child like Kassidy. Well, she refused to become discouraged. As time went on, and everyone got to know each other, the sessions were bound to get better.

The next parent introduced herself as Miranda Cooper. "And this is my son, Kevin, and my daughter, Debbie."

Neither child said a word. Heidi hoped her young students might be more talkative once they got busy making today's recipe.

The last parent stood and said her name was Ellen Blackburn, and that she was a single mother. She'd brought her ten-year-old daughter, Becky, to learn how to cook.

Becky's chin dipped toward her chest. No comment from her either.

Poor child, Heidi thought. *Becky must be shy, the way she's keeping her head down and not looking at anyone. It's probably best to keep things moving along.* "Thank you everyone, for your introductions. Now we'll begin making our first recipe."

Heidi went to the refrigerator, took out a tray of fresh fruit, and placed it on the table. "Today I'll be teaching you how to make a fruit salad."

"I hope it doesn't include oranges." Kassidy wrinkled her nose. "I can't stand the smell of oranges, and I'd gag if I tried to eat one."

"I do have oranges available for those of you who would like to include them, but there are other fruits to put in the salad, so you can pick and choose."

After Heidi had all the supplies set out, she asked the children to take turns washing their hands at the sink. Heidi watched in dismay as a couple of parents, obviously determined to be a part of the class, washed their hands too.

She stood at the end of the long table, holding a stack of index cards. "Here is the recipe I've written out for you to take home today." Heidi moved about the table and gave each child a card. She'd written a verse of scripture on the back, the way she'd done previously for her adult students, but she made no mention of it. Heidi hoped after the children got home, they would discover the verse and it would be meaningful to them.

Heidi had coaxed Marsha to take a seat beside Randy. Even though they couldn't read yet, she'd given them both a recipe card so they wouldn't feel left out. Then she returned to the head of the table to explain what they should do first.

Heidi first demonstrated how to hold and cut up an apple. The children picked up their dull paring knives and apples, and copied what she did on their cutting boards.

Like a mother hen, Miranda moved in close to her boy. "Kevin isn't used to cutting up food. I do all the meal preparations at home." The woman almost reached for the knife, but pulled back.

"I can do this, so don't worry, Mom." Kevin's tongue shot out and rested against the side of his mouth, while he cut up the apple into good-sized chunks.

"He's doing a fine job." Heidi stepped over

to watch him and the other children. She wasn't sure how this was going to play out. Heidi could see that some of these children didn't have a lot of experience in the kitchen.

Darren shifted in his seat. He felt ill at ease, being the only man here with his child. In order to hide his embarrassment, Darren concentrated on his son and how he responded to Heidi's instructions.

Next, Heidi showed the children how to peel an orange. Darren wasn't surprised when Kassidy held her throat as though gagging and looked away. Then lowering her voice, she muttered, "That's so easy. Anyone with common sense can peel an orange."

Darren held back a snicker when Kevin took half an orange and squeezed the juice in Kassidy's direction. She responded by sticking out her tongue. "Ha! Ha! You missed me."

"That's enough, Kevin," the boy's mother reprimanded.

Darren was glad it wasn't Jeremy who'd squirted the orange. So far, he'd been minding his manners.

"Children, as long as you are here taking my classes, you will need to be kind to one another," Heidi said. "That includes no intentional squirting or sticking your tongue out at anyone."

Aside from a little more awkwardness with

everyone in the room, the kids, for the most part, remained well behaved.

One thing that annoyed Darren a little, though, was the blond woman—Ellen. Instead of allowing her daughter to participate on her own, Ellen did everything for Becky. The girl simply sat, watching her mother take part, when she should have been doing by herself what Heidi instructed. Not only did Becky watch what her mother was doing, but she shyly glanced around at the other kids, who were cutting the fruit on their own.

Darren looked at Heidi. She was also watching Ellen. He assumed from her sober expression that she saw it too. *Maybe I'll say something to Ellen once the class is over. Would she be offended?*

After all the fruit was prepared, Heidi explained how to mix the two juices and ginger and then pour it over the fruit to lightly toss. The fruit salad looked good, but it would need to chill for half an hour.

Once everyone had put their bowl of fruit salad in the refrigerator, Heidi explained a little about the upcoming classes and what to expect. She told the parents that unless they felt they needed to be there, they weren't expected to stay during the classes. The lessons would last for two hours, so if the parents had something they'd like to do in the meantime, they could return for their children at noon.

Darren figured maybe next time he wouldn't stay, but he'd wait and see first what the other parents did.

After the cooking class ended, Heidi helped clean off Kassidy's shoe, as well as the mess on the porch. Denise apologized once more for the mess her daughter had left, but Kassidy remained silent as she stood and watched, her cheeks crimson.

Heidi didn't mind tending to the job, for she'd learned early in life how important it was to be kind and patient. Maybe this would help the contrite girl to be a little nicer. Heidi could only imagine how it would be to have a daughter as bold as Kassidy. While different from a shy child, Kassidy too could use some help learning how to act around others.

Kassidy seemed a bit more pleasant now that her shoe had been cleaned up. Denise nudged her daughter's arm. "What do you say to Heidi?"

"Thank you," Kassidy mumbled.

"You're welcome." Heidi handed the shoe to the girl.

Kassidy went over to retrieve the other shoe, and slipped it on her foot.

Not long after, Heidi waved as Denise and her daughter got in the car and pulled out of the driveway. Then Heidi grabbed the hose and turned on the water, giving the porch one more good washing.

Soon Randy and Marsha came outside and took a seat on the porch swing.

"How did you like learning to cook with the English kids today?" Heidi asked the children. "Did you both have a good time?"

"I liked eatin' the salad, but it was hard to cut up the fruit." Randy looked at his sister. "It was too hard for Marsha, but I'm glad she gotta taste the salad."

"The next class will be two weeks from today, and then we'll learn to make something else." Heidi put the hose away. "I'm going in the house now to get our lunch started. Do you two want to come inside or stay out here on the porch?"

"Think we'll stay out here awhile." Randy clasped his sister's small hand. "Me and Marsha wanna sit on the swing."

"Okay. I'll call you when lunch is ready." Heidi went inside. As she took a loaf of bread out to make sandwiches, she heard a shrill scream. Dropping the bread to the counter, Heidi rushed out the front door.

Chapter 7

When she stepped out on the porch, a blast of water shot Heidi in the face. Holding her hands like a shield, she gasped.

"Uh-oh." Randy quickly lowered the hose, holding the nozzle so it pointed toward the nearest flowerbed.

Marsha, who stood sobbing across from him, was drenched from the top of her blond head all the way down to her little bare toes.

Heidi wasn't sure what to do—scold Randy or comfort his distraught sister. She shook her finger at the boy, then quickly turned off the nozzle at the end of the hose. "I'm ashamed of you, Randy. What made you squirt your sister with water?"

He gave an undignified grunt. "Marsha said she was hot, so I cooled her off."

"I don't believe being soaked with cold water from the hose was what she had in mind." Heidi placed her hand on Marsha's wet head. "Now, Randy, please put the hose back where it belongs and make sure the spigot where the hose is connected is turned off."

"Okay." Randy paused and looked at his sister. "Sorry for gettin' you wet. Are ya mad at me?"

Still sniffling, Marsha shook her head.

As Randy stepped off the porch, Heidi leaned down and clasped the little girl's hand. "Looks like I got a little bath too. Come inside with me, and we'll get out of our wet clothes." She was thankful the social worker hadn't shown up for a surprise visit in the middle of all this. If Gail had seen what had just happened, it would not have made a good impression.

Marsha looked up at Heidi with such a sweet expression, it almost melted her heart. Truth was, she had begun to think of these children as her own.

"I don't see why we have to eat here," Kassidy grumbled as the hostess showed them to a table at Der Dutchman restaurant. "I told Hillary I'd be home before one o'clock. She was gonna come over and swim in our pool today." Kassidy reached back to flip her red ponytail.

Denise clicked her freshly manicured finger-nails against the table. "In the first place, it's not warm enough to go swimming yet. In the second place, you should not have invited your friend without checking with me first. So settle down, because we are not going home until we've eaten lunch."

Kassidy slumped in her chair. "Are you trying to punish me 'cause of what happened to my shoe?"

"Your shoe is inconsequential. What upset me

today was your attitude. You were rude and acted like a spoiled three-year-old child instead of an eleven-year-old girl who should know better." Denise released an exasperated sigh. "I've never been so humiliated in all my life."

"Well, what about me? You shouldn't have signed me up for that stupid cooking class. I already know how to cut up fruit, and everything about the class was boring."

"Is that so? First of all, you need to stop thinking of yourself all the time, and boring or not, you will be taking the next five classes." Denise spoke with clenched jaw and forced restraint. "As far as Hillary is concerned, you can call her right now and say she can't come over because you're on restrictions until you learn to have a better attitude."

Tilting her chin down, Kassidy frowned. "That's not fair, Mom. I was looking forward to spending the afternoon with my friend."

Shaking her head, Denise held firm. She'd given in to her daughter too many times in the past, and it had done nothing to improve the girl's haughty attitude or tame her temper. "Kassidy, I was looking forward to us being at the cooking class together, and look how that turned out. So get on your cell phone and call Hillary right now."

Frowning, Kassidy reached into her pocket. "My phone! It's not here."

"Did you leave it in the car?"

"No, I—I must have left it at that Amish woman's house." Kassidy's face contorted. "I remember setting it down on the table when we were eating the fruit salad. I bet it's still there." She pushed her chair aside and stood. "We've gotta go back, Mom. We need to go there now and get my phone."

"Sit down, Kassidy and quit making a scene." Denise pointed to the menus on the table. "We'll go after we've had lunch."

"But what if something happens to my phone? Those kids Heidi's taking care of are little. If one of 'em fools around with the phone, they might mess up the settings." Eyes narrowed, Kassidy's voice rose as she clutched the neckline of her blouse.

Denise put her fingers to her lips. "Calm down. I'm sure Heidi would have found your phone and put it in a safe place."

"But what if she didn't? What if—"

"All the 'what ifs' in the world won't change a thing. We'll find out about your phone when we get there." Denise pushed the menu closer to Kassidy. "Now make a decision on what you want, or I'll order for you."

Kassidy pouted, but grabbed the menu. After looking it over, she muttered, "Nothing looks good, so I'll just have a burger and fries."

Denise felt relief when a waitress came to take their order. Maybe once her daughter had food in her stomach, she'd be in a better mood. *I know I will be.* She picked up her water and took a drink. *I'm more than ready to eat lunch, and despite whatever Kassidy thinks, everything on the menu here looks good to me.*

Berlin

"What did you think of the cooking class today?" Miranda asked her children.

"I liked it, but I don't care much for Kassidy." Debbie's lips curled. "She wants her way all the time."

"Maybe since we were all strangers to one another, everyone was a little uncomfortable. I'm sure it will get better once we all get to know each other." Miranda had to admit that Kassidy was one spoiled child. *I'm glad my children aren't like that.* "How about you, Kevin? What did you think of the cooking class?"

"Guess it was all right, but I had more fun when that nice man showed us the animals after the class was over."

"It was kind of Mr. Troyer to give you a tour of their barn."

As Miranda drove toward home, she recalled how Heidi's husband had been so patient, answering the children's questions about all the animals they had on the farm. One thing that had really impressed Miranda was when Lyle glanced lovingly back at his wife, and how Heidi smiled at him, watching as he and the children ventured toward the barn.

Miranda blew a breath from her lips. *I remember when Trent used to look at me that way. When did it all go wrong?*

Before returning home, Miranda wanted to make a stop, so she pulled into the local market in Berlin. "Hey kids, how about we go in here and get some things to make toasted cheese sandwiches for our lunch?"

"Sounds good," Debbie and Kevin said in unison.

"We'll need to make it quick, though. We have to get home and let Blondie out."

Blondie was their poodle, and she got the name because of her light-colored, curly fur. Blondie was a friendly, good-tempered dog. The kids loved her, and she'd become an important part of the family.

After picking out some different cheeses, fresh bread, and a bag of potato chips, they returned to the minivan, and Miranda drove the three miles to their home.

When she pulled into the driveway, she spotted Trent's shiny red truck parked by the garage. Her husband stood in the backyard, throwing a stick for Blondie to fetch.

"Dad's here!" Debbie yelled, quickly getting out of the van after it came to a halt.

Kevin was close behind her, and they both ran to greet their father.

Miranda got the bags of groceries out of the back and headed toward the house. Like a faithful friend, the poodle ran up to greet her.

"Hey there, Blondie. Did you miss us?" Miranda smiled as the dog raised up on her hind legs and tried to sniff inside the bags. "Don't worry. I got something for you too."

As if the dog understood, Blondie gave an approving bark.

After chatting with their dad a few minutes, the kids called to Blondie and continued the game of fetch.

Miranda stopped as Trent approached. He wore a light beige shirt and a pair of darker beige, stylish slacks. While some people might think her husband was average looking, to her, no other man was as handsome as Trent. The first two buttons of his shirt were open, revealing dark curly chest hairs that matched his thick eyebrows. Miranda's face grew warm, as she willed her eyes to rise up and meet his gaze. Even with all the problems between them, she still remembered, and longed for, the way things had been before he'd begun seeing another woman. Of course, Trent denied having had an affair. He insisted the relationship hadn't gone that far before he'd broken things off. But Miranda lost faith in him and wasn't convinced he was telling the truth.

"Nice of you to stop by when we weren't home." Miranda couldn't keep the sarcasm out of her tone. "Why are you here anyway? I thought you were scheduled to work today."

"I did work this morning, but I got off at noon. Oh, by the way, I didn't know you weren't going to be home."

"Don't you remember?" Miranda sighed heavily. "We were at the cooking class I told you about when I called to see if you could take the kids." *Trent never remembers anything I tell him.*

"Oh, yeah, right, I forgot."

Big surprise. "So, why did you stop by?"

"I want to get some of the music CDs I left here when you kicked me out." Trent shifted from one foot to the other. "I have a CD player, but no music to play in it."

"Oh, I see." Miranda's body temperature rose, and it wasn't from the heat. "Then I guess it wasn't because you wanted to see the kids."

"Now don't try to make something out of nothing, Miranda." Trent kept his voice lowered. "Figured when I got here, I'd spend a little time with Debbie and Kevin." He reached out and took one of the grocery sacks.

Miranda didn't want to argue, especially in front of the children, so she invited Trent to stay for lunch. That would allow him some time with the kids.

"Thanks for the offer, but I'll have to take a

rain check." Trent looked toward the children, who were still playing with the dog. "I had a busy morning at the dealership. In fact, I sold three cars. So I'm tired and want to get home and relax. If it's okay with you, I'll pick out some CDs and be on my way."

"Sure, take whatever you want." She waved her hand to shoo him on.

"Look, Miranda, I'm trying to be cordial. Quite frankly, when I realized you weren't home, I could have just gone in the house, got the CDs, and left. But I hung around, hoping you and the kids would be home soon. That's why I came out here with Blondie. Figured I'd mess with her a bit while I waited for you."

"Well if you'd paid attention, you would have remembered that I said the cooking class would be over at noon."

"Okay, I admit, I forgot." Trent rubbed the bridge of his nose.

"By the way," she added, "the next cooking class is in two weeks, and I have to work that Saturday. So can you take the kids?"

"I'm scheduled to work, too, but I'll see if I can switch with someone."

"Thanks."

Miranda and Trent entered their ranch-style house. While she put the groceries away, he went to the living room to get what he'd come for.

Debbie and Kevin came running into the kitchen. "Where's Daddy?" Kevin asked.

Miranda nodded toward the living room. The children hurried in to be with their father. *Those poor kids miss their dad so much. I'll never understand that man. If he hadn't messed up, he could still be living here.*

Blondie, who'd been left outside, whined and scratched at the door.

"Did they forget about you?" Miranda held the door open as Blondie pranced in. The cute dog stayed with her in the kitchen, sitting patiently and wagging her pom-tipped tail.

"What do ya say now?" Miranda held her hand out, hiding a surprise.

"Woof! Woof!" Blondie rose up in a begging position, reaching her front paws up as high as she could.

"Good girl." Miranda rewarded her with a chewy bone.

She watched the pretty poodle go over to her doggie bed, spin in a circle, and lie down with the bone. Shortly thereafter, Trent, holding a few CDs in his hand, entered the kitchen, with both kids trailing behind.

"Can't you please stay, Daddy?" Debbie held onto her father's arm.

"Sorry, honey. Some other time. I want to go back to my apartment and put up my feet." Trent patted the top of Debbie's head.

Kevin stood silently, not saying a word, but his look of disappointment said it all.

Sugarcreek, Ohio

"Why are we stoppin' here?" Jeremy asked when Darren pulled his rig into the parking lot of a restaurant in Sugarcreek.

"We're going to stop for lunch." Darren glanced in the mirror at his son sitting in the back seat, wearing a scowl. "I'm hungry and figured you would be too."

"Yeah, okay. Guess I could eat something. That dumb fruit salad I had to make during the cooking class didn't fill my stomach. Especially when I had to share it with you."

Darren chuckled. "You wouldn't have eaten it in front of me, would ya?"

"Naw, I was only kidding."

"Are you feeling better about taking the class now that you know you're not the only boy?"

"I guess so, but the other guys are just little kids. I don't have much in common with Randy or Kevin."

"That's okay. You don't have to become best buds. It's just kind of nice to know there are three boys in the class, which evens things out, since there are three girls."

"Four, if you count the little girl who lives with Heidi."

"True." Darren opened the door on his side of the vehicle. "Let's go inside the restaurant and see what's on the menu."

They had no more than stepped into the restaurant when Darren spotted Ellen and her daughter, Becky, sitting at a table near the window. He thought about how the two of them had hurried out the door after class ended today, preventing him from telling Ellen what he thought about her not giving Becky a chance to learn on her own. It was probably for the best, though. No point creating a problem—especially when they'd be seeing each other again at the next cooking class.

Ellen glanced up from perusing her menu and was surprised to see Darren Keller enter the restaurant with his son. When Darren looked her way, she offered a casual wave. He nodded in her direction, before following the hostess to a table. Ellen turned back to Becky. "Did you enjoy the cooking class today?"

Becky lifted her shoulders briefly. "It was okay, but I didn't like two of the boys who were there."

"Which two?"

"Kevin and Jeremy."

"How come?"

"Well, Kevin kept doing things to irritate that girl, Kassidy, and Jeremy kicked me under the table a few times."

"I'm sure he didn't kick you on purpose." Ellen glanced across the room, where Darren and Jeremy sat. They were too far away to hear what Becky had said, especially since she'd spoken so quietly.

"Mom, do they have pizza here?" Becky asked.

"I don't think so." Ellen pointed to the menu. "I'm going to order the baked chicken wrap. You should order something healthy too."

"Okay I'll have a wrap."

"We'll have pizza soon," Ellen promised, seeing Becky's defeated expression. "I know pizza's your favorite food. Whenever we decide to have it, maybe instead of ordering a pizza, we can make one together. How's that sound?"

"Okay."

Ellen felt better when Becky nodded in agreement.

"Mom, when I go to the next cooking class, you can just drop me off at Heidi Troyer's and come back when it's done to pick me up."

Ellen shook her head. "I wouldn't feel right about that. I'd prefer to stay during the class." She glanced at Darren again, and was surprised when he left his seat and headed in their direction. Ellen moistened her lips. *I wonder what he wants.*

Chapter 8

I'm surprised to see you here." Darren smiled as he stood beside Ellen's chair. "Do you come to Sugarcreek often?"

"No. I heard about this restaurant and decided to stop for lunch before heading home." She fiddled with her napkin, nervous all of a sudden. The depth of Darren's blue eyes seemed to bore right through Ellen as he held her steady gaze. "How about you? Have you and your son eaten here before?"

"Nope. It's our first time too. Got a recommendation from another fireman who lives in Sugarcreek." He grinned. "If anyone knows a good place to eat, it's a guy who puts out fires for a living."

She chuckled. Darren was not only good looking, but he had a sense of humor, something she'd always appreciated in a man—or anyone else for that matter. As a nurse, she'd learned from observing her patients that laughter and a positive attitude were good medicine.

Darren gestured to the empty chairs at Ellen's table. "Say, would it be okay if Jeremy and I joined you? It might be nice to get better acquainted."

Ellen looked at her daughter, wondering how she would feel if Darren and his son sat at their table. When Becky said nothing, Ellen looked back at Darren. "Sure, that'd be fine."

Darren turned and motioned for his son to come over. Jeremy remained in his seat a few seconds, then got up and tromped across the room. "What's up, Dad?"

"We're going to sit here and eat lunch with Ellen and Becky."

Jeremy's brows furrowed. "I thought we had our own table."

"We did, but I decided we should sit over here and visit with Becky and her mother."

"Okay, whatever." Jeremy took a seat next to Becky and slouched in his chair.

She gave him a sidelong glance, but didn't say a word either. Ellen hoped her daughter wasn't holding a grudge against Jeremy because he'd kicked her under the table.

Darren seated himself in the chair beside Ellen, then glanced over at her menu. "I hear the French dip sandwich is pretty good here."

"I'll probably have a salad." Ellen pushed the menu closer to him. "Do you want to take a closer look?"

"Nope. I know what I want." He handed the menu to Jeremy. "You'd better make up your mind soon, 'cause a waitress is headed this way."

"I made up my mind when we were sittin' at

the other table." Jeremy nodded in that direction. "I'm gonna have a personal-size pizza."

"I thought they didn't have pizza here." Becky looked at Ellen with furrowed brows. "If he gets to have pizza, why can't I?"

Feeling a headache coming on, Ellen rubbed her forehead. "Okay, Becky, you can have whatever you want. I must have missed seeing pizza listed on the menu."

After the waitress took their orders, it grew uncomfortably quiet at the table.

"Did you enjoy the cooking class?" Darren asked at the same moment Ellen threw out the same question.

He chuckled. "You go first."

"Yes, despite the fact that no one knew each other, I thought things went well for the first class."

"I thought it was a little awkward, though." Darren glanced at Becky, then back at Ellen. "Hopefully the next ones will go better, and the kids will be more comfortable with each other. Don't you think so, Jeremy?" He nudged his son's arm, but all Jeremy did was nod his head.

"Did you like the class, Jeremy?" Ellen asked.

"It was okay." Jeremy glanced at Becky, then looked quickly away.

"How about you, Becky? What did you think?" Darren questioned.

"It was all right," she mumbled without looking at him.

Darren chuckled. "Well, at least our kids think alike where that topic is concerned."

Ellen smiled. "You mentioned another fireman had recommended this place to eat." She took a drink of water the waitress had put on the table. "Are you also a fireman?"

"Yeah. It's what I've always wanted to be." He grabbed his glass of water and took a big swallow. "I tried college after graduating from high school, but only got as far as acquiring my associate's degree in business management."

"I see." Ellen leaned her elbows on the table.

"I knew sitting behind a desk was not for me." Darren didn't want to talk about himself anymore. "How about you? What do you do?"

"I'm a nurse in the pediatric ward at the hospital in Millersburg."

He smiled. "Guess that means you must like kids."

"I do." Her face sobered. "It saddens me, though, to see a severely sick or injured child."

Darren slowly nodded. "It's hard for me to see kids who have been burned or injured because of a fire. So in some ways our jobs are similar."

"Yes, I suppose." Ellen rested her hands beneath her chin.

"Don't mean to change the subject, but are you

planning to come to all the cooking classes with your daughter?"

"Yes, I am."

Darren came close to voicing his opinion on that subject, but the waitress arrived with their food. *Maybe once he'd gotten to know Ellen better he would feel free to interject his thoughts.*

Walnut Creek

"Are ya still mad at me for playin' with the hose?" Randy asked Heidi as she sat in the kitchen with him and Marsha, eating lunch.

She reached over and gave his shoulder a tender squeeze. "No, Randy. You apologized and I forgave you." Heidi looked at Marsha, her lips covered with peanut butter. "Your sister accepted your apology too."

"I won't touch the hose again." Randy shook his head vigorously. "Promise."

Heidi smiled. "Sometimes Lyle or I might ask you to turn on the hose, and then it will be okay. I just don't want you spraying anyone with water."

"Okay." He pointed to the cookie jar on the counter. "Can Marsha and I have a *kichli*?"

"Yes, but not until you've finished your lunch. There are only a few oatmeal cookies left, but you and Marsha can help me make more."

Marsha grinned, and Randy bobbed his head. It was good to see him becoming more receptive to her. It also pleased Heidi that Randy had used the Pennsylvania Dutch word for cookie. He was beginning to catch on to more Amish words. When he started school this fall, Randy would have an advantage over the other children, since he already knew the English language. It would be easier for him to make friends and communicate with the other children before and after class if he spoke Pennsylvania Dutch. Marsha wouldn't start school for a few more years, so Heidi would have plenty of time to work with her if she and Lyle were allowed to continue caring for the children.

What a privilege it was to take care of these precious youngsters. *And to think, if one of my previous students hadn't mentioned the need for foster parents, Lyle and I never would have considered such a thing.* It still amazed Heidi how the Lord had worked things out on their behalf, as well as the children's. Despite the disappointment she'd felt over not being able to adopt Kendra's baby, everything had turned out well.

Seeing that the children had finished their sandwiches, Heidi scooted away from the table and went to get the ingredients to make oatmeal cookies. She set a carton of eggs on the counter and was about to get out the oatmeal, when a knock sounded on the front door.

"I'll be right back." She hurried from the room.

When Heidi opened the door, she was surprised to see Denise and Kassidy on the porch.

"Sorry to bother you." Denise's tone was apologetic. "My daughter thinks she may have left her cell phone here."

Kassidy lifted her chin. "I don't think it, Mom. I know I left it here. I had my phone with me when I was in Heidi's kitchen."

"The children and I just finished eating lunch, and I didn't see any sign of your cell phone in the kitchen. Perhaps you left it somewhere else," Heidi suggested.

The girl's face turned crimson, as she shook her head. "I only took it out when I was sitting at your table, because I wanted to see if I had any text messages."

"Okay, well, let's go to the kitchen and take a look." Heidi led the way.

When they entered the room, where Randy and Marsha still sat, Kassidy scanned the table.

"Your phone's not here," Denise pointed out. "Are you sure you left it on the table?"

Kassidy nodded curtly.

"Maybe one of the others who was here at the class saw the phone and moved it someplace else," Heidi suggested.

"Or maybe someone took it." Kassidy planted both hands on her hips, glaring at Randy and Marsha.

"Now, don't go making accusations, Kassidy."

Denise stepped between her daughter and the table.

Kassidy's face tightened. "I need my phone, and I want it back!" She skirted around her mother and leaned close to Randy's chair, looking him right in the face. "I bet you took it, you little thief. You have guilt written all over your dirty face."

"My face ain't dirty." He glared back at her.

"Yeah, it is. There's purple jelly on your chin and a smudge of peanut butter on your cheek."

Heidi was on the verge of intervening, when Denise spoke again. "Kassidy, you can't go around accusing people of taking your things when you have no proof."

"But I do have proof," she insisted. "I left my cell phone here, it's gone now, and the little runt looks guilty."

Feeling the need to end this, Heidi looked at Randy and said, "Did you take Kassidy's phone?"

He started to shake his head, but then slowly nodded. "It was on the table when she left, so I picked it up."

"What'd you do with it?" Kassidy's nostrils flared like an angry bull about to charge.

"I—I put it in my room so I could look at it later."

"You'd better not have played with the buttons or messed up any of my settings." The girl's cheeks turned a deeper shade of red.

"Randy, please go to your room and get Kassidy's phone." Heidi was embarrassed by his behavior and disappointed because he had taken something that wasn't his, without asking. She wondered if his parents had taught him right from wrong.

"Okay, I'll get it." Randy leaped from his chair and bolted out of the room.

"I apologize for his behavior." Heidi looked at Denise. "He's young and doesn't always think about what he's doing."

"Believe me, I understand." Denise gave a sidelong glance toward her daughter.

A few minutes later, Randy returned with Kassidy's cell phone. Before he could utter a word, she snatched it out of his hand and looked it over.

Randy backed away from Kassidy and took a seat next to Marsha.

"Everything seems okay with my phone. Can we go now, Mom?" Kassidy put the phone in her pocket.

"Yes, but before we do, you need to tell Randy you're sorry for talking so sharply to him."

"Okay, whatever." Kassidy went over to where Randy sat, and mumbled. "Sorry for what I said. And you should be sorry, too, for taking my phone." She moved across the room and stood with both hands on her hips.

Denise turned to face Heidi. "Sorry for the

interruption and especially for my daughter's rude behavior. We'll look forward to seeing you in two weeks." Denise and Kassidy went out the back door this time.

Heidi looked at Randy. "I'm not going to punish you this time, but if you ever take anything that doesn't belong to you again, there will be consequences. Understand?"

"Jah." Randy scrubbed a hand over his face and turned his head away quickly.

Heidi wished she could do something to reach the boy. One minute things were going along okay, and the next minute Randy misbehaved. Was it the pain he still felt over losing his parents that caused his naughtiness, or did Randy dislike living here? One thing was certain: this had not been a good day for the boy.

That evening before the children went to bed, Heidi would read to them the verse she'd written on the back of the recipe card for fruit salad. Both Randy and his sister needed to understand the importance of obedience.

Chapter 9

Velma Kimball stood at the back door of the run-down double-wide she shared with her husband, Hank, and three of their children. They'd moved from Kentucky to Ohio a month ago but hadn't yet made any real friends.

The sun shone brightly this ninth day of June, but Velma's emotions swirled like a brewing storm. Nothing seemed to go right for her family. Seventeen-year-old Bobbie Sue had dropped out of school six months ago, and worked as a dishwasher at a restaurant in Berlin. It would be time for Velma to pick her up soon.

Velma was glad they'd gotten Bobbie Sue out of Kentucky, for her boyfriend there had been a bad influence, encouraging her to quit school, smoke, and sneak out of the house. Velma hoped things would be better now that Bobbie Sue was away from Kenny.

Clem, their oldest son, had left home two years ago, when he'd turned eighteen. They hadn't heard from him since. Then there was Eddie, their ten-year-old son. The boy had a chip on his shoulder and often got in trouble at school. Maybe now that summer was here, Eddie would settle down and make some new friends. Peggy Ann, age eight, was Velma's clingy child, which sometimes got on Velma's nerves. The girl also needed friends, or at least something to keep her busy during the summer months.

To make matters worse, Velma's husband, Hank, a truck driver, was often gone from home, leaving her to cope with the kids on her own.

As her frustration mounted, Velma kicked the rickety screen door with the toe of her worn-out sneaker. She'd been dealt a bad hand most of her life, and it was getting old. She longed for something better and hoped by moving they'd be getting a new start. Of course, leaving Kentucky wasn't just about getting Bobbie Sue away from Kenny. Most of it had to do with the rift they'd had with Velma's folks. It was sad to have to cut ties with one's folks, but for Hank's sake, Velma had done just that.

Velma's mouth twisted as she balled her hands into fists. *Maybe I shoulda married someone else—a man my parents approved of, at least. Well, it's too late for regrets. It's time to focus on our new life here in Ohio and hope things go better for me, Hank, and our kids.*

With a gentle breeze blowing in her face, Heidi headed down the road in her open buggy toward Walnut Creek Cheese. She inhaled deeply. It was a warm, dry wind—the comfortable kind of breeze that didn't give you goose bumps and wasn't too humid.

Holding the ends of her covering ties between her teeth so her *kapp* would stay in place, she gripped the reins firmly to keep her horse from sprinting at full speed. Heidi hadn't used Bobbins, their chestnut mare, for a few days, and she seemed eager to run.

It was hard to believe almost a week had gone by since her first children's cooking class. With her second class just a week from tomorrow, she needed to make sure she had everything on hand. Since Heidi would be busy with other things the first several days of next week, today was the best time to get some shopping done. Lyle didn't have an auction, so he'd volunteered to stay home with Marsha and Randy, which allowed Heidi to shop with no interruptions. It wasn't often that she had time to be by herself these days, and she appreciated his willingness to supervise the children. No doubt, they would be good for him.

Their social worker had dropped by yesterday morning, and they'd had a good visit. Gail seemed pleased that Randy and Marsha were getting along well, and when Heidi told her about the cooking classes, Gail said it sounded like an interesting venture and wouldn't mind taking cooking lessons herself sometime.

Driving along, Heidi saw a woman from their church district out mowing her lawn. She waved at Irene, and her neighbor responded with a hearty, "Nice to see you, Heidi!"

The heavy smell of fresh mowed grass filled Heidi's senses, and an image of herself during childhood days came to mind. As a young girl, she loved being cushioned by the sweet-smelling grass and watching big white clouds float slowly across the sky. *I'll have to introduce Marsha and Randy to cloud watching some afternoon.* Heidi smiled. *Another thing I'm sure they would enjoy is a picnic in our backyard.*

The thought of an evening meal of fried chicken, baked beans, potato chips, and sweet tea made her mouth water. Randy and Marsha would no doubt enjoy eating those too.

Heidi figured the children were due for a reward of some kind. Ever since the incident with the hose last Saturday, plus being caught with Kassidy's phone, Randy had been on his best behavior. Marsha too, but then the quiet little girl always did as she was told. A family picnic seemed like a valid way to show her approval. Plus, her husband was a pushover when it came to her crispy, coated chicken.

She thought about the other night. When she'd tucked the kids into bed and read them the verse from the Bible about obedience, they'd promised to be good. Heidi hoped the other children who'd received a card would also take the verse to heart.

Despite the wind that had increased, the

warmth of the sun felt pleasant to Heidi as she continued in the direction of the store. Sunlight always brightened her mood, and today was no exception. Since Randy and Marsha had come to live with them, Heidi had a renewed sense of hope for the future. She hadn't spoken to Lyle yet about the possibility of trying to adopt the children, but hoped to talk to him soon. He'd become a father to their foster children in every way, so Heidi felt sure he would want to make Marsha and Randy legally theirs. She couldn't imagine him saying anything but yes.

After Heidi pulled into the parking area and secured her horse, she headed into the cheese store. Grabbing a basket by the door, she moved along the refrigerator case, eyeing the many types of cheeses they offered.

Heidi noticed an English family picking out some different items. She wondered if they were tourists or lived in the area. The mother and father were soft spoken as they talked to the two children, allowing them each to pick out a treat. The boy seemed content as he chose some cheese and crackers. His sister took longer deciding, until she reached out for a small container of bear-shaped graham crackers.

Heidi turned away and tried a sample of habanero cheddar. It was so hot she couldn't finish eating it, and ended up spitting it in a tissue she pulled from her purse. *I hope no one saw me do that. Lyle might like the hot cheese, since he enjoys putting spicy salsa on some things we eat at home, but it's certainly not for me.* Waving her hand in front of her mouth, in the hope of cooling off, Heidi wished she'd brought her water bottle inside with her.

Not long after, she saw her friend Loretta and visited with her for a bit. They decided to go to another shop in the area and look around, since neither of them had their children along.

As Heidi walked beside Loretta, they shared the latest news, while looking at some of the gift items. Then they stopped for a dish of ice cream before going their separate ways. Of course, Heidi bought a gallon of ice cream that she put in a small cooler she'd brought along so she could take home a treat for Lyle and the children. She would serve it after supper.

Berlin

"Are you ready to head for home?" Velma asked Bobbie Sue as she climbed into the passenger's seat of Velma's older model, mid-sized car. Eddie and Peggy Ann were in the back seat.

Bobbie Sue's face reddened as she crossed her arms. "Oh, I'm ready, all right. The boss just fired me, so I won't be comin' back to this stupid diner anymore." She scrunched her nose. "What a cruddy way to end the week."

Velma blinked rapidly. "Why would Marilyn let you go?"

"Said I was mouthin' off." Bobbie Sue's nostrils flared as she shook her head. "I think she made it up so she can hire her niece who moved here last week from Cincinnati."

"Did she come right out and say that?"

"No, but it don't take no genius to figure it out. All's I did was tell the boss lady that I was sick and tired of gettin' stuck with all the dirty work. I wanna wait on people, not be stuck washing dishes, cleaning tables, and sweeping the floors." Bobbie Sue paused long enough to draw in a quick breath. "Marilyn plays favorites anyways, and when I heard her niece was here and would need a job, I had a feeling I'd probably get fired."

Velma's jaw clenched. Maybe Bobbie Sue was telling the truth, but since she often mouthed off, Marilyn may have let her go for a legitimate reason.

"Would you like me to talk to your boss? With any luck, maybe I can talk her into giving you your job back."

Bobbie Sue shook her head. "Don't bother, Mama. I'm sick of the job anyways."

"Well, like it or not, you need to be working and paying room and board, like I did when I was your age."

Her daughter just stared straight ahead.

· · ·

"How long till we get to Uncle Patrick's house?"

Keeping her concentration on the road ahead, Ellen responded to her daughter's question. "It will be awhile. Probably about two hours to go yet." Ellen couldn't believe how busy Berlin was today.

"Yeah, but I can wait." Becky folded her hands and rested them in her lap. "I wonder what we will have to eat tonight."

"Your uncle said something about grilling hot dogs and burgers." Ellen smiled. When Becky first learned they were going to her aunt, uncle, and cousins' place for the weekend, she'd been excited. With Ellen's brother and his family living in Wheeling, West Virginia, they didn't get to see them regularly. Since Becky tended to be a bit shy around other children, it was good for her to spend time with her cousins, Alisha and Connie. Ellen was thankful she'd been able to get two days off in a row so they could make the trip. When she'd gotten off work today, she had gone home, put their suitcases in the car, and headed out with Becky. They would return home early Sunday evening, since Ellen's shift on Monday would begin at six o'clock in the morning.

The traffic became heavier, no doubt due to the number of people getting off work, not to mention all of the tourists. And because it was Friday, everyone seemed anxious to get to wherever they were going. Already, one driver had cut in front of Ellen to gain some headway. She found an easy-listening station on the radio and turned the volume down to a soft level, hoping it would help soothe her nerves as she and Becky traveled the rest of the way. She was just as anxious as her daughter to see her brother and his family.

Patrick was two years older than Ellen, and their brother, Dean, was five years older. Because of their close ages, she and Patrick had always had a stronger relationship while growing up. They had a lot in common too. He was a doctor and she a nurse. They both enjoyed people and shared the same bubbly personality. Patrick had a strong relationship with God, and so did Ellen. Unfortunately, their older brother had strayed from his faith, and it had affected his marriage. Dean and Shelly were now divorced, and their three children lived with her in Texas.

I hope my older brother gets back on track before it's too late, Ellen thought as she approached a stoplight. *Shelly hasn't remarried, so maybe there's a chance that they could get back together.*

Ellen noticed a compact car as it started through the intersection as the light turned green. At the same time, an older-model vehicle on the right sailed through the light without stopping. She gasped at the horrible sound as the vehicles collided, breaking glass and crunching metal.

From the backseat, Becky screamed.

Concerned that one or more of the passengers in either car might be hurt, Ellen pulled onto the shoulder of the road and turned off the ignition. "There, there Becky. It's going to be okay." This was the first time her daughter had witnessed an accident such as this. "Stay right here, though. I need to see if anyone was injured and call for help."

Chapter 10

"A re you all right?" Velma's heart pounded as she reached across the seat and touched her daughter's arm.

"I—I think so. My neck kinda hurts, though. How about you, Mama? Are you okay?" Bobbie Sue's voice trembled as she sat slumped in her seat.

"I'm not sure." Velma swiped at the wetness on her forehead, certain that it was bleeding. She found a lump there, but no blood, just perspiration.

Quickly, Velma turned in her seat to see if her two younger ones had been injured. "Are either of you hurt?"

Wide eyed, and with her chin trembling, Peggy Ann shook her head.

"I'm okay too," Eddie said.

Velma heaved a sigh of relief. Then the door on her side of the car opened, and a pretty woman with blond hair looked in. "Are any of you hurt?"

Velma shook her head. "There's a small lump on my forehead from where I hit the steering wheel, and my oldest daughter said her neck hurts a bit, but my kids in the back are okay too. Thank goodness those safety seats kept them secure."

"I've called 911, so help should be here soon." The color of the woman's brown eyes deepened. "The man in the vehicle you hit passed out and it wouldn't be wise to try and move him until the paramedics get here and can determine his injuries."

Velma sucked in a deep breath. If the man died it would be her fault, for she had plowed through the intersection without stopping at the light. Thank goodness she'd paid the car insurance premium on time this month.

"It's going to be okay. My name is Ellen Blackburn, and I'm a nurse. I'll stay with you until help arrives." The woman's voice was calm, and she spoke with reassurance. The way the sun shone on her blond hair, it almost appeared as if she were an angel. Not that Velma had ever seen an angel. Truth was, she'd never been a religious person and could only imagine what one looked like.

"Wonder what Papa's gonna say when he finds out what happened." Bobbie Sue's forehead wrinkled as she looked over at Velma.

"He won't be thrilled, that's for sure." Velma moved in the seat, trying to loosen the tight belt that held her in. "This ancient car is our only transportation, other than your dad's semitruck, and I'm sure ole Bessie will need a lot of repair—if she can be fixed at all."

"There's a lot of smoke coming up out there." Her daughter pointed toward the rising fog.

She glanced in the direction of the moving cloud. "Actually, that isn't smoke; it's the radiator steaming. It probably has a crack in it from the accident." Velma groaned and shook her head.

"That's another reason for me to get a new job, and soon." Bobbie Sue popped a stick of gum in her mouth. "We're gonna need more money to afford another car."

"I hope the other driver will be okay. It was stupid of me to have driven through that stoplight." Velma's eyes teared up.

"Mama, it was only an accident. You didn't do it on purpose." Bobbie Sue patted her arm.

"I know what you are saying, but I'm worried about the other driver and wish there was something I could do. I wonder what other folks do in situations like this. All we can do is sit here and wait to hear how they're doing."

"Maybe they pray."

Velma rested her hands against the steering wheel. Although she rarely prayed, Velma sent up a quick plea on the other person's behalf.

"I feel bad for you, having to listen to Papa blow a gasket 'cause you wrecked the car," Eddie spoke up.

Velma groaned. She could only imagine.

• • •

Ellen felt relief when the paramedics arrived. She directed them to the passenger in the smaller vehicle first, since he seemed to be hurt the worst. Two of the medics headed in that direction, while a third man went over to see about the passengers in the older-looking car. Two patrol cars arrived a few minutes later, and Ellen waited in her car until they were ready to talk to her.

"What's going on, Mom?" Becky's eyes were wide with fear. "Are the people in those vehicles hurt bad?"

"I don't know, Becky, but now that help is here, they will be looked after and taken to the hospital if necessary."

Becky blinked rapidly, then squeezed her eyes tightly shut. "I'm glad our car wasn't hit."

"Same here." Ellen patted her daughter's arm. "God was watching over us—that's for sure."

When Ellen saw one of the officers approach, she stepped out of her car.

"I'm assuming you must have witnessed the accident?" he asked.

She nodded.

"Would you mind giving me your statement?"

"No, I don't mind at all, but could you tell me how the people involved are doing? Were any of them seriously injured?"

"Other than a couple bumps and bruises the

women and children in the one car seem to be okay, but the guy driving the van is still unconscious. He's being taken to the nearest hospital."

Ellen sent up a silent prayer, asking God to be with the injured man, as well as those in the older vehicle.

Canton

"Kassidy, would you please set the table? It's almost time for supper." Denise took the meat loaf out of the oven and placed it on top of the stove. When no response came, Denise turned to see what her daughter was doing. Kassidy sat in the chair at the roll-top desk across the room, doing something on her cell phone.

"Please put that phone away and do as I asked."

Kassidy looked up and wrinkled her nose. "I'm in the middle of something, Mom. Can't you set the table yourself?"

Tapping her foot, Denise took a deep breath. Apparently her daughter had not read the verse Heidi wrote on the back of her recipe card about children obeying their parents. If she had, she'd chosen to ignore it.

Denise marched across the room and snatched the phone out of Kassidy's hands. "I want you to set the table—now!"

Kassidy gripped the sides of her head, as if

to cover her ears. "You don't have to yell. I'm sitting right here."

Denise's jaw clenched as she shook her finger. "Don't you talk to me like that, young lady. When I ask you to do something, I expect you to do it with no back talk or rude comments." She set the cell phone on the counter. "If you cooperate, you can have it back tomorrow morning."

Kassidy's mouth fell open. "But, Mom, I—"

"No arguments or you won't get it back tomorrow either." Denise turned toward the hallway door. "I'm going to let your father know supper is ready. By the time I get back, you'd better have the table set."

When Denise entered the living room, she found her husband in his recliner, watching TV.

"Supper's ready, Greg. But before we go in to eat, I want to talk to you about our daughter."

"Can't it wait? I had a long day in court, and I'm too tired to deal with any problems Kassidy may have."

Denise rolled her shoulders in an effort to relieve some of the tension. "You're not the only one who's had a long day. I showed five houses to the pickiest couple I've ever met, and then I came home, made supper, and had to deal with our spoiled daughter."

He picked up the remote and turned off the TV. "Whose fault is it that Kassidy's spoiled? You're the one who's always buying her things."

"This isn't about things. It's about her disrespectful attitude and refusal to obey when I ask her to do even a simple chore."

"Guess it's something you need to work on then." He pulled the lever on his chair and sat up.

Denise moved closer to him. "I've been thinking about this over the past week, and you know what the biggest problem is, Greg?"

"No, but I'm sure you're going to tell me."

Ignoring his sarcasm, she said, "You and I have been putting our careers first. We're both too busy for our daughter, so she acts out to get attention. It's time we call a halt to her temper tantrums and self-centered ways."

"What brought this on all of a sudden? We've never had this discussion before."

"Going to the cooking class last week with Kassidy got me thinking. She acted like a spoiled child, embarrassing me to no end. Truthfully, that's exactly what she is."

He stood, shoving his hands into his pants' pockets. "Our jobs keep us busy, and if it weren't for our jobs, we wouldn't be able to give Kassidy all the nice things she's come to expect and appreciate."

"You're right. She does expect them, but I'm not sure our daughter appreciates anything we do for her." Denise massaged the bridge of her nose. "Maybe we need to work less and spend more quality time with Kassidy. Except for the obsession with her phone, it's apparent all this stuff we give her means nothing."

Greg tipped his head, looking at her through half-closed eyes. "If you want to cut back on your workload and spend more time with our daughter, that's up to you, but I'm not in a position to do that right now." He moved down the hall toward the kitchen, leaving Denise alone, shaking her head.

I can't do this by myself, Greg. If we want Kassidy to grow into a mature young woman who respects her elders and doesn't respond negatively when she can't have her way, it's going to take both of us giving her more of our time and attention. Her chest tightened. *I just hope you realize that before it's too late.*

Walnut Creek

Humming one of the songs they frequently sang at family gatherings, Heidi checked on the baked beans in the oven. The fried chicken cooled on a large platter, while Lyle was outside tending the grill. When shopping, Heidi had also purchased some early fresh corn on the cob. Lyle smothered the ears with butter, wrapped them in foil, and heated them on the hot coals.

Heidi's mouth watered as the smell of seasoned chicken reached her nostrils. "Yum. I can't wait to sink my teeth into that meat." Whether hot or cold, fried chicken was a perfect picnic choice for their supper.

With the scent of grilling smoke wafting through the open window, she could hear the children's laughter and Rusty's excited barking. Heidi breathed in a contented sigh. When she'd gotten home a few hours ago, she was pleased to hear what a good time Lyle and the children had together. Randy was eager to share with Heidi how he and Marsha helped Lyle in the barn. Marsha bobbed her head as Randy explained how fun it was to clean the cat's dishes and fill them with fresh water and food. Lyle also piqued their enthusiasm with his plan of purchasing some chickens. The kids seemed excited when they learned their responsibility would be to help collect eggs once the hens started laying. But first Lyle had to ask Eli about building a chicken coop for them, as well as a sturdy fenced enclosure. It would not only keep the chickens in, but help to protect them from predators.

Heidi had to admit, getting some chickens was a good idea, and having farm-fresh eggs to collect every day was a bonus. It would also teach the children responsibility.

Randy and Marsha had been with them six months and were settling in more comfortably. Even Randy's negative attitude had turned more positive, and Marsha was talking more. Here at the Troyer residence, it was starting to feel like they were a real family. Heidi hoped the children might someday open up more about their parents—especially Randy, since he was older and had more memories of his mom and dad. Marsha was still pretty young and probably didn't remember as much. In time, the memory of her folks would fade. But Heidi would not push the children to talk about their past until they were ready.

Heidi thought about the photo albums tucked away in her and Lyle's bedroom closet, which they'd received when Randy and Marsha came to live with them. They belonged to the children's parents, Fred and Judy. All the other belongings from the Olsen household had been auctioned off after they'd passed away. But social services felt these photo memories were important to keep with the children. Heidi and Lyle agreed. Those pictures were part of the children's life, and the only tangible things they had left of their parents. When the time was right, Heidi planned to go through the albums with the children so they could talk about the photos.

When the agency had given Heidi the albums, they had looked pretty worn. Heidi could only assume they'd been looked at many times throughout the years. Along with the family album, inside the box was their parents' wedding album and the children's baby albums. Heidi had scanned through the baby books, consisting of details from the children's birth to one year of age, before putting them in the closet.

As she pulled the casserole dish of baked beans out of the oven and put it on the counter, Heidi heard the crunch of tires on gravel as a vehicle pulled into the driveway. Glancing out the window, she saw a minivan park, and was surprised when one of the students from her second cooking class got out of the passenger's side.

"Oh my, it's Allie Garrett." Heidi wiped her hands on her apron and quickly covered the beans and chicken with foil. She hadn't heard from or seen Allie since early December, when their final class ended.

When Heidi stepped out to the porch, a man in a police uniform was getting out of the driver's side. Heidi assumed it was Allie's husband, Steve, and was glad for the opportunity to finally meet him.

Allie and Steve wore big smiles as they walked up to Lyle standing by the grill. After they introduced themselves and shook his hand, Allie ran over to greet Heidi as she approached.

"Oh, Heidi, it's so good to see you." Allie reached out for a hug. "I picked my husband up from work, and we're heading to Millersburg to eat and do some shopping at Hershbergers' Farm and Bakery." Allie looked over at Steve. "We were going right through Walnut Creek, and I told Steve it would be a shame if we didn't stop. The kids are at church camp for a few days. Otherwise, they'd be with us."

"I'm so glad you came by." Heidi draped her arm around Allie's shoulder as they walked over to join their husbands.

"Heidi, this is my husband, Steve." Allie's eyes shone brightly as she looked at him. "And Steve, this is Heidi—the best cook in Holmes County."

"So nice to meet you, Steve." Heidi shook his hand. Steve's was a gentle, but firm handshake.

"I've heard a lot about you, Heidi. I'm enjoying being Allie's taste tester every time she makes a new dish." Steve patted his stomach. "If I'm not careful, though, it's going to show."

"Tell me about it." Lyle thumped his own belly. "It's a good thing this farm and the auctions I oversee keep me active. Otherwise, I'd have to buy bigger clothes."

Everyone laughed.

Allie scanned the yard. "How are things going with the children?"

"Very well." Heidi smiled, and Lyle nodded. "They're around here somewhere, playing with the dog. When Rusty and those two get together they're inseparable."

At that moment, their dog came bounding from the other side of the house, wagging his tail as he approached the visitors, with Randy and Marsha following.

"Here they are now." Heidi pointed.

When the children got closer and spotted the Garretts, their laughter and giggling halted, and Randy stopped in his tracks. Marsha took one look at Steve, held out her arms, and shouted, "Daddy!"

Chapter 11

As fast as her little feet could go, Marsha ran up to Steve and wrapped her slender arms around his legs.

Steve and Allie looked at each other in bewilderment, while Heidi stood beside Lyle, too stunned to say anything. As Steve squatted down to be eye-level with Marsha, she looked him square in the face.

"Now what do we have here?" Steve touched the end of Marsha's nose. "Aren't you a cute little girl?"

As quick as she had been eager to greet Steve, Marsha was even faster to pull away. Sobbing, she turned and ran over to her brother, hiding her face in his chest.

Even at five years old, Randy was protective of his sister, so it didn't surprise Heidi when he guided Marsha up to the porch, and they went inside the house together.

Heidi looked at Lyle, who appeared to be as bewildered as she was right now. "Allie and Steve, I'm so sorry. I'm not sure what just happened."

"It's okay." Allie turned to Steve. "We'd better

go." Then giving Heidi another hug, she said, "I'll catch up with you soon, Heidi, and I hope the children are okay."

After the Garretts' van pulled out, Lyle turned off the grill and joined Heidi on the porch. "I wonder what was going on with Marsha." He reached under his hat and scratched the back of his head.

"I don't know." Heidi rubbed her hand down her cheek and rested it at her throat. "It's not like Marsha to run up to a stranger like that. She's normally pretty bashful. And did you hear her call Steve, 'Daddy'?"

"Jah. It surprised me too. Maybe Steve resembles the children's father."

"We better go check on them."

When they went into the house, Heidi heard whimpering coming from the living room. As they walked in, she saw Randy consoling Marsha, as he gently patted her back. "It's okay Marsha. Don't cry." Even though Randy was trying to be the big brother, they both looked so small, huddled together on the couch.

Heidi went over and sat next to Marsha, then held out her arms. Marsha quickly climbed onto her lap and put her face against Heidi's neck.

Lyle sat next to Randy. "Did something frighten you outside?" he asked.

"Kinda." Randy kept his head down, lips quivering like a leaf in the wind.

"Do you want to talk about it?" Lyle touched the boy's arm.

Randy took a shuddering breath. "When I saw that man in a uniform, it made me think of my daddy. He wore a uniform at his job too."

"What was your daddy's job?" Heidi questioned.

"He worked at the shoppin' mall." Randy looked at Heidi with such seriousness in his eyes.

"You mean, like a security guard?" Lyle leaned closer to the boy.

"I . . . I think so, but I'm not sure. When we saw him standin' there, my sister thought it was our daddy. Then she got scared when she heard his voice. That's when she knew it wasn't Daddy. Guess it was his clothes that made her think it was Daddy." Randy sniffed. "Wish it had been. And I wish Mama was with him too."

"I understand." Heidi clasped both children's hands. Tonight, before bed, she would get out the photo albums in their closet and share them with the children. This was definitely the right time.

"You know, sometimes we think we see someone we know, and it turns out being someone else," Heidi continued.

Marsha sat up and looked at Heidi, rubbing her tearful eyes.

"I'll bet there is someone out there who looks just like you." Heidi smoothed the blond hair back that had come loose from Marsha's ponytail. Then she kissed the little girl's forehead.

"How about we go back outside and have that picnic now?" Lyle suggested. "The corn on the cob should be done, and I'll bet Heidi has the chicken and beans ready too."

"Yes, and after we've had some ice cream for dessert, I'll share something special with you and your big brother." Heidi smoothed the wrinkles in Marsha's dress. Her heart ached for Randy and Marsha. This was the first time Randy had mentioned anything about where their dad had worked. He too had clearly been shaken seeing Steve in uniform. But children were resilient and could usually get over things faster than most adults. Hopefully, Randy and Marsha would find it easier to talk about their parents after looking at the pictures in the album, and their emptiness would slowly wane. Heidi would do everything in her power to make these children feel loved and to give them a sense of belonging.

Dover

It was a slow day at the fire station. "How are things going with you these days?" Darren's friend Bruce asked as they hosed down one of the fire trucks at their station.

"Everything's fine." Darren moved to the front of the truck. "I took Jeremy to a cooking class a

111

week and a half ago, and we'll be going to class number two this coming Saturday."

Bruce's eyebrows lifted. "How come you're taking a cooking class? As I recall, you get around the kitchen pretty well."

Darren shook his head. "It's not for me. Jeremy's taking the class from an Amish woman, along with four other kids, plus the Amish woman's two foster children."

"If it's for kids, then why are you going with Jeremy?"

Darren shrugged. "I wasn't planning to at first, but the other parents stayed instead of dropping off their children, so I figured I would too. Also, it gives Jeremy and me something fun to do together." He watched a volunteer fireman pull in for his shift. "I thought my son could learn something new with kids his age and have a good time."

"Did you watch or take part in the cooking class?"

"Like many of the other parents, I was mostly a spectator, but there was a young single woman who did just about everything for her daughter." Satisfied that the truck looked clean enough, Darren turned off the hose and put it away. "I ran into Ellen . . ."

"Ellen?" Bruce cocked his head to one side.

"Yeah, her name's Ellen." Darren shrugged his shoulders. "As I was saying, I ran into Ellen and her daughter, Becky, at a restaurant in Sugarcreek when Jeremy and I went for lunch after the first class. We ended up sharing a table with them and got to know each other a bit better. Found out we have a few things in common, which was kinda nice."

Bruce looked at him through half-closed eyelids. "Is something going on between you and this woman? And if so, aren't you moving a little fast?" He picked up a drying towel and began working.

Darren flapped his hand. "Nothing is going on, so get that notion out of your head. My heart belongs to Caroline, and I have no desire to begin a relationship with another woman. Besides, I barely know Ellen. Our kids will be together in this cooking class for a total of six weeks, and it's nice to get to know the other parents." He grabbed a towel and moved along, helping to dry the vehicle. "When we get the truck dried off, we'll need to do some inventory. Oh, and I'm gonna fix a hearty casserole for the guys this evening."

"Sounds good, since we'll be here awhile on our shift." Bruce stood back and studied his work. "Think this rig is ready to go."

"If we get any calls, I'll pop the casserole in the oven on low." Darren finished drying a few streaks of water they'd missed.

Their conversation was interrupted when a call came in about a fire on the other side of town.

Darren paused to send up a prayer, just as he did every time he went out on a call. Then, with all other thoughts pushed aside and his focus on the task at hand, Darren and the other men on duty gathered up their gear and headed out, all thoughts of the casserole forgotten.

Berlin

Miranda, dressed for work, tapped her foot in annoyance. Trent was supposed to pick up the kids to take them out for pizza half an hour ago. She hoped he hadn't forgotten.

Miranda clenched her fists. *That man can be so undependable.* She reached for the phone and punched in his cell number. *If only Trent could put others first and try to be less self-absorbed.*

A few seconds later, Trent answered. "Hey, hon, I was just gonna call you."

Her jaw tightened. They'd been separated since the end of April. Why did he still call her "hon"? Did he think she'd be impressed with the endearment and welcome him home with open arms? Well, she'd be a lot more impressed if Trent would show up on time when he promised to take the kids somewhere.

"Where are you, Trent? You were supposed to be here thirty minutes ago. What happened—did you forget about your promise to take Kevin and Debbie out for pizza this evening?"

"I did not forget, and if you'd let me get in a word, I'll explain why I'm not there."

Holding the phone slightly away from her ear, Miranda moved away from the window and took a seat at the kitchen table. "Okay, what's your excuse?"

"It's not an excuse. It's a fact. I'm locked out of my apartment, and the keys to my car are inside."

She lifted her gaze toward the ceiling. "Are you kidding?"

"Wish I was, but I'm not. I would ask the apartment manager to let me in with his key, of course, but he's out of town till tomorrow evening. Can't you explain things to Kevin and Debbie? We'll do pizza some other time."

"It isn't as simple as that. I got called in to work to fill in for someone who's sick, and I need to leave soon. What am I supposed to do about the kids if you can't drive over here to pick them up and spend the evening with them?" Miranda waited, but only heard silence at the other end. "And besides, what were you going to do, now that you're locked out of your place?" she questioned.

"I'm not sure. Haven't figured that out yet." He groaned. "Guess I can call a locksmith, but it would be a while before he arrived, and I have to be here in person to meet him. Why don't you call your sister, and see if she'll watch the kids while you're at work?"

Miranda grimaced. "Do I need to remind you that Kate lives in Akron? For goodness' sake, Trent, it would take her at the very least, forty-five minutes to get here."

"Okay, I get it, but if you need me to watch the kids this evening, you'll have to drive over and get me."

Her chest rose and fell in a heavy sigh. "I'll call my boss and let her know I'll be late, because I have to pick up my kids' sitter."

"Your kids' sitter? Is that all I am, Miranda?" His voice grew louder. "Why not just tell her you're picking up your husband so he can be with the children?"

"Let's not get into an argument about this. The kids and I will be there soon to pick you up. Goodbye, Trent."

Wheeling, West Virginia

"It's sure nice to have you here, sis." Ellen's brother, Patrick, wrapped his arms around her in a hug. "Between your busy life as a nurse and mine as a doctor, we don't get to visit each other often enough."

She thumped his back. "You're right, and I miss all of your teasing."

Patrick grinned and squeezed Ellen's hands before turning to Becky. "And how's my favorite niece?"

Becky snickered. "I'm your only niece, Uncle Patrick. Your brother has two boys, remember?"

Patrick slapped his forehead. "Oh, of course. How could I have forgotten something so important?" He winked, then gestured toward the hall leading to the upstairs. "Glad you're here. We were wondering what was holding you up." He gestured to Becky. "Your cousins are upstairs. Why don't you go on up and say hello? Or would you rather I called them down here?"

"I'll go up." Becky grinned shyly and headed upstairs.

"Where's Gwen?" Ellen asked her brother.

"She's taking a shower. Since we weren't sure what time you'd get in, we decided to take you out for supper, rather than cooking something here. I hope you're okay with that."

Ellen smiled. "Going out to eat is fine with me."

Patrick moved toward the living room. "Let's sit and visit while we wait for Gwen."

Ellen followed and took a seat on the couch, while he seated himself in a leather recliner.

"How was the drive here?" Patrick asked, reaching down for the lever to put the footrest up.

"Well, before getting too far from Berlin, we witnessed an accident." Ellen grabbed a throw pillow and wrapped her arms around it. "We would have been here sooner, but being a nurse, I couldn't leave."

"How bad was it?"

"It could have been a whole lot worse." Ellen explained the details. "So while Becky waited in the car, I called 911, and checked on the people involved. We stayed until the authorities came and took my statement. Fortunately, the rest of the way here was uneventful."

"Glad to hear that. It was good of you to stop and help out." Patrick smiled. "Your daughter's grown a bit since I last saw her. Pretty soon she'll be a teenager, going out on dates and keeping her mom awake at night, trying not to worry."

Ellen grunted. "Don't remind me. I'm not looking forward to any of that."

He brushed her comment aside. "You've done a good job raising her. I doubt you'll have anything to worry about."

"I'm doing the best I can." Ellen sat silently for several seconds. "When I first adopted Becky, I never dreamed there would be so many challenges in being a single parent."

"You're right, but then any parent, single or not, faces challenges when they are raising their—"

Ellen heard a gasp, and she and Patrick both turned their heads toward the archway. There stood Becky, her mouth gaping open. Ellen briefly closed her eyes. *Oh no, what have I done? It's too late to take back my words.*

Becky came into the living room and stood

right in front of Ellen. "Adopted? I'm adopted?" Her shrill voice reverberated throughout the room. "How come you never told me this? Does everyone know except me?" Tears pooled in Becky's eyes as she scrutinized Ellen.

Ellen swallowed hard. She could hardly look at her daughter. *What am I going to tell her? How do I explain why I kept her adoption a secret all this time? I took a chance speaking to Patrick about it with Becky in the house. This was not how I planned for her to find out.*

Chapter 12

Ellen's throat felt so swollen she could barely swallow as she crossed the room and reached out to touch her daughter's arm. "Let's take a seat, and I'll explain things to you." She moved toward the couch, hoping Becky would follow. The child, however, remained standing like a statue, with her arms held tightly against her sides.

Ellen looked at Patrick, hoping he would say something, and she wasn't disappointed. Speaking softly, he smiled at Becky. "Please take a seat. You and your mother need to talk."

Shuffling her feet across the carpet, Becky took a seat in the rocking chair. Except for the grandfather clock striking the half-past hour, the room was uncomfortably quiet.

Ellen couldn't hide her disappointment. Her desire was for Becky to sit beside her, so she could wrap her arms around the girl and explain her reasons for keeping the adoption a secret.

Becky shot Ellen an icy stare. The daughter who was usually so pleasant, showed no sign of that trait. "Did you ever plan to tell me the truth?"

"Of course, when you were old enough to

understand it all, I planned to tell you, but—"

"Who are my real parents?" Becky's voice cracked. "I . . . I can't believe you hid this from me."

Ellen clutched the folds in her skirt. She had put herself in this position by keeping the truth from Becky, and that had obviously been a mistake. Her daughter was clearly upset, with good reason.

"I don't know your biological parents, Becky. I never met them." Ellen paused to clear her throat, hoping to dislodge the lump that had formed. "The adoption took place through an agency, and as far as I'm concerned, I am your real mother."

"But you're a single mom. Didn't you want me to have a dad?"

"It was not my intention for you to be raised without a father, but . . ." Ellen shifted on her seat. "I've always loved children and wanted some of my own. Since I had no serious boyfriend or any promise of marriage, I decided to adopt a child on my own."

Becky got the rocker moving and gave Ellen her full attention. "So what was the big secret? How come you didn't want me to know?"

Speaking slowly and with conviction, Ellen told how, when she was in high school, her best friend, Lynn, had learned she was adopted. "Lynn was upset and wanted to know about the woman who'd given birth to her," Ellen explained. "My friend's adoptive parents wouldn't tell her much and refused to help her look for her birth mother. Lynn was angry and moved out of their house and found a job after she graduated. It was sad, but she cut all ties with the parents who'd raised her, and as far as I know, she never went back." Tears welled in Ellen's eyes. "I was afraid if you knew you'd been adopted, it might cause problems between us too. I realize now that I made a huge mistake. I should have been honest with you as soon as you were old enough to understand. Will you forgive me, Becky?"

The ticking of the clock seemed to grow louder in Ellen's ears as she waited for her daughter's response. Finally, Becky nodded. With tears coursing down her flushed cheeks, she rushed across the room and into Ellen's arms. "I still love you, Mom, and I always will."

Ellen breathed a sigh of relief. She never wanted to lose her daughter and would do anything to protect what they had together. She closed her eyes and lifted a silent prayer: *Lord, thank You for a daughter like Becky. Please continue to help me raise her according to Your purpose. Amen.*

"Someday, when you're a bit older, I'll help you search for your biological parents if that's what you want." She opened her eyes and patted her daughter's back. When Ellen looked across the room where her brother sat in another chair, he smiled and gave her a thumbs-up.

Berlin

"How come you're in Mommy's closet?"

Trent whirled around at the sound of his son's voice. "I'm looking for some of my clothes."

"Why?"

"Because I'm locked out of my apartment and need a place to spend the night."

"Are you gonna stay here?" Debbie questioned, giving Trent's shirttail a tug.

"Yes. I'll be sleeping on the couch downstairs."

Jumping onto the foot of the bed, Kevin frowned. "But you used to sleep in here with Mommy."

"You're right, but we don't live together anymore, remember?" Trent ruffled his son's hair.

"If you and Mommy don't fight this time, maybe you can spend another night at our house." Kevin's expression brightened.

"I rather doubt it," Trent mumbled under his breath.

"Try to get along better with her, Daddy." Debbie stepped closer to him and took hold of his hand. "I wish we all lived together like we did before you and Mommy started fighting so much."

"Yeah, me too," Kevin added.

Trent swallowed hard. He remembered those days well and knew how hard it had been on the kids when Miranda had asked him to move out. He wished he could erase the past and start over again, but he'd done many things that had gotten him in trouble with his wife—one in particular. Trent needed to work on this matter—not just for the kids, but also for him. "I can be nicer to your mom, but I'm not sure she'll want me back." He squeezed his daughter's fingers. "Let's take it one step at a time and see how it goes."

When Miranda awoke the next morning, she was greeted with the aroma of coffee. It took a few moments to remember that Trent had spent the night on the living-room sofa. But the smell of coffee was the reminder she needed.

She rose from the bed and stretched both arms over her head. Miranda would never admit it to Trent, but it was kind of nice having him in the house again. She felt protected and knew the kids were happy to have their daddy there too. It was evident last evening, after he got settled in and they ate popcorn together while watching TV. If only things could be different. If she and Trent could have learned to get along and settle their differences peacefully instead of hollering at each other all the time, maybe he wouldn't have gotten interested in another woman. She still found it hard to believe Trent's protests that his relationship with that person had never developed into an affair. Miranda's heart held no trust where her husband was concerned, and she was still contemplating if divorce was the best option.

I can't think about all this right now. I need to get downstairs and start breakfast. After slipping on her robe, she opened the bedroom door. Miranda heard some contagious laughter rising from the room below. When she entered the kitchen a short time later, she found Debbie and Kevin, all smiles, sitting at the table, each with a glass of milk in front of them. Trent stood at the stove with his back to her.

"What's going on?" she asked.

When Trent turned around, she couldn't believe he was wearing her springtime floral apron. "Our children were laughing at their father's choice of cooking attire," he announced, before turning back to the stove.

Miranda stifled a chuckle. "I can see why there was so much giggling going on."

Kevin grinned and pointed to the bottle of maple syrup sitting in the center of the table. "Daddy's making us pancakes."

"Is that so?" She pressed her lips together to keep from asking Trent why he never fixed breakfast for the kids when he was living here. Was he trying to butter her up via the kids, in the hope of worming his way back in?

Miranda grabbed a mug and poured herself some coffee. *Well, it won't work. Trent hasn't changed. If he had, he'd start by going to church and setting a Christian example for his family. He'd also prove he was responsible and be true to his word.*

Trent looked over his shoulder and smiled at Miranda. "After breakfast, would it be okay if I borrow your car so I can meet up with the locksmith whom I called first thing this morning? I need to get into my apartment again."

"I guess that'll be okay. Today's my day off, so I won't need the car unless I decide to run to the store for something later on."

He flipped one of the pancakes and gave her a wide grin. "Thanks, hon. I appreciate that."

Miranda looked away. *There he goes, calling me "hon" again.* She'd have called him on it, but not here in front of the kids. Miranda would save her accusations for another time when she could speak to Trent alone.

Walnut Creek

After breakfast, Lyle hitched the horse and buggy and set off to Eli's place. He wanted to make arrangements to have a coop built before they purchased some chickens. "I sure hope Eli has time to build one for us." Lyle said to himself, and Bobbins nickered in return. Last evening, after their picnic when things had settled down a bit, Randy talked excitedly about the chickens they would soon be getting. This morning at the kitchen table, even Marsha seemed excited. Brother and sister talked about who would feed the chickens and who would collect the eggs.

Lyle had been relieved that the children recovered so quickly after Steve and Allie stopped by and knew Heidi was happy about it too.

"Those poor kids." Lyle shook his head, letting Bobbins take the lead. It was hard enough to lose one parent, let alone both at the same time. Lyle felt blessed that his and Heidi's parents were still around. If Lyle could do anything to ease the children's grief and help them understand about losses, he would do it, whatever it took.

It hadn't been that long ago when Lyle thought it was God's will for him and Heidi not to have any children. In fact, he had convinced himself that if it was to be that way, he would be content. But since he and Heidi had become foster parents, he couldn't imagine even a day without Marsha and Randy. Heidi had told him several times that she felt the same way about the children. Last night, before going to bed, they'd even discussed the possibility of adopting Marsha and Randy. Of course that would depend on several things, including how well the kids adjusted to living with them.

Nearing Eli's farm, Lyle breathed in the fresh

air as the *clip-clop* of Bobbin's hooves put him in a mellow mood. So clear was the sky, uninterrupted by any clouds for as far as the eye could see.

Pulling into the Millers' lane, Lyle noticed Loretta waving from the yard where she was hanging up clothes.

"*Guder mariye.*" Lyle tipped his hat after he secured the horse to the hitching rail.

"Good morning to you too." Loretta smiled as she walked to the edge of the yard. "What brings you here on this beautiful morning?"

"I have a project to ask Eli about. Is he around?"

"Jah, he's there in the shop." Loretta pointed. "I'm sure he'll be glad to see you."

"Okay, danki. Have a *gut* day." Lyle turned and walked toward the woodshop. When he entered, he found Eli staining a porch chair.

"Hello, my friend."

"Oh, you startled me." Eli bent to pick up the paint brush he'd dropped.

"Sorry, I thought you may have heard me out there talking to Loretta."

"Nope. I've been concentrating on my work in here." Eli grinned, picking a piece of straw off the brush. "It's good to see you and a fine morning it is, jah?"

"Sure is." Lyle stepped closer to his friend. "Don't want to keep you from your work, but I came to see if you might have time to do a project for me soon."

"Sure thing. I have one other chair to finish for a customer, but no coffins to make right now. So, what did you have in mind?"

Lyle explained about the need for a chicken coop, and was pleased when Eli said he'd be happy to build it. In fact, Eli said he would be able to start by Friday or Saturday of the coming week. Lyle also agreed when Eli suggested the structure be built right there at Lyle and Heidi's place. That way they wouldn't have to worry about transporting the completed coop once it was finished. And Randy and Marsha could watch the progress.

On the way home, feeling like a kid himself, Lyle whistled. He was anxious to tell the children and couldn't get Bobbins to go fast enough.

"You did what?" Velma's husband's face contorted.

"You heard me, Hank. I ran a stoplight and hit another vehicle." Velma stared at her lukewarm coffee sitting on the kitchen table. Ten minutes ago, Hank had returned home with his truck, after being gone three days, and she'd just given him the news that their car was totaled. *Why couldn't that man of mine be a little more sympathetic? Sometimes I feel like I'm married to a grumpy ole grizzly bear.*

Hank pounded his fist, vibrating the table. "What in tarnation were ya thinkin'? You shoulda been payin' attention to your driving."

"I don't know. Guess I was thinking about Bobbie Sue and how she lost her job yesterday afternoon."

He hit the table a second time. "Now isn't that just great?"

Velma drew a sharp breath. "Aren't ya even gonna ask if anyone was hurt? Or do you care more about your precious vehicle than your wife and kids?"

He scrutinized her. "I can see by lookin' at ya that you ain't hurt. I saw Bobbie Sue outside when I pulled my rig into the yard. She looked fine to me."

Velma pulled in a few more breaths, hoping to calm her nerves. Hank had a temper, and while he'd never hit Velma, she often wondered if he might someday. She figured her one saving grace was him being on the road so much. If he wasn't home when something unpleasant occurred, she wouldn't have to hear him blow his stack.

Velma handled most situations with the kids on her own, without him ever knowing about it. However, hitting another vehicle was something she couldn't very well hide, especially since their one and only car had been totaled.

"Eddie and Peggy Ann were in the car too, and luckily, none of us was seriously hurt." She paused for another breath. "But the driver of the other vehicle was taken to the hospital by ambulance. I heard later that he wasn't in serious condition, so that's something to be thankful for."

His eyes glazed over. "That's good news about the other driver, but you're lucky the cops didn't haul you off to jail for runnin' a stoplight."

Oh boy, here we go . . . Mount St. Helens is erupting again. Velma sniffed, struggling to hold back tears. "I did receive a citation—a pretty hefty one at that."

"Great! So now we have that to pay for too." Hank's face reddened further, and a vein on his neck protruded. "You do realize that we only have liability insurance, so even though our insurance company will pay for the other guy's vehicle and injuries, our car won't be covered. Not to mention our insurance will go up with surcharge points, all because of this accident."

Gulping, she nodded. *Doesn't he know he's making me feel even worse by his continued ranting?*

"So now, on top of daughter number one bein' out of a job and unable to contribute to our finances, I'll have to work twice as hard hauling with my semitruck in order to earn enough money to replace the car."

"I can look for a job."

Hank shook his head vigorously. "Your job

is here, takin' care of the kids while I'm on the road." He glanced around. "Where are they, anyhow?"

"Eddie and Peggy Ann are still in bed, and as you already know, Bobbie Sue's outside, hanging up the laundry because we can't afford to buy a dryer."

He raked his fingers through the ends of his thinning brown hair. "That's right, and now, because of your careless driving, a new dryer goes to the bottom of our list."

Velma rested her head on both hands. "I don't know how, but we'll get through this, Hank. We always have."

Chapter 13

New Philadelphia, Ohio

Trent sat at the kitchen table, staring into his empty mug. Thanks to the locksmith he'd called a few days ago, he was back in his dinky apartment. But after spending a night and part of a day with Miranda and the kids in a home he was still paying the mortgage on, he felt depressed. Here in his humble abode, these rooms were too quiet for him.

"Shouldn't be living here alone," he mumbled. "I miss my wife and kids and want to go home."

Trent's apartment was big enough for one person, but it had few furnishings and absolutely no personality. It was drab and dull, and he missed seeing the little touches Miranda had placed around their house. A vase of flowers, little knickknacks, framed photos of the kids— those were the kind of things missing in this dreary place.

"Even my walls are bare." Trent lifted his hands in despair. "But why bother with all that stuff when I'm here all alone?" He first believed his stay here would be only temporary. Now he had serious doubts. "I wonder if Miranda will make good on her threat and file for divorce."

Trent glanced at his cell phone. He had just enough time for another cup of coffee before heading out to pick up the kids for their cooking class in Walnut Creek. It would be good to see them again. *Maybe I can get Kevin and Debbie to work on their mother. If they tell her how much they miss me, maybe Miranda will say I can move back to the house. Sure wish I could do something to prove I wasn't disloyal to her.* He tugged his ear. *Well, maybe I was, but I didn't have an affair. I broke things off with Isabelle before it got that far.*

Trent was about to reach for the coffeepot, when his cell phone rang. The sound made him jump up. Seeing it was his buddy Rod Eckers, he answered.

"Hey, Rod, what's up?"

"I heard you had the day off and wondered if you'd like to meet me for a game of racquetball this morning."

Frowning, Trent tilted his chin down. *Sure wish I could.*

"Trent, are you there?"

"Yeah." He moaned. "But I'm not free this morning."

"How come?"

Resting his elbows on the table, while holding his head in his hand, Trent made it short and sweet. "Gotta take my kids to some cooking class. Miranda has to work today, and she pretty much insisted it was my turn to take them."

"Aw, that's too bad. Let me know when you have your next day off. Hopefully, we can work something out."

"Okay, I'll give you a call. Talk to you later, Rod."

Trent hung up and groaned. When he and Miranda first separated, he'd thought he would have more time to do the things he liked. But moving out of the house didn't make his responsibility to the children disappear. So he would take the kids to Walnut Creek, but he wasn't going to stick around. He planned to drop them off and pick them up when the class was over. Truthfully, Trent had no interest in watching some Amish woman teach a bunch of rowdy kids how to cook or bake something.

He stood up and straightened his button-down shirt. *I need to get going.* Trent poured himself a cup of coffee and took a couple of sips. "I wish a game of racquetball could fit into the time frame of the kids' cooking class." He shut off the coffee maker and carried the mug to his bedroom. Setting his cup on the windowsill, Trent thumbed through the closet, sorting through his insufficient supply of shirts. He really should bring the rest of them over from the house.

"There's my favorite racquetball shirt. Too bad

I can't put it to good use today." Trent picked up his cup again and took a drink as he deliberated. *It can't hurt if I sneak away and have some "me" time would it? I deserve a break today from my expected duties.*

Walnut Creek

Lyle stepped outside onto the porch and noticed Eli's horse and buggy at the hitching rail. "I wonder when he showed up." Lyle figured his friend wanted to get an early start.

Lyle had an auction yesterday, but he was free today. It worked out well, since the building where some of his auctions were held was closed today, due to repairs. Since Heidi had a cooking class, Lyle planned to give Eli a hand with the chicken coop.

Lyle unleashed Eli's horse and walked it to the barn. He was surprised Eli hadn't taken care of it himself. After giving Blossom a few scratches behind her ears, Lyle put the horse in an empty stall and headed out to the yard where Eli was working. "Guder mariye, Eli." Lyle approached him. "I didn't hear you arrive."

"Guess I shoulda let you know I was here, but I wanted to get right to work. And if my calculations are correct, the chicken coop should be finished soon."

"You got a lot done on it yesterday." Lyle

reached out to hold the board Eli was preparing to hammer to the frame.

"I had a good little helper." Eli chuckled. "That Randy was sure eager to be a part of this project, and I couldn't let him down. So I asked him to hand me nails when I needed them, as well as some other little things he could handle."

Lyle chuckled. "It's all he's been talking about since we told him and Marsha about getting some chickens."

Eli grinned and shook his head. "It'll be good for the kinner to have a part in this. Randy told me yesterday all about the responsibility he and his sister will have: feeding the chickens and collecting eggs."

"Jah. You know how it is when you're young." Lyle reached for another board and handed it to Eli. "Heidi and I hope this will be good for the children and give them an even better sense of belonging. They sure seem eager to help."

"Believe me, I know." Eli finished putting the nails in the board. "Loretta's two are the same way. Whenever there's a project to do at our place, one or both of 'em are eager to help."

"How are Conner and Abby doing these days?"

"Doin' well. They're both like two wound-up pups. Don't know where they get their energy. They'll be at their grandparents visiting soon. And Loretta . . . Well, she's been scurrying around like a busy bee painting each of their bedrooms. She wants it to be a surprise when they get home and see their favorite color on the walls of their rooms."

Lyle pondered things as Eli sawed a few more boards to length. *Maybe it would be a good idea to paint Marsha and Randy's bedroom walls and let them choose the color. That way each of their rooms will feel as though it's really theirs. I'll take care of that soon.*

As Velma walked along the shoulder of the road with Peggy Ann and their dog, Abner, she found herself beginning to relax. The scent of blossoms from a gorgeous rose garden in a nearby yard filled her senses with sweetness. It was nice walking with her daughter, too, and doing some deep thinking. *Boy, I really needed to get away from the house for a while.*

The last few days had been stressful, and the fresh air and sunshine felt good. Walking the dog was a good excuse to be outside on a day such as this.

Facing the sun, she closed her eyes for a second and let the sun's warmth penetrate her skin. The only sounds for the moment were the birds singing and the jingle of Abner's dog tags as he pranced along in front of Velma's daughter.

Peggy Ann insisted on holding Abner's leash, and Velma didn't object, because the black Lab was behaving himself.

"How come you're so quiet, Mama?" Peggy Ann asked, skipping to keep up with the dog.

"Oh, just enjoying the surroundings and thinkin' is all."

"What about?"

Velma shrugged. "Nothing much."

"Wanna know what I'm thinkin' about?"

"What's that, honey child?"

"Papa." Peggy Ann stopped walking so the dog could sniff something on the ground. "I wish he didn't have to be gone all the time. Bet you miss him, too, huh, Mama?"

Velma slowly nodded. She wouldn't admit it to any of her children, but it was a relief when Hank left early this morning to pick up a load with his semitruck. He'd be gone several days, so she wouldn't have to listen to him harp on the issue of the accident she'd caused and them having no car. Velma was the person inconvenienced. Having to walk or ride one of the kid's bikes was certainly no fun for her. Neither was living with disharmony in their home. Velma wanted a good solid marriage. She needed some answers to fix her dilemma, because right now, nothing seemed right. *Maybe it would help if I had a friend— someone to bounce things off of.*

Velma glanced at a well-kept farm across the road. *Too bad we don't have a horse and buggy like those Amish people do. At least it would get us where we wanna go without worrying about having money to fill the gas tank.* She wrinkled her nose. *Guess keeping a horse wouldn't be cheap, though. It would cost money to feed it too.*

As they came parallel to the driveway leading to the Amish house, a Brittany spaniel started barking from the yard. Abner responded with a few *Arf! Arfs!* Then, jerking the leash out of Peggy Ann's hand, the dog broke free and darted across the street.

"Come back here, Abner!" Velma and Peggy Ann shouted at the same time.

Both dogs were now chasing each other around the yard, yipping and yapping so loud Velma felt like covering her ears.

"What should we do, Mama?" Peggy Ann began jumping up and down.

Only one thing to do. Go into the yard after her dog.

"I don't wanna learn cookin' today." Randy's lower lip protruded. "Wanna be outside watchin' Eli work on the chicken coop."

"You got to watch and help him yesterday when he started the project," Heidi reminded the boy. "And remember, as soon as Eli finishes building the coop, we'll get some chicks." She pointed to the recipe cards lying on the table. "This morning you'll enjoy making mini corn dogs with the other children, and we'll get to eat them afterward."

"But I was helpin' Eli, and what if he needs me again today?"

"I'm sure Eli will understand. Lyle will be helping him today. Now that he has your rooms painted, he has some free time."

Out of the blue, Marsha spoke up. "I like corn dogs."

Heidi smiled. "I think most kids do—and even some adults like me and Lyle."

The little girl looked up at Heidi with such a sweet smile. "Lyle's my *daadi*, and you're my *mammi*."

"No, they're not." Randy shook his head. "Our mommy and daddy are in heaven."

Marsha squinted, while tipping her head, as if trying to process what her brother said. They'd talked about this before, but apparently Marsha had forgotten.

Before Heidi could offer an explanation, a ruckus coming from outside drew her attention to the window. She was surprised to see Rusty being chased by a black Lab she didn't know. A leash clipped to the Lab's collar trailed behind.

"Oh, dear." Heidi opened the back door and stepped outside. Clapping her hands, she called for her dog, but Rusty kept running and barking, oblivious to her command. This was unusual for her normally obedient dog.

Then a woman with scraggly blond hair dashed into the yard, hollering, "Stop, Abner! Come

141

here right now!" When she picked up a stick and shook it, the Lab quit running and crawled to her on his belly.

"Don't hit him, Mama. Please don't hit Abner." A young girl with reddish-blond hair worn in pigtails ran up to the woman and clutched her hand.

"I ain't gonna hit the mutt. Just wanted to scare him so he'd quit running." The woman picked up the dog's leash, holding it firmly. Then she turned to face Heidi. "Sorry for the intrusion. My daughter and I were takin' Abner for a walk, and when he saw your dog and heard it barking in your yard, he took off like a flash. Peggy Ann couldn't hold him, and the leash slipped out of her hand."

By this time, Rusty had also quit running and was lying on the porch by Heidi's feet, panting. Lyle came out of the barn. "Everything okay up there?"

Heidi waved. "Jah, we're good." She smiled when he nodded, and he went back into the barn.

Heidi came down the porch steps. "It's all right. I understand how dogs can be sometimes." She smiled. "I'm Heidi Troyer. Are you new to the area? I don't recall seeing you or your daughter before."

"Yeah, we moved here from Kentucky about a month ago. My name's Velma Kimball, and this is Peggy Ann. I have two more kids at home:

Bobbie Sue—she's seventeen—and Eddie, who's ten. We live down the road apiece in a double-wide."

Heidi wasn't sure she could get a word in, with the woman talking so fast, but she was finally able to say, "It's nice meeting you." Now that she thought about it, she had seen the mobile home set back off the road. It had been for sale a while ago, but she hadn't realized it had sold or that anyone was living there now.

Still holding her dog's leash, Velma reached out her other hand to shake Heidi's. "Nice to meet you too. Have ya got any kids?"

"None of my own, but my husband and I have two foster children."

"I see. Well, maybe my kids will get to meet them sometime." Velma glanced at her daughter, then looked back at Heidi. "Peggy Ann's kinda shy, and she hasn't fully adjusted to our move. I think it'd be good if she makes some new friends."

Heidi noticed how their dog had begun to pant. The animal's pink tongue hung out the side of its mouth. "Peggy Ann, there is a bucket over by the porch. Why don't you get the hose and fill it with water for your dog? He looks thirsty."

After Peggy Ann filled the bucket, she carried it over and set it down by the Lab. As if the dogs were best friends, Rusty and Abner, heads together, lapped the water at the same time.

"Now would you look at that?" Velma grinned

when both dogs laid down in the cool grass together. "Abner's never taken to any dog like that. Seems he's already made a new friend."

Heidi was about to respond, when a car she hadn't seen before pulled in. A few seconds later, Kevin and Debbie got out of the vehicle. Heidi saw a man in the driver's seat, but she'd never met him before.

"I'm sorry to cut our conversation short," she said, looking at Velma, "but I teach a cooking class every other Saturday, and some of my students have arrived."

Velma pursed her lips. "Those kids are your students?"

"Yes, that's Kevin and Debbie. The others aren't here yet but should arrive soon, I expect." Heidi nodded. "It's a cooking class for children, and today will be their second lesson."

Velma rubbed her chin with a thoughtful expression. "Hmm . . . Are the classes expensive?"

Heidi quoted the price and Velma grimaced. "Unfortunately, I don't have any extra money right now. It's a shame, too, 'cause I think learnin' to cook with a bunch of other kids would be real good for my Peggy Ann."

"I may teach more classes for children in the future," Heidi said. "If I do, I'll let you know."

Velma snapped her fingers. "Say, ya know what? I have an idea."

Heidi glanced at Kevin and Debbie. They stood next to the car, talking through the open window to the man who'd brought them. *I need to go introduce myself to him, but I don't want to be rude to our new neighbor.*

"Would ya like to hear my idea?" Velma seemed eager to share her plan.

"Umm . . . certainly."

"I was thinkin', since I can't afford to pay for Peggy Ann to take your classes, I could do some work for you in exchange for you teaching my daughter."

"Well, uh . . ." Heidi moistened her lips with the tip of her tongue. "I'm not sure . . ."

"I'll do any kind of chore you need to have done. I can clean your house, do yard work, and even chop wood. I'm very handy, believe you me, and strong too." Velma's voice trembled a bit. "Oh, please don't say no. Peggy Ann would surely benefit from takin' your class."

"Well, I suppose it would be all right. Peggy Ann can join the class today, and afterward I'll make a list of some things I need to have done. Then you can choose."

Velma's face broke into a wide smile. "Thanks, Heidi. Thanks so much."

Heidi wasn't sure if agreeing to let Velma work for her in exchange for Peggy Ann joining the classes was a good idea, but she didn't have the heart to say no. Velma seemed almost desperate, and her daughter looked so forlorn. Perhaps she would have the opportunity to minister to them in some way, as she had in the past with many of her previous students.

Heidi looked over at the Cooper children again and was disappointed because it appeared that the man in the car was getting ready to leave.

Excusing herself from Velma, Heidi hurried across the yard.

Chapter 14

When Heidi approached the car, the man sitting in the driver's seat offered her a friendly smile. "Hi there, I'm Trent Cooper—Debbie and Kevin's dad. And you must be their cooking teacher."

She nodded. "I'm Heidi Troyer."

"Daddy brought us today 'cause our mom has to work," Kevin spoke up. "I asked him to come inside and watch us cook, but he said he has to go somewhere."

"That's right," Trent agreed, "but I'll be back around noon to get the kids. That's what time the class ends, right?"

"Yes, but—"

"Good. See you later then."

Debbie and Kevin jumped back from the car as their father hastily pulled out of the yard, giving Heidi no chance to say anything more. Walking beside the Cooper children, she headed for the house, where Velma and her daughter remained by the porch.

Barely giving Velma and her daughter a glance, Kevin poked his sister.

"Hey, stop it!" Debbie moved to his other side.

Velma's dog tried to jump up on Kevin, but Velma yanked Abner's leash. "I'd better take this mutt home now." She looked at Peggy Ann. "You go on in the house with Heidi and get acquainted with the other kids. I'll be back to get you when the class is over."

"Except for Debbie and Kevin, none of the other children are here yet," Heidi explained again.

Velma waved her hand. "Well, never mind about that. Peggy Ann can sit with these two and wait till the others show up."

Peggy Ann gripped her mother's hand. "I thought you was gonna stay with me, Mama."

Velma shook her head. "Not this time. I have some things I need to do at home, but you'll be fine. I want to get Abner home too." Holding the dog's leash, Velma turned and headed toward the road.

Heidi's jaw clenched. That made two parents who wouldn't be with their children today. She wasn't sure how she felt about the parents participating or not. With the addition of another child to teach, she might need a helping hand. Although with the exception of Ellen, none of the other parents had been very helpful during the first class. Looking back on it, Ellen had actually done too much for her daughter. Becky needed the chance to learn things on her own without her mother taking over. So maybe it was best if the parents didn't stay. That's what Heidi had expected in the first place.

She opened the front door. "You three can go on into the living room. Randy and Marsha are inside. I want to put Rusty in his pen, and then I'll be right in." Heidi waited until the children stepped inside and shut the door behind them.

"Come on, Rusty, let's go to the pen." Heidi clapped her hands.

The dog lifted his head, then flopped back down with a sleepy grunt.

"Sorry, mister, you're going in the pen. My other students will be here soon, and I don't want you creating anymore ruckus."

Rusty got up and ambled down the steps behind Heidi. They were halfway across the yard when he darted to the left and made a beeline for a mud puddle in the driveway. It had rained during the night, leaving several puddles of water in various places throughout their yard.

Heidi cupped her hands around her mouth and whistled, but Rusty ignored her. Now he was chasing a butterfly he'd spooked near the puddle. Jumping up as he gave chase through the damp grass, Rusty's attempts to catch the colorful insect failed. She didn't understand what had come over him today. He was normally so well-behaved.

Well, she couldn't spend any more time watching Rusty's shenanigans. He'd gotten himself into too much mischief already. Heidi didn't want to leave him free to roam in the yard. Plus, she had to get back inside to make sure Randy and Marsha were getting along with the other children.

Heidi clapped her hands and said firmly, "Rusty, come here, boy."

The dog turned in her direction, but when a car pulled into the yard, he plodded down the driveway to greet them.

"Watch out, Mom. There's that stupid mutt coming toward our car." Kassidy tapped Denise on the shoulder from the back seat.

Denise turned to look at her and frowned. "I hope he gets out of the way. Sure wouldn't want to hit Heidi's dog." She slowed the car and crept forward just a bit, waiting to see what the Brittany spaniel would do. It was a pretty dog but not very bright. She was surprised the Troyers hadn't trained it to stay away from cars. *Of course,* she reasoned, *the dog's probably not used to many cars coming onto their property, since their main mode of transportation is by horse and buggy.*

Denise couldn't imagine having to hitch a horse to a buggy, not to mention traveling so slow compared to riding in a car. Whenever she went anywhere, she wanted to get there as quickly as possible.

"What's wrong with that dog, anyways?"

Kassidy complained. "Why won't it get out of our way?"

"Just be patient. The dog will eventually move."

"Look, Mom. Heidi's coming now to get the dog." Kassidy pointed again.

Denise stopped the car, waiting for Heidi to approach. Once Heidi had a hold of the dog's collar and had guided him off the driveway, Denise moved her vehicle forward and parked it near the barn. She and Kassidy opened their doors and got out at the same time. But just as Kassidy started walking toward the house, Heidi's dog got away from her. The animal raced across the yard and jumped up, putting his dirty feet on Kassidy's chest. Kassidy screamed so loud, it must have frightened the dog, for it raced off and darted into the barn.

A few minutes later, Heidi's husband came out, carrying the spaniel. He said a few words to Heidi, then put the dog in its pen. In the meantime, Kassidy sat on the front porch steps, crying hysterically. Denise went immediately to her side.

"Calm down, Kassidy. The dog didn't bite you, did he?"

"No, but he did this!" She motioned to the muddy paw prints and wet grass stains on the front of her cream-colored blouse. "We've gotta go home, Mom. I can't go in there looking like this."

Heidi joined them on the porch with a pained expression. "I am so sorry, Kassidy. I tried to hold Rusty, but he got away. Don't know what's come over him today. He's normally better behaved."

Lowering her gaze, Kassidy folded her arms. "My blouse is ruined, and I'm not in the mood to learn how to cook anything today. Every time I come here, there are problems with your dog. First, my shoe. Now this." Kassidy pointed to her blouse. "I bet the stains will never come out!"

"Your blouse isn't ruined," Denise spoke up. "I'm sure the mud and green stains will wash out. I'll take care of it as soon as we get home."

Looking up, Kassidy blew out a noisy breath. "What am I supposed to do in the meantime? I look a mess!"

"I'd offer to loan you one of my dresses, but they'd be too big for you." Heidi tucked a stray piece of hair back under her white head covering. "I do have an apron you can wear today. It will cover the front of your blouse."

Kassidy looked at Heidi as if she had two heads. "I wouldn't wear one of your—"

"Thank you, Heidi," Denise interrupted before Kassidy could say more. She gave her daughter a look, daring her to say another word. "We seem to be the only ones here so far, so let's go inside. You can put Heidi's apron on before anyone else arrives. Then you won't have to be embarrassed about anyone seeing the mud on your blouse."

"Actually, a few of the other students are inside," Heidi said.

"Oh, great." Kassidy looked down, mumbling something else under her breath.

"What was that?" Denise nudged her daughter's arm.

"Nothing, Mom."

Denise smiled. For the moment at least, it appeared that she'd won this battle of the wills. She hoped Kassidy would be cooperative during the cooking class today.

"Sure hope we make something good this time." Jeremy leaned over the seat and bumped Darren's arm as they turned up Heidi's driveway.

"I'm sure it will be good. The salad you made during the first class was pretty tasty."

"I guess—if you like a lot of fruit chopped up in one bowl. I'd rather eat a banana or an apple by itself instead of with other fruit."

Darren didn't comment. He was too busy watching Ellen and her daughter get out of their vehicle. Ellen was not only pretty, but from the few times they'd visited, she seemed intelligent and well grounded. He wanted to get to know her better.

"Say, Dad, I've been wondering about something."

"Umm . . . what's that, Son?"

"Do you know why the Amish wear such plain clothes?"

"No, I don't. Why don't you ask Heidi?"

"I don't know. She might think it's a dumb question."

Darren parked next to Ellen's vehicle, turned off the engine, and hopped out. "Hey, it's good to see you again." He offered Ellen what he hoped was a pleasant smile. "How have you been?"

She smiled in return. "We've been fine, and we're looking forward to another cooking lesson." Ellen looked at her daughter. "Isn't that right, Becky?"

The girl shrugged. She wasn't a very talkative child. Not like Jeremy, who had been known to talk nonstop when it came to something he was interested in, such as playing soccer, going fishing, or teaching his dog new tricks.

"How are things going with you?" Ellen asked.

"Good. Jeremy and I are going hiking next week. We're looking forward to that."

Ellen's eyes brightened. "Sounds like fun. I've enjoyed hiking since I was a young girl. Used to go on hikes with my dad, and sometimes we went fishing."

"Now isn't that something? Jeremy and I both like to fish." Darren looked at Becky. "Do you enjoy fishing?"

Without meeting his gaze, she mumbled, "It's okay, I guess."

Darren couldn't help noticing the face Becky made as she turned and looked toward the house. Ignoring Ellen's daughter, he continued. "Maybe the four of us could go fishing sometime. We could make a trip to one of the lakes or ponds in the area and take a picnic lunch along. We'd park the car some distance away, and hike in, of course." He grinned. "It'll make it more fun that way."

Jeremy tapped Darren's arm, and said in a low voice, "Can we go inside for the class now?"

"Just a second, Son." He rested his hand on the boy's shoulder.

Ellen repositioned her purse's shoulder strap and nodded. "That does sound like an enjoyable outing. After we get inside, I'll give you my phone number. When you have a date in mind to go fishing, you can let me know, and then I'll see if Becky and I are free to go."

"Dad, we need to get to the class. I'm sure Heidi's waiting." Jeremy kicked at a pebble.

Darren looked at his watch. "We're fine. We've got a few minutes yet."

Becky looked up at her mother through half-closed eyes but said nothing. Darren had a feeling the girl wasn't thrilled about the idea of going fishing with them. For that matter, based on the frown his son wore right now, he guessed neither one of the children wanted to go. Well, it didn't matter. If he and Ellen could work out a day when they were both free, the kids would have to go along whether they liked it or not. Maybe some time fishing and enjoying the great outdoors would be good for all of them.

Chapter 15

Once everyone gathered around the kitchen table, Heidi introduced her newest student. "I'd like you all to meet Peggy Ann. She and her family live down the road a ways, and Peggy Ann will be joining us today, as well as the next four classes we have." She placed her hands on the young girl's slender shoulders. "Please make her feel welcome by introducing yourselves."

Denise, Ellen, and Darren went first, then their children.

"You met Kevin and Debbie when they first arrived," Heidi said.

After the introductions were made, Heidi explained that they would be making mini corn dogs. She was about to hand out the recipe cards, when Randy leaped off his chair and raced to the back door. "I hear Eli pounding with his hammer!"

"Eli's been out there a good while, and I'm sure Lyle is helping him. You can check on their progress after class is over." Heidi gestured to the table. "Please come back, Randy, and take your seat."

With slumped shoulders, the boy shuffled across the room and flopped into his chair with a grunt. "Eli's gonna wonder why I'm not helpin' like I did yesterday."

Heidi shook her head. "He knows we're having a cooking class today."

"Who's Eli?" Kevin asked, leaning closer to Randy.

"He's a nice Amish man, and he's buildin' a coop so me and Marsha can have some chickens."

Kevin grinned. "Oh, boy, that sounds like fun. Can I see your chickens when you get them?"

Randy bobbed his head. "Course ya can. I'll show 'em to everyone here if they want."

"I'd like to see them," Debbie put in.

"Me too." Peggy Ann nodded affirmatively.

"How 'bout you?" Randy asked, looking at Darren's son.

Jeremy shrugged. "Maybe."

Randy looked at Becky next. "Would you like to see the chickens?"

"I guess so," she said quietly.

"I don't want to see any stupid old chickens." Kassidy wrinkled her nose. "And I don't see what the big deal is either."

"Bet you don't have any chickens." Randy looked Kassidy square in the eyes. "Me and my sister will get to gather eggs and feed the chickens."

"Oh, that sounds like so much fun." Kassidy rolled her eyes. "Chickens are smelly, and even if you paid me, I'd never want any."

"Well, ours won't be smelly." Randy crossed his arms. "I'll keep their coop nice and clean."

Kassidy answered by holding her nose, and her mother looked fit to be tied.

Heidi figured it was time to get back to the topic of making the corn dogs, before an argument started. "As you can see on your recipe cards, in addition to a package of hot dogs, we'll be using white flour, cornmeal, baking powder, salt, shortening, butter, and milk."

"How come so many things just to make hot dogs?" Peggy Ann blinked rapidly, and when she tipped her head, one of her braids fell across her face.

Marsha giggled and pointed at her. "You look funny."

Heidi shook her head. "Marsha, it's not nice to make fun of others."

"But she's right." Kevin snickered. "Peggy Ann looks like she's wearin' a giant mustache."

All the kids laughed—even Becky, who up until this time had seemed quite sullen. Peggy Ann, on the other hand, pressed a fist to her lips, as though holding back tears. Or maybe she was trying to refrain from saying something mean back to Kevin.

Heidi was certain if the boy's mother had been

here, she would have scolded him for teasing. Perhaps his father would have as well. But neither parent was here today, so Heidi felt it was her place to say something.

"Now, Kevin, I'm sure you wouldn't want someone to poke fun of you, so you shouldn't do it to anyone else. Don't you think you should tell Peggy Ann you're sorry?"

He leaned his elbows on the table. "Don't see what for. I didn't say anything bad. Just told the truth."

Debbie poked her brother's arm. "Quit arguing and just say you're sorry. If you don't, I'm gonna tell Daddy when he picks us up."

Frowning, Kevin glanced at Peggy Ann, then looked away. "Sorry," he mumbled.

It wasn't much of an apology, but it was better than nothing.

"So now," Heidi said, after clearing her throat, "Let's begin our lesson."

Berlin

As Trent wandered around Heini's Cheese Chalet, tasting samples of various cheeses, he thought about the kids and wondered how they were doing. If he'd had more time, he would have driven to New Philly and joined his buddy for a game of racquetball. But if he went there, he'd be late picking up the kids and felt sure one or both of them would tell their mother about it.

Trent checked his watch, wondering if there would be time to go anywhere else, but he thought better of it. Two hours could go by quickly, especially if a person wasn't paying attention, so he would just browse around here a little more.

Trent grabbed a clean toothpick, and took another sample of cheese. *This stuff's good. Maybe I'll buy a few packages and give one to Miranda. I've got to do something to get back in her good graces again.*

He put two packages of baby Swiss in his shopping basket, along with some mild cheddar and a package of Gouda. As he neared the cash register, he spotted some milk-chocolate bars and put those in the basket for the kids. *If I give 'em candy to eat on the way home, they might be less apt to tell their mother I bailed on them this morning.*

While the clerk rang up the customer ahead of him, Trent thought he might make another stop. *Maybe I'll go to a store nearby for a homemade pretzel. That'd be good, because I'm still hungry. All those cheese samples did was whet my appetite. I may even indulge in a double scoop of ice cream.* That was one thing nice about living where the tourism was hot—plenty of businesses selling his favorite treats.

Walnut Creek

Ellen stood quietly, watching as Becky mixed the butter, shortening, and milk in with the dry ingredients Heidi had given each of the children. *I wouldn't mind taking a cooking class myself. It's fun to watch the children, although it is hard to resist doing my daughter's work.* Ellen was making an effort not to take over for Becky as she'd done during the first cooking class. With Becky being her only child, sometimes it was difficult not to smother her.

Even though Becky had said she loved Ellen and forgave her for keeping the adoption a secret, things weren't quite the same between them as they had been before the visit to Patrick's. Becky seemed withdrawn and disinterested in most things. *I know I've betrayed my sweet daughter's trust, but I must believe that in time the Lord will help me with this.*

Ellen bit down gently on her bottom lip as she stole a quick glance at Darren. *Hiking and fishing with him and Jeremy would be something fun for us to do. I hope we can work things out with our schedules so we can make it happen. I, for one, am looking forward to it—not only for the fresh air and exercise, but I'd like the chance to get to know Darren better.*

Ellen noticed a bee come into the room and fly

to the kitchen window. "Um, Heidi, do you have a fly swatter around?"

"Yes, I do. I'll get it." Heidi retrieved the swatter hanging in the corner of the kitchen.

"Hey, everybody, look there. Heidi is gonna swat that ole bee." Peggy Ann piped up.

"Wish I could kill it." Kevin hopped down from his seat.

Heidi took a swing and missed the insect the first time. The bee flew around the room and came back to the window. All eyes seemed to be on the fly swatter, as well as its target. Heidi's arm drew back like a loaded spring, then she released it with a *smack!* The bee hit the sink and didn't budge. Kevin cheered and everyone else clapped. Heidi scooped the insect onto the weapon of its undoing and carried it outside. When she returned, she washed her hands and came back to the table.

"Now that everyone has their ingredients mixed well, it's time to roll out the dough." Heidi owned three rolling pins, which she'd previously placed on the table. "We'll take turns rolling the dough before we cut it in rounds. She handed one rolling pin to Debbie and one to Kassidy. The other one she used to demonstrate the correct way to flatten and roll out the dough.

"Can I go check on Eli while I'm waitin' my turn?" Randy asked.

She shook her head. "It won't take long to get your dough ready for the hot dog, so I want you to remain at the table and watch the others."

Randy bent his head forward, sitting in a hunched position, but at least he stayed seated.

After Heidi demonstrated with the rolling pin, she watched as Kassidy and Debbie rolled theirs. They both did it easily, and then it was Randy and Kevin's turn. The boys, being younger, needed a bit of assistance, but once their dough was rolled out adequately, the rolling pins were given to Becky and Jeremy.

"This looks easy." Jeremy glanced at Becky, through half-closed lids. "Bet I can get mine rolled out before you do."

With a determined expression, Becky began rolling hard and fast.

"Slow down, sweetie. There's no need to hurry." Ellen touched her daughter's shoulder.

Becky shrugged and kept rolling.

Lips pressed tightly together, Jeremy rolled his dough so hard that it split down the middle.

"Now look what happened." Darren shook his head slowly. "You're too competitive, Son."

Heidi was at a loss for words. She couldn't understand what the problem was between the two children or why there would be competition. But then Heidi didn't understand a lot of things these days—such as why, whenever Marsha called her mammi, or Lyle, daadi,

Randy seemed upset. She doubted that he would ever call them anything except their first names. But it was okay. At least his overall attitude had changed for the better, and as with the chicken coop, he'd taken an interest in more things.

Heidi smiled when she saw Marsha, kneeling on a chair, while reaching over to touch the dough Debbie had rolled.

"Are we makin' a pie?" the little girl asked.

"No, dear one," Heidi explained. "The dough we mixed up is sort of like what we'd make for a pie, but it'll be wrapped around our mini corn dogs."

Eyes wide, Peggy Ann spoke up. "Ain't the dough too big for a little bitty frankfurter?"

Heidi smiled, biting back a chuckle. "Our next step, Peggy Ann, is to cut out the dough in a circle, and then we'll place the small frankfurter in the center of it."

"How we gonna cut it—with a pair of scissors?"

"No. We'll use the lid from a canning jar," Heidi responded. "It's simple enough, and everyone, even Marsha, should be able to do it."

Heidi moved across the room to get a few of her wide-mouth canning lids, but was interrupted by pounding on the back door. She went to answer it, thinking either Lyle or Eli wanted something. *Of course,* she reasoned, *if it were Lyle, he would not have knocked.*

Heidi opened the door, and Velma, dressed in what looked like a pair of men's overalls, stepped inside. Strands of blond hair stuck out from under the red paisley hankie scarf tied at the back of her neck, and she seemed out of breath. "I know it's not time for the class to be over, but I'm here to do whatever work ya need done. After I got Abner taken care of, I changed and came right back."

"Well, I'm right in the middle of class." Heidi tilted her head. "Didn't you say you had things to get done at your place?"

"Oh, that." Velma waved off Heidi's question. "Those chores can wait. This is more important to me."

Oh, dear. Heidi massaged her forehead. She hadn't expected Velma would want to get started so soon, and truthfully, she hadn't had a chance to even think of what she might want to have done.

With the door still open, Randy must have seen this as his chance to escape, for he leaped off his chair, and raced outside before Heidi could call out to him.

The class was only half over, and already things seemed topsy-turvy. Heidi wasn't quick enough to stop Marsha from taking a chunk of dough from Debbie's rolled-out piece, and popping it in her mouth, like it was candy. Once more, Heidi wondered if teaching a children's cooking class had been a good idea. If she continued teaching classes, she might stick to adults only. At least they weren't so impulsive—although some of her previous students had other problems.

Chapter 16

Now that's some chicken house you're makin' there."

Heidi turned at the sound of Velma's voice. She hadn't realized the woman had followed her into the yard where Lyle and Eli had moved the structure and were now working on its roof.

Heidi hated to be rude, but she hoped Velma wouldn't take up too much of her time talking. She was halfway through today's class and needed to get back inside.

"Yes, indeed." Velma slapped her knee. "I've built a few chicken coops in my time. We had a really nice one when we lived in Kentucky. Housed enough chickens to give us plenty of eggs for our use, plus enough to sell." She paused long enough to draw a quick breath, then kept talking. "I need to get one built at our place. Just haven't made the time to do it yet. But I'd be glad to help you finish this one if ya like."

When Velma quit talking, Eli jumped in. "I appreciate the offer, miss, but Lyle and I are almost done here, and everything's under control."

Before Velma could comment, Randy stepped

forward, giving the leg of Eli's trousers a tug. "You said I could help ya finish up with the coop." He pointed to the house. "But I'm stuck in there makin' some dumb old corn dog."

Eli tapped the boy's shoulder. "As soon as you're done, you can come out and help us put the finishing touches on."

"And don't forget," Lyle added, "you'll get to go with me to pick up the chickens next week."

Randy's face brightened. "Can Marsha go too?"

"Of course she can." Lyle gestured to Heidi. "I think my *fraa* might want to accompany us as well."

Heidi nodded. "I wouldn't miss it."

"Okay!" Randy grinned.

Heidi felt relief when the boy started back to the house, swinging his arms. She smiled at the men. "There'll be enough corn dogs to eat when they are done, so if you two would like to join us, you're more than welcome."

"Sounds good." Lyle thumped his stomach. "I've been working up an appetite. How about you, Eli?"

Eli grinned. "Same here, but I think I might pass on the offer. I'll be taking Loretta out for an early supper this evening, and I want to save plenty of room for the Farmstead Restaurant's buffet."

"Okay, well, I'd best get back to my class."

Heidi looked at Velma. "You're welcome to come watch if you like."

"I would, but I came here to get started on some chores for you, like I promised." Velma shifted from one foot to the other. "What about your garden? Does it need to be weeded?" She looked toward the yard where the garden was planted, then tucked a strand of wayward hair back underneath her scarf.

Heidi glanced toward her garden. "I do appreciate the offer, and I would say yes, but the weeds aren't too bad yet." She could see by the downward curve of Velma's mouth, that she was disappointed.

Since Heidi wasn't sure what she wanted to have done, nor did she want to take the time to show Velma right now, she said, "Why don't you plan on coming over one day next week to do a chore? By then I'll have a better idea what I'd like to have done."

Velma's forehead wrinkled as she hesitantly nodded. "Guess that'd be okay. All right then, I'll go inside with you and watch the proceedings."

"Where's Heidi? When is she coming back?" Kassidy's chin jutted out as she pointed to the clock on the far wall. "It'll be time for us to go pretty soon, and we won't have made a thing."

"Don't be so impatient," Denise reprimanded. "I'm sure Heidi will return soon. Besides, we

170

don't have any plans for the rest of the day, so there's no hurry."

Kassidy frowned. "I don't wanna be here all day, Mom. I might want to get together with one of my friends."

Jeremy glanced her way. "Ya know what, Kassidy? You whine too much."

"Do not."

"Yeah, you do."

"No, I don't, and you should mind your own business."

Before a full-blown argument could brew, Denise quickly changed the subject. "Who likes mustard on their corn dogs?"

"I do." Peggy Ann's hand shot up. Little Marsha followed suit.

"I don't like mustard," Debbie said, "but I do like plenty of relish."

"I like ketchup," Kevin announced.

"Same here." Jeremy nodded.

"How about you, Becky?" Denise asked. "What's your favorite thing to put on a corn dog?"

"Ketchup, I guess." The girl spoke quietly. "Sometimes I like mustard."

"I'll bet Heidi has ketchup and mustard." Darren looked at Ellen and smiled. "What's your favorite condiment?"

"I'm okay with ketchup and mustard, but what I really like on my regular hot dogs, or even a corn dog, is sauerkraut."

"Same here." Darren's smile widened. "Looks like we have one more thing in common."

Denise suppressed a smile. It didn't take a genius to see the fireman was infatuated with the nurse. She remembered back to when Greg used to look at her like that. With both of them absorbed in their busy careers, they'd drifted apart. He rarely took the time to really look at her anymore, much less with such a happy expression.

Denise's contemplations came to a halt when Heidi entered the kitchen with a frumpy looking woman with faded blond hair sticking out of a red paisley hankie scarf. The woman reminded her of a funny card she'd seen at the store recently. Except for not wearing a straw hat or having missing front teeth, Denise could swear it was the same lady pictured on the hilarious birthday card.

"Everyone, I'd like you to meet Velma Kimball. She's Peggy Ann's mother."

"Sorry for the interruption," Velma said, "but Heidi said it was okay if I came in and watched." She gestured to Denise, as well as the other two parents. "Looks like I'm not the only adult here, though."

"That's right," Heidi agreed. "This is Denise McGuire, Darren Keller, and Ellen Blackburn. Ellen's daughter, Becky; Darren's son, Jeremy; and Denise's daughter, Kassidy, are my students."

172

She motioned to the boy and girl sitting across from Kassidy. "And you've met Debbie and Kevin Cooper. Neither of their parents is here today."

Velma nodded. "Yeah, I was outside with you when their dad dropped them off." She placed her hand on top of Marsha's blond head. "And this cute little girl I've already met, along with her brother." Velma reached out, as if to touch Randy, but he slunk down in his chair. Denise figured the boy was either shy around strangers or didn't care much for Velma. *Maybe she reminds him of someone he knows and doesn't like.*

"Okay, now, let's start where we left off." Heidi washed her hands at the sink and handed each of the children a wide-mouthed canning jar lid. "Just press it into your dough and when you lift it off, you'll see that you've made a circle. Keep doing that until you have several circles."

"What about the dough Marsha pulled off of mine and ate?" Debbie glanced at Heidi with a look of concern.

"It's okay," Heidi reassured her student. "You still have plenty of dough." Heidi shook her head at Marsha. "Please don't eat any more dough, okay? It's not good for you."

Slowly, Marsha nodded.

"Now what do we do?" Jeremy asked after he'd made his circles.

"You will place half a hot dog on each of the

circles. Then bring the sides of the dough up and pinch it in the center." Heidi took one and demonstrated.

"This is easy-peasy," Kassidy said. "If you want my opinion, it's baby stuff."

Jeremy squinted. "Nobody asked for your opinion."

"Oh, yeah, well, for your information—"

Heidi broke in quickly, as though hoping to divert a confrontation. "The next step will be to place the frankfurters wrapped with dough on a greased cooking sheet. We'll set the oven temperature to 350 degrees and bake them for twelve to fifteen minutes. Once they have cooled sufficiently, we can take the mini corn dogs outside and eat them at the picnic table."

"Got any potato chips to go with 'em?" Peggy Ann wanted to know.

Heidi smiled. "Yes, I certainly do. We can also have some cold lemonade to drink."

Peggy Ann clapped her hands. "Oh, good! It'll be like a picnic. It's been a long time since we had a picnic, huh, Mama?"

Velma nodded.

"We used to do picnics all the time before our daddy moved out of the house." Kevin looked over at his sister. "Ain't that right, Debbie?"

She scowled at him. "*Ain't* isn't good English, and you shouldn't be blabbing stuff about us. It's nobody's business but ours."

Kevin sneered at his sister. "Well, it's not like I'm makin' stuff up or anything. It's the truth. We did a lot more fun things when Daddy lived with us."

Denise felt sorry for these children whose parents were obviously separated, or maybe even divorced. She wondered if Kassidy knew how good she had it.

After everyone's corn dogs were adequately browned, Heidi provided paper plates and suggested they take the food outside. "I'll bring out the condiments, and if some of you parents don't mind helping, you can bring the lemonade, chips, and some napkins."

"I'll bring the chips," Darren offered.

"And I'll get the lemonade."

Denise smiled. "Guess that leaves me to carry the napkins."

"What about paper cups? Do you have any of those?" Velma asked.

"Yes, of course." Heidi didn't know why she felt so mixed up today. She'd had everything planned out ahead of time, but things hadn't turned out the way she'd expected—starting with Velma and her daughter showing up before class.

"Always be prepared for the unexpected," Heidi remembered her father saying.

It's hard to be prepared for things you weren't planning to happen, she mused.

After the children went outside with their plates filled, Heidi and the parents followed them out the door with the rest of the items. When Heidi saw Lyle look her way, she motioned for him to join them at the picnic table.

She was about to suggest that everyone bow their heads for silent prayer, when Jeremy picked up the plastic bottle of ketchup and held it over one of his corn dogs. Nothing came out, so he gave it a good squeeze. This time, though, he angled the container, while at the same time, looking at something across the way. The next thing Heidi knew, ketchup squirted out of the bottle and all over the front of Becky's shirt.

Becky gasped, and so did all the adults. But, with the exception of Becky, the children must have thought it was funny, because they all laughed.

Becky started crying and raced for the house. Ellen followed.

Heidi cringed. *So much for a nice picnic lunch.* She debated on whether to go inside to check on Becky or stay put and let the girl's mother handle it. She didn't have to think about it long, for Darren got up and grasped his son's arm. "Come with me, Jeremy. You owe Becky an apology."

The boy shook his head. "Don't see why I have to say I'm sorry. It was an accident, Dad. I didn't mean to squirt her with ketchup."

"That may be so, but you're the one who

caused it, so you need to apologize." Darren held his ground and led his son up to the house.

"Eww . . . Mom." Kassidy pointed. "Look what a bird just did on your shoulder."

"Goodness, gracious." Denise turned her head and grimaced when she saw a white blob on the navy-blue blouse she'd worn today. Taking a napkin, and trying to rub it off, Denise only managed to smear it.

"Guess when we get home you'll have to soak your blouse and mine." Kassidy snickered. "Maybe Heidi should have given you an apron to wear too."

Heidi closed her eyes briefly. She would be glad when this day was over.

Chapter 17

New Philadelphia

The next Wednesday morning, Trent sat at his kitchen table, mulling things over. Although Kevin and Debbie hadn't made a big deal out of him not staying for their cooking class last week, he felt guilty for bailing on them. At the time, he didn't feel like sitting through the class, but in hindsight Trent wished he had hung around. He also knew if the kids had told Miranda, it would give her one more reason to be upset with him.

Trent rapped his knuckles on the table. There had to be something he could do to redeem himself with her. He'd had enough of living alone and cooking his own meals. Of course, that was only part of the reason he wanted to come back home. Truthfully, he missed his wife and kids. So it was time to take stronger measures in getting Miranda to let him come home.

Let's see . . . What does she like? He snapped his fingers. *Flowers. Miranda loves flowers. Probably not a good idea to get her a bouquet of cut flowers, though. Those don't last long.* Maybe he could find some nice potted flowers to plant. He'd be on the lookout for roses the same color as the ones Miranda had carried in her wedding bouquet.

Trent glanced at his watch. He didn't have to be at work until noon today, so he had all morning to put his plan into action. And he knew exactly what it would be. He just hoped Miranda would like it.

Walnut Creek

"Them little chickens are sure cute." Randy leaned close to the pen and peered in. Marsha had gone inside with Heidi soon after returning from Baltic, where they had gone to purchase the poultry.

"They're fun to watch, aren't they? Lyle leaned in, observing their cute behavior. "We have a good variety of breeds here. I especially like the Plymouth Rocks, but the Araucana chickens and Rhode Island Reds are nice too."

"Those brown striped ones are sure neat lookin'." Randy pointed at one and smiled. "I could watch 'em all day. Can I hold one again?"

"Sure, go ahead. The one you are after is a Rhode Island Red chick. We'll get nice brown eggs from it when it's fully grown." Lyle knelt next to Randy.

The boy scooped up one with care and stroked

the soft brown, down feathers on its back. "I like having these babies around to take care of." Randy looked closer at the fluffy chick. "Are these its feathers growing out on its back?"

"Yep. They're called pin feathers, and in no time, these little guys will grow them all over their bodies." *Randy and I have something fun we can do together now.* Lyle smiled, observing the boy's delight.

"It sure wants to move around in my hands." Randy petted the chick.

"Taking care of these peepers will be a big responsibility," Lyle said. "Are you sure you're up to it, Son?"

"Umm . . . I guess so." Randy's forehead wrinkled a bit as he looked up at Lyle, while holding on to the peeping fledgling. "What all am I supposed to do?"

"Well, you'll need to feed and water the chicks and keep their pen clean." When Lyle saw the boy's perplexed expression, he quickly added, "Would you be willing to let me help you? We can do the chores together until you have the routine down. Then, when you feel more comfortable with it, you can do the chores on your own. How's that sound?"

"Sure, I'd be glad for the help till I know what I'm doin'." Randy's expression changed to one of obvious relief. At the moment, the little fellow looked much older than his six years.

Lyle smiled. No way he'd let Randy take care of the chickens all by himself—at least not until he felt confident enough to take on the responsibility alone.

At times like this, Lyle felt as if Randy was actually his son. He didn't think the feeling was mutual, however, because the boy kept a safe emotional distance most of the time. Lyle noticed Randy's guard lowering, even though it may have been for brief moments. He hoped in the near future, he and Heidi would gain this young man's trust.

Lyle hadn't brought up the topic of adoption to Heidi for some time, and he certainly didn't want to rush into anything where Randy and Marsha were concerned. But here lately, he'd begun to think adopting these special children might be the best thing—for Randy and Marsha, as well as for him and Heidi.

"Hi there. Is Heidi at home?"

Lyle rose to his feet and turned around. He'd been so preoccupied with Randy and the chickens that he hadn't realized anyone had come into the yard. He recognized Velma right away, though. She wore the same pair of baggy overalls she'd had on last Saturday, but this time she had a dark blue hankie scarf on her head.

"Yes, my wife is here," he responded. "She's in the house."

Velma joined them by the chicken coop. "I

see ya got your chicks. They're not as little as I thought they'd be."

"That's right." Lyle nodded. "These chickens are four weeks old, so they should be fine out here in the coop."

"I can tell by their color that those ones there are Rhode Island Reds." Velma whistled, pointing to the brown striped ones. "You picked some good breeds. They're not only good egg layers, but they are good eatin' too."

"No one's gonna eat my chickens." Randy looked up at Lyle and blinked. "Are they?"

"Definitely not." Lyle raised his eyebrows at Velma. "These chickens are strictly for egg laying."

"That's good." Randy crossed his arms and lifted his chin.

"Don't blame ya none." Velma pointed to the chicks. "I'd rather have the eggs too." She ran her fingers across the chicken-wire enclosure. "It's good you made a place so they can be outside for some sunshine and bug pecking." She tucked her unruly hair back under her scarf. "Chickens need that, ya know."

Randy looked up at her and tipped his head. "You seem to know a lot about chickens."

"Yep. I've raised my share of poultry over the years. Even when I was growing up, we had chickens. We raised Leghorns mostly. They lay lots of eggs." She swatted at a fly buzzing around her head. "Whelp, guess I'll go on up to the house and talk to Heidi now. Came here to do some work for her today."

She sprinted toward the house so quickly Lyle didn't have a chance to say anything more. Although a bit unconventional and seemingly impetuous when she spoke, Velma seemed like a decent sort of person. He had a hunch she would work hard at whatever chores Heidi gave her to do.

Velma stepped up to the door, and seeing it was open a crack, she knocked once and stepped inside. Tipping her head to one side, she heard voices coming from the kitchen.

Velma moved in that direction. "Hello!"

Eyes wide, Heidi stepped out of the kitchen. "Oh, you startled me, Velma."

"Sorry about that. The door was open so I came right in. That's how it is at our place." Velma's lips twitched. "If a door's open it means folks are welcome to come in."

"I see. Well, come into the kitchen. Marsha and I are baking cookies. Perhaps you'd like one."

Velma smacked her lips. "You bet I would."

Heidi led the way. When they entered the kitchen, Velma saw little Marsha sitting on a stool at the table, forming cookie dough into balls with her delicate hands. "Well, aren't you the big helper?" Velma placed her hands on Marsha's shoulders, but the little girl shrugged them away.

"Sorry about that," Heidi said. "She's still a little shy around strangers."

"I can understand that." Velma moved away from the table, putting a safe distance between her and Marsha. "My Peggy Ann is a shy one until she gets to know ya."

Heidi held a plate of ginger cookies out to Velma. "Here you go."

Velma didn't have to be asked twice. She grabbed a cookie and took a bite. "Yummy. Yummy. This is one good cookie. And your kitchen sure smells good from all the baking that's been going on."

Heidi smiled, brushing off some flour clinging to her apron. "Would you like another?"

"It's real tempting, but I'd better not. I can't stand around all day, shootin' the breeze and eatin' all your cookies. Came to work, so what have ya got for me to do?"

Heidi went over to her desk and picked up a piece of paper, which she handed to Velma. "I've written a few things down and thought you could decide which of the jobs you'd prefer to do."

Velma studied the list. "Let's see now . . . Gather the cut-up wood out behind the house and stack it by the barn. Dust the living-room furniture and shake out the throw rugs. Wash all the lower windows, inside and out. Paint the

184

porch railing. Put new stain on the picnic table."
She paused, clamping both hands against her
hips. "I don't have to choose. I'll do at least
one of those chores each week to pay for my
daughter's cooking classes."

"Oh, no," Heidi was quick to say. "I don't
expect you to do all the chores. I only made the
list so you could decide what you would rather
do."

Velma shook her head vigorously. "Nope. I
insist on doin' everything you mentioned. It's the
least I can do to repay your kindness."

Millersburg

Gathering up her keys, Ellen hollered up the
stairs for her daughter to hurry. If she didn't drop
Becky off at the sitter's soon, she might be late for
work.

"Okay, Mom, you don't have to shout. I'm
coming." A few minutes later, Becky plodded
down the stairs. She carried along a tote with a
drawing tablet and colored pencils inside. "I have
a book on animals, and I wanted to try drawing
horses like the ones out by Heidi's place."

"That sounds like a good idea. I can't wait to
see your picture when we get back home this
evening."

Ellen was almost out the door when her cell
phone rang. She pulled it out of her purse, and

when she looked at the caller ID, she didn't recognize the number. Figuring she ought to answer anyway, she said, "Hello."

"Hi, Ellen. It's Darren Keller. I hope this isn't a bad time to call."

"Well, I was about to head out the door, Darren, but I have a few minutes to talk." She glanced over at her daughter.

Becky looked upward, rolling her eyes.

"I found out I don't have to work this Friday, and wondered if you and Becky would be free to join me and Jeremy for a day of hiking and fishing."

Ellen's face grew warm as she glanced at her work schedule, pinned to the bulletin board in the kitchen. "As a matter of fact, I have Friday off too. So yes, we'd be glad to join you."

"That's great. If you'll give me your address, we'll be by around nine Friday morning to pick you up. Or is that too early for you?"

Ellen tried to swallow, but her throat had gotten dry. She grabbed the water bottle close to her purse and took a drink. "No, nine will be fine. I'll pack a picnic lunch for the four of us."

Darren laughed. "I was just going to say that I'd be happy to furnish our lunch, but if you really don't mind, I'll leave it up to you."

"I don't mind at all. Is there anything special you or Jeremy would like?"

"Naw. Just throw some sandwiches together and we'll be content."

"Any particular kind?"

"I'm not picky, and neither is Jeremy—except for tuna fish. He doesn't like tuna sandwiches at all."

"No worries. I won't fix tuna fish."

"Okay. See you Friday." Darren paused. "I'm looking forward to it, Ellen."

"Me too. Bye, Darren."

When Ellen hung up, Becky clasped her arm. "Why'd ya tell him we would go, Mom? I don't want to go fishing with Darren—and especially not Jeremy."

"How come? You enjoy fishing. I'm sure you'll have a good time."

"No, I won't. Jeremy is a know-it-all, and he doesn't like me." Becky held her stomach as though she was in pain. "The truth is, I don't like him either."

"Don't be that way, Becky. Do you remember the Bible verse Heidi wrote on the back of the corn dog recipe card? It's 1 John 4:7."

"No, not really. What'd it say?"

"Beloved, let us love one another."

"It's hard to like some people, and I could never love Jeremy." Frowning, Becky shook her head. "He gets on my nerves."

"It's not always easy to love or even like some people, but as Christians we are commanded to

187

love one another. And who knows, once you and Jeremy get better acquainted, you might see him in a different light."

"Can't I stay with one of my friends on Friday? You can still go fishing with Darren and Jeremy, if that's what you really want."

Ellen shook her head. "Darren invited both of us, and I already said yes, so we're going."

Becky rushed out the door and trumped down the porch steps. She was obviously not happy about this. But she would get over it once they got to the lake and started fishing. At least, Ellen hoped that'd be the case.

Chapter 18

Berlin

The minute Miranda stepped out of her car, she knew something in the front yard was different. The space where she'd thought about planting some dahlias was now full of pink-and-white roses.

"What in the world?" She scratched her head. "Where did those come from?" Miranda couldn't imagine how this happened. What a treat to find such gorgeous colors at home in the once empty spaces bordering her walkway.

Not only did she favor the color of the flowers, but for a special reason, roses were her favorite. Their beauty drew her toward them, and the intoxicating scent coming off the velvety petals made her bend closer to inhale the fragrance. Miranda stared at the beautiful roses a few more seconds, then hurried into the house. There, she found Debbie and Kevin watching TV with Carla, their middle-aged babysitter. "Hey, kids. Do either of you know where those roses came from in the front yard?" Miranda questioned.

Carla pulled out her earbuds and gave Miranda a blank stare. "What's up?"

Miranda repeated her question.

"Daddy did it." Kevin bobbed his head. "He said it was a surprise for you."

Carla gave a twisted smile. "It was supposed to be a nice gift for your mother."

"Yeah," Kevin agreed, "but I think he did it 'cause he felt bad that he didn't stay at Heidi's last Saturday to watch us cook."

Debbie's elbow connected with her brother's arm.

"Ouch," Kevin rubbed the spot. "Hey, what'd ya do that for?"

"You weren't supposed to say anything about that. You have a big mouth."

Kevin squeezed his eyes shut and covered his mouth. "Oops! I forgot."

Miranda's skin prickled as agitation took over. "If your dad didn't stay with you during the cooking class, where did he go?"

Kevin shrugged. "Don't know. He never said."

Debbie shot him an icy stare. "You've already ratted on Dad, so you shouldn't be lying to Mom now." She looked up at Miranda. "Dad went to the cheese store in Berlin. He said he bought some cheese for you, but then he decided to keep it for himself. Guess that's because he didn't want you to know he dropped me and Kevin at Heidi's and then went off to do whatever he wanted."

Miranda glanced at Carla. She was a pleasant woman, and Debbie and Kevin both liked her, but she tended to be a bit of a gossip. The last thing Miranda needed was for the kids' babysitter to blab around the neighborhood, or even at church, anything about the Cooper family. It was bad enough that most of their friends and family knew Miranda and Trent were separated. Too many well-meaning people had already offered their unsolicited thoughts and opinions about the situation.

"Umm, we can talk about this later, kids." Miranda gestured to the TV. "I'd like you to turn that off and go into the kitchen so you can help me get supper going."

After Debbie hit the remote and she and Kevin had left the room, Carla rose from her chair. "Now that you're home from work, you won't be needing me anymore this evening, so I'll head for home."

"Thanks, Carla." Miranda smiled. "I'll see you next Monday, when I'm scheduled to work again, and I'll pay you then if that's okay."

"Sure, no problem." Carla gathered up her purse and started out the door with a farewell wave.

Miranda paused to think and offer a quick prayer before heading for the kitchen. She did not want to say anything negative to the children about their father. She would, however, have a talk with Trent when Debbie and Kevin weren't around. He needed to know that he couldn't buy her love or work his way back into her good graces through the act of planting flowers—especially ones that reminded her of their wedding day.

Walnut Creek

Heidi was getting ready to start supper when she heard a familiar *thunk* and knew wood was being chopped. Assuming Lyle had returned home, she went outside to tell him what time their evening meal would be ready. Instead of Lyle, however, she found Velma by a stack of uncut wood, holding Lyle's axe in her hands.

"Velma, what are you doing?" Heidi walked across the yard, swatting at a cluster of gnats that seemed to form out of thin air. "When I asked you to stack the wood that had already been chopped, I didn't expect you to do this." She gestured to the pile Velma had already cut.

Velma lifted her hand, encased in a pair of dilapidated-looking work gloves, and slapped the dust off her overalls. "Well, I got the other wood stacked, so figured I may as well add some more to the pile."

Heidi shielded her eyes from the evening sun—and the annoying bugs. "I appreciate you wanting to do some work as payment for Peggy Ann's cooking classes, but you've worked several hours already and should really go home. I imagine your children are getting hungry and expecting their mother to fix supper."

Velma's head moved quickly from side to side. "Naw, I won't be cookin' supper tonight. It's Bobbie Sue's turn in the kitchen."

"I see." Although Heidi hadn't met Bobbie Sue, she knew from talking to Velma that her oldest daughter was seventeen, certainly old enough to cook a meal. If Velma's children had been with her right now, Heidi would have invited them all to stay for supper. Perhaps some other time she would extend an invitation. It would be nice to meet Mr. Kimball too.

"I appreciate the work you did here today." Heidi smiled. "It more than covered Peggy Ann's first cooking class. In fact, it probably covered two."

"Naw." Velma touched the side of her face, leaving a smudge of dirt behind. "I plan to do several chores and work at least one day each week that my young'un comes here for a class. It's the least I can do for your kindness." She leaned the axe against the side of the woodshed, and rubbed her eyes when more bugs aimed for her face. "Boy, these gnats are relentless. It must be gonna rain." Velma swatted at them, but it seemed to aggravate the insects even more. "Well, I've had enough of this. Guess I'm a little sweaty, and I am gettin' kinda hungry, so think I'll call it a day and get on home."

"Okay. Thank you, Velma. I'll see you sometime next week."

As Velma headed down the driveway, swinging her arms, Heidi paused and said a prayer for the woman. Moving into a new neighborhood in an unfamiliar state would be difficult for anyone—especially when they were having financial difficulties. Heidi planned to speak to Lyle about the Kimballs' situation. Perhaps they could think of other ways to help. Allowing Velma to do some work in exchange for her daughter's lessons was simply not enough.

Walking briskly toward home, Velma whistled, glad that the bugs had finally dispersed when she got to the road. She hadn't minded working for Heidi today. Despite the pesky gnats, and the sore muscles she expected to end up with, it felt good knowing she was able to pay for Peggy Ann's classes by helping the Troyers with things needing done. She'd meant to ask how Peggy Ann did during Heidi's second cooking class, but she'd forgotten to say anything about it. Hopefully her daughter hadn't missed too much by not attending the first class.

Velma reflected on how nice it would be to have a beautiful flower bed growing out front of her place, like the one Heidi had. It would take a lot of time and work, but it'd be worth it. However, she couldn't afford to spend extra money right now—unless it was a necessity.

As Velma continued her journey, she thought about Hank. He'd be home, either late tonight or early tomorrow, and would probably stick around a few days. In some ways, she looked forward to him being there, but in other ways she dreaded it. He'd no doubt start harping at her again about the accident that had totaled their car.

"Well, I won't let him get under my skin," she murmured. "Everyone makes mistakes, and he's sure not perfect."

Velma remembered how one Fourth of July, Hank had thrown a firecracker into her birdbath and blew it to smithereens. Of course, that didn't compare to wrecking a car. But the birdbath had been a birthday gift from Velma's sister, Maggie. Velma was quite upset when Hank ruined it, although she'd decided not to make a big deal out of it. What was the point, anyway? Fussing and fuming wouldn't bring back her birthday present, and it would have only made Hank mad. What really riled her, however, was Hank never even apologized for what he'd done. At least she'd had the decency to say she was sorry about wrecking their car.

Life sure has its ups and downs, she thought. *Wish I'd been lucky and was born with a silver spoon in my mouth. But no, my folks were poor as church mice.*

Soon Velma's driveway came into view, and as she turned to start heading toward their mobile home, she spotted a motorcycle parked near the small storage shed to the left of the trailer-house. She recognized the skull and crossbones insignia on the back of the cycle. It belonged to Bobbie Sue's boyfriend, Kenny Carmichael. Her muscles tensed, and she bit the inside of her cheek so hard she tasted blood. *What's he doin' here? That fellow never was anything but trouble.*

Velma hurried her footsteps. She planned to march right in there and send the old boyfriend packing.

Velma was almost to the door when Kenny stepped out, with Bobbie Sue clutching his arm. "Look who came to see me, Mama." Bobbie Sue gave Velma a wide grin, then looked adoringly back at Kenny.

"Nice to see ya again," Kenny mumbled.

With a curt nod, Velma waited.

Kenny put his arm around Bobbie Sue and pulled her close to his side. "I sure have missed my girl. Wish you all hadn't up and moved."

"I'm goin' for a ride with Kenny." Without waiting for Velma's response, Bobbie Sue followed him over to his motorcycle and climbed on the back.

Velma was almost too dumbfounded to say

anything, but she found her voice before Kenny had a chance to start up the cycle. "You can't go anywhere right now, Bobbie Sue. It's time to eat supper, which you should have ready for us by now."

Bobbie Sue shook her head. "I was thinkin' about starting something when Kenny showed up. We're going to the burger joint in Berlin."

Anger bubbled in Velma's soul, and she slapped both hands against her hips. "Oh, yeah? Who says you're goin' anywhere?"

"Well, I . . ."

"Aw, come on Mrs. Kimball," Kenny interrupted. "It's been way too long since I saw my girl. Ya can't be mean enough to try and keep us apart."

"I am not trying to be mean." Velma spoke slowly, curbing her anger. "I've been workin' hard most of the day for one of our neighbors, and my daughter was supposed to fix supper for all of us tonight. Then I show up here, dog-tired, and she wants to run off and spend the evening with you, which would mean I'd have to do all the cooking." Heat flooding her face, Velma tapped her foot a couple of times.

Kenny pulled his fingers through the ends of his black, shoulder-length hair. "Now don't go gettin' yourself all worked up over nothin'. If ya don't want Bobbie Sue to go out with me to grab a bite, I'll eat supper here with your family."

Velma blinked. *The nerve of that boy! Just who does he think he is?* She drew a deep breath and silently counted to ten. *I suppose having Kenny here for the evening would be better than my daughter going out with him on that motorcycle and leaving me stuck with the cooking. At least if he's here, I can keep an eye on things.*

She forced a smile and said, "Sure, Kenny, you're welcome to join us for supper. You'll get to see what kind of a cook my daughter is." *You just won't be staying long after we're done eating,* she added silently as Bobbie Sue gave her an icy stare.

Chapter 19

Canton

Denise stood at the living-room window, watching as Greg pulled out of their yard. Her husband had been in such a hurry to get to the office today he hadn't even taken the time to eat breakfast.

She glanced at the stately grandfather clock across the room, gonging on the half hour. In a few minutes it would be time to take Kassidy to her friend's house for the day. After she dropped her off, Denise would be hosting a Realtors' open house for a new listing. If this home sold at the price it was listed for, she could make upwards of thirty thousand dollars.

Better not get my hopes up too high, at least not yet, she reasoned. Still, given that it was Friday, Denise hoped they'd have something to celebrate soon.

After pulling her sleeve back to check the time on her diamond-studded wristwatch, Denise turned and was about to call her daughter down from upstairs, when Kassidy burst into the room.

"Just look at my blouse, Mom. Those stains

you said would come out are set in for good. I even tried scrubbing the blouse when I found it on the floor of my closet this morning, but it didn't do any good." Frowning, Kassidy held out the item in question. "It's ruined, and now I'll have to throw it away."

Denise's gaze flicked upwards. "If you had put it in the laundry when we got home from the cooking class last week, like I told you to, I most likely could have gotten the stain out." She swept her hands impatiently. "I don't have time to debate this with you. We have to go right now or I'm going to be late for my open house."

Kassidy stomped her foot. "Mom, you're not listening to me—my blouse is ruined."

"Yes, I heard you—loud and clear. But there is nothing I can do about it, so get your things and let's go."

"I need a new blouse, and I want one today." With an angry-looking scowl, Kassidy tossed the blouse on the floor, then grabbed her backpack and stomped out the door.

I think Greg and I created a monster by allowing our daughter to get away with her temper tantrums since she was a little girl. Denise picked up her purse and followed. There would have been a day she'd have given in to her daughter's demands, but not anymore. Until Kassidy learned how to ask for things nicely, she would not be getting anything new other than necessities.

Millersburg

"I sure like this weather we're having," Darren commented as he walked beside Ellen on the trail leading to the lake he'd chosen for fishing today. Tall trees—a mix of evergreens and hardwoods—shaded the pathway, while a warm breeze tickled Darren's bare arms. He wasn't sure if it was the weather or strolling down the footpath this close to Ellen that seemed to make his senses tingle.

She looked over at him and smiled. "You're right. We couldn't ask for a better day." Ellen turned and called over her shoulder, "Hurry up, Becky. You're falling behind."

Darren paused. "Maybe we're walking too fast."

Ellen shook her head. "She's been dawdling since we got out of the car."

"Not Jeremy." Darren pointed ahead. "He acts like he's rushing to a fire or something." He chuckled and started walking again. "My boy's always enjoyed going fishing with me. I'm sure that's why he's running ahead. Probably thinks if he gets to the lake first he'll catch the most, or biggest, fish."

"Maybe he will." Ellen stopped walking and looked at her daughter again. Becky had almost caught up to them, but the grim twist to her mouth let Darren know she was anything but happy to be here today. Ellen had said previously that Becky enjoyed fishing and hiking, so he figured her lack of enthusiasm might be because of him or Jeremy. *Does Becky feel threatened by my interest in her mother? Or is it simply that she doesn't like my son very much?* Either way, Darren was determined to win the girl over, because he definitely liked Becky's mother. Maybe things would go better once they reached the lake.

When they arrived at the spot where Darren suggested they set up, Ellen couldn't believe how beautiful it was. The area felt like some secret place, undiscovered by anyone but them. Wild grass grew up to the water's edge, with trees surrounding the sides and far end of the lake. All the way around, the body of water looked promising to fish from its bank.

"It's so pretty here." Ellen glanced over at Darren as she set the picnic basket down, along with the duffle bag that held the blanket. "Do you and Jeremy come here often?"

"As much as we can. We've been to other places, but we like it here best." Darren pointed to a trash can several feet away. "Other people fish here, too, because there's usually evidence in the can. But we always seem to time it right and usually have this spot all to ourselves."

Darren walked over to a level area under the shade of a tree. "How about we spread your blanket out here for later, when we have lunch?"

"Sure, this looks like a good place." Ellen looked toward the water again, taking in the alluring reflection from the sun and clouds over-head.

"I can tell you this. Jeremy and I have pulled some good-sized fish out of this lake."

"Regardless if I catch a fish or not, it's just nice being here." Humming, Ellen rolled her shoulders forward. Up above, a robin sang its cheery melody, and a frog began croaking.

"I know exactly what you mean." Darren took the fishing rods over to a log near the water, then came back to get his tackle box.

Unfolding the large blanket she'd purchased a few years ago at a yard sale, Ellen glanced over at her daughter. Tight-lipped, Becky stood with her arms folded. Ellen was about to suggest that her daughter grab the other end of the blanket, to help her spread it out over the grass, when Jeremy ran up to Becky. "Do you know how to skip stones over the water?" Jeremy held a few flat stones in his hand.

"Course I do." Becky put her hands on her hips, giving him quite the stare.

"Well then, come on. Let's see who can make one go the farthest." Jeremy handed Becky a few stones, and off to the water's edge they both ran.

"Here, let me help you, Ellen." Darren reached down and took the other end of the blanket. After they had it spread on the ground, they got a few things out of the basket.

"Kids. Always trying to outdo each other." Darren chuckled, looking over his shoulder at Becky and Jeremy. Their stones skimmed over the water's surface before disappearing.

"I hope they don't scare the fish." Ellen knelt on the blanket to get a few snack bags out.

"Nah, Jeremy skips rocks every time we come here, and it never seems to bother them."

Once Ellen made some snacks available, Darren reached his hand out to help her up. "Come on, let's do some fishing."

It was a peaceful morning, and while Darren and Ellen sat on the log, talking and keeping an eye on the red-and-white bobbers floating in the middle of the lake, her body relaxed. Jeremy and Becky were fishing, yards apart, over on the bank toward the right. Neither of them wanted to use a bobber, but preferred to throw their line out, then slowly reel it back in. It was easy to see they were competing again, only this time with casting their fishing lines.

"I hope if anyone catches some fish, it's the kids." Ellen smiled. "Right now, at least, they seem to be tolerating each other."

"Yeah, kids can be funny—one trying to

upstage the other." Darren looked out where his line went into the water. "So far, I haven't gotten any bites."

"Don't feel bad. I haven't either." Ellen chuckled. "But who cares?"

Just when all seemed content, Jeremy yelled, "I got one!"

"So did I!" Becky squealed a few seconds later.

"Bet mine's bigger than yours." Jeremy struggled, reeling his line in until it revealed a nice trout flopping on the end.

Ellen watched as Becky pulled her fish in next. "Oh, she got a nice one too."

Darren and Ellen got up to check out the fish. Jeremy walked over to Becky, proudly holding up his catch. Becky did the same, placing hers right next to his.

"Looks like a tie to me." After eyeing the trout, Darren picked up a stick and held it next to his son's fish, then did the same to Becky's. "Now, how about that? They are exactly the same length."

Ellen smiled as Darren took the fish off their hooks, put them on a stringer, and set them back into the water along the shoreline.

"I'm glad they each got a trout, but now I'll bet they'll both try for a bigger one." She pointed as Becky and Jeremy ran back to their fishing spots.

Darren strolled back to the log, while Ellen

continued to watch their children. Jeremy cast his line out. Becky put more bait on the end of the hook and extended her arm back to cast. What looked to be a good fling of her line, ended up getting snagged on a shrub behind where she stood.

"Oh great! My line is tangled." Becky groaned.

"Here, let me help you." Jeremy offered, setting his fishing pole down.

Ellen walked over to Darren, raising her eyebrows. "Will you look at those two?"

"Jeremy's a good kid. Sometimes it just takes him awhile to warm up to someone." Darren looked fondly at his son as he helped Becky free up her line.

Ellen recognized the proud feeling Darren had for Jeremy, for she felt the same about Becky. "Looks to me like we are both fortunate parents."

"You've got that right." Darren's lips parted slightly as he moistened them with his tongue. "Mind if ask you a personal question?"

"No, not at all."

"How long have you been a single mom?"

"Well . . ."

He pulled his fingers down the side of his face. "Guess what I really wanted to ask is, are you a widow or a divorcee?"

"I'm neither." Ellen briefly explained how she'd adopted Becky, leaving out the part about not telling her daughter until recently. "How about you?" she asked. "I assume you were once married."

"Yes, my wife died from a brain tumor two years ago." Darren pressed a fist against his chest. "Losing Caroline was difficult for me, as well as Jeremy." He paused, staring vacantly across the lake. "I do my best with Jeremy, but my son needs his mother."

Ellen reached out and touched his arm. "I'm sorry for your loss."

"Thanks. I'm doing better, but there are still times when I think about Caroline and all we had."

"While I've never lost a mate, I struggled with depression after my grandma died. We were very close, and I still miss her."

"Loss of any sort is hard, but life goes on, and all anyone can do is keep pressing forward and try to focus on the good things—like those two." Darren pointed to Becky, who had made a successful cast now that her line had been untangled. Jeremy stood a little closer to Becky than before, and a few giggles erupted as they talked.

Ellen couldn't help hearing part of the kids' conversation, and was surprised when her daughter said, "Thank you, Jeremy, for untangling my line."

"You're welcome." Jeremy grinned, although he kept his focus on the water.

This day was turning out better than she imagined. Ellen felt comfortable around Darren as they opened up to each other and also discovered some more things they had in common. Ellen couldn't remember the last time she'd felt so lighthearted. She wondered if Darren might ask to see her again, and hoped if he did that Becky and Jeremy would continue to get along.

Walnut Creek

Velma's fingers clenched around her coffee mug so tightly that her veins protruded. Soon after she and the children had eaten breakfast this morning, she'd found a note on her desk in the kitchen. Reading it for the second time, before starting lunch, her nose burned with unshed tears.

Dear Mama,

I'm sure you won't like this, but I'm running away with Kenny. In two weeks I'll be eighteen, and we're gonna get married.

Don't worry about me. Kenny and I will both get jobs, so we'll be fine. Once we're settled, I'll send you our address and phone number. I love you, Mama, and I hope you and Papa will forgive me for doin' this. I love Kenny and wanna be with him.

Love,

Bobbie Sue

Velma let go of her mug and slammed her fist on the table. "I knew that snake was up to no good when he showed up here two days ago. Shoulda sent him packin' like I wanted to do."

"What's going on, Mama?" Peggy Ann asked when she and Eddie entered the room. "Who were you talkin' to?"

"Myself. I was talking to myself."

Eddie glanced around, as if looking for answers. "How come?"

"Because I'm upset." Velma picked up the note and waved it about. "Found this awhile ago, and I just finished reading it again."

Peggy Ann tipped her head. "What is it?"

"It's from your big sister. She ran off with Kenny Carmichael sometime during the night." Velma swallowed hard. "And ya may as well know, there's a good chance we'll never see her again."

"What?" Peggy Ann lowered her head and started to wail.

Eddie scrunched up his nose. "Just wait till Papa gets home. Bet he'll go after Kenny and punch him in the nose."

The words were no more than out of his mouth

when Velma heard the roar of an engine. Rising from the table, she went to the kitchen window and peered out. Sure enough, Hank's rig had pulled into the yard.

"Oh, great." Velma blew out a quick breath and turned to face her children. "Not a word to your dad about Bobbie Sue. Understood?"

Peggy Ann's forehead wrinkled. "How come, Mama? Papa's gonna know somethin' ain't right when he asks where she is."

"I realize that. I just need to be the one to tell him. So when he comes inside, you can both say hello, and then I want you to go to your rooms till I call ya for lunch."

"Okay, we'll zip our lips." Eddie bumped his sister's arm. "Right, Peggy Ann?"

She pushed him away. "You're not my boss, so don't be tellin' me what to do."

"I wasn't."

"Uh-huh."

Velma stepped between them. "That's enough, you two. Ya don't want to be bickering when your dad comes in, now, do you?"

Both children shook their heads.

A few minutes later, Hank entered the house and came into the kitchen. "Hey, how's my little brood?" He leaned over and patted Eddie's head, then scooped Peggy Ann into his arms. "Have you two been good for your mama while I was gone?"

"Yes, Papa." Peggy Ann wrapped her arms around his neck and gave it a squeeze.

"How about you, Son?" Hank looked down at their boy.

"I've been good too." Eddie looked up at Velma. "Right, Mama?"

She nodded. "Now, why don't you and your sister skedaddle to your rooms? I'll call ya when it's time to eat."

Hank set Peggy Ann down, and she scurried out of the kitchen behind her brother.

"Would ya like a cup of coffee?" Velma asked, moving across the room to the stove.

"Sure." He followed Velma and placed a sloppy kiss on her cheek. She took it to mean he wasn't angry with her anymore.

After she'd poured coffee into his mug and handed it to him, Velma suggested they take a seat at the table.

"Aren't you gonna fix me some lunch?" Hank asked.

"I will shortly. But first, we need to talk."

Turning his head, he cleared his throat. "If it's about the car . . ."

"No, it's not the car. It's Bobbie Sue."

"Where is that girl anyway? Is she at work? Did Bobbie Sue find another job while I was gone?"

"No." Velma pulled out a chair and sat.

Hank took the seat across from her. "What's

this about? Do those creases in your forehead mean somethin' is wrong?"

"Afraid so." Velma took in a gulp of air and quickly relayed how their daughter had run off with Kenny and left a note.

Hank's nostrils flared, and sweat beaded on his forehead. "Why that no good so and so." He stood and pushed back his chair with such force it toppled over. "I'm gonna get back in my rig and go lookin' for Bobbie Sue. And when I find that girl, I'll drag her right back home."

Velma lifted her hands. "What good would that do? Bobbie Sue will be eighteen in two weeks, and then she can do whatever she pleases."

Hank shuffled back a few steps. "Oh, that's right. I'd forgotten her birthday was comin' up soon."

"I don't like this any better than you do, Hank, but I think it's best we leave well enough alone. Hopefully, our daughter will smarten up and come home on her own. She'll soon find out how rough it is out there in the real world with no support from her family."

Squinting, Hank rubbed the back of his neck. "If she takes after her older brother, we won't see any sign of her again."

Moaning, Velma held both hands tightly against her body to keep from shaking. Hank's final words had pierced her soul. If she was honest with herself, Velma would have to admit that she may never see Bobbie Sue or Clem again. The mere thought of it took away any appetite she may have had this morning. But life didn't stop because they'd been thrown another curve ball. For the sake of her two younger children, she'd fix lunch and somehow muddle through the rest of the day.

Chapter 20

Berlin

As Heidi sat in the waiting room at the dentist's office Monday morning, she took a notepad from her purse and made a list of the ingredients she would need for Saturday's cooking class. Marsha sat quietly next to her, looking at a children's picture book, while Randy had his teeth cleaned and saw the dentist for an evaluation. It would be Marsha's turn next, but since she was so young and insecure, Heidi intended to go in with her.

She chuckled to herself, thinking about Randy's independence when she asked if he wanted her to go with him when it was his turn. Putting on a brave face, he'd shaken his head and said, "Nope. I'm a big boy and don't need no one to sit beside me."

When the children's appointments were over, Heidi planned to take them to lunch at one of her favorite restaurants. Afterward, they would stop for ice cream at Walnut Creek Cheese.

A smile reached Heidi's lips, remembering how many years she'd dreamed of doing these things with her own children. Having Randy and Marsha in her life had turned out to be the most precious blessing, and she prayed it would keep getting better.

Heidi glanced out the window in the waiting room. There wasn't a cloud in the sky. After a weekend of off-and-on rain, it was nice to see blue skies again. The buggy ride here had been pleasant, with warm breezes pushing away the damp air. The only evidence of the soggy weather was puddles of water that hadn't dried up yet. *Guess Velma was right last week when she mentioned rain might be coming.*

Pulling her attention back to her notebook, Heidi wrapped her fingers around the pen as she thought about this Saturday and how she would teach her young students to make strawberry shortcake. Since there were plenty of ripe strawberries in her garden right now, this would be the perfect dessert to make. She was sure everyone would like it—especially since she planned to make some homemade whipped cream to put over the top of the berries after they were spooned onto the shortcake.

The verse she planned to write on the back of their recipe cards this time was Proverbs 20:11: "Even a child is known by his doings, whether his work be pure, and whether it be right." No one had said anything about the scriptures she'd included so far, but Heidi hoped one or more of the children in class, or perhaps a parent, might memorize the verses and find help through them.

"Mama, what are they doin' to Randy?" Marsha placed her small hand on Heidi's arm.

"The hygienist is cleaning his teeth, and then the dentist will look in your brother's mouth and let me know if there are any problems. You will go in after Randy comes out."

Marsha shook her head. "Don't want no one lookin' in my mouth. Only you can brush my teeth."

"I'll be right there with you when they clean your teeth. I've had mine cleaned many times." Heidi patted the little girl's hand. "It'll be fine. I promise. They will most likely give you a new toothbrush too, and even let you pick out the color you want."

Marsha looked up at her with a dimpled grin. "Okay, Mammi."

Heidi's heart nearly melted. Even though Marsha was not her biological daughter, every day spent together seemed to draw them closer.

Walnut Creek

In order to keep her mind off her runaway daughter, Velma decided the best remedy was to stay busy. She had more work to do at the Troyers', of course, but didn't want to leave Peggy Ann and Eddie by themselves. Her plan was to work for Heidi this Saturday, while Peggy Ann took part in the cooking class. Since Bobbie Sue was no longer around and Hank was on the road again, no one would be home to keep an eye on Eddie. So Velma would enlist his help on whatever chore Heidi gave her to do. It was either that, or let the boy attend the class with Peggy Ann, which wasn't a good idea. Quite often, Eddie could be quite mischievous. No telling what kind of trouble he might cause that could interrupt Heidi's teaching. No, it was safer to keep him close by Velma's side.

Velma thought about Heidi and the way she and other Amish women in the area dressed. *Sure can't picture myself wearing a long dress while building a chicken coop. I like Heidi. She's a good person, and her ways, even though they're different, aren't bad.*

Velma's contemplations came to a halt when she looked out the window at the clean sheets flapping in the breeze. *Guess it's time to get some work done around here. It would go a lot quicker if my wayward daughter was still with us.* Her eyes misted.

She went outside, took the bedding off the line, and hauled it inside. Velma paused to inhale the fresh fragerance. "Now those are some nice smellin' sheets for Eddie's bed." She carried them to his room.

Coming in through the door, the not-so-nice

smelling bedroom needed a good airing. Velma dumped the sheets on the bed and opened the window as wide as it would go. The curtains swayed back and forth with the fresh breeze entering the room.

Turning her attention to Eddie's twin-size bed, Velma began searching through the bedding for the pillowcase to put on, but it was not there.

She hurried from the room and found it lying in the hallway on the worn carpet. "Even the laundry isn't cooperating today." Velma picked up the pillowcase and headed back to Eddie's room, trying to focus on something positive.

Yesterday, in between rain showers, Velma had begun building a chicken coop in their backyard, so that was positive. She hoped to finish it today. Velma had seen some laying hens advertised in the local paper for a reasonable price and planned to pick them up on Wednesday. Having fresh eggs to eat, and maybe sell, would be nice. Any little extra income in their pockets would surely be beneficial.

When Abner barked excitedly, Velma opened the front door and glanced toward the road. Hope welled in her chest as she heard a noisy vehicle approach. It sounded like a motorcycle. Maybe Bobbie Sue had changed her mind and come home.

But as the cycle sped by, Velma realized it didn't belong to Kenny. The elderly man driving it waved, and so did the woman in the sidecar. They were a happy-looking couple—probably reliving their youth and enjoying every moment they had together.

Velma envied them. It had been a long time since she and Hank had done anything purely for fun. With his long days on the road, plus their lack of money, she couldn't envision them doing anything fun in the near future either. Fact was, with her two oldest children leaving home, Velma had been left with a huge void in her life, so nothing seemed enjoyable anymore. She felt like an unfit mother who had driven her children away.

Dropping to her knees, just inside the door, Velma gave in to her tears. Had she done something in her past to deserve such misery? Had she failed her children somehow? Maybe their negative behavior was because of how she'd raised them.

Berlin

Miranda said goodbye to Carla and the children, then headed out the door. She didn't have to be at work for another hour and a half but needed to run a few errands on the way.

She'd no more than stepped out the front door when she saw a silver-gray SUV pull in. At first, she wasn't sure who it was, until Trent got out of the vehicle. It made sense after she noticed the license plate with the dealership's name on it. Since her husband sold cars, he sometimes drove a demo instead of his own. While this might not be the best time to confront Trent about the flowers he'd planted, she wouldn't pass up the opportunity.

Miranda brought her hand up to the strands of hair grazing her forehead, waiting until Trent finished dabbing a spot off the car. Then she stepped up to him as he approached.

"Hi, how are ya doing?" He gave her a dimpled grin—the kind of sweet smile that used to cause a stirring in her heart.

"Okay, I guess. Nice car you're driving."

"Wish it were mine, but it's only a demo." Trent continued to smile, never taking his eyes off of her. "You look great, Miranda."

A shiver went through her as Trent's gaze slowly roamed from her head, down to her toes, and back to her face again.

"Is that a new shade of lipstick you're wearing?"

She lifted her chin and gave him a probing gaze. In all the time they'd been married, he'd never once mentioned her lipstick. Or much of anything else about her appearance, for that matter. Why the sudden interest now? *I bet he's trying to butter me up.*

"It's not new." Miranda spoke slowly,

deliberately. "I've worn this same lipstick many times in the past."

"Okay then, but you do look nice this morning. Are you on your way to work?"

"Yes, I am. And what might you be here for? Did you come to plant more flowers?" Miranda couldn't keep from speaking in a tone of sarcasm.

Trent lifted both hands. "All right, you've found me out. I did plant the roses. Do you like them?"

She slowly nodded. "They're beautiful, but I'm not happy about the reason you put them there."

He tipped his head slightly. "What do you mean?"

"Don't act innocent, Trent. You felt guilty for not staying with the kids during the cooking class, so you—"

"Okay, okay, I admit it. I did feel bad about not sticking around. But the real reason I planted the roses was to remind you of our wedding day. Remember the beautiful bouquet you carried as you walked down the aisle toward me—your eager groom?"

Miranda shifted her weight, clutching her purse close to her side. "Of course I remember."

"I still love you, honey, and I want to come home."

She swallowed hard, hoping he wouldn't know how close she was to letting her tears fall. Thinking back to their wedding day, Miranda recalled how she'd thought she and Trent would always be happy together, making beautiful memories throughout the years. But those hopes and dreams had gone out the window when her husband admitted he had feelings for another woman and wanted to pursue a relationship with her. It wasn't long after Miranda insisted he move out of their home that Trent said he was sorry and pleaded with her to forgive him. Of course, Miranda said no. She couldn't trust him anymore. And with good reason. He couldn't even keep a simple promise to take the kids to cooking class.

She bit her bottom lip. *Trent did take them. He just didn't stay there like I expected him to. And he asked the kids not to tell. That's deceitful behavior from a man who claims to love me.*

"Well, aren't you going to say anything, Miranda? Can I come home or not?"

Trent's question pulled her back to the present. "No. I can't believe you think that just because you planted some roses in my flower bed, our marriage should be back on track and everything would be peachy—or should I say rosy?"

Trent huffed impatiently. "What's it gonna take to convince you to give me another chance? What do I have to do to get back in your good graces?"

"For one thing, you'd need to take an interest

in spiritual things." Her chin jutted out. "And I don't mean just going to church."

"What exactly do you mean?"

"You need to make a serious commitment to God and become the spiritual leader in our home."

He spoke as though his words were chosen deliberately. "I am not a bad person, Miranda. And I'm getting sick and tired of you making me feel like one. Just because I almost got caught up in an extramarital affair doesn't mean I'm headed down the road toward—"

She held up her hand. "I don't want to discuss this with you anymore, Trent. And I won't be late for work on account of you."

He glared at her. "Why do you always have to blame me for everything? Did it ever occur to you that your holier-than-thou attitude might be part of our problem?"

Trent's words stung like a slap across the face. If she didn't leave now, Miranda knew she would either say something mean or break down in tears. "Sorry, Trent, but I have to go. Debbie and Kevin are inside with their babysitter if you want to say hello." Miranda hurried to her car and opened the door. Short of a miracle, she doubted that she and Trent would ever live together again.

Miranda closed her eyes and took in a breath. *I just wish the children weren't affected by all of this. They deserve two parents who love the Lord, as well as each other.* She sniffed deeply. *Perhaps that's too much to hope and pray for, but I have to trust God to help me get through this without losing faith and becoming a bitter person.*

Chapter 21

Kevin leaned his elbows on the table and stared at Miranda as she fingered the handle of her teacup. "Mommy, are you mad at Daddy?"

She blinked. "Why would you think that?"

" 'Cause he said so when he came by the other day."

Debbie poked her brother's arm and put one finger against her lip.

"What's going on?" Miranda asked. "Has your father been talking about me behind my back?"

Debbie dropped her gaze to the table, while Kevin slumped in his chair.

"Okay, kids—out with it. What did he say?"

"Just said you was mad at him for plantin' the flowers."

Miranda felt a flush of heat on the back of her neck. She took a moment to gather her thoughts before responding to her son's statement. *What I wouldn't do for a God-fearing husband in this house. If only Trent would get his act together and be that kind of man for his family.* "I am not mad at him for that." She spoke in a soft tone, glancing at her watch. "And you know what? You two need to go brush your teeth so we can leave for Heidi's on time. You don't want to miss her third cooking class."

After finishing his glass of orange juice, Kevin pushed away from the table. "Wonder what she'll teach us to make today."

"I hope it's something good." Debbie left her seat too.

Kevin wrinkled his nose. "The corn dogs we made last time were okay, but they were so little."

"Course they were, silly. That's why Heidi called them 'mini corn dogs.'"

"I ain't silly."

"Are so."

"Huh-uh."

Miranda put her cup in the sink and turned the water on full blast, hoping to drown out Debbie and Kevin's bantering. She'd been tempted to tell them the reason she was mad at their father, but stopped herself in time. It wasn't right to involve the children in her and Trent's problems, and she certainly didn't want them to take sides. Their separation was hard enough on the kids, and she disliked even asking them what their father had said. They were already in the middle of this mess, and the last thing either child needed was to become an informer.

Miranda turned off the water. She heard the faucet running in the bathroom and knew one of them was in brushing their teeth. She combed her fingers through her shoulder-length hair, and watched a pair of turtle doves in the yard. She thought about Trent's comment that she was partly to blame for their relationship falling apart.

"It might be true," she murmured. "I may have done things to drive him away." Miranda lifted her hands with intertwined fingers, bowing her head in prayer. *Lord, if it's meant for Trent and me to be together again, please show us both what we need to do in order to work things out. And help me learn to be more forgiving.*

Millersburg

"Are you ready to go, sweetie?" Ellen called to her daughter. "We don't want to be late for class number three."

"Okay, I'm ready, Mom." Becky met Ellen at the door with a smile. "How do I look in my new blue-and-white-striped shirt?"

"You look nice, and a little nautical with your red sneakers." Ellen winked, pointing to Becky's feet.

She was happy to see her daughter in a good mood this morning. It seemed she was looking forward to the cooking class, which was a pleasant change. Ellen had a hunch it had something to do with the way things had gone when they'd been fishing with Darren and Jeremy. It had turned out to be a fun day for all, and for the first time since Becky met Jeremy, they'd actually gotten along.

Ellen smiled as she grabbed her cell phone and put it in her purse. She looked forward to seeing Darren today and appreciated the things they had in common. In addition to being single parents, they both enjoyed the outdoors, shared Christian beliefs, and had careers of a helpful nature. It might be too soon to think this way, but Ellen could almost see a future with Darren. It was the first time since she'd adopted Becky that she'd been seriously interested in a man.

"Are we going, or what?" Becky tugged on her mother's arm.

"Of course." Ellen followed her daughter out the door, locking it behind them. *I wonder if Darren's been thinking of me.*

Dover

Darren eyed his son, sitting across the table from him, staring at his bowl of cold cereal. "Aren't you hungry this morning?"

Jeremy shrugged. "I guess."

"You guess you're not hungry, or did you mean you are?"

"I'm not hungry. My stomach doesn't feel right, Dad. Think I might be comin' down with the flu."

Darren wasn't sure whether to take his son seriously, since Jeremy sometimes feigned sickness to get out of doing something. "You wouldn't be trying to get out of going to the cooking class, would you?"

Jeremy lowered his head, rubbing his hand through his messy hair.

"I thought now that you and Becky are getting along better, you wouldn't mind going."

"She's not my best friend, Dad." Jeremy dropped a piece of his toast on the floor for his dog.

Darren didn't approve of feeding the dachshund table scraps but decided not to make an issue of it this time. Bacon looked like he needed some more meat on his bones. "I wasn't insinuating that you and Ellen's daughter are best friends, Jeremy. I just thought—"

"Can we talk about somethin' else?"

"Sure. What do you want to talk about?"

"I don't know. Anything other than Becky or her mother."

"Okay." Darren drummed his fingers on the table. *Does my son have something against Ellen. Do I dare ask?*

Clearing his throat, Darren blurted the question. "How do you feel about Becky's mom? Do you like her, Jeremy?"

"She's okay, I guess." Jeremy rubbed his forearms. "She did catch a nice trout the day we went fishin'."

"That she did." Darren chuckled, remembering

Ellen's surprised expression when she reeled in the fish. "So you wouldn't mind if I ask Ellen to go out to dinner with me—just the two of us this time?"

Jeremy blinked rapidly. "How come?"

"Because I enjoy being with Ellen, and I'd like the chance to get to know her better."

"Okay, sure, whatever."

"Maybe we can plan it so you can spend the night with one of your friends."

Jeremy frowned. "I'm not a baby, Dad. I can stay here by myself."

Darren shook his head. "You're not even close to being an adult yet. And until you're a few years older, I will not leave you alone for a long period of time."

Jeremy tossed the dog another piece of toast. "Guess if you think you have to see Ellen alone, I'll talk to my friend, Todd. See if I can spend the night with him."

"Good. I'm glad we got that settled. Now finish your breakfast so we can get on the road. I don't want you to be late for Heidi's class."

"Sounds like you're the one who's excited about going," Jeremy mumbled, picking up his spoon. "Bet the only reason is so you can see Becky's mother again."

Ignoring his son's comment, Darren changed the subject. "I still need to shave, pick out a shirt, and comb my hair."

"Okay." Jeremy spooned some cereal in his mouth.

Darren couldn't deny it. Ever since their time spent at the lake the previous week, Ellen had been on his mind. So much so, that he'd decided to sit in on the cooking class again today. And if he had the opportunity to speak to her privately, before or after the class, he planned to bring up the idea of a dinner date.

Canton

"I don't want to go to Heidi's today. Something bad will happen to me like it did before." The muscles along Kassidy's jawline tensed.

"Life is full of ups and downs, Kassidy." Denise handed her husband a cup of coffee when he took a seat at the kitchen table. "Isn't that right, Greg?"

"Absolutely." He brushed his fingers across his mustache and looked over at Kassidy. "So you'd better get used to it, because you'll be faced with many obstacles over the course of your life."

Kassidy's face slackened as she hunched over. "Well, if that's how it is, then life really stinks."

Denise placed her hand on Kassidy's shoulder. "It does stink sometimes, but if we keep a positive attitude and try to do what's right, it will be easier to deal with problems when they come along. Besides, you'll learn over time the challenges we experience give us a chance to do things better the next time around." Denise thought about her own situation, where the owners of the expensive house she'd hoped to sell had changed their mind and taken it off the market.

Kassidy picked up her glass of milk and took a drink. "It's kinda hard to have a positive attitude when people make fun of my red hair or think it's funny when something bad happens to me. Some of the kids at Heidi's cooking class thought it was hilarious when my blouse got grass and mud stains on it." Her forehead wrinkled deeply. "I don't like any of those kids, and I wish I didn't have to take any more of Heidi's classes."

"Just remember this." Denise touched her daughter's arm. "No matter what age we are, we're never too old to gain knowledge and learn from our mistakes. Same goes for the other kids in the class."

Kassidy grunted. "Well it doesn't seem like they've discovered how to be nice yet."

"Perhaps you could start by setting a good example. Did you read the Bible verse Heidi wrote on the back of the recipe card she gave you during the last class?"

Kassidy shook her head.

Denise rose from her seat and returned to the table with the card. "This is what it says: 'Beloved, let us love one another.'"

Greg looked at her through squinted eyelids.

"Is that Amish woman teaching cooking classes or doing a Bible study?"

"We are not studying the Bible, Greg. The Amish are God-fearing people, and I think Heidi just wants to share a little of her faith with the class."

"Yeah, well, that's fine and dandy. Just don't let it go to your head so you end up coming home in a preaching mood." Greg pushed his chair away from the table. "I've got to head out. I'm supposed to meet my friend Arnie at the golf course today." He bent and kissed Denise on the cheek, then landed a quick peck on Kassidy's forehead. "You two have fun at the cooking class."

Kassidy's eyes brightened a bit as she looked up at him. "Okay, Dad, I'll try."

Chapter 22

Walnut Creek

Heidi popped a fresh strawberry in her mouth. Its sweet, juicy flavor made it tempting to eat more, but the others in the bowl were for the strawberry shortcake they'd be making today. She looked forward to another class. Her doubts about teaching children had been erased, for she'd soon learned what a pleasure it was to spend time with them, watching as they learned to make a new recipe. The mouthwatering smell of sweet shortcake she'd made for dessert tonight rose from the oven and brought back memories of Heidi's childhood when her mother made the tasty dessert for their family during the warm summer months.

Looking out toward the garden, an image of Marsha came to mind, with the red stain of strawberries all over her face and hands. Heidi chuckled, thinking how much fun Randy and Marsha had helping her yesterday as they picked the plump berries. The children had eaten more than they picked, but that was the fun of it all.

Heidi had started washing the breakfast dishes when Randy dashed into the kitchen. Sliding to a halt in his stocking feet, he announced, "Someone's car is pulling into the yard out front."

"Okay, thanks for letting me know. Now, please head upstairs and put your shoes on. My students will be here soon for the cooking class."

Randy nodded. "I'll make sure Marsha is wearin' her shoes too."

"Good idea, Randy. I appreciate you being so helpful."

He scampered out of the kitchen, and Heidi dried her hands on a paper towel, then hurried to the front door to see whose vehicle had pulled in. Since her class wouldn't start for another half hour or so, she figured it wasn't one of her students. But it could be their mailman, Lance, bringing a package to the house, as he often did.

When Heidi went out to the front porch, she was delighted to see Kendra getting out of her car. She waited in anticipation as the young woman opened the rear door and took her ten-month-old baby girl out of the safety seat. Kendra looked like she'd lost all her baby weight, and she was wearing a pretty, floral dress with pink sandals.

As she watched them approach, Heidi realized this was the first time she'd seen her little namesake without her heart being filled with regrets. Kendra had a right to raise her own child, and Heidi's life had become filled with the joy of taking care of the Olsen children. She and Lyle had talked earlier this week and decided to move forward in taking the necessary steps to adopt Randy and Marsha. It had been over six months since the children's parents died and they'd become wards of the state. In all that time, no relatives had come forth to seek custody, so Heidi felt safe in seeking to adopt Marsha and Randy.

"It's good to see you." When Kendra stepped onto the porch, Heidi greeted her with a hug. "How are you and your little one doing these days?" She reached out and touched the sweet child's silky hair.

Kendra grinned, hoisting her daughter a bit higher on her hip. "Real well. As you can see, little Heidi is growing by leaps and bounds."

"Yes, I can certainly tell."

"If you're not busy, I'd like to come in. I have some exciting news to share with you."

"I'll be teaching another cooking class today, but my young students aren't due to arrive until shortly before ten, so please come in." Heidi opened the front door. "Let's take a seat in the living room and we can visit awhile."

"Okay." Kendra glanced at her watch. "But I'll only stay a few minutes. I apologize for not calling ahead."

"It's not a problem. I'm always pleased to see you and the baby." Heidi reached out her hands. "May I hold her?"

"Of course." Kendra handed her daughter to Heidi, and they both took a seat on the couch.

Heidi stroked the little girl's soft cheeks. "I'm eager to know. What is the exciting news you want to share with me, Kendra?"

Kendra extended her left hand and pointed to the sparkling diamond ring on her finger. "Brent and I got engaged last night. We're planning to be married this December."

Heidi clasped Kendra's hand. "That's wonderful news. I only met Brent the one time when Bill stopped to introduce his son, but he seemed like a nice young man."

"You're right about that, and he's so good with the baby. I think he'll make a great father for little Heidi, not to mention a wonderful husband for me. I'd like it if you and Lyle could come to our wedding in December. I'll send you an invitation as the time gets closer."

"It would be so nice to be a part of your special day."

"I can't stop looking at my ring." Kendra wiggled her hand back and forth as the light caught the diamond and made it sparkle. Then she pointed at the box of toys across the room. "I'm guessing you and Lyle are still foster

237

parents to the children who came to live with you toward the end of last year."

"Yes, we are. Marsha and Randy are upstairs, putting on their shoes. Lyle and I have become quite attached to those two." Heidi leaned closer and lowered her voice. "We are seeking to adopt them, but they don't know yet. No living relatives came forward after their parents died, so we assume that either there are none, or no one wanted the responsibility of raising them. Now, we're just waiting to see if our application gets accepted."

"Now that is good news." Kendra reached into her purse and pulled out a tissue, then wiped a wet spot off the baby's chin. "Sorry about that. She's on the verge of cutting another tooth, so she drools a lot."

Heidi nodded. "They do grow quickly, don't they?"

"You can say that again. It won't be long before my daughter will be toddling all over the place. Ever since she learned how to crawl, the little stinker's been getting into things." Kendra looked at little Heidi with such adoration. "Course, I am not complaining. I'm enjoying every phase of my daughter's babyhood, and so are my folks, as well as my sisters."

"And that's how it should be." Heidi chuckled when the baby stuck her thumb in her mouth and made loud sucking noises.

Kendra rolled her eyes. "She doesn't know about good manners yet."

A forceful knock on the front door interrupted their conversation. Heidi glanced at the clock. It was a quarter to ten. She hadn't heard any vehicles pull into the yard, and figured it might be Velma, since she'd previously come on foot.

"Excuse me, Kendra. I'd better answer that." Heidi handed the baby to her mother and hurried across the room. When she opened the door, she found Velma on the porch with Peggy Ann, as well as a young boy with dark brown hair and eyes that matched.

"I'm here to do more work for you, while Peggy Ann takes her cooking class." Velma motioned to the boy. "This here's my son, Eddie. I didn't want to leave him home alone, so he's gonna be helping me today."

"Oh, I see. Well, perhaps he'd like to come in and take part in the cooking class with his sister."

With a pinched expression, Velma shook her head. "I can't afford to pay for Eddie's lesson, and believe me, it's best that he helps me outside. I'll chop some more wood, and he can stack it for me. Unless there's something else you'd rather have done today."

"No, that's fine. You can start with that. I'll be out later to tell you what else I'd like to have done. That is, if you have time to do anything more than chop wood today."

"I'm sure I'll have the time." Velma dropped her gaze to the wooden planks on the porch. "Workin' helps take my mind off the troubles that seem to keep coming my way."

Heidi was about to comment, when Velma gave her daughter a little push. "You go on inside now, Peggy Ann. And you'd best do whatever Heidi tells you during the cooking class, ya hear?"

Looking up at her mother, Peggy Ann nodded.

Velma turned, took hold of her son's arm, and stepped off the porch. "Come on, Eddie. Let's you and me get to work."

Shoving his hands into the pockets of his bib overalls, the boy mumbled something Heidi didn't understand, but he went along with his mother, kicking a few pebbles in the dirt. It was obvious Velma's son did not want to be here today. He'd probably rather spend the day doing anything other than work.

Back inside, Heidi introduced Peggy Ann to Kendra, then suggested the young girl choose a toy to play with until Randy and Marsha came downstairs or some of the other children arrived.

Kendra gathered up her purse and stood, holding her baby daughter. "Looks like things are gonna get busy around here, so I'd better go. I'll let you know when Brent and I have set an exact date for our wedding. And again, we'd be honored if you and Lyle could be there."

Heidi smiled. "It would be an honor for us to attend." She wrapped Kendra in a warm hug and watched as the young woman went out the door.

A few seconds later, Randy and Marsha appeared, both fully dressed, including their shoes. Without saying a word, they took a seat on the floor next to Peggy Ann. It pleased Heidi to see them interact with the girl. Since Peggy Ann was new to the area, she needed a friend or two.

"I hope that stupid mutt of Heidi's isn't running around the yard today," Kassidy muttered as they approached the Troyers' driveway. "I'm glad I don't have any pets."

Denise glanced in the rearview mirror at her daughter. "What do you mean? Have you forgotten about Tokai?"

"She's not my cat, Mom. She's yours." Kassidy's nose crinkled. "Besides, Tokai doesn't jump on me with dirty paws."

Seeing no other vehicles parked in Heidi's yard, Denise pulled up close to the house. She figured if the dog was running around outside somewhere, the front door wouldn't be too far for them to go.

Seeing no sign of the dog, Denise signaled Kassidy to get out of the car, and she did the same. They were almost to the house when a young dark-haired boy, wearing a pair of faded overalls and a T-shirt with several holes in it, stepped in front of them. "Hey, I'm Eddie. Who are you?"

"My name is Denise McGuire, and this is my daughter, Kassidy. Are you here to take Heidi's cooking class?"

He shook his head briskly. "No way! Cookin' is for girls, not boys."

"How so?" Kassidy crossed her arms.

"My papa says a man's place isn't in the kitchen."

Narrowing her eyes, Kassidy's face tightened. "Oh, yeah? Well, for your information, there are three boys taking Heidi's class. And besides, sometimes, when he has the time, my dad likes to cook too."

He sneered at her. "So what? Don't mean I wanna cook, so just leave me be."

"Hey, you're the one who approached us. And you know what?"

"What?" Eddie asked, squinting at her.

"You look dorky in those bibs you're wearing." Kassidy's hands went quickly to her hips. "I wouldn't be caught out of the house in those faded old things."

Just then Rusty came bounding around the house. The dog ran up to Eddie and sat by his feet. Eddie knelt on one knee and talked to the dog. "You're a good boy, aren't ya?"

"I see you made a furry friend." Kassidy snickered. "You two mutts deserve each other."

Eyes narrowing into tiny slits, Eddie stood up, but before things could escalate, Denise grabbed her daughter's hand. "You're being rude. Let's go inside."

Kassidy gave Eddie a dismissive nod and quickly stepped onto the porch. Denise followed, giving the boy a backwards glance as he and the Troyers' dog disappeared around the side of the house.

Denise pointed her finger at Kassidy. "What you said to that boy was uncalled for. And let me remind you, young lady, you own a pair of bib overalls yourself."

"But mine are the latest style. They aren't faded and tattered, like his are."

"You haven't learned a thing, have you?" Denise grew more disappointed as she looked at her daughter, wanting to say more. Instead, she turned and gestured to the door. "Let's drop it for now, but don't think this discussion is over."

It was a good thing Eddie wasn't taking part in today's class. Those two would probably go at it the whole time. Kassidy had certainly met her match.

When Darren pulled his SUV into Heidi's yard, he was pleased to see Ellen getting out of her car.

This would be the perfect opportunity to talk to her alone.

As soon as Darren got out of his rig, he called out to Ellen. She turned and smiled.

"Can I talk to you a minute, before you go inside?" he asked.

"Certainly." Ellen looked at Becky. "Why don't you go ahead in?"

The girl shook her head. "That's okay. I'll wait till you're ready to go in the house."

Oh, great. Darren struggled not to give an impatient huff. *Should I ask Ellen for a date, with her daughter standing here?* Of course, Jeremy had gotten out of the car now, too, and stood near Darren, shifting from one foot to the other. *Well, it's better to have it out in the open with Becky and Jeremy here,* Darren decided, since he'd already discussed it with his son.

He moved closer to Ellen. "I was wondering if you'd like to go out to dinner with me one night next week. Just the two of us this time."

Ellen glanced at Becky, then looked back at Darren. "That sounds nice. Would Friday night work for you?"

Nodding, he grinned. "That'd be great. I'll pick you up at six, if that's okay."

"Six will be fine."

Whew, that's a relief. Darren closed his eyes briefly. When he opened them again and saw the obvious displeasure on Becky's face, the joy he felt seconds ago was replaced with concern. Apparently Ellen's daughter wasn't thrilled about him dating her mother. *Well, our kids will have to deal with it, because Ellen and I have the right to date whomever we choose.*

Chapter 23

I wish you and Daddy could both take us to the cooking class," Kevin announced from the back seat of Miranda's minivan. "Then we could all learn to cook together."

"Mommy already knows how to cook," Debbie put in. "Besides, Daddy has to work today."

Kevin spoke again. "I miss him and wish he'd come home to live with us, like he did before."

Miranda cringed. Sometimes she felt guilty for asking Trent to move out, especially knowing how much the kids missed him. Even so, she couldn't let him come waltzing back until she saw a true change in his behavior. Sending gifts and making promises he might not keep in order to lure her in simply wouldn't do.

Shifting mental gears, Miranda turned into the Troyers' driveway. Seeing that three other vehicles were already there, she hoped she and the children weren't late.

New Philadelphia

Trent had only been at work an hour, when a stabbing pain started on his right side, radiating to his back, and making him feel nauseous. As he rubbed the area, and took a deep breath, Trent tried to recall what he might have done to make it hurt this much. But he hadn't done anything strenuous lately, except being on his feet several hours at work yesterday.

Oh no! Trent rubbed the bridge of his nose as he leaned against a shiny new car in the showroom. *I hope this isn't another kidney stone.* Trent remembered all too well the stone he'd passed a few years ago. It was the worst pain he'd ever experienced, and he'd hoped he would never have to go through anything like that again.

As Trent headed toward his boss's office, he felt relief that for a Saturday, no customers had shown up yet. He found Herb sitting at his desk going over some papers. "Trent, come on in and sit down. It's been a slow morning so far, hasn't it?" Herb got up to pour himself a cup of coffee. "Would you like a cup?"

"No thanks." Trent inhaled sharply as the pain grew worse. "Think I need to head home. I'm not feeling well all of a sudden."

"Sure, sure, Trent." Herb's thick eyebrows furrowed. "I can handle things here. Do you think you're coming down with something?"

"I can't say for sure, but I believe I'm having a kidney stone attack."

"Oh my, you'd better get on home then. My brother gets kidney stones, and I know from what he's told me, how bad they can be—especially if they're difficult to pass." Herb's brows came together in a frown. "Do you want me to drive you home?"

"Thanks, but my apartment isn't far from here." Trent started to leave, then turned back. "Hopefully, if I pass this stone quickly, I'll be back to work on Monday."

"Just let me know." Herb waved him off. "Get going now, and be careful driving home."

Walnut Creek

"Now that the Coopers have arrived, let's all go into the kitchen." Heidi led the way, and everyone followed.

Ellen noticed her daughter's solemn expression as she took a seat at the table. *Becky doesn't want me to go out with Darren. She's had me all to herself since she was a baby and obviously feels threatened by me dating for the first time in ten years.*

Ellen took a step away from the table, contemplating things further. *Should I tell Darren I've changed my mind about going out with him and end this relationship now, before it goes any further?*

Ellen felt trapped between wanting to please Becky and fulfilling her own needs. She could see herself perhaps having a future with Darren, but not if Becky wouldn't accept him. *I'm thinking ahead too far,* she berated herself. *It's too soon to know if there's even a possibility of a future with Darren.* She tipped her head. *I wonder how Jeremy feels about his dad going out with me. If I give this relationship a try, maybe Becky will come around and be okay with it. I certainly hope so, because the more I get to know Darren, the more I like him.*

"As you can see, everything you will need to make the shortcake is on the table." Heidi gestured to the dry ingredients, as well as the milk, vanilla, softened butter, and one egg for each child. "Now, the first thing you'll need to do is cream the sugar and butter in your mixing bowl."

Peggy Ann's pale eyebrows squished together. "How are we supposed to make the sugar and butter turn into cream?"

Heidi smiled at the child's innocent question. "It won't turn into cream, Peggy Ann. When I said 'cream the sugar and butter,' I meant, stir the ingredients in the bowl until they are creamy."

Peggy Ann's cheeks puffed out as she huffed. "Why didn't ya just say that then?"

Heidi lifted her hands and let them fall to her sides. "You're right. I should have explained it better. So now, let's all get our butter and sugar mixed." Heidi stood next to Marsha and helped her put the ingredients in the bowl and stir them around.

Marsha looked up at Heidi and grinned. "This is fun, Mammi."

Heidi smiled in return. "I'm glad you're enjoying it, and I hope everyone else is too."

"Not me. I think this is boring, and if you ask me—"

Denise poked her daughter's arm. "Kassidy, I'm warning you."

Kassidy's mouth clamped shut, and she picked up her wooden spoon.

While Heidi couldn't say she noticed much improvement in the young girl's belligerent attitude, she did see a change in Kassidy's mother's behavior. Denise seemed more determined to make her daughter behave. Kassidy was one of the oldest children taking this class, but so far, she wasn't setting a good example for the others. Heidi could only hope that in time things would improve, but she wished there was something specific she could say or do to make it happen quickly.

Once the children had finished the first step, Heidi asked them to add the milk, egg, and vanilla, and then mix well. She was impressed with Randy and the younger children in their determination to do a good job and keep up with the older students.

"This smells good. I can't wait to eat the cake when it's done." Kevin smacked his lips. "Bet my daddy would like it, and I think he'd be proud of me for learnin' how to cook."

Heidi smiled. "I'm sure he would, and I'm pleased that you followed directions."

"What do we do next?" Debbie wanted to know.

"You'll add the dry ingredients." Heidi was pleased that none of the parents here today stepped in and took over for the children—although it was nice to have their assistance when needed.

Once everyone had mixed their dry ingredients, Heidi showed them how to pour the batter into their baking dish. "We can bake four at a time, and when those are done, the other three can go in. Who would like to be first?"

Peggy Ann's hand shot up, and so did Randy's. "Okay, why don't we let the younger children bake their cake first? That would be Peggy Ann, Randy, Marsha, and Kevin."

"How come they get to go first?" Kassidy's eyes narrowed. "I shouldn't have to bake mine last just because I'm older than them."

"Kassidy . . ." Denise spoke firmly, and her daughter backed down.

"Okay, whatever."

"While the first pans are in the oven, you children can chop and sweeten the berries. As you're doing that, I'll whip the whipping cream with my egg beater."

Peggy Ann's face scrunched up. "What's an egg beater?"

"This is what I'm talking about." Heidi held up the device. "When you turn the handle really fast, it will stir things up quickly."

"My mom uses an electric mixer to make whipping cream and stuff like that." Becky snickered. "One time she beat the cream too long and ended up with butter."

Ellen's cheeks grew pink. "Guilty as charged, I admit. That's what can happen when a person starts thinking about one thing while doing something else."

"What were ya thinkin' about?" Peggy Ann asked.

"Well, that happened some time ago, and I don't remember what it was. All I know is we couldn't use the whipping cream on our pudding that night."

Heidi glanced at Jeremy. While he'd done everything she asked and had his cake batter ready to go into the oven, the boy hadn't said one word since he'd come into the kitchen. And he hadn't so much as cracked a smile—not even when someone said something funny.

I wonder if he's upset about something. Or maybe Jeremy isn't feeling well today. Heidi was on the verge of saying something to the boy, when he grabbed his stomach, leaped out of his chair, and raced for the bathroom. The other children sat with their mouths partially open, while Darren ran down the hall after his son. Heidi wasn't sure what to do.

Finally, after gathering her wits, she helped the younger ones put their cake pans into the oven. Hopefully, Jeremy wasn't seriously ill, and things would go better for the rest of this class.

New Philadelphia

The drive from the dealership was short, but with the pain Trent was in, the road seemed to stretch for miles before he got home to the comfort of his apartment. All he wanted to do was take an ibuprofen, lie down on his bed, and wait for the pain to subside. *I wish Miranda was with me right now. I need some TLC.*

Sometime later, after the stone had passed, Trent collapsed on his bed, exhausted.

Like the last time after the kidney stone passed, Trent had a few bouts of pain, but it didn't compare to what he'd just been through. "Guess I won't go back to work today," he mumbled. "I better take it easy till Monday."

Trent fluffed up his pillow and stared at the ceiling. *Wonder how the kids are doing at the cooking class this morning? Maybe I should surprise them and drive to Heidi's. It would probably surprise Miranda, and she might even think it was nice if I showed up.*

But after thinking it through, Trent realized he wasn't up to going anywhere right now.

After resting for an hour in a comfy pair of sweatpants, he got up, made his way to the kitchen, and fixed himself a cup of coffee.

"What am I gonna do now?" Rubbing his hand through his thick hair, Trent looked around his too-quiet apartment. *Maybe I'll clean my golf clubs and wash the towels that are in the bag.* "I'm sure they need it."

Trent still used the clubs and bag Miranda had bought him on their first anniversary. He smiled, remembering the day she'd surprised him with this special gift.

Sipping at his coffee, he took each of the clubs out and laid them on the table. Then he went through the different compartments and pulled out the terry-cloth towels. He held them up to his nose. "Oh yeah, these definitely need to be washed."

Trent went to another pocket of the golf bag and unzipped the closure. Reaching in, he pulled out an envelope. Inside was the anniversary card Miranda had given him many years ago with the golf clubs and bag.

Trent smiled as he fondly remembered that day. They were so much in love and enjoyed every minute of being together. His smile faded. *What went wrong anyway?*

He looked at the front of the card with two

doves holding a heart. Then he opened it and read the hand-written message Miranda had included inside the card:

Trent,

Happy Anniversary to my wonderful husband. This first year of our marriage has been like a fairy tale for me, because you are in my life.

I know, as the years go by, we may have problems or challenges to face, but as long as we can work through them together, our relationship will only grow stronger.

Thank you for giving me a wonderful first year.

I am so blessed knowing I'll be spending the rest of my life with you.

I'll love you forever,

Miranda

Closing the card and holding it against his chest, Trent blinked tears from his eyes. His heart felt empty without Miranda. He missed his wife, he missed his kids, and he missed doing things together as a family. It was scary being sick all alone this morning, remembering how his wife had fussed when he'd dealt with his first kidney stone.

How could I have been so stupid as to jeopar-

dize our marriage like I did? Somehow, I have to prove to Miranda that it will never happen again. I have to gain her trust, and maybe now, I know how.

Chapter 24

Walnut Creek

Darren waited outside the bathroom until Jeremy finished emptying his stomach. He felt like a heel, forcing the boy to come to class when he'd complained earlier that his stomach bothered him. But Darren figured his son might have been using it as an excuse to stay home. If he'd had any idea Jeremy was really sick, he would have called Heidi and left a message, explaining their absence.

When Jeremy stepped out of the bathroom, his pale face and sagging features said it all. "Dad, I'm sick. My head hurts, and my belly's still churning."

Darren placed his hand on Jeremy's shoulder. "Sorry, Son. I should have listened to you this morning when you said you weren't feeling well." He handed Jeremy his keys. "Why don't you go out to the car and wait for me? I'll explain the situation to Heidi, and let her know that I'm taking you home."

"Okay." Holding his stomach, Jeremy made his way down the hall and out the front door.

As Darren headed back to the kitchen, he berated himself for not paying closer attention to Jeremy. What made it worse was he knew the reason.

Unwrapping a piece of peppermint gum, he popped it into his mouth. *I didn't want to miss seeing Ellen today. That's the real reason I ignored my son's complaint.*

When Darren entered the kitchen, he crossed over to Heidi and said, "Jeremy is sick, so I'm taking him home. Someone else can enjoy his shortcake when it's done."

"I'll finish Jeremy's dessert and then bring it by your house after class," Ellen offered.

Darren smiled. "That's nice of you, but I don't think Jeremy will be up to eating much of anything the rest of the day."

"It will keep in the refrigerator for a few days," Heidi spoke up. "Since I've made extra, I'll give one to Ellen for you too."

"Okay, thanks." Darren hesitated, wishing he could speak to Ellen privately. But then if she was coming by later, he'd have a chance to talk to her then. Right now, he had to get his son home. Darren said a quick goodbye to everyone and headed out the door.

"I bet that kid has the flu." Kassidy blew out a breath that rattled her lips. "And now everyone here will probably get it, because he was spreading his germs all over the place."

Denise tapped her daughter's shoulder. "You can't be sure. It might be something else that upset Jeremy's stomach. Besides, if he does have the flu, it doesn't mean the rest of us will come down with it."

"That's right," Ellen agreed. "In my years of nursing, I have seen many patients get sick with the flu, while none of their family came down with it."

Kassidy made an unladylike grunt and looked the other way.

"Mom, you're not going inside when you drop off Jeremy's dessert, I hope." Becky clasped her hands together, positioning them under her chin.

Ellen shook her head. "I'll take the shortcake up to the door, and you can wait in the car."

"Okay, but don't get too close to Jeremy. Like Kassidy said, he could be contagious."

"I'm sure it won't be him who comes to the door," Ellen assured her daughter. "Besides, didn't you hear what I said about the flu? If it even is the flu Jeremy has come down with."

Becky bobbed her head. "I heard, but I think Kassidy's right. We could all end up sick because of him. He shoulda stayed home today."

"Bet he didn't feel sick this mornin'," Peggy Ann spoke. "I threw up at school once, but I felt fine when I first woke up."

Feeling the need for a topic change, Heidi

broke in. "Let's finish baking our shortcakes and cutting up the berries. Then, when the cake is cooled enough, we can go outside and sit at the picnic table to enjoy the dessert."

Velma paused from chopping to see how Eddie was doing. He'd taken a wheelbarrow full of wood around the corner of the barn fifteen minutes ago and still wasn't back. She reached under her scarf and scratched her head. *I'm sure it couldn't have taken him that long to unload that kindling.*

She set the axe aside, pulled a hanky from the back pocket of her overalls, and wiped her sweaty forehead. Then Velma grabbed her bottle of water and took a swig. Still no sign of Eddie.

"Ouch." Velma winced, almost choking on the water. Throwing the bottle aside, she leaned down and picked up the axe that had fallen against her knee. Pulling up her pant leg, she rubbed the spot where the handle hit. *I'll probably have a black-and-blue spot by nightfall. At least it was the handle, and not the blade, that walloped into me.* She rubbed her knee a few more times, then pulled her pant leg down. *Don't even wanna think about what coulda happened if the blade of the axe had hit my knee.*

Making sure she propped the axe in a safer position, Velma looked around. *I wonder what that boy is up to. Wouldn't be surprised if he's not off somewhere, playin' with the Troyers' dog.*

Velma limped toward the woodshed, and was halfway there, when she spotted Eddie squatted beside the chicken coop with his nose pressed against the screened enclosure. "What are you doin' out here?" Velma came alongside of him. "You're supposed to be stacking wood."

"I did stack what I put in the wheelbarrow. But when I was done I decided to come look at the chickens." Eddie pointed. "They're sure scrawny-lookin', ain't they, Mama?"

"That's 'cause they're not fully grown." Velma knelt next to him. "Why, by the end of summer, these chicks will be fully grown—just like the chickens we'll be gettin' soon."

"Havin' chickens means a lot of work, don't it, Mama?"

"Yeah, but we'll all take turns feeding them and cleaning their coop. It'll pay off, too, when they start layin' eggs."

Eddie tipped his head to one side as he looked at her. "Who's 'we all,' Mama? Papa ain't home that much 'cause of his job, so there's just you, me, and Peggy Ann to do everything. It ain't fair."

"I know, Son, but we'll manage."

"Sure wish Bobbie Sue wouldn't have run off." With tears gathering in his eyes, Eddie's shoulders drooped. "Guess she don't care about us no more."

"No, I don't think it's that."

"Maybe she left 'cause you yelled at her so much. It ain't fun to be hollered at all the time, ya know."

Velma's chest ached, and tears blurred her vision. Eddie was right. She did yell a lot. Once more, she felt like an unfit mother, who probably should have never had any children. She sure wouldn't be getting any mother-of-the-year awards. That she knew was a fact.

After everyone's shortcake had cooled sufficiently, Heidi asked if Ellen, Miranda, and Denise would oversee the children while they each cut up their berries. Then, everyone would go outside.

Denise smiled. "Of course, I'd be glad to do that."

Ellen nodded. "Same here."

"I'm fine with it too." Miranda got up from her chair. "You do whatever you need to do, Heidi. We're more than happy to help out."

"Thanks, ladies. While you're doing that, I'll go outside and see if Velma and Eddie would like to join us at the picnic table. I'm sure they could use a break from the work they've been doing for me this morning."

"That makes sense," Miranda said. "You go right ahead."

When Heidi entered the backyard a few minutes

later, she was surprised to see Velma and Eddie kneeling beside the chicken coop. As she drew closer, she realized they were both crying. Heidi hesitated, wondering how best to approach them.

She didn't have to ponder things long, for Velma must have heard her coming. Sniffing, she reached up and dried her eyes, using an old hanky, then quickly stuffed it back in her pocket. "Sorry about that. You caught me bawlin' like a baby, when I shoulda been workin'." She rose to her feet, pulling Eddie up as well. "We'll get right back to work."

Heidi shook her head, watching Eddie swipe a finger under his nose. "There's no need for that. It's time for you both to take a break. In today's cooking class we made strawberry shortcake, and we're going to eat it out on the picnic table soon. I came out to invite you and Eddie to join us."

"That's real nice of you, but I think we'd better pass." Velma gestured to the smudges of dirt on her face. "I must look a mess."

"I'm not worried about that, and I'm sure it won't bother the others either. What I am concerned with is why you've been crying. Is there something you wish to talk about?"

A crimson flush crept across Velma's cheeks. "I don't wanna take up your time with my problems. You've got better things to do than listen to me bellyaching."

Speaking softly, Heidi touched Velma's arm.

"I don't mind listening at all. Talking about your problem might help you feel better."

Velma turned her head toward the house when three ladies and the children filtered out the door toward the yard. "O–okay." She looked at Eddie. "You go on over to the picnic table and join the others. I'll be there shortly."

"Ya mean I get to have some cake?" Eddie looked at his mother first, then over at Heidi.

Heidi smiled. "Yes, you sure do."

The boy didn't have to be told twice. He whirled around and took off toward the picnic table like a bee was in hot pursuit of him.

Velma grunted. "My boy has more energy than he knows what to do with. Maybe that's why he gets into so much trouble at times."

Heidi motioned to a wooden bench Lyle had built and placed under the shade of a maple tree. "Let's take a seat over there, and you can tell me what has caused you to feel so troubled."

Velma followed Heidi silently to the bench, and once they were seated, she proceeded to pour her heart out. She began by sharing details of how her oldest son had left home a few years ago, and they'd lost contact with him.

"Oh my, this is so hard to talk about." Tears slipped from Velma's eyes and rolled down her blotchy, red cheeks. The dirt on her face ran down as well, and smeared like wet paint that had been thinned too much. Reaching into her pocket she took out the hanky and wiped it across her cheek. "Then to make things worse, my oldest daughter, Bobbie Sue, ran off with her boyfriend one night last week. She didn't bother to tell her dad or me, face-to-face, of course—just left a note that I found the next day."

Velma paused long enough to wipe her nose with the hanky. "I feel like a terrible mother, who must have let her kids down. I mean, why else would Bobbie Sue and our son Clem have run off without tellin' us why? They both must have hated their life at home. We'll probably never see either of them again."

Heidi tugged her ear, thinking about the best way to respond. She certainly didn't want to say anything that would make Velma feel worse. *Help me, Lord. Please give me the right words.*

"I'm scared outa my wits, Heidi. If things don't change for our family soon, I fear my two youngest kids might run off during their teen years too."

Heidi reached for Velma's hand and gave it a tender squeeze. "Do you attend church anywhere, and is there a minister you can talk to about all this?"

Velma shook her head. "Never been one to go to church. Hank don't go, neither. He thinks it's a waste of time and says there are too many hypocrites in church." She chuckled.

"My thoughts are, if the church is full of hypocrites, then I guess there's room for two more, because me and my husband sure ain't perfect. If we were, our kids wouldn't have turned out so bad."

"I think you're being too hard on yourself. None of us is perfect, and life can be difficult, even when we are trying to do what is right." Heidi paused to collect her thoughts. "Even for those of us who attend church regularly and try to set a Christian example, we have no guarantee that our children or other family members will not go astray. We do the best we can, and ask God daily for wisdom and strength to endure the trials we sometimes must face. And when things go wrong, and we feel like we can't cope, we reach out to others and ask for help." Heidi slipped her arm around Velma's shoulder. "I'll be praying for you, and whenever you need to talk, please feel free to share your burdens with me. It always seems to help when I'm upset about something if I talk it out."

Velma pressed both palms to her chest. "Whew, I feel like I've just been to church and heard a great message—one I needed to hear, mind you. Thanks, Heidi."

"You're welcome." Heidi rose from the bench. "Now, should we join the others for a refreshing dessert?"

"Yeah, that'd be nice."

As they made their way across the grass to the picnic table, Heidi sent up a silent prayer. *Heavenly Father, please show me something specific I can do to let Velma and her family know how much You love and care about them.*

Chapter 25

Dover

"How do you even know where Darren and Jeremy live?" Becky asked when Ellen turned off the main highway and into Dover.

"He gave me their address the day we went fishing with them."

"Oh."

Ellen glanced back at Becky, slouched in her safety seat. "We had a good time that day, huh?"

"Yeah, I guess."

"It was good to see you getting along better with Jeremy. I think he's a nice boy, especially when he untangled your fishing line."

Becky hunched her shoulders. "He's okay."

"Darren's nice too. I enjoy being with him."

"Yeah, I can tell."

Ellen turned left at the next street, drove a few blocks, and stopped. "This must be their place. I see Darren's SUV parked out front." She turned off the engine, picked up the plastic containers on the seat beside her, and opened the car door. "I'll be back in a few minutes."

As Ellen walked across the yard, she couldn't

help admiring Darren's tan-colored, split-level home with a brick facade. It had a welcoming feel, and so did the well-manicured yard. She wondered how he found the time to keep it looking so nice.

When Ellen stepped onto Darren's front porch, she was surprised to see a pot filled with petunias hanging next to a hummingbird feeder. She smiled. Feeding the birds and appreciating flowers added to the list of things she and Darren had in common.

As Ellen stood quietly, she heard a buzzing sound she thought was a bee. But when she turned slightly, she saw a hummingbird hovering near her head. It flicked back and forth mere inches from her face. Then just as quickly, it swooped down and landed on the feeder. Ellen had to suppress a giggle, watching the tiny bird's beak dart in and out between sips. Then another hummingbird appeared out of nowhere and dive-bombed the one at the feeder, giving chase to it up toward the trees.

Turning back, Ellen was about to ring the doorbell when the front door opened, and Darren, with a little dog following him, stepped out to greet her. "I was watching a hummingbird at your feeder." Ellen pointed to the trees. "Then another one chased it off."

"They're at each other constantly." Darren shook his head. "I even put another feeder out back, hoping they could feed without being so territorial, but they chase after each other there too."

"Aw, what a cute little dog." Ellen looked down at the dachshund, which was sniffing her shoes.

"This little fella is Jeremy's dog, Bacon." Darren's cheeks colored. "Well, he's kinda my dog too. I can't help but love the pooch." He reached down to pick the dog up.

Ellen giggled when Bacon licked doggie kisses all over his face. Then she asked, "How is Jeremy doing?"

"About the same. He's running a fever, so I'm almost sure it's the flu."

"Sounds like it. Be sure to give him plenty of fluids."

Darren grinned. "Yes, Nurse Ellen."

Her cheeks warmed. "Sorry about that. Whenever anyone is sick, my nursing instincts kick in."

"It's okay. I don't mind." His brows furrowed. "If Caroline were still alive she'd be playing nursemaid, and I wouldn't have to do anything more than worry."

Ellen saw the pain in Darren's eyes. No doubt, he still missed his wife. Hoping to lighten the mood, she handed him two plastic containers filled with strawberry shortcake. "Heidi sent one for you, and one for Jeremy, when he feels up to eating."

"Thanks. I'll enjoy mine tonight, but it may be a day or so before Jeremy eats his."

Ellen shifted her weight. "Well, I'd better go and let you and your dog get back inside."

"Okay, and thanks for coming by." Darren touched her arm. "I'm still planning to take you out for dinner next Friday, but if Jeremy isn't better by then I'll let you know."

She moved her head slowly up and down. "I'll be praying for him, and if there's anything I can do, please let me know."

"I will." Darren pulled his hand aside. "Have a good weekend, Ellen."

"You too." She turned and hurried to her car. *Oh, Darren, you're such a nice man. Where have you been all my life?*

Berlin

When Miranda pulled her minivan into her driveway, she spotted Trent sitting in a silver-gray mid-sized car. *No doubt another vehicle from the dealership where he works. I wonder what Trent wants this time.*

"Daddy's here! Daddy's here!" Kevin shouted from the back seat. "I hope he brought us something."

Miranda grimaced. Trent's gifts, even for the kids, meant nothing to her. She wished he would realize that.

She'd barely turned off the ignition, when Debbie and Kevin hopped out of the van and ran up to greet Trent as he stepped out of his vehicle.

By the time Miranda joined them, he was squatted down with his arms surrounding both kids. "What are you doing here, Trent?" she questioned. "This is not your weekend with the children."

"I am well aware." He stared at her intently. "I came by to give you something."

Miranda stiffened. "No thanks. The last time you brought me something there were strings attached. You can talk to Debbie and Kevin for a while if you want to, but I've got work to do inside." Without waiting for a response, she whirled around and hurried into the house.

As Miranda marched off, Trent stood, clenching his jaw. *Why couldn't she have at least given me a chance to show her the card I found? Maybe I should give it to one of the kids and ask them to show it to their mom.* His forehead wrinkled. *Or would it be better to wait for another time, when Miranda's in a more receptive mood? Of course, that may never happen. What does she want from me, anyway? Am I supposed to sit up and beg like a dog?*

Kevin tugged on Trent's hand. "How come you're frowning, Daddy? Don't ya like what I said?"

Trent swept a hand across his furrowed brow. "Sorry, Son, I must've missed it. What did you say?"

"I was tellin' you what we made at the cooking class today."

"Oh? What was it?"

"Shortcake, and we put strawberries from Heidi's garden over the top."

"And don't forget the whipping cream," Debbie interjected. Her eyes looked as bright as shiny new pennies. "It was sure good."

"I'll bet it was." Trent's thoughts went to Miranda again, and the delicious strawberry shortcakes she'd made over the years. In addition to wishing for his wife's companionship, he missed her great cooking.

"Did ya bring us anything, Daddy?" Kevin asked, pulling Trent's thoughts aside once more.

"Uh, no. Not today, Son. I did bring your mother something, though."

Debbie frowned. "Mommy doesn't like it when you bring her gifts. I heard her say so when she was talking to Grandma on the phone the other day."

Trent resisted the urge to say something negative about his mother-in-law. The kids loved their grandparents, and he wasn't about to spoil their relationship. He could only imagine, though, what Alta's response was when Miranda told her that. Whenever Trent had been around

Miranda's folks, he'd always felt that he never quite measured up. It was like they—especially, Alta—felt as though their daughter could have done better in choosing a husband. He wasn't sure if it was his job they didn't approve of, or maybe his personality rubbed them the wrong way.

"I don't think your mom will mind what I brought for her today." Trent opened the car door and reached inside, where he'd placed the card on the passenger's seat. He'd kept it in its original envelope so it wouldn't get wrinkled. "Would you please see that your mom gets this?" He held the envelope out to Debbie.

She hesitated at first, but finally reached for the card.

"Thanks, sweetie." Trent bent down and hugged both kids again. "I should get going now, but I'll see you guys next Saturday."

"Why can't you stay, Daddy?" Debbie's soulful eyes looked directly at him.

"I would, honey, but this morning I wasn't feeling well. I passed a kidney stone, so I'd like to go home and rest a little more."

Kevin looked up at Trent with a hopeful expression. "Are we gonna do anything fun when you pick us up next Saturday?"

"Yeah. I'm not sure what yet, but I'll come up with something you and your sister will enjoy." He opened his car door, but then turned back around to face Debbie. "Don't forget to give your mom the card."

"Okay, Dad."

Trent got in the car and sat watching as the kids went into the house. Clenching his fingers around the steering wheel, he murmured, "I hope that card jogs Miranda's memory and she comes to her senses. If this doesn't do the trick, I'll have to come up with something else."

Walnut Creek

After setting lunch on the table, Heidi stepped outside to call Marsha and Randy. It was no surprise when she discovered them standing by the chicken's enclosure.

"Lunch is ready." Heidi put a hand on top of both of their heads.

"Can we come back and watch the *hinkel* after we eat?" Randy asked.

Heidi smiled. It was a pleasure to hear him using the Pennsylvania Dutch word for chickens. "Of course you can. And a little bit later, you can give them fresh water and more food."

Randy grinned up at her. "I like takin' care of the hinkel."

"You've been doing a good job." She pointed to the house. "But right now, lunch is waiting."

"Okay." Randy grabbed his sister's hand. "Let's go, Marsha!"

Heidi followed, but she'd only made it halfway to the house when Lyle's driver pulled into the yard. She waited until Lyle got out of the van.

"How'd your class go today?" he asked, joining her on the lawn and slipping his arm around her waist.

"For the most part it was good, but one of my young students got sick and had to go home. I think Jeremy may have come down with the flu."

"That's too bad. I hope no one else gets it." Lyle handed Heidi his lunch pail. "Would you mind taking this into the house while I go out to the barn to check on our horse? She was favoring one of her back legs before I left for the auction this morning, and I want to make sure she's okay."

"No problem. I hope Bobbins is all right. But before you go, I'd like to ask you a question."

He paused. "Sure, what's up?"

"Well, today, when I went out to invite Velma and her son to join us for strawberry shortcake, I found her in tears. Him too."

He tipped his head. "Oh? Did she tell you what was wrong?"

"Jah. Apparently, Velma's teenage daughter ran off with her boyfriend recently, and Velma is quite depressed. Her oldest son also left home a few years ago, and they've had no contact with him since."

Lyle shook his head. "What a shame. It has to be difficult for Velma and her husband."

"It is, and also for the younger kids too. As I've mentioned before, they've had some financial problems since they moved here, which I'm sure has contributed to Velma's emotional state. I'm wondering if there isn't something we can do to help that family."

"I'll have to give it some thought, but in the meantime, why don't we invite them over for an indoor supper or an outdoor barbecue some evening? It will give us a chance to get to know them better," Lyle suggested. "I've seen her husband a few times, but all we did was wave at each other. If we spend some time with them, it might give us a better idea of their needs and how we might help out."

Heidi nodded. "Good idea. I'll contact Velma sometime next week and extend an invitation to supper."

"Oh, and speaking of next week . . . Don't forget about the auction coming up on Saturday. There will be lots of good food available and some interesting things to see. I think it will be a fun outing for Marsha and Randy."

Heidi smiled. "I believe you're right. And now, I'd better get inside and make sure the kids washed their hands before sitting down at the table."

Lyle slipped his arm around Heidi's waist

again, hugging her tenderly. "I'll be in soon to join you for lunch."

Before heading inside, Heidi glanced toward the birdhouse at the far end of their property. The other day, while watering her flowers, she'd watched a pair of bluebirds catching bugs and taking them into the birdhouse—a sure sign they had a family to feed.

As Heidi walked slowly across the yard, she squinted her eyes to get a better look. "Hmm . . . Now why does it look so odd?"

When she drew closer to the little house Lyle had attached to a fence post, Heidi realized one of their barn cats sat upon the roof of the birds' dwelling. Little tweets and chirps came from inside, as the parent birds frantically swooped toward the cat, then landed in the nearby tree. Their loud and frantic *chit, chit, chit* let Heidi know the bluebirds were not happy with this intruder so close to their home with babies inside.

Scurrying to get there quickly, Heidi picked up her pace. Just as the cat reached a paw inside the small entrance, Heidi clapped her hands. "Oh no you don't! Shame on you. Now scat!"

The orange-colored feline had been so intent on trying to get the baby birds, the sound of Heidi's clapping startled him. It was hard to suppress her giggles when the tabby jumped off the roof, with his paw still inside the opening, and dangled there in midair a few seconds before dropping to the ground. It looked like a streak of orange as the cat made a beeline toward the barn.

"That will teach you." Heidi watched a few more minutes, as one of the bluebirds flew into the little house. A few seconds later, it zipped out again, while the other parent bird sailed in with a bug in its mouth.

Satisfied, after hearing little chirps coming from the hungry babies inside, Heidi hummed as she made her way back to the house. Next week would be busy, but she didn't mind. Between doing something neighborly for Velma and her family, and spending time with the children, she felt sure it would be a satisfying week.

Chapter 26

How come you're limpin' 'round the kitchen, Mama?" Peggy Ann asked as Velma moved slowly about the room, getting supper ready.

"I told you before—my knee hurts from where the handle of the axe fell against it today." Velma grunted. "Don't ya listen to anything I say?"

Peggy Ann's hair hung in her face as she lowered her head. "S–sorry. Guess I forgot."

Shuffling over to her daughter, Velma pulled the child into her arms. She wished she could take back her harsh words. "No, I'm the one who should be sorry. Didn't mean to be so cross. I'm just tired, hurtin', and hungry, to boot."

Eddie burst into the room. "I'm hungry too. What's for supper, Mama?"

She pointed to the stove. "I'm heating some leftover vegetable soup, and we'll have cheese and crackers to go with it. Nothing exciting, but at least it'll fill our bellies."

"Will we be havin' any dessert?" Peggy Ann wanted to know.

Velma shook her head. "Nope. You two had your dessert at Heidi's, remember?"

Eddie smacked his lips. "It was sure good."

"That it was. And since your sister came home with the recipe, we can make strawberry short-cake sometime. I'm sure it'll be as good as what we had today." Velma took three bowls down from the cupboard. "You two go wash up now, while I dish out the soup."

The children scampered out of the kitchen, and Velma hobbled over to get the soup ladle.

Pulling and tugging, Velma blew out an exasperated breath. "Now why won't this stubborn drawer open?" She rattled it and jiggled it in every direction, but it wouldn't budge. "Come on you stupid thing. Don't I have enough troubles already?"

Velma stopped for a minute to catch her breath. She hoped Hank would be home soon with some money. Their food supplies were running low, and some things needed to be fixed around the house—including now, this kitchen drawer.

Once more, Velma wished she could look for a job. But what would she do with Eddie and Peggy Ann while she was at work? She couldn't leave them home by themselves. That would be asking for trouble. And then there was her need for transportation. If she took a job at one of the stores or restaurants anywhere—even one of the small towns here in Holmes County—it would require a car.

Staring at the drawer, Velma knew it wouldn't

open itself. She grabbed the handle one more time, and with one final tug, the drawer flew open, almost sending Velma backward to the floor. Apparently the soup ladle had been stuck, keeping the drawer from opening. It was bent, but, at least, still usable. "Why can't anything ever be simple?" she mumbled.

"Cause it ain't."

Velma jumped at the sound of her husband's booming voice. "Hank, I—I didn't hear your rig pull in. How long have ya been here?"

"Long enough to say hi to the kids." He moved toward Velma. "What's the matter with you, woman? Are ya goin' deaf? That truck of mine's loud enough to wake the dead."

Velma's chin quivered. "You don't have to holler, Hank. I'm standing right here."

His eyes narrowed. "What's going on? You look like you're gonna start bawling."

"I'm tired, and I've had a rough day." She motioned to the pot of soup on the stove. "The kids and I are about ready to have supper. Have you eaten yet?"

"Nope."

"Okay, I'll set you a place." Velma took out another bowl and put it on the table where Hank normally sat when he was at home. "Can I talk to you about something?"

"Sure, what's up?" He pulled out a chair and sat down.

Velma moved to stand beside him. "I was talkin' to Heidi today—told her about our two oldest running off."

His face tightened. "Ya got no call to be tellin' other people our business. What happens in the Kimball home stays right here." Hank slapped his hand on the table. "A nosy neighbor starts gossiping, and pretty soon the whole county will know what's goin' on at our place."

"But Heidi isn't like that. She's not a nosy neighbor, and I doubt she will tell anyone what I told her."

"*Puh!* I wouldn't be so sure about that. The Amish don't have TVs or run around in motorized vehicles. What else do they have to do all day but spread gossip?"

Velma's fingernails bit into her palms as she fought for control. "You are not being fair. Are you prejudiced against the Amish?"

He shook his head vigorously. "Course not. I just know how people like to talk—not just the Amish, but anyone with a waggin' tongue."

"Well, like I said, I don't think Heidi would gossip about us. When I talked to her today, she seemed to truly care." Velma drew in a quick breath. "Heidi mentioned church too."

"What about it?"

"She asked if we attended church or had a minister we could talk to about our problems."

"Humph! Church is the last thing we need.

Now, if you wanna start goin', I won't stop ya, but there's no way I'll step inside a church building." Hank pushed his chair aside and strode across the room. After opening the refrigerator door, he took out a carton of milk and poured himself a glass. "Is this all the milk we have?" He shook the carton.

"Yes, it is, and I could use some money to go grocery shopping."

"Figured you'd be askin' for money." He lifted the glass to his lips and took a big drink. "You really oughta find a job."

"We've been over this before." She sighed. "If I went to work, I'd need to pay someone to watch the kids—not to mention some form of transportation."

"Eddie and Peggy Ann are big enough to stay by themselves."

"No they're not, Hank. They're just children."

He took another drink. "Yeah, well, when I was Eddie's age, I was helpin' my pa at the lumber mill."

She plopped her hands against her hips. "Just because your dad trusted a boy to do a man's job doesn't mean we should leave our kids alone while we're both off working." Velma could see by her husband's placid expression that she wasn't getting anywhere with him. She was stubborn, but Hank was even more hard-headed. He rarely agreed with her on anything.

Hank flopped back in his chair. "So, are we gonna eat now, or what?"

"Yeah, I'll go get the kids." Velma clenched her fists as she limped out of the kitchen. No kiss on the cheek today when Hank got home. It seemed they were getting further and further apart. "Guess absence doesn't make the heart grow fonder, like some people say," she muttered. Nothing would probably ever change for the better in her life, so she may as well accept it. *I bet he didn't even notice me limping.*

Berlin

Miranda was getting ready to climb into bed when someone tapped on her door. "Who is it?"

"It's me, Mommy. Can I come in?"

"Of course, sweetie," Miranda called.

The door opened, and Debbie stepped into the room. "I have something for you. It's from Daddy, and I promised to give it to you, but I forgot until now."

Miranda's lips pressed together. *Oh, boy, here it comes.* "What did your father ask you to give me?"

"This." Debbie held out a cream-colored envelope. "I was supposed to give it to you when me and Kevin came in the house after Dad left. But then you told us we should change clothes before lunch, so I put the envelope on my dresser and forgot about it till now."

"Okay, thanks." Miranda took the envelope and hugged her daughter. It wasn't Debbie's fault Trent was using her to deliver his gift. "Did your dad visit with you and your brother a little before he left?"

"No. Daddy said he had to go home and rest. Something about a kidney stone."

"Your father had a kidney stone?"

"Yep, I think he said he passed it, whatever that means."

Miranda didn't ask her daughter any more. "Now off to bed you go."

"Night, Mommy. Sweet dreams."

Miranda smiled. "Sweet dreams to you too."

After Debbie left the room, Miranda took a seat on the bed and opened the envelope. She recognized the card right away. It was one she'd given Trent on their first anniversary, when they were so very much in love. She'd written such lovely things to him—promising, no matter how many struggles they might encounter, or how difficult or challenging situations may get, they'd always work things out together.

I wonder if I should call him to see if he's okay. The last time he had a kidney stone attack, it lasted for two days. No, I better not. Trent would have called if it had been too bad.

Tears welled in her eyes and dripped onto the card. Miranda couldn't deny that she still loved Trent. She just wasn't sure they could be together again.

Chapter 27

Charm, Ohio

I'm glad your son is feeling better." Ellen smiled at Darren from the passenger seat of his SUV.

"Me too. He was only sick about twenty-four hours, so I'm pretty sure he had a stomach virus and not the flu." Darren slowed as they drove through the small village of Charm. "I'm glad neither you nor Becky got sick, and I hope none of the others who were at Heidi's that day came down with it."

"I hope they didn't, either. So where is Jeremy this evening?" she asked.

"He's spending the night with one of his friends. I'll pick him up in the morning sometime after breakfast. The boys will probably go to bed late and sleep in Saturday morning. I may just catch some extra z's myself—that is, if Bacon lets me." Darren glanced over at Ellen. "What's Becky doing tonight?"

"A friend of mine from church came over to be with her. Of course, Becky thinks she's too old for a babysitter, but as far as I'm concerned, she is not old enough to be left alone for any length of time—especially after dark."

Darren bobbed his head. "We're on the same page regarding that. Say, I hope you like the Bavarian-style food they serve here," he said as he pulled his vehicle into the parking lot of the Chalet in the Valley restaurant. "I should have asked."

"Yes, I do, and I've actually been here a few times with Becky." Ellen smiled. "Believe it or not, she likes bratwurst with sauerkraut, which is also one of my favorites."

"That's a dish I enjoy eating too." Darren chuckled. "Your daughter has good taste. Guess she must take after her mother."

"Yes, she does in many ways." Ellen's face sobered. "Just not in appearance. But then, that's because she's not my biological child."

He tipped his head. "Most people would never guess it, though."

"Probably not." Ellen shifted in her seat. "Becky didn't know she'd been adopted until recently. It came out when she overheard a conversation I had with my brother."

"How'd she take it?"

"Not well. It was quite a shock."

"Why did you wait so long to tell her?"

"I was afraid for her to know the truth." Ellen explained, "You see, when I was a girl, I had a friend who found out she was adopted, and it ruined the relationship that had been established with her adoptive parents."

Ellen's eyebrows gathered in. "I regret not telling Becky sooner. I'm afraid it's put some distance between us."

"Really? If so, it's not obvious—at least not to me."

Ellen sighed. "Well, things are better, but not quite how it was before Becky found out the truth."

"How are things different?"

"For one thing, Becky's not as talkative as she was with me before. And she spends more time alone in her room than she used to."

Feeling her frustration, Darren reached over and clasped Ellen's hand. It felt warm to the touch, making him wish he could hold it all night. "I'll bet things will go back to the way they were once she's had enough time to work through it."

"I hope so. Thanks for listening. It helped to be able to share this with you."

"That's what friends are for, Ellen." Darren's lips parted slightly as he struggled with the temptation to pull her into his arms and offer a kiss. But it may be too soon for that. Before their first kiss, Darren wanted to be sure about Ellen's feelings for him.

The feelings stirring within Darren surprised him. Ellen was so beautiful, and at the same time, looked so vulnerable after revealing her concern over Becky. All he wanted to do was hold her and make everything right.

Ellen's stomach rumbled softly, and she quickly placed her hand on it. "My tummy seems to be talking to me. Guess we need to go into the restaurant so I can feed it."

Darren gave Ellen a thumbs-up. "I'm all for that."

Walnut Creek

Velma stepped into the bedroom she shared with Hank and stopped. Wearing the most faded, threadbare jeans in their closet, he lounged, shirtless, on the bed.

"What are you doing? You need to get dressed or we'll be late for our supper at the Troyers'." She stood at the foot of the bed, squinting at him.

He yawned, stretching both arms over his head. "Wish you hadn't told 'em we'd go there tonight. I don't get much time at home these days, and I'd planned to kick back and relax all evening."

Her pulse quickened. "Then ya shoulda told me that before you agreed to go."

"Wasn't thinkin' much about it at the time. I was probably half asleep when you asked."

Velma stared straight at Hank as she pushed her shoulders back. "Well, the invitation was extended, and we accepted, so ya may as well get up and get dressed, 'cause we're goin'." Velma wasn't normally this assertive with her husband, but with the way things were going between them lately, her nerves were on edge. Truth be told, she was looking forward to spending the evening with Heidi and her family—and Eddie and Peggy Ann were excited about going there too.

"Okay, okay . . . Don't get so pushy." Hank pulled himself off the bed, ambled across the room, and opened a dresser drawer. The T-shirt he pulled out caused Velma to gasp.

"You're not gonna wear that old thing, I hope."

He shrugged his broad shoulders. "Don't see why not."

She shook her head. "It's not appropriate."

"It is to me." He slipped the dingy white shirt with a couple of small holes in it over his head.

She recoiled, wrinkling her nose. "You have better T-shirts to choose from. Please wear one of those colorful ones in your drawer. Or better yet, how about a long-sleeve cotton shirt that will cover up your tattoos?" Velma glanced at the cotton dress she wore, hoping it looked presentable.

Hank gazed at the tattooed panther on his left arm, then gestured to the eagle on his right arm. "You think your Amish friends will have somethin' against my tats?"

"I'm not sure what they'll think, but whether they do or not, I'd appreciate if you would wear somethin' decent."

He planted his feet in a wide stance. "Either I wear what I've got on, or I ain't goin'."

Velma's posture sagged. "Okay, Hank, wear whatever you want." She could only imagine what the Troyers would think of her sloppy, boisterous husband.

"This is some mighty good tater salad." Hank emitted a loud burp, then reached under his T-shirt and scratched his belly. "Mind if I have some more?"

"No, not at all." Heidi handed the bowl to Lyle, who passed it on to Hank. "I'm glad you like my salad. It's a recipe that's been in our family for a long while, and it has been handed down to each generation."

"Everything is good." Velma pointed to the barbecued chicken. "You and Lyle outdid yourselves on our account, and we thank you for it." She glanced over at her husband as if expecting him to agree, but he was silent. Heidi figured Hank's appreciation was being shown through the manner in which he was eating the food, as he sat there licking barbeque sauce off his fingers.

"I understand you're a truck driver." Lyle looked over at Hank.

"Yep." The man bobbed his head and shoveled another spoonful of potato salad into his mouth.

"That's why Hank's away from home so much," Velma put in. "Sometimes he's gone for just a few days. Other times it could be a week or longer."

"Me and Peggy Ann don't like it when Papa's gone," Eddie spoke up. "It means more work for us to do." He glanced at his mother, then looked quickly away.

"Yep, I got word before we came here that I have to leave tonight on a run," Hank added. "And I probably won't be back till Monday sometime."

Both Eddie and Peggy Ann groaned, while Velma grew silent.

Heidi wanted so badly to come right out and ask Velma if they could do anything for her family, but she didn't want to embarrass her in front of everyone. She knew from some of the things Velma had told her that money was tight and they were in need of a car. A vehicle was something she and Lyle couldn't help with, but maybe they could loan the Kimballs some money. Of course, that might be a touchy subject. Some folks didn't want to be beholden to anyone, and she had a feeling Hank might be one of those people.

Heidi touched the base of her neck, where a

mosquito had landed moments ago and left its mark. *Guess this is one more thing I need to pray about. Hopefully, something will come to me soon about the best way to help the Kimballs.*

Chapter 28

Between Berlin and Charm

By the time Heidi and the children arrived at the Doughty Run School Auction on Saturday, things were in full swing. Lyle had gone early, since he was the head auctioneer, but Randy and Marsha didn't get up in time for them all to go with him. So right after breakfast Heidi hitched her horse to their open buggy, and she headed to the auction with the children.

They arrived at eight thirty, in time for the auction to begin, but missed the breakfast that had been served at seven. School auctions were important to the Amish community, and Heidi was glad she could bring Randy and Marsha here today. Randy would attend the Amish schoolhouse near their home toward the end of August, and she and Lyle would be involved in many functions centered on the school. Parental involvement was important to the children, teachers, and Amish school board.

After guiding her horse and buggy into the area reserved for parking, Heidi climbed down and secured Bobbins to the hitching rail provided.

She felt thankful the mare's leg was now better. Then she clasped the children's hands and headed to where the action was. In addition to all the activity in the auction tent, vendors were selling barbecued chicken, root beer floats, ice cream, and lots of baked goods.

"I smell somethin' good." Randy pointed to a booth selling kettle popcorn. "Can we go get some?"

"We will a little later." Heidi smiled. "I thought we would go into the auction tent for a bit and see how things are going. You'll get to see Lyle there too."

"Can we talk to him?" Marsha asked.

"Probably not. He will be busy auctioning items and making sure everything is running smoothly." Heidi led the way to some benches, where they all took a seat. She enjoyed watching as several handmade quilts were auctioned, as well as some nice pieces of furniture made by one of the local Amish men. She caught a glimpse of Loretta and Eli across the way and waved.

Randy and Marsha both giggled.

"What are you two laughing about?" Heidi smiled as they pointed at Lyle.

"He's talkin' funny." Randy smirked. "And really fast."

Heidi explained about how auctioneers talked when they were bid calling.

Hearing her name called, Heidi glanced to the

right. She was surprised to see Allie Garrett in the row directly across from them.

Heidi smiled and waved. Allie waved back, and then she left her seat and came over to where Heidi sat. "It's good to see you," Allie whispered. "Can we find a place to talk for a few minutes? It'd be nice to get caught up."

Heidi glanced at Randy and Marsha. They both seemed intent on watching as Lyle got the crowd bidding on a beautiful oak desk. She leaned close to Randy. "Will you two be okay if I go outside the tent for a few minutes to talk to my friend?"

Randy moved his head up and down.

"Okay. Just stay right there on the bench. I'll be back soon." Heidi stood and followed Allie out of the tent.

"I have some good news." Allie spoke excitedly. "Steve's taken a desk job, so he won't be patrolling or out on the streets where his life has been in constant danger." She leaned closer to Heidi. "He's spending more time with me and the kids now, and it was his idea to bring me and the kids here today."

Heidi tenderly squeezed Allie's shoulder. "I'm glad things are working out."

"So how are things going? I saw your foster children sitting on the bench with you."

Heidi nodded. "Marsha and Randy are adjusting pretty well."

"That's wonderful, Heidi. Did the officials ever find out if the children have any living relatives who might want to raise them?"

"No, and because we love Randy and Marsha so much, Lyle and I have decided to adopt the children. It's a process, and we're waiting until things are closer to being finalized before we tell the kids."

"I'm sure everything will move forward without a problem. After all this time, any relatives would have come forward." Allie hugged Heidi. "You and your husband will be good parents for those children."

"We will do our best, and we're looking forward to the days ahead—watching Randy and Marsha grow up, and hopefully both of them someday joining the Amish church."

"That time we stopped by your place, we felt bad after we left, seeing how upset the children were—especially little Marsha."

"Apparently your husband reminded the children of their father until he spoke," Heidi explained. "It was his uniform. Apparently their dad was a security guard at the mall."

"Oh, my. How traumatic for them to see someone who resembled their dad."

"It's okay. We had a picnic that evening, and afterward I was able to sit down with Randy and Marsha and look through a photo album that had belonged to their parents." Heidi paused. "I believe it helped for the children to be able to talk about their mom and dad as they looked at all the pictures."

They chatted a bit longer, until Heidi said she should go back and check on the children.

"Yes, I should check in with my family too." Allie hugged Heidi once more, and they walked back inside together. "Please let me know how everything goes with the adoption."

Heidi nodded. "I certainly will."

Loudonville, Ohio

"You kids are gonna have a great time here today," Trent said as he pulled his newer-model truck into a large parking lot. He was glad the parking was free, because there was an admission fee for the event. The cost was minimal, however, and they'd probably be here most of the day, so he would get his money's worth.

"I like when you let us sit up front with you, Daddy." Debbie grinned.

"If I had some safety seats, you'd be sitting in the seat behind me. But the seat belts have you good and secure."

Kevin, who sat beside Trent, tapped his arm. "I forgot. What'd ya say is goin' on here today?"

"It's the Great Mohican Powwow. We're going to see all kinds of Native American events and activities."

"Like what?" Debbie peered around her brother, looking curiously at Trent.

"There will be things like singing, dance and drum competitions, tomahawk throwing, fire starting, storytelling, flute making, and most likely lots more." Trent wiggled his brows. "I found out about this event on the internet, and it said there would be over forty traders, artisans, and craftsmen."

"Will there be food to eat?" Kevin wanted to know.

"Yep. There'll be plenty of that."

"How come the Native Americans get together like this?" Debbie asked.

"It's a chance for them to sing, dance, renew old friendships, and make new friends too," Trent explained. "It's also a time to reflect on their ancestors' old ways and preserve their people's heritage."

Kevin's eyes gleamed. "Can we get outa the truck now?"

"In a minute, Son. I need to ask your sister a question first." Trent leaned around Kevin so he could see his daughter's face. "Did you take the envelope I gave you last Saturday to your mother?"

She nodded.

"What'd she say when she opened it?"

"I don't know, Daddy. I just handed it to her and said it was from you. Then I headed back to my room 'cause it was time for bed."

"Did your mom say anything about it the next day?"

"Huh-uh."

Trent sagged against his seat. If the words Miranda had written on the card still meant something to her, surely she would have contacted him this past week. He would have to come up with some other idea now to win Miranda back.

Walnut Creek

Slicing a pineapple she'd purchased at the market yesterday, Velma sighed. She'd already been up a few hours after a fitful night of little sleep. She'd tossed and turned, done a lot of crying, and punched her pillow numerous times as well. So early this morning she'd risen from bed before the sun had come up.

After sprucing up the living room and kitchen, while Peggy Ann and Eddie were still sleeping, Velma had gone to the living room, opened the drawer of an end table, and pulled out a dull white album that held her and Hank's wedding pictures. Since they could not afford a professional photographer back then, Hank's brother, who lived in South Carolina, had offered to take the pictures for them. A few weeks later, after the film was developed, her brother-in-law mailed them the pictures, which were inserted in a standard off-white album. Enclosed was also an envelope with the negatives, along with a card telling them the album and wedding pictures were his wedding gift to them. Velma remembered feeling grateful because his gift saved them a lot of money.

Her mouth puckered as she bit into a slice of pineapple. *So long ago.* Velma heaved another sigh, flipping through the worn-out pages of the album. They were decent enough photos, and a few were exceptional. Years ago, Velma had intentions of purchasing an actual wedding album, picking out a few of the better prints, and having the pictures enlarged to put in a special keepsake album. After looking at many beautiful scrapbooks in the local card store, she gave up. There always seemed to be something more important to spend the money on, since the keepsake albums were not cheap.

"Humph!" Velma mumbled out loud as she glanced around the small kitchen. "Like a lot of things I'd always hoped for, that wedding album never happened."

Looking at the pictures took her back in time. Except for the birth of her children, Velma couldn't remember a happier moment than the day she married Hank. She sniffed and grabbed a napkin from the holder to wipe at a tear rolling down her cheek. Today was their twentieth wedding anniversary, and she'd be spending another one without her husband, since he was out on the road.

The first couple of years of their marriage, Hank made sure to take the day off. He'd do something simple on their special day. Sometimes it was giving her a bouquet of cut flowers or some other sweet memento, along with a nice card. Velma still had every card Hank had given her. Sometimes they would start celebrating early and attend Fourth of July events around their hometown, with the evening ending in a stunning fireworks display. But as time went on, his romantic gestures waned, until their anniversary became like any other ordinary day.

Things sure do change, Velma brooded. At times it really tore at her heart. *Guess I should be used to it by now, though.*

Eddie chose that moment to come bounding into the kitchen, his brown hair uncombed and unruly. "Mornin', Mama." He grinned at her before getting the carton of milk out of the refrigerator, and then slid in his stocking feet all the way to the small pantry for his favorite box of cereal.

Velma got up and put the album back, then went to the kitchen to get a bowl for her son.

"Is cereal all ya want for breakfast? I can make an egg and toast if ya like, or even some pancakes."

"Nope, cereal's fine." Eddie winked one of his chocolate-colored eyes.

"I'll have cereal too." Peggy Ann skipped into the kitchen.

"Goodness." Velma lifted her eyebrows. "You two are mighty chipper this morning."

After pouring milk on his cereal, Eddie handed the carton to his sister. "It's Saturday, Mama, and our favorite cartoons are on." He scooped up a spoonful of colorful crunchy puffs and put them in his mouth.

Peggy Ann nodded while stirring the milk through her bowl of honey-flavored oats.

"Okay, but you can only watch TV for an hour. Then I have some chores for you both to do."

Without argument, her children looked at her and nodded. *That's odd.* Velma looked at her daughter, then her son. *Normally they would fight me on doing chores.*

"You can take your bowls to the living room and set up TV trays, if you'd like to eat there. Also, here are some slices of pineapple to have with your cereal." Any other time, Velma didn't allow them to eat in the living room, but this morning, she made an exception.

"Oh yummy." Eddie took a slice of the fruit and had it eaten before he bounded out of the kitchen.

"Thank you, Mama." Peggy Ann put her pineapple slice on a napkin, then followed her brother.

Velma got a bowl of cereal for herself and sat back down at the table. She could see the kids through the open doorway, sitting quietly, eating, and watching TV. *I wonder if those two heard me crying during the night. It wouldn't surprise me as loud as I got. Maybe that's why they were bein' so nice.*

Canton

"I don't see why I have to go with you today," Kassidy complained as they headed to the home where Denise would be conducting an open house in the afternoon. "I'm old enough to stay by myself, you know."

Denise clicked her newly manicured fingernails against the steering wheel. "How many times must we have this discussion?"

Kassidy said nothing.

Some parents might be comfortable leaving their eleven-year-old at home alone for a good chunk of the day, but Denise wasn't one of them. Besides, bringing Kassidy along would give her daughter something to do besides fooling with her cell phone. Denise still didn't understand why Greg thought it necessary to give their daughter her own phone at such a young age. It would make more sense if Kassidy was older, and had a car or a job. As far as Denise could tell, the only thing Kassidy used her phone for was

306

texting friends, taking selfies, and sharing them with friends. Occasionally, she found her playing a game, but were those things reason enough to pay for the extra phone?

"You know, someday when you grow up, you might decide to become a Realtor, so helping me at the open house today can be beneficial."

"I don't see how, Mom. All I'm gonna do is just stand around. Good thing I brought my cell phone along so I'll have something to do."

Denise shook her head. "You are not going to play on that phone today. In fact, when we get there, I want you to give it to me."

"What?" Kassidy groaned. "How come?"

"Because it's a distraction you don't need. Today I'll need you to keep an eye on the brochures I will have set out, and if the pile goes down, you can replace them with more from my briefcase."

"That's gonna be boring." Kassidy kicked the back of Denise's seat.

"You can also make sure the plate of cookies I brought gets refilled as needed." Denise glanced in the rearview mirror. "And please stop kicking my seat. It's distracting."

"Okay, whatever. What I wanna know is what are you gonna do the whole time during the open house?"

"I will be answering the door and showing prospective home buyers through the house."

"That sounds like more fun than what I'll be doing."

Denise released a puff of air as she turned up the driveway leading to the house with the For Sale sign. This home would also bring a good commission if she found a buyer willing to pay the full asking price.

At least Kassidy wasn't putting up too much of a fuss at this point. Denise parked the car. *Maybe the scripture verse Heidi put on the back of a previous recipe card about children obeying their parents is getting through to my daughter. I wonder what verse Heidi will share with the class next week when we go to her house.*

Walnut Creek

After lunch, Velma pulled weeds, while the kids gathered up their toys that were strewn all over the yard. Something strange was going on, but she wasn't about to question anything. It was rare when the kids did what she asked without moping about it or suddenly making themselves scarce.

Earlier, after watching their favorite cartoon, Peggy Ann and Eddie had actually cleaned their rooms and even removed the sheets from their beds so Velma could put fresh linens on.

To the best of her knowledge, Hank wasn't due home until sometime Monday. *I'll bet he doesn't even call to give me an anniversary wish.* As she pulled some stubborn dandelion stems out of the dry dirt, her thoughts went back to their wedding day.

Velma had been nineteen when she walked down the aisle to the man she had fallen in love with. The man she wanted to make dreams, have children, and grow old with.

Back then they'd started with nothing, and twenty years later, they still had very little. Except for having children, not many of their dreams had come true.

"You'd think after this many years, we'd be further ahead in our life." Velma stood up, wiping a dirty hand across her sweaty forehead. Her knee still hurt, but not as bad. Still, she was careful not to put a lot of pressure on it and cause more problems. They certainly couldn't afford any unnecessary medical bills.

Hearing a horn honk, as an unfamiliar car pulled into the driveway, Velma shielded her eyes from the sun and watched the vehicle come to a stop. She could barely see someone waving through the tinted glass.

Wiping her hands on the back of her coveralls, Velma started walking toward the car, when a woman wearing sunglasses, and dressed in a stylish blouse with neatly pressed twill slacks, got out.

"Velma!" The woman hurried in her direction.

"Nellie!" Velma recognized her voice. "Is it

really you?" Meeting her halfway, she smothered her childhood friend with a huge hug.

"Oh, Velma, it's been way too long." Nellie's voice caught. "But life gets in the way sometimes. I'm just glad you sent me your change of address when you and your family moved here from Kentucky."

"It's wonderful to see you. I had no idea you were coming."

"Sorry, I should have called, but I wanted it to be a surprise."

"I'm surprised, all right. So glad I'm home today." Velma took Nellie's arm and steered her to the plastic resin picnic table under their one and only tree. "My, my . . . Just look at you. Except for your hair being styled a bit shorter, you haven't changed one bit."

"Oh, I don't know about that." A blush crept across Nellie's cheeks.

"Look at me. I'm a mess." Velma quickly crossed her arms to hide her dirty hands. "Can I get you something to drink, or have you had lunch yet?"

"Maybe something cold to drink. I stopped at a restaurant for lunch about an hour ago."

"Come inside with me while I wash these grungy hands, and afterwards I'll make us some lemonade. We can come back out here and catch up with each other at the picnic table."

Nellie grinned. "Sounds wonderful."

After Velma mixed the lemonade and poured them each a glass, she and Nellie headed back out to the yard.

"Come here, Eddie and Peggy Ann," Velma called to her kids once she and Nellie got seated. "I want you to meet someone special."

When the children ran up to them, Velma introduced Nellie. "Peggy Ann and Eddie, this is my friend Nellie Burns." Velma touched Nellie's arm. "We grew up together when we lived in Kentucky, and were very close, almost like sisters. Nellie moved away before you two were born."

"Hello." Peggy Ann grinned shyly.

"Nice to meet ya," Eddie said with a nod.

"Well it certainly is nice to meet you both, as well." Nellie reached out and shook the children's hands.

"Okay, you two, go on in and pour yourself some lemonade, and then continue with what you were doin'. Afterwards, you can relax; you both did a good job today." Velma smiled as they ran toward the door, each trying to get inside first.

After the kids went inside, Velma looked at Nellie. "I've thought about you often over the years. Wondered how you were doing. Did you ever get married again after Ted died?"

Nellie shook her head. "I never remarried. I've been single so long now I'm sort of used to being on my own." Nellie took a sip of her drink. "What about you? What's happened with you since we last saw each other?"

Velma lowered her head. "Not much to talk about. I'd hoped when Hank suggested we move here, things would get better for us."

"And they haven't?" Velma saw pity in her friend's eyes.

"Nope." Velma went on to tell Nellie about her two oldest children leaving home. "Most recently, our teenage daughter, Bobbie Sue, left a note and ran off with her boyfriend, Kenny, saying she plans to marry him as soon as she turns eighteen. Who knows—they're probably hitched by now."

Nellie didn't say anything but continued to listen.

"Bobbie Sue's boyfriend would not have been my choice for our daughter, but then it's sorta fitting I guess. My parents didn't approve of Hank either, but I still married him. You know the ole saying: what goes around comes around." Velma stopped talking and sniffed. "Hank owns a semitruck and is gone a lot, so it's been kinda lonely since we moved here. Other than an Amish woman who lives down the road, I haven't made any friends."

Nellie placed her hand on Velma's arm. "I'm sorry. I wish I'd kept in better touch."

"Yeah, me too." Velma released a lingering

sigh. "To make matters worse, today is Hank's and my wedding anniversary."

"I really should have called ahead. I hope I'm not in the way of any plans you and your husband have for today."

Velma shook her head. "Plans? What plans? Hank's not here to help me celebrate, and he didn't even leave me a card before he headed out on the road." A lump formed in Velma's throat, and she swallowed a couple of times, hoping to push it down.

"That's too bad." Nellie gave Velma's arm a motherly pat.

"So, what brings you to Ohio? I'm sure you didn't come here just to see me." Velma asked, not wanting to talk about her husband anymore.

"Well, I'm actually heading to Pittsburgh, where my son, Dale, lives. He and his wife, Kay, had a baby boy recently, and I'm anxious to meet the little guy." Nellie smiled. "They want me to move there, and I'm seriously considering it. Being close to family will be better than living alone."

Velma nodded. "I hope it all works out."

"Same here." Nellie turned her head in the direction Eddie and Peggy Ann were pointing at something in the yard. "Peggy Ann reminds me of you at that age."

"You think so?"

"Definitely."

When a cloud floated over the sun, a moment of cool air passed through the leaves above them. Velma lifted her head toward the limbs overhead. The air felt so refreshing. Then she looked back at Nellie. "Ya know, even though me and Hank have had some struggles along the way, things could always be worse."

"Velma, I'm really sorry for all you've had to go through." Nellie patted Velma's arm again. "I wonder if there is such a thing as a perfect marriage. It seems everyone I know who's married, even those who seem to have a good relationship, has something they're dealing with—either in their marriage, with their children, or even the in-laws."

"Well, it's hard, but I'm tryin' to do my best with the situation we're in." Velma waved her hand, as she motioned around the yard. "We don't have much, but I keep hopin' for some sort of miracle, and that our situation will look brighter someday."

"I know there are people who seem to have it all: a big expensive house, nice cars, and all the other bells and whistles one would think makes a person happy. But you know what? Those folks are some of the saddest people I know." Nellie's head moved slowly up and down. "So don't go thinking those objects bring happiness into a person's life, 'cause they don't."

"Guess you're right," Velma agreed. "We have our health, and I pray our two youngest children don't leave us too."

"You know Velma, there seem to be many opinions floating around these days on how to raise children, but I doubt there is one book ever published that explains how to do it right all the time." Nellie spoke in a calming voice.

"Well, I'm tryin' to improve and do some things differently."

"Such as?"

"For one thing, starting tomorrow, I'll be takin' the kids to church." Velma went on to explain about Heidi and what an influence she'd made on her. "Yep. She's opened my eyes to a lot of things, and the realization that I've been missing something important without God in my life. I'm hopin' if these kids of mine can learn something by going to church, maybe they'll end up with a better attitude about life than our two older children did."

"What about you, Velma?" Nellie's expression was one of concern. "Do you have any expectations for yourself?"

"I'd like to finish high school someday. Maybe take a few night courses and get a decent job." Velma looked toward her children again. "It'll have to be when they're older though."

"Don't you miss the good ole days when we were growing up together?"

"Sure do. Things were so simple back then. We didn't have much when we were kids, but as I look back on it, I can see that we had what was important."

Velma and her friend visited awhile longer. Then Nellie looked at her watch. "I hate to rush off, but if I'm going to make it to Pittsburgh before suppertime, I'd better hit the road."

"Okay, Nellie. Thanks for stopping by. It's been so nice to catch up." Velma wrapped her arm around her friend, and they walked to the car. Eddie and Peggy Ann ran up to them.

"Are ya leavin' now?" Eddie asked.

"Yes, I'm heading to Pittsburgh." Nellie ruffled his hair. "Maybe you all can come to visit me and my family sometime."

"Can we?" Peggy Ann asked, standing close to Velma.

Velma put her arms around both of the kids. "God willing, we'll sure try—especially if Nellie moves to Pittsburgh."

Nellie and Velma shared a parting hug.

"I think you are heading in the right direction by going to church tomorrow." Nellie smiled. "My life would have no meaning if God wasn't a part of it."

"I'm hopin' my life will have more purpose. I just hope the roof doesn't cave in when I walk through those doors tomorrow morning." Velma giggled and grabbed Nellie's hand. "Your visit meant more to me than you will ever know. Let's stay in touch now, okay?"

"For sure." Nellie gave Velma's hand a final squeeze before getting into her car.

As Velma watched her friend's vehicle pull onto the main road, she felt as hopeful as she had after Heidi talked with her.

Dear God, I have no right to ask this, since I've ignored You all these years, but please bear with me, and help me to be strong for my kids, my marriage, and even myself. Show me the way to keep hope alive, and please forgive me for all the mistakes I've made.

Velma looked up toward the sky, and a sense of peace came over her. As she headed inside, she knew what she was going to do first. It had been many years, but she said a little prayer that her grandma's old Bible would give her some answers.

Chapter 29

Seated in the back row of the community church she and the kids had walked to this morning, Velma felt conspicuous and as out of place as an elephant in a candy shop. Hank hadn't made it home yet, but he would have refused to join them anyway. Of course, Velma didn't let that stop her. She was determined to follow Heidi's suggestion and give church a try. After all, what did she have to lose?

Velma glanced to her left, where Peggy Ann sat, clinging to her hand. The girl's reddish-blond ponytail bounced as she bobbed her head in time to the music. *Maybe coming here will be good for my little girl. She seems to be enjoying herself.*

Velma didn't recognize any of the songs being sung. But then she hadn't set foot in church since she was a young girl. Velma's parents were not the religious type, but her maternal grandmother was. She'd taken Velma to Sunday school a few times when she came to visit on some weekends. She remembered singing songs like "Jesus Loves Me," "Down in My Heart," and "The Lord's Army." But none of those were being sung here today. One of her favorite songs had been "Onward Christian Soldiers."

She pursed her lips, staring at the songbook in her lap. *Guess that's what I get for stayin' away from church so long. I'm out of touch with everything that goes on.*

Eddie, sitting on the other side of Velma, nudged her arm. "I'm bored. When are we goin' home?"

"Shh . . . Be quiet." Velma glanced around, hoping no one heard what her son said.

Eddie crossed his arms and slumped farther down on the benched pew seat.

Velma had hoped she and the kids would make a good impression, in case they decided to come back again, but they weren't off to a very good start.

When the music stopped, and the people on the platform who'd led the singing sat down, a man dressed in a dark blue suit stood in front of the congregation and offered a prayer. Velma closed her eyes, hoping her children would do the same. But no, Eddie decided to start chomping real loud on his gum. She opened her eyes, and was about to whisper for him to take the gum out of his mouth, when he blew a rather large bubble. The next thing Velma knew, the bubble popped, leaving gum all over her boy's face.

Velma quietly opened her purse and fished around for the small pack of tissues. Nudging her son's elbow, she frowned. With a sheepish look on his face, Velma watched Eddie pull the sticky gum off his mouth and put the wad in the tissue she held out to him.

The prayer was still going on, but Velma noticed several people around them had opened their eyes and were looking in their direction with disapproving expressions. *They probably think we're hicks from the sticks.*

Velma groaned inwardly. *So much for making a good impression. This may be the first and last time we ever visit this church. Why can't Eddie be as well behaved as the other children sitting around us?*

Berlin

"It's good to see you. How are things going these days?" Miranda's friend, Shelly Cunningham, greeted her as soon as she and the children entered the church they regularly attended.

"About the same as usual. I'm still cashiering part-time at our local grocery store." Miranda gestured to Debbie and Kevin. "And these two completed their third cooking class a week ago, Saturday."

Shelly squeezed both children's shoulders. "That's great. Are you two enjoying the class?"

Debbie nodded, but Kevin merely shrugged. Then, seeing his friend Scott enter the building,

Kevin ran over to greet him. A few seconds later, Debbie wandered off in the direction of four young girls about her age.

Shelly rolled her eyes. "Kids—you gotta love 'em."

"You're right," Miranda agreed, as she and Shelly stepped away from the front entrance. "I'm just glad my two like coming to church—even if the main attraction is to see their friends. Some parents have a difficult time getting their kids to go to church—especially when their father refuses to go and doesn't set a Christian example."

"Are you thinking about Trent?"

"Uh-huh. If he could only see how important it is for him to be the spiritual leader in our home." Miranda sighed. "He's been trying his best to get me to take him back, through gifts and preying on my sympathy."

Shelly tipped her head. "Are you considering it?"

"No. I won't go back to the way things were. There would need to be a heartfelt change in my husband before I'd consider trying again."

"What about a marriage seminar? Do you think Trent would consider going to one?"

Miranda turned her hands palms up. "I'm not sure. Do you know of one in our area?"

"Sure do. In fact, it will be taking place here at this church in August." Shelly reached into her purse and pulled out a brochure. "All the information is right here. Look it over, and if you think it's something the two of you should attend, you might talk to Trent about it. If he's serious about wanting to get your marriage back on track, then maybe he will consider going."

"Okay, thanks." Miranda put the pamphlet in her purse.

Shelly hugged Miranda. "I've been praying for you, my friend, and I'll keep on until God gives you clear direction."

Miranda appreciated her friend's concern. Maybe this marriage seminar was the miracle she'd been hoping for.

Walnut Creek

"The kinner are sure quiet back there," Lyle commented as he guided their horse and buggy toward home after leaving Eli Miller's, where church was held that morning. "I wonder if they fell asleep."

Heidi turned and glanced over her shoulder. Sure enough, Marsha's head drooped against Randy's shoulder, and the children's eyes were closed.

She turned back around. "Jah, they're both snoozing."

"Guess they must need it." Lyle grinned. "It was nice seeing Randy and Marsha mingling with some of the kinner after our noon meal. I'm glad they're adjusting so well."

"Me too." Heidi released the tight grip she held on her purse straps and tried to relax. "I just wish we'd hear something from our lawyer soon about the adoption proceedings. It's difficult waiting for news."

"I agree, but the wait will be worth it. You'll see."

As they approached their home, Heidi noticed a car parked across the road. A gray-haired man stood beside it. But as Lyle began to turn the horse and buggy up their driveway, Heidi looked back and saw the man hurriedly get into his car.

"I wonder who that is." She looked over at Lyle. "Did you recognize him?"

Lyle shook his head. "Probably some tourist looking to get a few photos of Amish people. You know how it is. Sometimes curiosity gets the better of folks, and they stop along the road to stare at us or snap a few pictures." His face sobered. "Guess they don't realize we're just human beings like they are. We may dress differently and use a different mode of transportation, but in here, we're the same as everyone else." Lyle touched his chest.

Heidi's skin prickled. She wanted to believe the man was only a tourist, but she had an odd feeling that something wasn't right. She'd always been intuitive, and the way the man had hurriedly gotten into his car made her suspicious. She wondered if he'd planned to break into their house and rob them while they were gone. Perhaps his quick getaway was because they'd seen his face.

It wasn't unusual for robberies to take place. Plenty of accounts of break-ins and thievery appeared in the newspaper every month. Heidi thought about one of her previous students, Ron, and how he'd stolen some things from them while they were gone. Hopefully, Lyle was right about the man they'd seen by the road. Heidi certainly didn't need one more thing to worry about.

Chapter 30

No, please . . . You can't take them! They belong here with us."

Rolling onto his side, Lyle gently shook Heidi's shoulder. "Wake up, Heidi. You were talking in your sleep."

Her eyes opened, and when she sat up in bed, Lyle noticed his wife's nightgown was drenched in sweat.

"W–what time is it?" Heidi looked toward the window.

"It's morning, around the time we normally get up."

"I was dreaming." She blinked several times. "Oh, Lyle, it was a horrible nightmare, and it seemed so real."

He sat up next to Heidi and clasped her hand. "What was it about?"

"I dreamed some unknown relative showed up here and wanted to take Marsha and Randy from us." Heidi paused and drew a shuddering breath. "It was dark outside, and the man or woman— I'm not sure which—pulled the kinner into their vehicle. I hollered at them to stop and to leave the children with us, but they drove away into the night."

"It was only a dream." Lyle spoke soothingly, hoping to alleviate her fears.

Heidi swept a hand across her forehead. "Oh, Lyle, I'm so frightened. What if someone should show up and try to take Randy and Marsha from us?" Her voice trembled. "I don't think I could suffer another disappointment."

Lyle slipped his arm around Heidi and pulled her close. "It was only a bad dream. Your fears are unfounded."

"I suppose, but after Kendra decided to keep her baby and the adoption was called off, I can't help but worry that something will happen to prevent us from adopting Randy and Marsha."

Lightly stroking his wife's arm, and fumbling for the right words, Lyle whispered, "We need to trust God. If it's meant for us to raise those children, nothing will stand in our way."

She leaned her head against his shoulder. "Danki for listening, and especially for the reminder to trust the Lord. Sometimes, I find it easier to tell others how to strengthen their faith, but it's much harder when I'm dealing with my own problems."

"That's how it is with most people." Lyle kissed her damp cheek. "Now I think we'd better both say a prayer before we get out of bed."

Heidi bowed her head. Lyle did the same. *Heavenly Father,* he silently prayed, *please chase away my fraa's doubts and concerns. Help us be strong and accepting if something should go wrong and we're not able to adopt the children.*

Heidi stood in front of the kitchen sink, washing the breakfast dishes. It was hard to believe it was the middle of July and today was her fourth cooking class. She hoped the egg-salad sandwiches she would teach her young students to make would be appreciated. While some children might not care for egg salad, it had been a favorite of Heidi's since she was a young girl. Heidi's maternal grandma had given her the recipe she would share with the kids today. She was eager to teach the class, too, hoping it would get her mind off the horrible dream she'd had early this morning. Although she wanted to believe everything would work out, it was difficult to get rid of the niggling doubts.

"I need to trust God, like my husband said," she murmured. "Perhaps my faith is being put to the test."

Heidi glanced out the window and smiled when she saw Randy and Marsha feeding the chickens with Lyle. In addition to bringing both of the children much joy, their little poultry venture was giving Randy, in particular, a meaningful chore and something he looked forward to doing each day.

She hoped helping take care of the chickens was also causing Randy to draw closer to Lyle as they worked together. The boy still hadn't called Lyle "Daadi" or her "Mammi," but Heidi hadn't given up hope of that happening someday. She felt certain Lyle had begun to think of Randy as his son in every way.

She smiled, watching Marsha dart away from the chicken enclosure to chase a pretty butterfly. Heidi would have been tempted to join the little girl if she didn't need to get the dishes done before her young students arrived.

Randy and Marsha had brought them much joy. At times like this, Heidi's heart felt like it would burst with enthusiasm and hope for the future.

Millersburg

"Your breakfast is sitting out, Becky," Ellen called when she left the kitchen and stepped into the hall. "And if you don't hurry, we'll end up being late for the cooking class."

"I'll be right there!" A few minutes later, Becky entered the room. She stopped in front of the table and frowned.

"What's wrong?"

"I thought we were having pancakes today.

You mentioned it last night when you got home from the hospital, remember?"

Ellen nodded. "I had planned to make them, until I came into the kitchen and looked at the time." She gestured to the clock above the refrigerator. "So we wouldn't be late, I decided it would be better to have cold cereal this morning."

Becky sat down with an undignified grunt.

"Aren't we the grouchy one today? Didn't you sleep well last night?" Ellen pulled out a chair beside Becky.

"I slept fine. Just woke up grumpy."

"How come?"

"I don't know."

"Well, let's pray. Maybe you'll feel better once you've had something to eat."

They bowed their heads, and Ellen offered the prayer. "Dear Lord, please bless this food to the needs of our bodies, and give us a safe trip to Heidi's today. Be with the others who'll be traveling there too. Amen."

Becky remained quiet as they ate, even when Ellen tried to make conversation. "Is something wrong? Aren't you looking forward to the cooking class today?"

"Yeah, I guess. But I'm not lookin' forward to going to the Firemen's Festival with Darren and Jeremy later today."

"Why not, for goodness' sakes? From what

Darren told me, it'll be a fun event, and after it gets dark, there will even be fireworks." Ellen smiled. "That should be fun, right?"

"Maybe. I just don't understand why we have to see Jeremy and his dad twice in one day."

Ellen picked up her coffee cup and took a drink. "The Firemen's Festival simply happens to be on the same day as the cooking class, Becky. It's not like Darren planned it that way."

With only a shrug, Becky grabbed her spoon and started eating. Once more, Ellen wondered if Becky resented Darren and wanted to keep things the way they were between mother and daughter. Was there room in Becky's heart for a stepfather and stepbrother?

Ellen shook herself mentally. *Now where did that thought come from? I'm just beginning to know Darren, and there's certainly been no mention of marriage. I need to stop thinking about something that may never happen, especially if my daughter doesn't approve of me seeing Darren.* She added a bit of cream to her cup and stirred it around. *Hopefully, Darren will win Becky's heart, the way he's beginning to win mine.*

Berlin

Miranda had started clearing the breakfast table when she heard a vehicle pull into the yard.

"Bet that's Daddy!" Kevin leaped out of his

chair and raced for the back door. Debbie was right behind him.

Miranda was scheduled to work this morning, so Trent had agreed to take the kids to their cooking class again. She hoped this time he would stay with them and not go off on his own. When she got home from work this afternoon, she would quiz the kids about what went on.

Miranda placed the dishes in the dishwasher, and as she closed the door, Trent entered the kitchen, both kids clinging to his hands.

"Morning, Miranda. How's it going?" Trent's cheerful attitude made her wonder if he was up to something. She still hadn't asked him about attending the marriage seminar, but she'd wait to do it until he brought the kids home this afternoon.

"It's going," she responded. "How are you?"

"Doin' okay, but I'd be better if . . ." Trent stopped talking, let go of the kids' hands, and moved across the room. "If you're not doing anything this evening, I'd like to take you somewhere so we can talk."

I bet you would. Miranda bit her lip to keep from verbalizing her thoughts. "What do you want to talk about?"

He nodded with his head in the direction of Kevin and Debbie, who had moved over to stand by the back door. No doubt, they were eager to go.

"Is there a problem?" She spoke quietly.

He shook his head. "Not really, but there are some things we need to discuss."

I bet he wants to talk about a divorce and doesn't want our son and daughter to hear. Miranda's muscles tensed. "I'd need to get a sitter. Sure can't leave the kids here alone."

"No, of course not." Trent fingered the top button of his pale green shirt. "If you can line someone up to stay with the kids, I'd be happy to pay the sitter."

Miranda tilted her head from side to side, weighing her choices. If she and Trent were alone, regardless of his agenda, it would give her a chance to bring up the marriage seminar. *Maybe Trent wants a divorce. If so, he'll never agree to go to the seminar with me.*

"Okay, I'll go, but not till after the kids are in bed. I don't want them asking a bunch of questions."

"That's fine. I'll come by around nine. Will that be okay?"

She nodded. "I'll see you then."

When Trent went out the door with Debbie and Kevin, Miranda released a lingering sigh. *I hope I made the right choice agreeing to go somewhere with Trent this evening. Maybe I should have suggested he talk to me here, after the kids have gone to bed. But then if he should bring up the topic of divorce, it's not something*

I want the children to hear. They would have to be told, of course, but Miranda wanted to be the one to tell them. Hopefully, she could do it in a gentle way so they wouldn't be too stunned and could accept it.

Chapter 31

Walnut Creek

When Darren pulled his SUV into Heidi's yard, he glanced around, hoping Ellen would be there by now. But there was no sign of her car. He needed an opportunity to talk to her before the class but figured it could wait till later. He just wanted to make sure Ellen and Becky were still planning to go with him and Jeremy to the Firemen's Festival later today.

Darren set the brake, turned off the engine, and got out of his vehicle. When he turned to shut the door, he was surprised to see Jeremy still sitting in the back seat. "Hey, are you getting out or what?"

"In a minute." Jeremy fiddled with something in his hand.

"What have you got there?" Darren leaned over and stuck his head inside the rig.

"It's nothing, Dad. I'm gettin' out now." Jeremy hopped out and shut his door. Then, with his hands in his jeans' pockets, he strolled up to Heidi's front porch.

Darren closed the door on the driver's side and

followed. He wondered if Jeremy had brought his pocket knife along, even after he'd been asked to leave it at home.

Woof! Woof! The Troyers' dog bounded over from the other side of the house.

"Hey there, Rusty ole boy." Darren stopped to pet the dog's silky head, watching his stubby tail wiggle back and forth. "Are you the official greeter today?"

After a few more barks, Rusty ran up to greet Jeremy, apparently in need of more attention.

As Darren followed his son to the house, he realized the boy was in need of a haircut. Jeremy's thick hair curled around his ears and had even worked its way under his shirt collar. *When Caroline was still alive, she would have noticed our son's hair way before me and taken him to the barber. I might be an okay dad, but I fall short in the area of mothering.*

Allowing his mind to wander a bit, Darren imagined what it would be like to be married to Ellen. How would Jeremy take to the idea of having a stepmom? Would he appreciate all the motherly things she would bring to their home, or would he resent her?

Shaking his thoughts aside, Darren stepped onto the porch, joining his son by the door.

"Did you knock?" Darren asked.

Jeremy nodded.

A few seconds later the door opened. Randy

stood looking up at them. "Guess ya must be here for the cookin' class, huh?"

Darren smiled. "That's right. Are we the first ones?"

"Yep." Randy opened the door a bit wider. "Heidi's in the kitchen. Said I should tell ya to come in."

"Okay, thanks, we will."

When they entered the house, Randy darted away, and Jeremy excused himself to use the bathroom. Darren took a seat in the rocking chair. Glancing around the tidy room, his thoughts returned to his wife again. Caroline was an immaculate housekeeper, although she never nagged him about picking up after himself. If things got a little disorganized, she quietly put them away herself.

I should have been more considerate, he thought. *Too bad there are no second chances for me. If there were, I'd do a lot of things differently.*

Darren got the chair moving and sat quietly, until Jeremy came back to the room and took a seat on the couch.

Tap. Tap. Tap. Someone was obviously at the door. Darren hoped it was Ellen, but before he had a chance to see who it was, Heidi came into the room. "Hello, Darren. Hello, Jeremy. You're the first ones here, so just make yourself at home. I'm sure the others will be along shortly." She gave them a brief smile. "A few minutes ago Randy came into the kitchen to let me know you were here, but just now, I thought I heard someone knock on the front door."

He nodded. "You did."

Heidi's cheeks looked flushed, and she fanned her face with both hands. "Guess I'd better see who it is."

"Guess what?" Velma asked when Heidi greeted her at the door.

"I don't know. But from the looks of your cheery smile, I'd say it must be something good."

"Sure is." Velma looked down at Peggy Ann, standing beside her on the porch. "Me and the kids went to church last Sunday, and I think I'm gonna take 'em another time too."

Heidi smiled. "That's good. If you're planning to go again, you must have enjoyed the service."

Velma's head moved up and down. "Can't speak for the kids, but I sure did." She lowered her head a bit. "I didn't know any of the songs, though. They were nothin' like the ones I sang when I was girl and attended my grandma's church a few times. Guess after I go awhile, I'll catch on. Of course, I may try a different church next time."

"It may be a good idea to try a few until you find a church you are comfortable with." Heidi opened the door wider. "Why don't you two come inside and join Darren and his son? I assume Eddie didn't come with you today?"

"Nope. Hank's home for the weekend, so Eddie's there with him." Velma nudged Peggy Ann. "My daughter's here for the class, but I won't be comin' in. Came here to work, not sit around." She turned toward the yard, then looked back at Heidi again. "Got anything outside ya want me to do? It's a beautiful day for yard work."

Heidi tapped her chin. "Well, I suppose you could do some weeding in my vegetable patch. Those sneaky little weeds have a way of coming up a few days after you pull them."

"Did you and the kids get to do any weeding together? You'd mentioned it when I first started doing some tasks for you."

"Actually, we did work in the garden one afternoon, but the weeds keep growing, so it needs to be done again." Heidi stepped out onto the porch and gestured toward the garden plot.

"Well, just point me to your gardening tools and I'll get started on it."

"Everything is in the barn. If you'll follow me there, I'll show you where I keep everything."

"Sounds good." Velma tapped her daughter's shoulder. "You go on inside now and have a good time. You can show me what ya made after your class is over."

"Okay, Mama, but can't I stay outside till

everyone gets here?" Peggy Ann tipped her head back to look at Velma. "I wanna see how Randy's chickens are doing."

Velma looked at Heidi. "Is that okay with you?"

"Certainly. But if you step inside and speak to Randy and Marsha, I'm sure they'd like to go out to the coop with you." Heidi chuckled. "Those two never miss a chance to hang out by the chickens."

Peggy Ann grinned. "I'll get 'em!" She hurried into the house.

Velma slapped her knee. "That girl. She sure is eager to see them chickens."

Woof! Rusty plopped down in front of Heidi as they turned to head for the barn.

Heidi leaned down and patted the dog's head. "Okay, Rusty, you can come with us."

The dog must have understood, for he jumped up and ran ahead of them all the way to the barn.

"Poor pup." Heidi looked at Velma. "Since those chickens arrived and are getting all the attention, Rusty's been feeling kind of left out."

"He's a nice dog. How 'bout he keeps me company while I'm weeding your garden?" Velma asked. "If it's okay with you, that is."

"Sure. I'm positive Rusty would love it."

"I wonder what you'll be making today," Ellen said as she turned her car up Heidi's driveway.

In the back seat, Becky didn't answer. In fact, she'd said only a few words since they left home this morning. Ellen figured her daughter's gloomy mood might have something to do with her not wanting to go to the Fireman's Festival later. Once they got there, and she saw all the festivities, maybe she'd be more interested and have a better disposition. Ellen certainly hoped so, because she looked forward to spending the evening with Darren and wanted it to be pleasant.

She noticed Darren's SUV parked near Heidi's house and figured he and Jeremy must be inside. Eager to see him, she hopped out of the car, but Becky remained seated with her arms folded.

Oh, great. Now she's going into her stubborn mode. "Come on, Becky. Let's go inside."

"You go ahead. I'll be in soon. Randy, Marsha, and that girl with the pigtails are out by the chicken coop. I'm gonna go say hello."

"Okay." Ellen closed her door. It was nice to see her daughter wanting to socialize with the other children.

"The last time you were here, did your cooking teacher say what you might be making today?" Denise asked her daughter when they arrived at Heidi's and had gotten out of the car. "I don't recall."

Kassidy lifted her gaze toward the sky. "Are you hard of hearing?"

Denise pointed a finger at Kassidy. "Don't use that tone with me, missy. I asked you a question, so please answer me respectfully."

"No, Heidi never said what we'd be making today." Kassidy's upper lip curled. "It better be something good, though."

"I'm sure whatever she teaches you to make will be tasty."

When they got out of the car, Denise noticed Peggy Ann, Randy, Marsha, and Becky standing outside the coop. "Before we go inside, why don't we go over and see how much Randy and Marsha's chickens have grown?" she suggested.

"Why?" Kassidy wrinkled her nose. "It stinks over there, and chickens are dumb."

"Oh, really? Well, you don't complain when you're eating their eggs."

"That's different. Eating store-bought eggs is not the same as standing beside a smelly coop and staring at a bunch of dumb little clucking birds."

"Well, nevertheless, let's take a walk over there and say hello to the children who apparently do enjoy looking at chickens." Denise guided her daughter in that direction.

"Oh, no!" Kassidy pointed, then whirled around. "Here comes that mutt."

Denise looked where her daughter was pointing and saw Rusty running ahead of Heidi and Velma, who had just stepped out of the barn area.

Denise put her hand on Kassidy's shoulder. "Don't worry. Heidi's dog is friendly. Just be nice to him, and you'll see how fast he warms up to you."

"We'll see." Kassidy trudged toward the chicken coop as Rusty ran past, with a wagging tail.

"It's nice to see you both again." Heidi called, before gesturing to the coop. "Those chickens are going to get spoiled with all the attention they're getting."

"You're probably right." Denise cupped her hands around her mouth. "We'll be in shortly."

"Take your time. We have a few minutes before class starts."

As Denise walked toward the children, she glanced across the way and noticed Velma, pulling weeds in the Troyers' garden. She could barely hear the woman's soothing voice as she held a one-way conversation with the dog, who had made himself comfortable a few feet away. Rusty must have enjoyed the attention, as he tilted his head as though listening.

Denise had no more than stepped up to the chicken enclosure, when Kassidy looked over at Randy and blurted, "I don't know what you think is so special about your chickens. They're just dumb birds who eat bugs and scratch around in the dirt."

Randy's chin quivered. "I like my hinkel."

"Hinkel? What's a hinkel? Is that anything like a wrinkle?" Kassidy got right in his face.

Before Denise could say or do anything to correct her daughter, Becky stepped up to Kassidy and bumped her arm. "That was mean. Tell Randy you're sorry."

Kassidy stood rigid and sneered at her. "I am not sorry, and I don't have to say I am, either. Besides, I wasn't talking to you."

"Well, I'm talking to you, and you had better apologize." Becky clenched her fists.

Denise held her breath, certain that her daughter would back down. But instead of telling Randy she was sorry, Kassidy grabbed a handful of Becky's hair and yanked. The next thing Denise knew, Becky retaliated. After a few whoops and hollers, both girls were on the ground, rolling around. The other children stood with their mouths gaping open, except for Marsha, who clung to her brother's arm and sobbed.

"Stop! Stop that, you two!" Denise yelled.

Chapter 32

Hearing a ruckus outside, along with Rusty's barking, Ellen and Heidi rushed out the front door. Ellen could hardly believe her eyes. Her normally timid daughter was on the ground in a scuffle with Kassidy, while Randy and Peggy Ann looked on as though in disbelief. From where she stood, it appeared that Marsha was crying.

Ellen's fingers touched her parted lips. *What in the world could have brought this on? I've never known my girl to provoke a fight, much less do battle with someone like this. Did Kassidy do something to hurt Becky?*

Ellen dashed across the yard, with Heidi running along beside her. She saw Rusty down on his front paws barking at both of the girls. Denise shouted at Kassidy to stop, and as they drew closer to the area outside the chicken pen, Ellen did the same. But the hair pulling, slapping, and rolling about continued. Ellen was beside herself. Never had she been so stunned or humiliated by her daughter's actions.

With a determined set of her jaw, Heidi clapped

344

her hands and spoke in short, strong sentences. "Girls, you need to stop fighting right now. This is wrong, and it's not the way to settle a disagreement."

To Ellen's amazement, Becky let go of Kassidy's hair and Kassidy let go of hers. Then both red-faced girls stood up and moved to stand by their mothers.

"What is the meaning of this, Becky Blackburn?" Ellen struggled to keep from shouting. "I have never known you to do something like this." She gestured to the other children, huddled nearby. "And what kind of an example are you setting?"

"I didn't provoke it, Mom. She did." Becky pointed to Kassidy.

"You're the one who started it." Kassidy, breathing hard, sneered at Becky.

"Did not. You were making fun of Randy's chickens, and when I defended them, you grabbed hold of my hair." Becky blinked rapidly, placing both hands against her flaming red cheeks, and Rusty started barking again.

"She ain't lyin'." Peggy Ann pointed at Kassidy. "What she said about Randy's chickens made me so mad, I felt like punchin' her in the nose."

"Nobody should be punching or making fun of anyone." Heidi leaned down and took hold of Rusty's collar, which helped him settle down. "It was wrong for you two young ladies to become physical."

"I tried to stop them," Denise interjected. "But they wouldn't listen." She wiped her brow where perspiration had gathered, and looked at Ellen. "I apologize for my daughter's behavior."

Ellen had never seen the usual put-together woman look so distraught. She felt sorry for Denise. "It's not your fault." Ellen placed her hand on Denise's arm. "It's our girls who are at fault for not controlling their tempers."

By this time, Kassidy and Becky were both sniffling. But neither would apologize. Ellen was ashamed of her daughter. Becky knew better than this.

"Debbie and Kevin aren't here yet," Heidi stated. "We all need to go inside so Becky and Kassidy can wash up before the other children arrive." She picked Marsha up and gently patted her back. Fortunately, the little girl's crying had subsided.

No one argued the point as they walked to the house. Ellen could only imagine how the rest of the day might go. If not for her wanting to spend time with Darren, she would have canceled her plans and taken Becky home as soon as the cooking class was over.

I wonder if Becky did this on purpose so I would decide not to go. One thing's for certain—

when Becky and I do go home, a lecture and some form of punishment will be forthcoming.

From where she knelt in Heidi's garden, Velma had heard and seen what transpired between Kassidy and Becky. She was surprised her daughter hadn't been in the middle of the scuffle, knowing the temper she had. Velma had been about to set her weed pulling aside and break up the fight, but seeing Heidi and Ellen come out of the house, she'd decided to let them handle it. Since the fuss didn't involve her daughter, it really wasn't her business anyway. Seeing the way Rusty had carried on, Velma wasn't surprised when Heidi put the dog away in his kennel.

She remembered back to when she was a girl and had gotten into disagreements with some of her schoolmates. She was a scrapper and often ended up in a kicking or hair-pulling match. Seeing how Becky and Kassidy looked as they'd rolled about on the ground, caused Velma to feel shame for her childish and mean-tempered conduct all those years ago. It was her duty as Peggy Ann and Eddie's mother to teach proper behavior, and by attending church, it would give them a stronger foundation in knowing right from wrong.

Gripping the shovel and digging it into the dirt, Velma made a decision. In addition to going to church on Sundays, she would look for the old Bible she'd inherited from her grandma and read a few passages every day.

Another car pulled in, and Velma watched as Debbie and Kevin got out of the vehicle. The same man who'd brought them here a few weeks ago followed them up to the house. She assumed he was their father. He paused once, and looked in Velma's direction, then gave her a friendly wave. *Goodness, he just missed seeing a bit of excitement.*

"Step away from the window, Jeremy. They'll think you've been watching them." Darren gestured for his son to take a seat.

Jeremy's mouth slackened as he moved back to the couch. "Can you believe Becky picked a fight with that Kassidy girl? I can't wait to find out what she said to her. Never figured Ellen's daughter could be so tough."

Darren shook his head. "When they come into the house, you are not to say anything about what you saw."

"How come?"

"Because it would be rude. I'm sure their mothers are embarrassed by what their daughters did. I would be if you'd ended up in a scuffle with one of the other kids here today."

"So I can't ask Becky what happened?"

"Not here, Son. If you feel you must ask her,

then wait till we take Ellen and Becky to the Firemen's Festival."

Jeremy huffed and flopped onto the couch.

A few seconds later, Heidi stepped into the house, along with Ellen, Denise, and the children. Kevin and Debbie came in right behind them, along with a man Darren assumed was their father. The two older girls looked a mess—rumpled clothes smudged with dirt, hair sticking out at odd angles, and bright red faces. Darren had to admit he, too, was tempted to ask what had happened to cause the skirmish. But he bit his tongue. If Ellen or Becky wanted him to know, the topic would come up later. He hoped this little incident with Becky wouldn't affect their plans for the afternoon.

Heidi clasped the edge of the table, praying for a sense of peace here in her kitchen. Ever since they'd come inside there had been a chill in the air, and it had nothing to do with the weather. Becky and Kassidy had both gotten cleaned up and sat silently at the table. Heidi was disappointed that neither of them would apologize for their part in the scuffle. She'd never seen two girls carry on like that—and over such a small matter. While it wasn't right for Kassidy to make fun of Randy's chickens, it was not a reason for Becky to lose her temper. *There must be something more behind the girl's aggression,* Heidi thought. *If I knew what it was, maybe I could help.* Heidi could see that Ellen was embarrassed by her daughter's outburst, as she kept her gaze downward. Denise appeared more subdued than usual. No doubt, she regretted Kassidy's unpleasant behavior.

Since she couldn't do anything about this problem, Heidi began her class. "Today we'll be learning to make egg-salad sandwiches."

"Egg salad?" Kassidy lips puckered. "I don't like eggs all mashed up and spread on bread. I only eat fried or scrambled eggs at breakfast time. That's when they're supposed to be eaten." Her lips pressed into a white slash.

"This egg salad is different than most," Heidi explained. She refused to let Kassidy influence the other children. "It's from an old family recipe, and—"

"I don't want to make it." Kassidy shook her head determinedly. "And no one's gonna make me eat it!"

Heidi glanced at Denise, who stood behind her daughter, rubbing her forehead. Kassidy's mother didn't say anything for several seconds, then she stepped forward, placed both hands on Kassidy's shoulders and said, "I will eat the sandwich, but you're going to make it."

Peggy Ann's hand shot up. "I like egg salad. Mama said when the chickens we're gonna get start layin', we can make all sorts of things with them eggs. We're even gonna sell some 'cause we need the money. Someday, Mama's gonna buy another car." The girl shook her head. "Course it won't be a new one 'cause they cost too much."

"I'll never be poor, because my folks are rich." Kassidy looked at Peggy Ann with a smirk. "We have three cars, and when I turn sixteen and learn how to drive, my dad's gonna give me one."

Heidi wasn't sure how to respond, but Denise relieved her of that problem.

"Kassidy McGuire! If you don't stop bragging—"

"What?" Kassidy's tone grew louder. "Were you gonna say that you'd take me home? If so, then I'm glad, 'cause I wanna go home!"

"Oh, Kassidy, give me a break." Denise left the room, apparently out of patience.

"Kassidy," Heidi said in a firm voice. "I have a chair over there in the corner. Do you want to spend the entire class sitting in it, or are you going to be a good student?"

The girl squirmed and heaved a sigh. "Okay, whatever."

Heidi held her hands behind her back, wondering how she could get through to Kassidy or Becky. And then there was the Kimball family. They needed help too. *All I can do is pray for my students, but I don't feel it's enough.*

• • •

Trent sat back and listened. He'd felt the tension as soon as he walked into the house. Except for Darren, the parents seemed on edge.

I should have stayed the last time I brought the kids. It's strange, though, they never mentioned any problems going on within their class.

As Trent half-listened to what Heidi was instructing, he was glad everything seemed to have settled down. Denise had rejoined her daughter in the kitchen, and Ellen seemed more relaxed.

Once more, Trent's thoughts turned to his wife. He missed the life he used to have with her and the children. Even their occasional squabbles seemed minor now. Trent would overlook them if given the chance to begin again with Miranda. It was like watching the wheel of time turn round and round as he remembered their first kiss, then their wedding day, and later the birth of their children.

My wife is a wonderful mother, and she's the perfect wife. How could I have been so stupid as to get caught up in another woman's charms? No wonder Miranda is afraid to trust me. But how can I prove myself to her and show that I've learned my lesson and will never do anything like that again? Would I trust her if she'd done it to me?

Chapter 33

Heidi handed out recipe cards to each of her students, and then gave them the ingredients to make her special egg salad. She could see from a few of the children's expressions that they weren't too enthused. Well, it was too late to fix something else, but at least she noticed a few of her students turning the card over to read the Bible verse. This week she'd used Isaiah 54:13: "And all thy children shall be taught of the LORD; and great shall be the peace of thy children."

Maybe the verses are getting through to some of these children, or even their parents. Heidi hoped that was the case.

"Now the first thing we will do is boil some eggs." Heidi pointed to the egg carton, as well as the kettle she'd set on the table. "If you'll each take one and gently place it in the pan, I'll put it on the stove to boil. Be very careful, though. We don't want to break any eggs."

Heidi had no sooner spoken the words when Peggy Ann picked up an egg and dropped it into the kettle. The shell cracked on impact, and the yolk, mixed with white, seeped out.

Peggy Ann burst into tears.

Trent stared at the child in disbelief as she ran out of the room. He glanced at Debbie, staring at the broken egg with a sober expression. *Wonder how my daughter would have reacted if it happened to her.*

"What's that girl's problem?" Trent directed his question to Heidi. "It's only a broken egg. Seems overly emotional to me."

"Peggy Ann has many reasons to be emotional." Heidi spoke in a quiet tone. "She and her family are fairly new to the area and they've had a rough go of it since their arrival."

"What kind of problems have they faced?" he questioned.

"For one thing, Velma—Peggy Ann's mother— was in an accident and totaled her car. Her insurance won't cover the damages, and Velma and her husband don't have the money to buy a new vehicle." Heidi moved away from the table. "I need to check on Peggy Ann. Would one of you please take over until I get back?"

"I'll do whatever you ask," Ellen spoke up. "Should I see that the eggs get boiled?"

"Yes, thank you." Heidi hurried from the kitchen and found Peggy Ann crouched in one corner of the living room, tears streaming down her face.

Heidi knelt beside the little girl and patted her trembling shoulder. "It's okay. No harm's been done. You can start over with another egg."

"I can't never do nothin' right. My brother says I'm a klutz, and I guess it's true." Peggy Ann sniffed, swiping at her tears. "Mama always says we shouldn't waste food, but I wrecked a good egg."

"Don't worry about it, Peggy Ann. I've broken plenty of eggs too." Heidi shook her head. "And you're not a klutz. It was an accident and could have happened to anyone."

Peggy Ann blinked rapidly. "You think so?"

"Most certainly." Heidi gave the child a sympathetic squeeze. "Now let's go back to the kitchen." She rose to her feet and reached for the child's hand.

Peggy Ann blew her nose on the tissue Heidi handed her. "Okay."

Heidi smiled. At least one problem was solved. Now, if she could just get Kassidy and Becky to apologize to each other and act civilized, it would be a successful day.

As Trent sat between his children, waiting for the kettle of eggs to boil, he thought about the things Heidi had said concerning Peggy Ann's mother needing another car. While he couldn't provide her with a new one, he might be able to buy a reliable used car. It may not prove he was trustworthy yet, but it would be a good deed and could help gain points with Miranda, which, in turn, might pave the way further to a reconciliation.

Trent's tongue darted out to lick his lips. *Yep. Come Monday morning I'll get on it. I'm sure the right car that would fit my budget and work for the struggling family's need is sitting on my boss's lot, waiting for a new owner.*

Trent bumped his son's shoulder and grinned. *Hang in there, buddy. It won't be long and your dad will be coming home where he belongs. Then our family will be complete again.*

Denise looked over at her daughter, sitting with elbows on the table and wearing a smug expression. *Does my daughter think she's won the fight with Becky, or does she have something else up her sleeve?* Kassidy seemed to be making an attempt to get along with all the other children except Becky—and especially Jeremy.

"Do you have any pets?" Kassidy smiled sweetly at Darren's son, although her question sounded far from sincere.

"I have a dog named Bacon," Jeremy answered with little enthusiasm. "Thought I told you before."

"No, you never mentioned him to me," Kassidy said in an all-too-friendly tone. "You should bring him to class next time."

"Naw. That wouldn't be a good idea." Jeremy turned his back on Kassidy and made conversation with Randy. Denise couldn't blame him for that. He probably didn't care much for her daughter, with the way she acted.

When Heidi returned with Peggy Ann, Kassidy spoke up. "Are you okay now, Peggy Ann?"

The young girl nodded.

Denise watched with suspicion when Kassidy smiled, then turned her conversation to Debbie. "Maybe sometime you can come to our place, and we can spend an afternoon together."

"Maybe." Debbie glanced at her father, but he said nothing.

Denise felt pity for Becky, frowning and fidgeting in her chair as she eyed Kassidy. *I wonder what that poor girl is thinking.*

"Kassidy, quit disrupting the class and pay attention to Heidi," Denise whispered so that others wouldn't hear. She felt sure Kassidy was up to something, but couldn't figure out what.

Velma paused from weeding long enough to watch a mother robin pull a worm from the grass and feed her baby. Even birds and animals cared about their young and provided for their needs.

Her heart clenched. *I wonder where Bobbie Sue is living now. Is she doing okay? If we would only hear something from her I'd feel a bit better.* She squeezed her eyes shut, reflecting on her son, Clem. He obviously didn't care about his family anymore either. *Maybe I'm getting what I deserve.*

Velma thought about her parents and the falling-out she'd had with them before she and Hank packed up their family and moved to Ohio. It was a heated argument that never got resolved. Velma had been so upset when they moved, she'd decided to sever the relationship with her folks. They'd never approved of Hank, and her obligation was to him, so Velma felt she had to choose. Some days she thought about trying to make amends, but she wasn't sure they would want anything to do with her—especially after the horrible things that had been said on both sides. Hank was even angrier than Velma, and he'd made it clear when they moved that he never wanted to see her parents again. So if she chose to contact them, she'd have to do it secretly. It might be worth taking the chance, however. At least then, she wouldn't have to live with guilt.

When she heard her name being called, her eyes snapped open. She looked toward the house and saw Heidi heading her way. Velma stood, and wiped her face with her hanky, hoping there were no tears.

"I came out to tell you that the children have finished making their egg-salad sandwiches," Heidi said. "We made a few extras, so would you like to join us as we eat our sandwiches?"

"Oh, I don't know." Velma self-consciously brushed a splotch of dirt off her T-shirt. "I'm not really presentable for socializin'."

"It's okay. Nobody is dressed fancy, and since Kassidy and Becky have dirt and grass stains on their clothes, no one will even notice the soil on yours. Besides, a little dirt from the garden shows how hard you've been working."

"A sandwich does sound good." Velma stuffed her hanky into one of her overalls' pockets. "Before we go into the house, can I ask you a question?"

"Certainly."

"If you had a disagreement with your folks, and your husband didn't want you to have any contact with them, what would ya do?"

"That would be a difficult situation." Heidi rubbed the base of her neck. "Does Hank have a good reason for not wanting you to speak with them?"

Nodding, Velma groaned. "We had a fallin'-out with them before we left Kentucky, and some ugly words were said on both parts. Truth is, my parents have never cared much for Hank, so that makes it even harder."

Heidi placed a comforting hand on Velma's arm. "If I were in your situation, the first thing I'd do is pray about it."

"Yeah, I kinda thought I should be doin' that." Velma puckered her lips. "Prayin' don't come easy to me, though, and it may take some practice."

"You know, Velma, praying isn't anything more than talking to God. He wants us to talk to Him—not just about our requests—but to praise and thank Him for our many blessings."

"Guess you're right about that. I just don't feel worthy to even be talkin' to God. All these years I've pretty much ignored Him, thinkin' I could do things by myself. So why would He listen to me now?"

Heidi shook her head. "If we based our relationship with God on our worthiness, none of us would measure up. But He wants us to humbly come to Him in prayer and supplication, so we should never be afraid to approach the throne with our requests. No prayer is too small or unimportant in God's eyes."

Velma's lips parted as she leaned closer to Heidi. "Know what I think?"

"What?"

"I think you'd make a good preacher."

Heidi's cheeks flushed. "Oh, my, no. I'm not qualified for that. Besides, in our Amish faith, only men are chosen to be ministers."

Velma tipped her head. "Is that a fact?"

Heidi slowly nodded.

"And why is that?"

"We believe the Bible tells us that women are not to teach men. Our ministers, deacons, and bishops are chosen by lot, and women are never included."

"Looks like I've got a lot to learn. Especially about my Amish neighbors." *If Hank heard what Heidi just explained, I'm sure he'd agree with this Amish rule, but not for the same reasons.*

Chapter 34

As Heidi reached into the laundry basket to hang a towel on the line, she noticed a car at the end of her driveway. It just sat there with the engine running, but she couldn't make out the driver. Could it be the same vehicle she'd seen out by the road a few weeks ago? Was it the same color? She didn't remember.

Her heartbeat quickened. Today had been stressful and her nerves were on edge. She didn't need one more thing to worry about.

Should I walk out there and see who it is? Perhaps it's only someone who is lost and needs directions. Her fingers clenched as she dropped the towel back into the basket. *I wish Lyle were here right now. He'd know what to do.*

Heidi started walking toward the driveway, but the car backed out and headed down the road. She sighed and resumed her task. Then hearing the squeal of laughter, she glanced in the direction of the children, playing on the front porch. After her students departed today, Heidi had expected Randy or Marsha to mention the quarrel they'd witnessed between Becky and Kassidy. But surprisingly, neither child had brought it up. Heidi couldn't imagine it not bothering them, for it still disturbed her.

Apparently Marsha, who had been quite upset at the time, now had other thoughts on her young mind. Kassidy and Becky had not set a good example for the younger, impressionable children. This was all the more reason Heidi was determined to give Randy and Marsha a good upbringing. Oh, how she looked forward to the day those sweet children would truly belong to her and Lyle.

A flash of blue, along with frantic chirping, caught Heidi's attention. She stood motionless, holding the towel she'd dropped back in the basket moments ago, and watched two male bluebirds seemingly in battle. She assumed the one bird was guarding his territory. Heidi expected the baby birds would soon leave the safety of their box. Last evening at dinner, Lyle had told her he'd noticed the young birds sticking their little heads out the entrance. They seemed anxious to discover the world awaiting them.

She looked toward the nesting area and saw the female bird watching the ruckus from the roof of the bird box. The fighting males flew at each other, wings flapping and feet extended. They dropped to the ground and continued to challenge each other. Heidi feared one of them might break a wing as they flew at each other. Finally, the battle ended. The female's mate, with a few feathers ruffled, joined her on top of their little home.

Heidi could relate to those birds and how they took care of their family. Without a doubt, she and Lyle would do whatever it took to provide for and protect Randy and Marsha.

She finished hanging the laundry, hoisted the empty basket, and stepped onto the porch. "Would you two like a snack?" Heidi asked, smiling down at the children.

Marsha grinned as she bobbed her blond head. "Jah, Mammi. Do you have any kichlin?"

"As a matter of fact, I do. Would you like peanut butter cookies or chocolate chip?"

"I want the chocolate ones," Randy spoke up.

Marsha licked her lips. "Peanut butter."

"All right then, I'll set some cookies and milk on the table, while you two go in and wash your hands."

The children clambered to their feet and raced into the house. Chuckling, Heidi followed.

Millersburg

"I can't understand why you didn't want the kids to come along this evening." Miranda looked over at Trent as they neared the town of Millersburg. "And just where are you taking me?"

He glanced over at her and smiled. "It's a surprise. You'll see soon enough."

She fiddled with her purse straps. *Why do I have the feeling he's up to something again? First it was the flowers. Now, who knows what?*

Trent turned on the radio to an easy-listening station, and Miranda tried to relax. She moistened her lips with the tip of her tongue, wondering if she should bring up the marriage seminar or wait until they got to their destination. *Maybe I'll let him tell me whatever he wants to say about the kids before I mention the seminar.*

Twenty minutes later, they pulled up to Fox's Pizza Den, and Trent turned off the ignition. "We're here." He grinned over at Miranda.

Her brows furrowed. "We're having pizza? What's that have to do with our children?"

Trent's ears turned pink. "No, I—" He placed his hand on her shoulder. "Remember when we came here on our first date, and then we went bowling at Spare Things Lanes?"

She shook her head. "No we didn't, Trent. On our first date we went to LaPalma Mexican Grill. Bowling and the pizza place was our second date."

"Oh, boy. Guess I blew that one, didn't I?" Trent's blush covered his ears and down his neck. "So much for trying to impress you."

Miranda tugged her ear. "I didn't think we came here so you could impress me or take a walk down memory lane. I thought you wanted to talk about Debbie and Kevin."

"I do. Just thought . . ." He paused and cleared his throat. "The kids miss me, Miranda. They want me to come home, and I was hoping you might want that too."

Miranda felt trapped. Trent was using Kevin and Debbie to pry on her sympathies again. He should know by now it was not the way to win her back.

Miranda's muscles twitched as she clasped her hands tightly in her lap. "Our marriage needs an overhaul, Trent. There are so many weak areas, and nothing will be resolved by sweeping things under the rug."

"What exactly are you saying?"

"We need help."

Trent slapped his forehead. "Here we go. You want us to see a marriage counselor, right?"

"Maybe, but to begin with, I'd like you to attend a marriage seminar with me that my church is having next weekend. It starts on a Friday evening, and then continues on Saturday for most of the day." She held her breath, waiting for his response.

Trent clutched the steering wheel as if he were holding a shield. "I—uh—will have to think about it."

"Okay, but I'll need an answer by the first of next week so I can sign us up for the event."

"I'll give you a call Monday evening." Trent rubbed his chin. "Now, I'd like your opinion on something."

"What is it?"

"There's a young girl taking Heidi's cooking class. Her name's Peggy Ann."

Miranda nodded. "She lives near the Troyers, and her mother, Velma, does some work for Heidi to pay for her daughter's class."

"That's right, and from what I overheard, the family is struggling financially and they need a car." Trent made strong eye contact with Miranda. "So I was thinking I ought to look into getting a reasonably priced used car for Velma."

"It's a nice thought, but I doubt they could even afford a secondhand car."

He shook his head. "I'm planning to buy the car myself and give it to them."

"Really? Can you afford to do that?"

"Probably not, but I feel sorry for the family, and I want to do something to help."

Miranda touched the base of her throat. She'd never known her husband to be so generous, especially to a perfect stranger. Was he doing it as a genuine good deed, or could it be that Trent was only trying to impress her? For now, she would give him the benefit of the doubt. The real test would be whether he would agree to attend the seminar with her.

"Do you want to tell him, or should I?" Denise's forehead wrinkled as she handed Greg a platter full of baked chicken. Greg had been playing golf all afternoon with his lawyer buddies, so he had no idea what had transpired at the cooking class earlier that day.

"Tell me what?" Greg looked from Denise to Kassidy.

Kassidy picked up the ear of corn on her plate and chewed off the kernels, leaving several pieces stuck to her face.

"Your daughter got in a fight today before class started." Denise forked a piece of steaming broccoli and blew on it.

"A fight?" Greg looked at Kassidy. "Was it a verbal argument or an actual fist fight?"

"It wasn't a fist fight, Dad." Kassidy grabbed a napkin and wiped the butter dripping down her chin. "Just a bunch of shoving."

That girl makes me so mad. Denise inhaled slowly feeling her frustration mounting. "That fight involved more than shoving, and you know it. You were pulling each other's hair and punching. Furthermore, it doesn't matter what kind of fight or argument it was. You should never have let it happen."

"It was Becky's fault too," Kassidy retorted.

"Maybe you need to spend the rest of the night

in your room." Greg reached for an ear of corn off the platter.

"But Dad, I was good in class afterwards, and even tried to be nice to the other kids. But Mom keeps harping at me."

With furrowed brows, Greg looked at Denise. "At some point, all kids get into fights. Doesn't make it right, but that's part of growing up. I'm sure you had a fight at least once during your childhood."

"No, I did not. Besides, it's not the point. Our daughter didn't even apologize to Becky. I think she should be grounded for a couple of days, or maybe—"

Kassidy lifted her chin. "Becky didn't apologize either."

"You see." Greg wagged a finger. "The other girl's at fault too. Just let 'em work it out, Denise."

Denise wiped her mouth and took her plate to the sink. *Why bother to argue? As usual, Greg's mind is made up, and once again, Kassidy has gotten her way.* She reflected on the verse Heidi had written on the back of the recipe card she'd given Kassidy at the last cooking class. "And all thy children shall be taught of the LORD; and great shall be the peace of thy children."

Denise rubbed the bridge of her nose and sighed. *Perhaps Greg and I have made a mistake by not seeing that our daughter gets religious training. We have taught her nothing about God, and I have to wonder if we should all start attending church, in search of God's peace.*

Berlin

Darren slipped his arm around Ellen's waist as they meandered around the Fireman's Festival, looking for the best place to sit during the fireworks display. Their kids walked ahead of them, neither saying a word. Jeremy had been quiet all evening, and Becky seemed to be pouting. *She's probably still fretting about the encounter she had with Kassidy this morning.* Darren wished he felt free to talk to her about it, but he didn't know how Becky would take it. And Ellen might not appreciate him reprimanding her daughter.

Darren spread out the blanket he'd brought along and suggested they all take a seat. With hands in his pockets, Jeremy shook his head. "I'd rather stand."

"Okay, but make sure you're not blocking anyone's view." Darren was pleased when Ellen sat on the blanket, and he quickly took a seat beside her, watching to see what her daughter would do.

"I'm gonna find a restroom," Becky mumbled, looking down at her mother.

"Okay, but hurry back, or you might miss the fireworks."

"Have you enjoyed the festival?" Darren asked, leaning closer to Ellen.

She smiled. "Very much. I admire and appreciate what you and all the firemen in our area do. It's a difficult and sometimes dangerous occupation."

"Yeah, but I like my job, and I'm betting you like yours as a nurse too."

"I do, although there are stressful times. But I suppose that's true with most professions."

"Uh-huh." Darren looked up and pointed as the fireworks started, then he turned to look into Ellen's eyes. The glow from the exploding lights illuminated her beautiful face.

Almost of its own accord, Darren's hand reached out and caressed her cheek. When he tilted her chin upwards, everything around them seemed to disappear, except for Ellen's warm breath feathering his face. Darren slipped his other arm around Ellen's waist, lowered his head, and kissed her tenderly. He was pleased when she didn't pull away and returned his kiss. Ellen's lips were soft as rose petals.

The spell was broken when Jeremy returned to the blanket and plopped down in front of them. So much for the evening ending on a romantic note. Darren had to wonder if his son had seen them kiss, and intentionally interrupted.

Becky returned a few minutes later and sat in

front of Ellen as the fireworks continued to burst overhead.

"Say, I have an idea." Darren reached for Ellen's hand. "How would you and Becky like to go with me and Jeremy to the Farm at Walnut Creek next Saturday? It'll be fun to ride in one of their horse-pulled wagons and see all the animals roaming about."

"That sounds good, and my schedule just changed so that I don't have to work next Saturday," she replied. "And I'm sure my daughter would like to go too." Ellen nudged Becky. "Right?"

The girl shrugged.

Darren gently squeezed Ellen's fingers. He looked forward to spending more time with Ellen. Hopefully, their kids would be in better moods.

Chapter 35

Who wants a glass of cold lemonade?" Miranda asked when she and the children entered the house after running errands Monday afternoon.

"I do! I do!" Kevin shouted.

"I'd like one too," Debbie added. "And also some cookies."

"I think that can be arranged." Miranda chuckled. "Let me change out of my work clothes, and I'll meet you both in the kitchen." She hung her purse on the coat tree and hurried down the hall to her bedroom. It had been a busy day at the grocery store, and all she wanted to do was prop up her feet. Standing at the register all morning and afternoon, Miranda felt weariness set in.

When Miranda returned to the kitchen, she found Kevin sitting with his elbows on the table. Debbie had gotten out the cookie jar and set napkins out.

Miranda smiled. "Thank you, sweetie. You're such a big help."

"You're welcome." Debbie stared off into space.

Miranda wondered what her daughter was thinking about. She opened the refrigerator and took out the lemonade.

"Can I ask you something, Mom?" Debbie asked after Miranda gave her a glass of lemonade.

"Sure, honey, what is it?"

"Do I have to go over to Kassidy's house if she invites me?"

Miranda took a moment to think how best to answer, but Kevin spoke first.

"I'd never go over there." He held out his glass, while Miranda poured the cold drink. "I don't like Kassidy. She's mean."

"Never mind." Miranda tapped her son's arm, then turned to Debbie. "If she does extend an invitation, and you don't go, that's fine. I certainly won't force you to go someplace where you wouldn't be comfortable."

"Thanks, Mommy. I can't figure her out. She's been so nasty, and then all of a sudden Kassidy acts like she wants to be my friend. Makes me wonder if she's only being nice 'cause she wants something."

"It's hard to know what another person is thinking. Perhaps Kassidy has a hard time making friends. Or maybe she wants to change her ways, but doesn't know how." Miranda noticed that her children were looking at her intently. "Maybe if you're kind to Kassidy, she will be kind back."

Debbie tipped her head. "I can be nice during

the cooking classes, but I don't wanna go to her house. She'd probably brag about everything she has."

"Yeah," Kevin chimed in before reaching for a cookie. "That girl's a bragger, all right."

Miranda handed her son a napkin. "Let's wait and see what happens. Kassidy may forget about asking either of you to visit her home."

Miranda's cell phone rang, and she went to retrieve it from her purse. A quick look, and she knew the call was from Trent. "You kids finish up your snack while I take this call."

So they wouldn't hear her conversation, Miranda stepped into the utility room and closed the door. "Hello, Trent."

"Hi. What took you so long to answer? Figured I'd end up leaving a message."

"I was in the kitchen with Debbie and Kevin, and my phone was in my purse."

"Do you have a few minutes to talk?" he asked.

"Sure."

"I've been thinking about our conversation Saturday night, and your suggestion that we attend a marriage seminar."

Miranda stood silently waiting for him to continue.

"If you still want to go, I'm willing to attend it with you." His tone was upbeat, which gave her hope that he wasn't doing it out of some sort of obligation.

"Yes, I do want for us to go. Hopefully, we'll both get something good from it." She leaned against the washing machine, waiting for his response.

"I have no idea what to expect, 'cause I've never been to that kind of thing."

"And I never thought we'd need to attend something like this, but I've heard good things from others who went to previous seminars."

"What time should I pick you up Friday evening?"

"The event starts at seven, so if you could be here by six thirty, that would be great. I'll get a sitter for the children."

"Okay, sounds good. See you soon."

"Bye, Trent." Miranda clicked off the phone and closed her eyes. *Heavenly Father, please let this seminar be the beginning of a healing in my marriage.*

Canton

When Kassidy entered the living room, wearing a pair of navy-blue shorts and a white blouse, Denise set the real estate listings she'd been looking at aside. "Is Hillary still coming over to play tennis?"

"Yeah, Mom. She should be here soon." Kassidy flopped onto the couch. "I wish it wasn't so hot out, though. We shoulda played earlier in the day."

"That would have been fine if either your father or I had been home. But since we both had to work this morning, and you spent that time with my folks, it didn't work out for you to have your friend over until this afternoon."

Kassidy focused on her white tennis shoes. "When are you gonna realize I'm old enough to be left alone? Hillary, and some of my other friends, have stayed home by themselves lots of times." Her bottom lip protruded. "You and Dad think I'm still a baby."

Denise shook her head. "We don't think you're a baby, but you aren't an adult either."

"Yeah, I know." Kassidy pushed a strand of curly red hair behind her ear.

"You should be happy your dad said you could have Hillary over to play tennis. If it were up to me, you'd have been grounded this week because of the fight you had with Becky last Saturday." Denise leaned forward in her chair. "Where did you get that barrette in your hair? I've never seen it before."

Kassidy's cheeks colored as she reached up and touched the golden hair clip. "Um . . . I borrowed it from one of my friends."

"Which friend? Does it belong to Hillary?"

"No, it's uh . . ." Kassidy jumped up and raced to the window. "Think I heard a car pull in. Yep,

I was right . . . It's Hillary's mother, dropping her off." She hurried to open the front door and stepped outside.

That girl. Denise pursed her lips. *I wish she wouldn't borrow things from her friends. If she loses the barrette, she'll have to buy a new one, but the money to pay for it won't come from me. I will take it out of Kassidy's allowance. She needs to learn a lesson.*

Walnut Creek

Walking barefoot through the grass, Velma shielded her eyes from the late afternoon sun. Abner lay panting in the shade of a willow tree on the side of their mobile home. It had warmed up considerably yesterday, and today the weather was even hotter. They had no air-conditioning, and she dreaded going to sleep tonight. "Maybe you, me, and the kids oughta sleep outside," she said, bending down to pet the black Lab. "It'll be a lot cooler than in that stuffy old double-wide." Velma had given the kids vanilla ice cream after lunch, and it melted before they could finish what was in their bowls.

Abner barely lifted his head, looking up at Velma with sleepy brown eyes. The poor dog looked as miserable as she felt.

She knelt on the grass next to him, then fanned her face with her hand. The hot muggy air made her feel weighed down. If this warm weather kept up, with no rain in sight, their yard would turn brown.

Velma glanced toward the porch, where the kids were spread out on a couple of old cots Hank had picked up somewhere. No doubt the heat wave had gotten to them too.

Hearing a *cluck . . . cluck . . . cluck,* she turned her attention to the chicken coop she'd finished building this morning. Soon afterward, she had walked down the road about half a mile and purchased three hens. Then she'd walked back, carrying them in a metal carrier. When Hank got home with some money later this week, Velma hoped to buy a few more hens, as well as a rooster. She'd spent the last bit of cash Hank had given her before he left on the three chickens. Once again, she wished she could go out and get a job. Velma was tired of pinching pennies and barely having enough money to put food on the table and pay the bills. On top of that, she was lonely and wished her husband had a job that would allow him to spend more time at home. His being gone so much was hard on Peggy Ann and Eddie too.

Velma sat back, with both arms spread out behind her, drawing in a deep breath. Yesterday, being Sunday, she'd planned for her and the kids to try out a different church, but they'd all slept in, and by the time everyone had breakfast and gotten dressed, it was too late to make it to church on time.

She leaned her head back and looked up at the cloudless sky. *Maybe next week we'll go.*

The smell of chocolate permeated the kitchen, making Heidi's stomach growl. It brought back memories of her mother baking, when the warm sweet aroma of cookies seeped into every room of the house. Even though Heidi had baked chocolate chip cookies earlier today, the aroma lingered—probably from the warmth of the kitchen. In fact, the heat was almost stifling.

Moving over to the back door, Heidi glanced through the screen to check on Marsha and Randy. They'd gone out to play in the yard half an hour ago, but the sounds of laughter were no longer drifting through the kitchen window.

Seeing no sign of the children, Heidi opened the screen door and stepped onto the porch. She cupped her hands around her mouth and hollered: "Randy! Marsha! Where are you two?"

No response.

She caught sight of Rusty, lapping water from his dish near the back porch. It seemed strange the kids weren't with him, especially when they'd said they were going outside to play with the dog. *Now where did those children get to?*

Heidi called: "Come out, come out, wherever you are!"

Still no answer.

She ran around the side of the house, and then to the front. "Randy! Marsha!"

Maybe they're playing in the barn.

Heidi dashed across the yard and flung the barn doors open. "Marsha! Randy! Are you in here?"

The only sounds were the soft nicker of their buggy horse and the cooing of pigeons from the loft overhead. *I've warned them about it so many times—surely they wouldn't leave the yard.*

The hair on the back of Heidi's neck prickled as a dreadful feeling formed in the pit of her stomach and an image of the vehicle she'd seen twice by the entrance to their driveway came to mind. *What if my precious children have been kidnapped?*

Chapter 36

With sweat pouring down her face, and her chest so tight she could barely breathe, Heidi ran down the driveway toward the road. Over and over, she called the children's names. No reply. *Where are they? Dear Lord, please help me find them.*

When Heidi reached the end of the driveway, she looked up and down both sides of the road. An English man sped by in his noisy pickup, blowing her dress all about. She clenched her teeth and held onto her skirt. Some of the locals drove too fast on the back roads.

What should I do? Who should I call? Oh, I wish Lyle was here. He was auctioneering again today, and probably wouldn't be home until close to suppertime. This problem had fallen on Heidi's shoulders, and she needed to find Randy and Marsha. Her first course of action was to walk down the road and search for the children. If she couldn't find them, she would go back to the phone shack and call the sheriff.

As Heidi looked up and down the road, she bit down on her bottom lip. *Which way should I go— left or right?*

· · ·

As Velma pulled weeds on the back side of the mobile home, she thought more about her idea of sleeping outside tonight. Peggy Ann and Eddie would probably enjoy it, and they could pretend they were camping. It would be fun to look up at the twinkling stars in the coal black sky and watch fireflies coming up from the grass.

A sigh escaped Velma's lips. "Haven't had a good time with my kids in a while. We should sleep pretty good out here too."

Some giggling nearby broke the silence. Thinking it must be Eddie or Peggy Ann, Velma went to see what they thought was funny. She was surprised to see two young children dressed in Amish clothes in the front yard. It didn't take Velma long to realize it was Marsha and Randy. Heidi had stopped by with the kids last week to drop off some produce from her garden, so Randy and Marsha knew where she lived. However, Velma thought it strange that Heidi wasn't with them today.

She hurried over to the children. "What are you two doing here?"

Randy smiled up at her. "We came to look at the hinkel."

Marsha remained quiet as she bounced on her toes.

"What's a hinkel?"

"It's a chicken," the little girl spoke up.

After a bark of laughter, Velma asked, "Now, how'd ya all know I had any chickens?"

"Cause Peggy Ann said you was gonna get some."

Velma tapped Randy's shoulder. "Well, I guess she did. But where's Heidi?"

"Mammi's at home." Marsha looked up at Velma with all the innocence of a child.

"Does she know you're here?"

Randy shook his head.

"Oh, boy! You two need to skedaddle on back then." Velma reached for Marsha's hand. "I'll walk you both home."

"But I wanna see the chickens." Randy inched closer to Velma.

"Okay, you can take a quick look, but then I'm escortin' you back where ya belong. If Heidi knows you're gone, she's probably worried sick."

Marsha's forehead wrinkled. "Mammi's sick?"

"No, that's not what I meant. But she might feel sick if she worries too much." Velma led the way to the coop, surrounded by wire fencing. "Now hurry and take a peek."

Randy and Marsha stood giggling as the two hens chased each other around the enclosure. "They're funny." Marsha clapped her hands.

Several minutes later, Heidi rushed into the yard. "Oh, Velma, the children are missing. Have you seen any sign of . . ." She stopped talking, and her mouth formed an *O,* as she focused on

Marsha and Randy. "Oh, my!" She ran to the children, bent down, and grabbed them both in a hug. "What are you two doing over here? Don't you know how worried I was?"

"Came to see Velma's hinkel." Randy pointed to one of the hens. "They're bigger than our chickens, though."

Tears gathered in Heidi's eyes. "I'm glad you're okay, but you should not have left the yard without my permission." She shook her finger. "And never go anywhere outside of our yard without me or Lyle along. Do you both understand?"

Randy nodded, and Marsha's chin quivered. "S—sorry, Mammi. We didn't mean to make ya sick."

"What?" Heidi glanced at Velma.

"I told 'em if you discovered they were gone, you'd be worried sick," Velma explained. "And just so ya know—I was about to take 'em home when you showed up."

"I see." Heidi hugged the children again. "You're not in trouble, but please don't ever leave the yard again by yourselves. Something bad might have happened to you." She rose to her feet. "Let's go home now."

As Heidi left the yard with the children, she called over her shoulder, "Thank you, Velma. I'll see you and Peggy Ann a week from Saturday."

Velma watched as they walked down the driveway and turned in the direction of Heidi's house. She glanced toward the double-wide, surprised that Eddie and Peggy Ann were not on the porch. "Bet they're inside watchin' TV," she muttered, heading in that direction.

Dover

Darren entered Jeremy's bedroom to call him for supper and was surprised to see him standing in front of his dresser, rummaging through one of the drawers.

"What are you doing, Son?" Darren questioned.

"I—I'm just lookin' for something."

"What is it? Maybe I can help you find it." Darren stepped forward.

Jeremy's ears reddened as he quickly shut the drawer. "It's nothin', Dad."

"Really? Then why the guilty expression?"

Jeremy's gaze dropped to the floor, and he shuffled his feet on the carpet.

"Come on, Son, fess up. What were you looking for?"

Jeremy lifted his head. "I've been lookin' for that fancy doodad Mom used to wear in her hair."

"Do you mean the barrette I bought for her a few months before she died?"

"Yeah."

Darren rubbed a spot on his forehead, just above his brows. "Why would you be looking for it in your dresser?"

"Cause it's missing."

"I know that, Son. It went missing a few days before your mom passed away, and we never found it."

Jeremy lowered his head again. "I found it down the side of the couch last Saturday, before we left for the cooking class."

"Was that what you were fooling with in the car?"

"Yeah."

"Why didn't you tell me you'd found it?"

"I don't know. Guess I thought you'd be upset 'cause I wanted to keep it." Jeremy looked up at Darren with tears in his eyes. "I miss her, Dad, and I wanted to have something of Mom's to remember her by."

Filled with compassion, Darren pulled Jeremy into his arms. "We have lots of things in our house to remind us of your mother. I was planning to give you some of her personal things when you got married someday, but if there is something you'd like now, just let me know."

"I wanted the hair clip because I knew it was special to her." Jeremy's voice broke. "But now I've stupidly lost it."

"You had it last Saturday, though, right?"

Jeremy nodded. "It was in my jeans' pocket, except for the time I took it out and was looking at it."

"So maybe you lost it someplace at Heidi's.

And if that's the case, we can ask her about it when we go to your cooking class a week from this Saturday."

"Do we have to wait that long? Can't we go back there now?"

Darren shook his head. "I'm on call this evening and may have to fill in for one of the men who is sick. I work tomorrow, too, so we'll have to wait till Wednesday to go to Walnut Creek to see Heidi."

Jeremy flopped onto his bed. "If Heidi did find it, I bet she threw it away. I'll probably never see Mom's hair clip again."

"Don't give up, Son. If you lost it at Heidi's, I'm sure you will see it again." Darren gave Jeremy's arm a squeeze. "I'm going back to the kitchen to make myself a cup of coffee. Let me know if you need anything."

Jeremy nodded. "Okay, Dad. I'll probably go to the living room and watch TV."

When Darren entered the kitchen, he poured himself a cup of coffee and stood by the window. As he looked out, he thought about Jeremy and the special keepsake symbolic of his mother. It had been only a little over two years since Caroline's death, but certain things, like the mention of her barrette, brought back memories and kept the pain alive.

In Darren's eyes, his marriage to her had been no less than perfect. *Well, maybe not perfect,* he admitted. *But we were happy and filled with hope for the future until Caroline began having severe headaches.* The pain had been manageable at first, but then the headaches got so bad she found it hard to do anything except lie down. When Caroline went to the doctor after about a month of misery, he ordered an MRI and several other tests. The results were devastating. It was discovered that she had an inoperable brain tumor. The prognosis was that his wife had less than six months to live. Caroline declined having any treatments. She wanted to live life as normally as possible and didn't want the side effects of chemo.

Darren remembered how they'd explained things to Jeremy and the way his son had taken it like a little man. But Darren also remembered walking by his son's room one night, a few weeks later, and hearing him sobbing into his pillow.

Darren cried too, but privately. He wanted to be strong for Caroline. But no one was stronger than his precious wife. Her insistence on living life as normally as possible kept her going, even though she dealt with pain, dizziness, and disorientation. The doctor gave her a prescription for medicine that helped her function for a while.

About three weeks before she died, Caroline could no longer manage even the simplest of chores. She became couch-ridden, preferring to recline there rather than in the bed she had previously shared with Darren. She was so brave and beautiful from the inside out, even though the tumor wracked her body with pain. She lost weight but still had her beautiful hair, and that is why Darren bought her the barrette. She wore it every day, but no one seemed to notice when it fell out of her hair and apparently got lodged between the couch cushions. Her condition by then had grown hopeless. Jeremy and Darren cherished every last hour, minute, and second with Caroline.

Darren's thoughts took him back to the night when Jeremy had snuggled up to his mom on the couch and they had fallen asleep together. . . .

Darren sat in the dark, with only the light of the moon filtering in through the living room, watching his son and wife, with tears streaming down his face. Then sometime around two o'clock, Darren could no longer keep his eyes open, and he nodded off.

Sometime later, Darren was awakened when he heard Jeremy cough. He looked over at his wife and saw that she was looking at him.

Darren picked up his son and carried him to his room, being careful not to wake the boy. Then tiptoeing down the hall, he went back to the living room to be with his wife.

Caroline reached out and clasped his hand. "I need you to promise me something," she whispered.

"Of course, honey, anything."

"I want you to be brave and not mourn for me after I'm gone."

"I will try to be brave, but I can't promise not to mourn." Darren could barely speak around the lump clogging his throat.

She lifted a shaky hand and stroked his cheek. "Thank you for being such a wonderful husband and father."

"It's easy to do, since I love you and our son so much."

"And I love you, but I want you to move on with your life when you're ready to let go. Do not feel guilty if you find love again." Caroline paused and drew a shuddering breath. "I will always have your love with me right here." She touched her chest where her heart would soon stop beating.

Darren couldn't talk. He simply gathered his precious wife into his arms. She clung to him, and then took one last breath. He felt her body relax, and just like that, his beloved wife was gone.

. . .

Darren shuddered, and he wiped the corners of his eyes as his mind returned to the present. He never thought he would find love again, but now with Ellen, he knew that wasn't true. Given the chance, he was almost certain they could build a strong relationship.

As Darren finished his cup of coffee, now lukewarm, he stared out the window. It was something, how when a person left the earth, life still went on. Darren, like others who had lost loved ones, had been numb with grief. Each day he'd had to get used to waking up without Caroline. At times he could almost feel her right beside him. But on other days, he was afraid he would forget her beautiful face. As the weeks drifted into months, and the months into more than two years, the horrors of what he and Jeremy had gone through were replaced by all the memories they shared. Not a day went by when something didn't remind him of Caroline and her sweet ways or reflect on things they used to do as a family.

Now that he and Ellen were getting close, he had to put some thought into their relationship and decide how serious he wanted it to get—especially with how his son felt. If only Jeremy could learn to appreciate Ellen as much as Darren did.

Chapter 37

Walnut Creek

S ure hope if Heidi found Mom's barrette, she didn't throw it away." Jeremy sounded desperate.

"Try not to worry," Darren called over his shoulder, keeping his eyes on the road.

"But Dad, today's already Wednesday, and if she did find it someplace in her house, she wouldn't have known who left it." Jeremy grunted. "Most likely she'd have thought it belonged to one of the girls in our class. Someone could've already come and claimed it by now."

"Not likely, Son. Since it doesn't belong to one of the girls, there'd be no reason for them to claim it. Now stop fretting. We're almost there."

When Darren pulled into Heidi's yard, he spotted her on the grass, tossing a ball back and forth to the children. They looked like they were having a good time.

Darren parked the car, but before he could open his door, Jeremy hopped out and raced over to Heidi. Darren sprinted across the lawn to catch up with his son.

"Did you find my mom's barrette?" Jeremy stepped in front of Heidi after she threw the ball to Randy.

She quirked an eyebrow. "I'm not sure what you're talking about."

"Jeremy had his mother's hair clip with him last Saturday, and he thinks he may have dropped it someplace in your house or yard," Darren explained. "Did you happen to see it anywhere? The barrette was gold, with little red stones along the top."

"I haven't seen anything like that around the house or in the yard." Heidi gestured to Randy. "Have you seen a fancy hair clip?"

"Nope." Randy bounced the ball a few times.

Heidi looked at Marsha, and the little girl shook her head.

Jeremy groaned. "I had it with me Saturday; I know I did. Dad, remember when you asked me what I was holding in my hand, before I got out of the car?"

"Yes, I do remember." Darren felt his boy's frustration.

"You're welcome to look around out here if you like." Heidi made a sweeping gesture of the yard.

"Thanks." Darren pointed to the driveway. "Let's start where we parked the car that day." He headed in that direction, and Jeremy followed. Heidi joined them in the search. They looked everywhere Jeremy remembered walking, but found nothing.

"What about the house? Can I look in there?" Jeremy bit down on his bottom lip. "I've gotta find it. The barrette was special to my mom, and now it is to me."

Heidi suggested they all go inside and search for the hair clip. Marsha and Randy looked none-too-happy when she asked them to put the ball away and go into the house, but they did as they were told.

Darren and Jeremy followed her and the children in, and Jeremy retraced his steps. "I was here in the living room, and when everyone got here, we all went to the kitchen."

"All right, let's look in those two rooms," Heidi said.

"You also went to the bathroom," Darren reminded. "Why don't you look there, while I check out the living room?"

"While you two are doing that, I'll search in the kitchen." Heidi offered Jeremy a sympathetic smile. "If it's here in the house, I'm sure one of us will find it."

Another hour went by, but the barrette was not found. "I'm sorry." Darren clasped his son's shoulder. "We may as well give up and go home."

With shoulders slumped, Jeremy lowered his head. "Guess it's my fault for bringin' it to class with me. I shoulda put it somewhere safe in our house." He shuffled toward the front door.

"I'll keep looking, Jeremy," Heidi called. "If I find it, I'll let your father know right away."

Jeremy went silently out the door.

Darren turned to face Heidi. "Thank you for taking the time to help us look. Jeremy took his mother's death pretty hard, and on top of that, he's having a difficult time accepting the fact that I'm interested in another woman."

Curious, Heidi tipped her head to one side. "Ellen?"

"Yeah. To tell you the truth, I don't think her daughter's too thrilled about it either."

"Children, like adults, can find it difficult to move forward after losing a loved one. We can try to be patient and find ways to encourage them along." Heidi rested her hands against the front of her apron.

"I've been trying to be patient, and I'll keep at it."

"Dad, are you coming?" Jeremy called from outside.

Darren looked over his shoulder, then back at Heidi. "We'll see you soon."

Heidi stood by the front door, watching them get into their vehicle. *I need to keep Darren and Jeremy in my prayers. I can't imagine what it's like to be a single parent, and I pray that never happens to me.*

Millersburg

"I don't see why we have to see a bunch of animals with Jeremy and his dad this Saturday," Becky complained as she and Ellen filled the bird feeders in their yard. "I've been to the farm before with my class at school, and it wasn't that exciting."

"Really?" Ellen stopped what she was doing and placed both hands on her hips. "As I recall, when you came home that day, all you could talk about was the llama that spit, and how much fun it was to see the baby giraffe. I would think you'd want to go back and see how all the animals are doing. You'll get to feed them again, you know."

Becky folded her arms. "Well, it might be more fun if it was just the two of us. Jeremy will probably say a bunch of stupid things, and his dad . . ." She stopped talking. "Oh, never mind. I can tell you wanna go, so I'll get through it."

Get through it? Ellen could hardly believe her daughter's attitude. *Is she jealous of Darren? Does she think he will come between us?*

"Sounds like those birds are mighty hungry." Ellen looked toward the trees. "We have one more feeder to do, and then we're done." Ellen reached for the feeder, and slid open the top, while Becky held the funnel to fill it with seeds. If Becky's attitude toward Darren didn't improve, Ellen realized she may have to stop seeing him.

New Philadelphia

Trent sat at his desk in the dealership, staring at the paperwork for the sale of a mid-size car he was considering buying at a reasonable price. If he went through with the deal, he'd take the vehicle to the cooking class a week from Saturday and give it to the woman who needed a car. *I bet Miranda will be surprised that I went through with my plan. I hope Velma will be willing to accept my gift.*

From where his desk was positioned, Trent could watch the lot where all the new and used vehicles sat. It had been a slow day so far, and only an elderly couple browsed up and down the rows of cars.

Trent paused at what he was doing and held his breath. *Oh no, not that one.* The man and woman stopped at the car he was thinking of purchasing. He watched as they walked all around the vehicle and peered inside at the interior.

Should I go out and see if they have any questions? Truth was, he hoped they'd move on to another car. When he saw them reading the information sheet attached to the passenger window, Trent walked out and joined them.

"May I help you?" he asked, approaching the couple.

"We're looking for a used car, and this one caught our attention." The man smiled.

"I'm not sure I like it, though." The woman walked around the car again. "I was hoping for something a little smaller."

"My name is Trent Cooper." He extended his hand to the man. "I'll let you look around some more, and if you decide on anything, please come inside so we can talk."

"Thank you, Mr. Cooper." The man had a good grip. "My name is Howard Witmer, and this is my wife, Marie. We'll keep looking and let you know if we decide on a car."

"Okay, I'll be at my desk. It's to the left of the door."

Trent walked back inside. He hoped they would find another car better suited for their needs.

As he sat back down at his desk and watched the couple go down another row of vehicles, his thoughts turned to the seminar he'd agreed to attend with Miranda in two days. He didn't see how it could repair their marriage, but he was desperate to get Miranda back, and hoped by going it might be his ticket home. *And who knows. Maybe I'll learn something.*

Walking over to the water cooler, Trent filled a cup and took a drink. Glancing back outside, he saw the couple get into their car and drive off the lot. "Guess that takes care of that." Trent smacked his hands together and smiled as he walked back to his desk. "Looks like my plan for Velma is going to work out after all."

Chapter 38

Walnut Creek

L ook over there—here comes some animals eager to be fed." Darren pointed to the deer running toward the wagon where he, Jeremy, Ellen, and Becky were seated on a long wooden bench. An elderly Amish man drove the wagon, pulled by two sturdy horses.

Across from them sat five other people, all here for the same fun-filled tour. Everyone had been given a small bucket full of food to feed the animals.

"You must stay in the wagon at all times, and you'll need to remain seated whenever we're moving," the Amish man instructed. "Most of the critters will need to be fed by pouring some of the feed out of the containers and onto the floor of the wagon so they can reach it. However, the two-legged feathered animals with beaks can be fed directly from the bucket," he added. "Just be sure to hold on tight, because if the bucket drops we won't be able to stop and pick it up."

"Oh, look, there's a zebra coming," Ellen shouted, as several deer ate the food on the floor of the wagon. She was obviously enjoying herself, but Darren wasn't sure about Ellen's daughter. Even though Becky had poured food on the wagon floor, she sat with a placid expression. Darren watched Jeremy. He sat quietly too.

When the zebra came up to the wagon, Ellen reached out and stroked behind the animal's ear. "It feels so soft and silky." She gestured to Becky. "Why don't you try it?"

"No, that's okay." The girl shook her head. "I'll just watch."

Ellen turned to Jeremy then. "Why don't you pet the zebra? It's really . . ."

Jeremy's brows furrowed. "If I wanted to pet the critter, I would." He looked away.

Darren was stunned by his son's sharp tone. "Jeremy, you need to apologize to Ellen."

"Sorry," his son mumbled without looking her way.

Darren rubbed his forehead. This day was not going like he'd planned.

Next, they saw an ostrich with a long neck and pointed beak. Darren couldn't help but chuckle as he held his bucket out, allowing the ostrich to stick its beak in and get some food. In and out. In and out—the big bird's head bobbed back and forth.

Ellen laughed too. "I think this enormous bird is trying to eat all the food."

Jeremy and Becky remained quiet. It was obvious to Darren that neither of them wanted to be here. *I don't think Becky likes me, and Jeremy doesn't care for Ellen either.*

Darren looked at Ellen and swallowed hard. *Without our kids' blessing, this isn't going to work. As soon as I have a chance to speak to Ellen alone, I'm going to tell her that I think it's best if we don't see each other socially again.*

As the wagon tour concluded, Ellen's shoulders sagged. This outing could have been such a fun day, but Becky and Jeremy's disinterest put a damper on things.

Ellen bit the inside of her cheek. *If only my daughter could see Darren for the nice man he is and realize there's room in my heart for both of them. Becky hasn't given him a fair chance.*

She glanced over at Jeremy, staring at the wagon floor. *He's not happy about his father seeing me either. I bet it's just a matter of time before Darren says he doesn't want to see me anymore.* Ellen pulled in a quick breath and released it slowly. *Maybe it would be best if I break things off. The first opportunity I get to speak to Darren alone, I'm going to tell him I don't think we should see each other outside of the cooking class.*

Berlin

Trent squirmed in his chair, trying to find a comfortable position. Already it felt like he'd been here all day. Last night he and Miranda had attended the first two-hour session of the marriage seminar. Today's gathering, which had begun early this morning, would go on until late afternoon. Trent was glad there was more than one speaker. Listening to the same voice for hours on end would have probably put him to sleep.

He looked around at the other couples who had come here today and wondered if they were all having marital problems. Or perhaps, as one of the earlier speakers had pointed out, some had come to merely strengthen an already healthy marriage. Trent recognized a few of the people from Friday night's meeting. Some were young couples, and a few others looked to be around the same age as he and Miranda. What surprised him, though, was the elderly couples who'd come to the seminar. *I would think those old timers would have all the answers by now. But then, I guess a person is never too old to learn new ways to improve their marriage.*

So far, Trent hadn't gotten a lot out of the class, other than being reminded that a husband and wife should do nice things for each other and work on their communication skills.

Rubbing a hand across his forehead, he felt worry lines creasing his skin. *I've tried to be nice to Miranda, and where has that gotten me? And how am I supposed to communicate with someone who doesn't want to talk to me most of the time and thinks nothing I say is important?*

He glanced in his wife's direction, noting her serious expression as the speaker brought up a new topic.

"A husband's role as head of the house is to be the spiritual leader." The gray-haired man spoke with a tone of authority as he quoted a verse from Ephesians 5:25: "Husbands, love your wives, even as Christ also loved the church, and gave himself for it."

Trent leaned forward, listening intently as the minister read the thirty-third verse of the same chapter: "Nevertheless let every one of you in particular so love his wife even as himself; and the wife see that she reverence her husband."

Trent swallowed hard. *Oh, boy. How can I expect Miranda to respect me when I haven't earned her trust?* Trent leaned back in his seat, and when he glanced in his wife's direction, he saw tears dribbling down her cheeks.

"I love you with all my heart," Trent whispered, clasping her hand. "And with God's help, I want to be the spiritual leader in our home."

"Does that mean you'll start going to church

with us as a family?" Miranda spoke quietly against his ear.

He nodded and gently squeezed her warm fingers. It was too soon to ask if he could move back home, but when he'd proved himself and earned her trust, he would ask.

Miranda could hardly believe the words her husband had whispered to her. For the first time since she and Trent had separated, Miranda felt a ray of hope that there might be a reconciliation. It would take some time for him to prove he was serious about attending church and becoming the spiritual leader of their home, but at least he was willing to try. She also felt confident that once it was proven, learning to trust him would be easier.

She closed her eyes and offered a prayer: *Heavenly Father, please lead my husband down the path You want him to follow, and help me to be an encouragement to him. Help me say the right words whenever I speak to Trent, and grant me the wisdom to know when it is right to invite him to come home. If Trent and I resume our marriage, I want it to be for good this time.*

Walnut Creek

After they'd left the farm, Darren had stopped at an ice-cream stand, hoping it would ease some of the tension. All kids loved ice cream, and he'd anticipated Jeremy and Becky would be in a better mood after they had a sweet treat.

Unfortunately the kids' moods had grown worse, and now as they headed to Millersburg to take Ellen and Becky home, his vehicle was filled with nothing but silence. Darren rehearsed in his mind what he would say to Ellen when he dropped them off. He planned to walk them to the door and then, before they went into the house, ask Ellen if he could speak to her alone.

His insides twisted as he thought about saying goodbye and never having the chance to see where their relationship might take them. But he saw no way they could keep seeing each other without their children's approval.

"Hey, Dad, did ya hear those sirens?" Jeremy asked as they approached the road where they always turned off to go to Heidi's.

"Yes, I did." Darren looked in his rearview mirror and saw a fire truck approaching. Then another one, coming from the opposite direction, appeared.

Darren pulled his SUV onto the shoulder of the road to let them pass and was surprised when both vehicles turned up the same road where the Troyers lived. He turned to look at Ellen, sitting beside him with an anxious expression. "I hope you don't mind, but I'd like to follow the trucks and see what's going on. It might be someone we know or maybe they could use some extra help."

Ellen was quick to nod. "I hope nothing has happened at Heidi's place."

Chapter 39

The heat and flames that had started in the kitchen when she left a frying pan on the hot stove sent Velma screaming through her double-wide. She'd tried to put out the fire, but to no avail. "Peggy Ann! Eddie! Where are you? We've gotta get out of the house!" When neither child responded, Velma's fear escalated to panic.

Smoke filled Velma's lungs as she raced down the hall, coughing, disoriented, and calling her children's names. Thick smoke filled the air, and she groped her way along, until she reached her daughter's bedroom. The door was open, and she stepped inside. "Peggy Ann, are you here?"

Velma tipped her head when she heard a faint whimper.

"Peggy Ann!" Velma moved forward, trying to focus through the smoky haze.

Suddenly, her daughter was there, gripping Velma's hand. "Are we gonna burn up in the fire?"

"No, honey, we'll be okay." Velma swept a hand across her forehead. She needed to call 911, but was unable to get to the phone. "Where's your brother?"

"I—I don't know, Mama. Eddie said he was gonna take the dog for a walk, but I don't know if he went outside or not." Peggy Ann coughed. "Oh, Mama, I can't breathe."

Velma pulled her daughter to the floor and instructed Peggy Ann to hold tight to her arm. "Don't worry, baby. I'll keep my arm around you, and we'll crawl out together." She remembered hearing once that, when trapped in a fire, the safest place to be was on the floor, and that a person should try to follow the wall. Velma had to get Peggy Ann to safety and then find Eddie.

Hearing sirens in the distance, she felt a glimmer of hope. One of her neighbors must have seen the blaze and called the fire department.

"Look over there! Do you see the smoke?" Lyle pointed as he guided their horse and open buggy up the road in the direction of their house. They'd taken the children out for an early supper and were on their way home, never expecting to encounter such a tragedy.

Heidi tipped her head back. Lyle was right—there must be a huge fire up ahead. Dusk was approaching, and when they continued on, she saw a red glow in the sky. "Ach, I hope it's nobody we know, and I pray no one's been injured."

As they drew closer, two fire trucks came up behind them, sirens wailing, and horns blaring.

Lyle pulled the horse and buggy onto the shoulder of the road and waited for them to pass.

Their horse threw her head back and whinnied. "Whoa, Bobbins, steady, girl," Lyle said in a calming voice. The horse pawed the ground and snorted, but finally settled down.

Lyle pulled back onto the road, but they'd only gone a short distance, when Heidi recognized the location of the fire. "Oh, no! The Kimballs' double-wide is on fire! We need to see if they're all okay."

Lyle turned up the Kimballs' driveway and halted the horse near a tree that stood a safe distance from the burning mobile home. He turned to a wide-eyed Marsha and Randy and said, "You two stay in the buggy with Heidi, while I check on things." Lyle stepped down and raced across the yard.

Trembling, Heidi remained in the front seat, while the children stayed seated behind her, both whimpering.

Randy tapped Heidi's shoulder. "Are Velma and her kinner gonna die in the fire?"

"I hope not, Randy. I pray everyone has safely gotten out of the house."

"What about the hinkel?" Marsha asked. "Are they gonna be all right?"

"Jah, the coop is away from the house, so the chickens should be fine." Heidi felt bad that the children had to witness such a horrible sight, but no way could she and Lyle take them home until they knew if Velma and her family were out of danger.

Desperate to know what was happening, Heidi reminded the children to stay in the buggy, and then she got out. She needed to see for herself if the Kimballs were okay.

As soon as Darren pulled his vehicle into the yard of the burning mobile home, Ellen hopped out of the car. He could almost tell by the determined set of her jaw what she had in mind.

"Where are you going?" Becky leaned out the back window and shouted at her mother.

"Someone may be hurt, and since I'm a nurse, I need to see if I can assist in any way." Ellen turned to look at Becky. "I want you to stay right here in Darren's SUV where it's safe. Do you understand?"

"Okay."

"You stay put too, Jeremy," Darren instructed, before climbing out of the car. "I'm going to see if my help is needed." He waited until his son nodded, then sprinted across the yard.

"Is anyone in the house?" Darren hollered to one of the firemen he recognized.

"Don't know yet. Two of our men went inside when they heard someone screaming, but I haven't seen anyone come out."

Acting on instinct, Darren made a dash for the

door, but the fireman stopped him. "Sorry, friend, but you can't go in there. You're not suited up, and this fire is not in your district."

"I know, but—"

"There are no buts about it. You know the rules."

With a reluctant nod, Darren backed off. It wasn't in him to stand around and do nothing, especially when lives could be at stake. He glanced to his right and saw Ellen talking to Heidi Troyer and her husband. A few other Amish folk were milling about. He wasted no time in joining the Troyers. "Do you know who lives here?"

Lyle nodded. "It belongs to Hank and Velma Kimball."

Darren's brows shot up. "The same Velma whose daughter's been taking Heidi's cooking classes?"

"Yes, and this is their double-wide engulfed in flames." Heidi tugged the narrow ties of her head covering. "I wish we knew if Velma or any of her family is inside." She closed her eyes briefly. "I pray no one's been hurt."

Darren stood helpless with the others, as he watched the mobile home continue to burn, despite the firemen's attempts to put out the flames. As the water from the hose hit the scorching inferno, it made a sizzling sound mixed with the popping of things exploding inside. From where he stood, the mobile home was nearly consumed by the fire. And a harsh wind had picked up, making the firemen's efforts that much more difficult.

A few minutes later, one of the firemen exited the home with Velma and her young daughter. Darren looked at Ellen and mouthed the words, *Thank goodness.*

"Where are Velma's son and her husband?" Ellen clasped her hands in a gesture of prayer.

"I don't know. Let's go find out." Darren led Ellen over to where Velma and Peggy Ann stood trembling, despite the blankets draped across their shoulders. Neither appeared to be burned, but their hair and clothes were black with smoke.

"What happened, Velma? Where's your son?" Ellen shouted.

"I don't know," Velma rasped. "Peggy Ann said Eddie was gonna take Abner for a walk, and I pray he and the dog aren't still in the house."

Woof! Woof! At the sound of a dog barking, Darren rushed forward. He couldn't stand out here idly watching when the life of Velma's son could be at stake.

Velma shook her head vigorously, pushing aside the oxygen mask the paramedic tried to place over her nose and mouth. "I need to find my boy!"

"You need to calm down," the man insisted, holding firm to Velma's arm. "We can't let you

413

go back in the house. If your son is in there, one of the firemen will make every effort to find him."

Ellen and Heidi stepped up to Velma. "It's going to be okay," they said in unison.

Velma rocked back and forth as a wave of dizziness washed over her. "I don't know about that. Bad things always seem to happen to me." She gulped in some air. "Hank will never speak to me again when he finds out my carelessness with hot oil started the fire. And if anything happens to Eddie, it won't matter if he doesn't forgive me, because I'll never forgive myself."

Heidi put her arm around Velma's waist, and Ellen took hold of her hand. They tried to offer her hope, but Velma found no comfort at all. No matter how angry he might get with her, Hank was needed right now and she wished he was here instead of out on the road. He never seemed to be around when she needed him, though.

After what seemed like hours, Darren emerged from the front door of the double-wide, his face blackened with soot. He carried Eddie in his arms and Abner was at his side.

Velma rushed forward. "Is my boy all right?"

"He's inhaled a lot of smoke, but I think he's going to be okay."

The paramedics took over then, offering first aid to Velma and both of her children, while

Ellen and Heidi looked on. A fireman took their dog and checked him for injuries. Other than needing some oxygen, Abner was okay.

"You'll need to go to the hospital to be treated for smoke inhalation and observation," one from the medical team told Velma.

"But what about my dog?" Velma felt so disoriented she could barely think. Her home, along with everything in it, was gone, and Hank didn't even know what happened.

"That's my best friend and fellow firefighter, Bruce Ferguson, taking care of your pet," Darren informed Velma.

Abner was now wagging his tail as Bruce removed the oxygen mask. "Don't worry about Abner, Velma. He's in good hands, and I'll see that he's taken care of for you tonight."

Tears welled in Velma's eyes as she murmured a quiet, "Thank you." She had no home and didn't know what the future held for her family, but at least she and the kids were all alive. That was something to thank God for.

When Ellen and Darren returned to his vehicle, Becky and Jeremy got out and hugged their parents.

"We were so scared, Mom. Did anyone die in the fire?" Becky sniffed, clinging to Ellen's hand.

"No, Becky. Velma and her children are going to be fine. Their dog is okay too."

Running a jerky hand through his hair, Jeremy looked up at his dad. "I was worried you might be killed tryin' to save someone's life."

"I'm fine, Son. Just a little smoke ridden is all." Darren gestured to the black Lab at his side. "Velma's dog needs a home for the night. Think you might want to help me take care of him?"

"Bacon might not like having another dog in the house, especially one that's bigger than him. But I guess the poor mutt needs somewhere to go, so I'll help you take care of him."

Darren smiled. "Thanks, Son. I knew I could count on you."

Jeremy looked over at Ellen. "I'm glad you're okay too. Becky and I were worried about you and my dad."

"He's right, we were," Becky agreed.

Ellen felt a sense of relief. Not only were their children getting along better, but they seemed more cordial toward each other's parents. Maybe there was hope for a relationship with Darren after all. There might be no need for her to break things off—at least not tonight. Ellen would give it more thought before making a decision that could affect the rest of her life. Right now, she needed to concentrate on looking for a way to help Velma and her family.

Chapter 40

It had been a week since the fire, and Velma couldn't believe how much had happened since then. Heidi and Lyle had generously invited Velma, Hank, and the kids to stay with them until they could secure a new place to live. On top of that, when Hank came home and discovered their double-wide had burned, instead of being angry with Velma, his attitude toward her and the children actually improved. He was especially grateful for the Troyers' generosity, and even more so when Lyle told him their Amish community would help them build a new house on their property. Neither Velma nor the children had any serious ill effects from the fire, and that was something to be thankful for too.

Hank took some time off work to be with his family. Every day he and the kids walked down the road to their property. Randy and Marsha often went along to help feed the Kimballs' chickens, while Hank checked on the progress of things after the fire. Abner remained his playful self and was getting along well with Rusty.

Velma was amazed at how the Amish community pulled together to help after the flames destroyed everything. She and Hank, with the assistance of Ellen, Darren, and the Troyers, had gone through the ashes to see if anything could be salvaged. Unfortunately, the double-wide was like a matchstick, and the intense heat of the fire destroyed everything. A week later, most of the rubble had been cleared, making way for construction to begin.

Velma smiled as she dried the dishes Heidi had just washed. They would soon have a real house, and not just an out-of-date, rundown mobile home with creaky floorboards and peeling wallpaper. *Good things come to those who wait,* she told herself. *Maybe my life isn't such a train wreck after all.*

She placed the clean plates in the cupboard and shut the door. *Now if amends could be made with my folks and if our two older children would come home, or at least make contact with us, I'd feel complete.*

Velma glanced across the room at Heidi, who was busy setting out the things she would need for today's cooking class. *Such a sweet woman, with a generous spirit. I'm glad I've gotten to know her. Heidi deserves only the best.*

Heidi glanced at the clock on the far wall, then looked over at Velma. "My cooking class will start in half an hour, so I think I will go outside and check for phone messages before the students arrive."

Velma looked out the window. "I see Hank coming back with the kids. Wonder how everything's going at our place?" A contented smile spread across her face. "My husband sure enjoys your kids. As a matter of fact, I do too."

"Randy and Marsha have taken a liking to both of you as well." Heidi moved across the room. "Guess I'd better head out to the phone shack now."

"Okay. I'll finish drying the dishes and then get to work on the laundry while you teach your class."

"You're doing more than your share of work around here." Heidi paused near the back door. "Why don't you take it easy today and join the class? You might enjoy seeing what Peggy Ann and the others will be making."

Velma planted her feet in a wide stance, while shaking her head. "With all you and Lyle are doing for us, the least I can do is help out at your place. Besides, I still owe you some work to pay for my daughter's cooking classes."

"I'm not concerned with that, Velma. You've done enough work around here this past week to more than pay for Peggy Ann's lessons."

"I don't mind a'tall. I'd like to repay all your kindness to me and my family." Velma placed the dish towel on the counter, stepped over to Heidi, and wrapped her in a hug. "Some folks I know wouldn't lift a finger to help their neighbor, but you and Lyle have gone the extra mile."

"We just try to do what the Bible says: 'Be ye kind one to another.'" Heidi tapped Velma's arm. "I'm sure you would do the same if someone you knew needed assistance."

"You got that right." Velma opened her palms. "Course, in our current situation, we couldn't do much for anyone in need."

Heidi gestured to the clean dishes in the drying rack. "You've been doing helpful things for me."

A circle of red erupted on Velma's cheeks. "That's different."

"No, it's not. Your help is much appreciated."

"Thank you, Heidi. You've become a good friend."

Heidi smiled. "I think of you as my friend too."

Denise glanced in the rearview mirror at her daughter, sitting quietly in the back seat. Kassidy hadn't said more than a few words since they'd left home this morning.

"I wonder what you'll learn to make today. When your last class ended, did Heidi say what she would be teaching you today?"

"Nope, she never said."

Not much of a response, but at least Kassidy had answered. Denise decided to try again. "When we get home after class today, why don't you invite Hillary over?" Denise looked in the mirror again.

"She's not home. Hillary and her family are visiting relatives in Nebraska."

"You know, you should invite the kids from the cooking class sometime, like you mentioned two weeks ago."

"I changed my mind about that. I don't have anything in common with those kids. Besides, most of 'em don't like me, so I'm sure no one would come."

"You won't know unless you ask. If you spent a little more time with them, you might find you do have a few things in common."

Switching her gaze from the rearview mirror and concentrating on the road ahead, Denise clasped the steering wheel a little harder when Kassidy didn't respond. *Is there any hope for that daughter of mine? Why must she be so difficult and moody?*

"Here we are." Darren set the brake and turned off the engine. He glanced in the back and was surprised to see Jeremy slumped in his seat. "Come on, Son. A few other cars are here, so we need to get inside. I'm sure class is about to start."

"Sure wish I knew where Mom's barrette got to," Jeremy mumbled. "The last time I saw it, we were sitting right here, and I remember putting it in my pocket. I must've dropped it somewhere."

Darren's gaze flicked upward. *How many times is Jeremy going to bring this up? I know he feels sad about losing his mom's hair clip, but rehashing it won't change the fact that it's lost and he may never find it.*

Thinking a change of subject would be good, Darren turned in his seat to make eye contact with his son. "Before we go in, I'd like to clarify something with you."

"What?"

"On the way home last Saturday, after the fire at Velma's, you said you'd be okay with me continuing to see Ellen."

Jeremy slowly nodded.

"So when I see Ellen today, if I ask her for another date, you won't have a problem with it?"

"Said I wouldn't, so why do ya keep askin'?"

"Probably for the same reason you keep bringing up your mother's barrette."

"What do ya mean?"

"Seeing Ellen is important to me, and I want to be sure it's okay with you, because someday, if things work out the way I hope, I might ask Ellen to marry me."

"Seriously?" Jeremy's eyes widened.

Darren nodded. "Would you be okay with that?"

"If that's what you really want, Dad, I won't mess things up for you."

"I appreciate that, but I'm not sure yet if Ellen's the woman God wants me to have." Darren paused. "Before your mother died, she said she wanted me to find love again. I think I may have found it with Ellen."

Jeremy sat quietly for several seconds, then slowly nodded. "I'm goin' inside now, okay?"

"Yes, we need to do that. Sure don't want to hold up Heidi's class today." As they walked up to the house, Darren draped his arm over Jeremy's shoulder. *In just a few short years, my son will no longer be a boy. Oh, how I wish Caroline could have seen him grow up to become a man.*

Another car pulled in, and Darren stopped walking to see who it was. He recognized Denise's vehicle and watched as she and her daughter got out of the car. *I hope Kassidy doesn't cause any trouble today,* he thought. *That girl has a way of getting under people's skin.*

When Darren and Jeremy stepped onto the porch, Denise and her daughter joined them.

"Good morning." Denise smiled at Darren. "It's hard to believe, after this one, our children only have one more cooking lesson to go."

He was about to comment, when Jeremy pointed at Kassidy and shouted, "Hey, where'd ya get the barrette you're wearin'?"

"I found it in Heidi's driveway the last time we were here. It's beautiful, isn't it?"

Jeremy lowered his brows, and his cheeks

sucked inward. "That's my mom's barrette. I had it with me at the last cooking class and must have dropped it. You have no right to keep something that's not yours, and I want it back!"

Her lips pressed together as she shook her head. "My dad's a lawyer, and I heard him say once that possession is nine-tenths of the law."

"What's that supposed to mean?" Jeremy's eyes narrowed.

"It means I found it, so now the barrette is mine." As if to taunt him, Kassidy pushed her hair away from her face, letting her fingers travel over the hair clip. "If it meant so much to you, why didn't you come back and look for the hair clip?"

"We did come back. In fact, Heidi helped us look for the barrette. It's no wonder we couldn't find it, 'cause you had it all along."

Darren was on the verge of saying something, but Denise spoke first. "Kassidy, I want you to give this boy his mother's barrette right now. Do you hear me?"

Kassidy's lower lip jutted out. "What's he gonna do with a hair clip, Mom? It looks better in my hair than it would his."

"That's not funny." Denise reached out and pulled the barrette from Kassidy's hair. "I'm sorry, Jeremy. My daughter is rude and selfish." She handed him the hair clip. Then taking Kassidy by the arm she led her into Heidi's house.

Darren glanced at Heidi, standing in the open doorway, and wondered if she'd heard what just happened. He felt bad for Jeremy. Caroline's barrette meant a lot to him, and Darren was glad he'd gotten it back. He gave Jeremy's back a pat. "You okay?"

"Yeah." He handed Darren the barrette. "Here, Dad. You'd better hang on to this. Sure don't wanna lose it again."

Darren put the hair clip in his pocket and hugged his son. "I love you, Jeremy."

"Love you too, Dad."

With his arm draped over Jeremy's shoulder, Darren led the way into the house. "Now let's see what you'll be cooking today."

Chapter 41

Heidi couldn't help overhearing the conversation that had transpired between Jeremy and Kassidy. It was hard to understand why some children were so sweet and kind, while others, like Kassidy, wore a frown most of the time and tried to provoke others. Was it her parental upbringing, unhappiness at home, or did the girl merely enjoy making trouble?

Heidi didn't want to keep everyone waiting, so she asked her students to move into the kitchen.

"If it's all right with you, I think I'll wait in the dining room today while Becky takes the class," Ellen spoke up. "It would be good for her not to have me watching over her shoulder."

"Thanks, Mom." Becky headed straight for the kitchen.

"I'll go along with that and sit in the dining room too," Darren was quick to say.

Heidi looked at the other parents. "What would the rest of you prefer to do? I'm fine with whatever you decide."

"I'll sit with Ellen and Darren. It'll give me a chance to get better acquainted." Miranda smiled. "And my kids won't have to worry about their mom asking unnecessary questions or trying to help them too much."

"I'll stay with the other adults too," Denise said.

"What about you, Velma?" Heidi questioned. "Would you prefer to join us in the kitchen or stay in the dining room with the other parents?"

Velma tugged on the collar of the blouse Heidi had bought her Monday. In fact, she and Lyle had purchased a few sets of clothes for Velma and the children, since all their clothes other than the ones they'd been wearing the night of the fire had been burned. "I think it'd be best if I do the laundry while you're teaching Peggy Ann, like I said before. Eddie can occupy himself outside in the barn with Hank and Lyle."

It was clear to Heidi that Velma felt uncomfortable sitting among the other parents, so she went along. When the meatballs were done, she would invite Velma to join them for a taste test.

As the adults sat in Heidi's dining room, drinking iced tea and visiting, Denise only half listened to their conversation. She was more interested in what was going on in the other room. She heard Heidi say she was going to check on Velma, so when she left the room, Denise turned an ear in the direction of the children waiting in the kitchen for Heidi's return.

Through the partially opened door, Denise saw

Miranda's son, Kevin, sitting at the table beside Jeremy.

"How come only your dad and not your mom have come here with you?" Kevin bumped Jeremy's arm.

"My mom died of a brain tumor." Jeremy lowered his head.

"That's sad. Bet ya miss her a lot."

"Yeah. Everything changed after she died." Jeremy heaved a sigh. "Now, whenever my dad goes to work, he calls a lady from church to stay at our house with me."

Denise glanced sideways at Darren to see if he'd heard his boy's comment, but Jeremy's father seemed to be absorbed in something Ellen was saying to him.

"You're not the only one who gets stuck with a sitter, but the lady who stays with me when Mom's at work is nice." From where she sat, Denise couldn't see Becky, but she recognized her voice.

"When our mom has to work, Debbie and I have a babysitter too." Kevin bobbed his head.

"My mother leaves me alone sometimes," Kassidy said in her usual bragging tone. "But not for very long, of course."

Now where did she come up with that? I've never once left Kassidy alone at the house. Denise was tempted to intervene, but remained in the dining room, watching and listening to the children. *I'll bet my daughter wants to appear grown-up in the other kids' eyes.*

Kevin thumped the table with his knuckles. "If my daddy moved in with us again, he could be with me and Debbie sometimes when our mom has to work at the grocery store." He paused and sniffed a couple of times. "I miss him a lot and wish he and Mommy would get back together so we could be a family again."

Denise heard Miranda's intake of breath, and when she looked her way, tears glistened on her cheeks.

Denise realized that each family represented here today had their own issues to deal with, and so did she. Even families that appeared to be perfect often dealt with serious issues. She wished there was a simple answer that could fix everyone's problems. But life held no guarantees, and for some, the problems they faced might never be resolved. *Even mine,* she concluded with regret.

Denise caught a glimpse of Kassidy when she got up to get a drink of water. Except for her comment a few minutes ago, she was surprised her daughter hadn't said something hurtful to one of the children or bragged about how perfect her life was. In fact, she'd suddenly become abnormally quiet.

Denise thought back to earlier that morning, when she and Greg had a disagreement. She'd asked him to get some things done outside that morning, because a storm had been predicted for later in the day. The gutters needed to be cleaned, but Greg declined, saying he'd made arrangements to go golfing with one of his lawyer friends, and then out to lunch to discuss an upcoming case. Greg had also added that the gutters could wait.

Denise pursed her lips. *Greg was trying to justify going golfing. I'll bet whatever they had to talk about could have waited until Monday.*

She looked at Darren and Ellen again. They seemed oblivious to everyone else in the room. She couldn't remember the last time Greg had looked at her in the tender way Darren was fixated on Ellen.

Turning away, she gazed out the window. The sky had darkened, and storm clouds brewed in the distance. *I hope we get home before the rain comes. It looks as if it could get nasty.*

"All right, class, I'm ready to begin now," Heidi announced when she returned to the kitchen. "Today I'm going to teach you how to make some yummy meatballs."

When Heidi's class ended, and they were ready to eat what the children had made, it began to rain, and the muffled sound of thunder could be heard in the distance. "Since a storm is coming, we'll eat in the dining room today," Heidi said.

She asked Ellen to get out the cut-up vegetables she'd prepared earlier and put in the refrigerator so they would stay cool and crispy.

"I'd be happy to do that." Ellen rose from her chair.

"I'll help get things on too. Just tell me what to do," Miranda offered.

"Would you mind setting the table?"

"Not at all." Miranda went to the kitchen.

Denise pushed her chair aside and stood. "I'll help her."

"Thanks. I'll see if Velma, Eddie, and the men would like to join us." Heidi grabbed an umbrella and hurried out the back door.

A short time later, Velma sat with the other parents and their children around Heidi's dining-room table, enjoying the delicious meatballs and cut veggies. With the exception of Kassidy, the other children seemed pleased when they received compliments on the meatballs from their parents.

While listening to the conversation going on at the table, Velma's mind wandered. *Once we get settled in our new house, I'm going to get involved in some community and church activities. I also need to get better acquainted with the Amish and English folks in the area. Who knows, maybe someday I'll have an opportunity to help someone out.*

A knock sounded on the front door, and Heidi went to answer it. When she returned, a tall man with brown hair was with her.

"Trent—what are you doing here?" Miranda sputtered, nearly spilling her glass of iced tea. "I thought you had to work today."

"I worked this morning, and now I'm here on a mission." He looked at Velma and smiled. "I heard you and your family need transportation, so I brought you a secondhand car that is in good shape."

Velma blinked rapidly as her mouth slackened. "Oh, you shouldn't have done that. My husband and I don't have enough money to buy a car right now. You probably haven't heard, but a week ago, we lost our mobile home and everything in it." She dropped her gaze to the table. "Right now, we're in the worst financial shape we've ever been."

"You don't understand." Trent moved closer to the table. "The car is a gift. I don't expect anything for it."

Velma stared at him with her mouth slightly open. The words would hardly come. "I—I can't believe you would do that for a stranger."

Trent glanced at Miranda and grinned. "My wife told me about your situation, and then I learned more the day I came to the class with Debbie and Kevin." He looked back at Velma. "So, you're not really a stranger. I feel like I know you, and it's my pleasure to help out."

Velma placed both hands against her hot cheeks, barely able to swallow due to her swollen throat. "Thank you, Mr. Cooper. I humbly accept your wonderful gift." Overcome with emotion and gratitude, tears coursed down Velma's cheeks. *Thank You, God, for bringing so many good people into my life when I needed it the most.*

Chapter 42

Canton

Ever since they'd left Heidi's house around one, Denise had tried unsuccessfully to engage her daughter in conversation. It was probably for the best, since she needed to keep her focus on the road now that the rain had increased and the storm was overhead.

Denise had never liked driving in bad weather, and today was no exception. Since the wind had picked up, at times the rain came down sideways. Up ahead, she caught sight of a flapping plastic grocery bag caught on a tree branch. Dark clouds raced across the sky, and a jolt of lightning split the skies. Pools of dirty water quickly formed in low spots in people's yards and along the shoulder of the road.

Denise turned on the radio in time to hear a flash-flood warning. *Oh great.* She gripped the steering wheel, mentally calculating where all the creeks and streams were on the way home.

Denise glanced in the rearview mirror and saw her daughter flinch when a boom of thunder sounded so hard the car windows rattled. The windshield wipers slid back and forth in a futile effort to keep up with the pelting rain. Turning them on the highest speed didn't seem to help.

A vehicle coming toward them sent up a spray of water as it passed through a low spot quickly filling from the intense downpour. Denise pushed hard against the seat, as water hit the windshield with such force it sounded like a million pebbles.

"Did it break the window?" Kassidy screamed above the noise.

"Everything's okay. It just sounded bad. Stay calm." Inside, Denise was nothing but calm, but she didn't want to upset her daughter. "Just a little ways to go, and we'll be home."

Denise felt relief when she drove her car through the open gate at the entrance of their expansive driveway. They were almost there. She couldn't wait to put the car in the garage and get into the house, where she could relax with a cup of her favorite tea.

As she pulled her vehicle into their three-car garage, she was surprised to see Greg's parking spot empty. He certainly couldn't be out on the golf course in this horrible weather, with lightning and thunder all around. Then she remembered he'd mentioned having lunch with his lawyer friend after they finished golfing. Most likely Greg was still at the clubhouse, waiting out the storm.

After she'd parked the car in her bay, Denise

followed Kassidy into the house. "Thank good-ness the garage is attached to our home. Even with an umbrella, we'd both be soaked to the bone if we had to come in from outside."

Kassidy was silent.

"Did you get enough to eat at Heidi's, or would you like me to fix you a snack?" Denise tapped her daughter's shoulder.

"No, thanks. I'm goin' to my bedroom to watch TV," Kassidy mumbled without turning around.

"I'm not sure I'd put the TV on with the lightning this close."

"If I hear it thunder real loud again, I'll turn it off." Kassidy disappeared down the hall.

Denise made her way to the kitchen. Along with her beverage, she might indulge in a chocolate brownie.

After fixing a cup of chamomile tea, and placing a succulent-looking brownie on a plate, she took a seat at the bar where she often sat to eat breakfast. *Should I or shouldn't I?* She pondered the thought. *Oh, why not?*

Denise went to the refrigerator and got out a can of whipped cream. *What's a brownie without a little sweet cream?* Denise shook the can and squirted a layer over top of her treat. *Now I'm ready to indulge.*

Even though the rain was still coming down hard, she felt relaxed inside her cozy, well-equipped kitchen. Denise watched as water poured over the edge of the clogged gutters outside the window.

She took a bite of the whipped-cream-covered brownie and closed her eyes. "Yum . . . This is so good."

Taking a sip of tea, Denise read the recipe card for meatballs Heidi had given Kassidy today. She turned it over. Sure enough, a Bible verse had been written on the back. "'Pray without ceasing.' 1 Thessalonians 5:17." She read the scripture out loud and pondered it a few seconds. *Would God listen to me, even though I'm not a regular churchgoer? Does He care about my marriage, our daughter, the struggles we face? Maybe so. Maybe not. I don't know. We probably should attend church more often.*

Denise finished her brownie and was deliberating about whether to eat another one, when Kassidy rushed into the kitchen, wide-eyed and trembling.

"Kassidy, what's wrong?"

"I just heard on the news that a man got struck by lightning on the golf course—the one near our home. I think it's the place Dad belongs to." She sucked in a breath as beads of perspiration formed on her upper lip. "Oh, Mom, what if it's him who got hurt? People who get hit by lightning can die, you know." She clung to Denise's arm. "I don't want to lose you or Dad, like Jeremy lost his mom."

Denise pulled her daughter close and patted her back. "Calm down, Kassidy. Did the news reporter give the name of the man who was hit?"

"No, but Dad's not home yet, and that's why I think it could have been him."

"If it was, I'm sure we would have received a call." Denise patted the stool next to her. "Take a seat, and I'll get you a brownie with whipped cream and a glass of milk."

Kassidy flopped down and Denise went to get the milk and a brownie, which she set on the bar in front of her daughter.

Kassidy took a few nibbles, and then put the brownie back on the plate. "Are you and Dad gonna separate, like Debbie and Kevin's parents did?"

"Of course not. Why would you ask that?"

"Because I heard you two arguing this morning before we left for class."

"Parents sometimes have disagreements, but it doesn't mean we're going to leave each other." Denise reached for the phone and punched in Greg's cell number. A few seconds later, he answered.

"Hey, I was getting ready to call you. Things got pretty bad on the golf course today when the storm blew in."

"Are you okay?"

"I'm fine, but one of the guys I don't know well was slightly injured while playing golf."

"Oh, my! What happened?"

"Lightning struck a tree close to where he was playing. From what we were told, the man started back to get the clubs he'd left under the tree, and that's when the lightning hit." Greg went on to say that the power of the strike knocked the man to the ground, but other than ringing ears and tingly arms, he wasn't seriously hurt.

"That's good to hear. Kassidy and I were worried about you."

"Well, you can set your concerns aside now, because I'll be home soon."

When Denise hung up, she turned to Kassidy and smiled. "It wasn't your dad who got hurt, and the man who did is going to be okay."

"I'm so glad." Tears pooled in Kassidy's eyes, and she hugged Denise. Maybe today had been a turning point for her daughter. For all of them, really.

Berlin

Miranda couldn't get over Trent's generosity toward Velma and her family. She'd invited him over for supper to spend time with her and the children and as a way of saying thank you for his selfless deed. Although she still wasn't ready to invite Trent to live with them again, Miranda felt as if they might be headed in that direction.

She glanced out the kitchen window. The storm they'd had earlier had died down, but a steady rain continued. Tomorrow, if the sun came out, it would no doubt be humid.

"Well, that's what summer often brings," she murmured, turning on the water to fill the teakettle. At least the yards in the area were nice and green, unlike some years when they didn't get much rain at all.

"Who are ya talkin' to, Mom?" Kevin skipped into the kitchen and tugged on her arm.

Miranda tickled him under his chin. "I was talking to myself."

He giggled. "Do ya answer yourself too?"

"No, but sometimes I'm tempted to."

"Is Daddy still comin' for supper?" Kevin asked.

"Yes, and I'm trying to figure out what to fix. What do you think he would like?"

"Hot dogs and potato chips!" Kevin gave a thumbs-up.

Miranda lifted her gaze to the ceiling. "Tell the truth now, Kevin. Hot dogs and chips is what you'd like to have, not what you think your dad wants, right?"

He moved his head quickly up and down.

"Daddy likes hot dogs too."

"You're right, so maybe if the rain lets up we can sit outside around our portable fire pit and roast hot dogs. We can also have potato chips, and I'll make a yummy macaroni salad to go with it. How's that sound?"

Kevin's smile stretched wide. "Okay!" He turned and started out of the kitchen, but turned back around. "Is Daddy movin' back with us?"

Miranda bit the inside of her cheek. "I don't know, Son—maybe. But not tonight. Your dad and I still have some things we need to work through."

Kevin grabbed her hand and squeezed it. "I'm goin' to tell Debbie the good news."

Miranda shook her head. "Please, Kevin, don't say anything about the possibility of your dad moving back home. I'll tell you both if and when anything is decided."

He looked up at her and grinned. "No worries, Mommy. I was only gonna tell Debbie we're havin' hot dogs tonight." Kevin darted out of the room.

Miranda set the teakettle on the stove and turned on the burner. She hoped things would work out between her and Trent, for it would be difficult to disappoint the children.

Chapter 43

Millersburg

Ellen and Becky had left the grocery store, and were heading to the car, when Becky stopped walking and clasped her mother's arm. "I can't quit thinkin' about something, Mom."

"What is it, honey?"

"During the last cooking class, Jeremy was talking about how his mom died, and it was really sad. It got me to thinking about the woman who'd given birth to me. I keep wondering if she's alive, and if so, where does she live?"

Ellen moistened her lips. "Let's talk about this in the car."

"Okay."

Once the groceries were put in the trunk, and Becky was seated in the back seat, Ellen slid in next to her. This was the first time Becky had brought up the topic of her birth mother since learning she'd been adopted.

Ellen reached for Becky's hand. "There are usually ways for a person to locate their birth parents, and as I've mentioned before, when you

442

are older and ready to do that, I'll help you with it."

"Thanks, Mom." Becky squeezed Ellen's fingers. "Even if I do find my birth mother, you'll always be my mom."

Ellen swallowed hard. "And you, sweet Becky, will always be my daughter."

Walnut Creek

"I still can't believe this beauty is ours. Sure never figured someone we don't know would up and give us a car." Hank tapped the steering wheel of their secondhand vehicle, then ran his hand over the dash. They'd had the car a week already and driven it someplace almost every day since. This morning Velma and Hank went to the grocery store to pick up a few things for Heidi and had just now returned.

Velma looked over at her husband and touched his tattooed arm. "There's something I need to ask you."

"Ask away."

Velma wadded up the tissue she'd pulled from her overalls' pocket—the only pair she had left from before the fire.

Hank's forehead wrinkled. "What's wrong? You look so serious all of a sudden."

"I'm kinda nervous."

"Whatcha got to be nervous about?"

"The question I'm about to ask."

He swatted her arm playfully. "Never had any problems askin' me questions before."

"This is different. You might not like what I'm about to say."

He grabbed hold of her hand. "For heaven's sakes, woman, just tell me what's on your mind."

She drew a quick breath, hoping to calm the fluttering in her chest. "It's about my folks."

"What about them?"

"I'd like to call them, Hank. They need to know about the fire that destroyed our home, and I'd like to ask if they've heard anything from Clem or Bobbie Sue." There, it was out. Velma released a breath of air that lifted the hair off her damp forehead.

Hank rubbed his jaw then moved his hand to the back of his neck. "Guess it would be all right. It's been a long time since you talked to your ma and pa. It's not been fair of me to come between you and your folks."

Releasing her hand from his grasp, Velma sagged against the seat, pressing both palms against her cheeks. "Thank you, Hank. Think I'll go out to the Troyers' phone shed and make a call to my mama right now."

"Okay, and while you're doin' that, I'll haul the groceries in, and see if Randy and Marsha wanna go with me, Eddie, and Peggy Ann to our place to feed and water the chickens."

"Sounds good. I'm betting the kids will be eager to help." She grinned. "Randy never has to be reminded to care for his chickens. Heidi and Lyle are doin' a good job raising him and his sister."

"Yeah. They're sure cute kids, and polite too. They've had a lot to deal with in their young lives. Let's hope when Marsha and Randy get older they don't decide to up and run off the way our two oldest did."

Velma shook her head. "I'm sure they won't. Heidi and Lyle love those kids, and they're raising them well. Teachin' them all about God too." She opened the car door. "Well, I'd best get on out to the phone shed. I'll let ya know later what my mama has to say." Velma hopped out. Truth was, she could have stayed here all day talking with Hank. But things needed to be done—beginning with a long-overdue phone call to Kentucky.

Velma entered the small wooden building and took a seat on the folding chair. Her fingers tingled as she picked up the receiver. *What if Mama doesn't want to talk to me? What if she hangs up the phone as soon as she hears my voice?* They'd had a pretty nasty argument with Velma's parents before moving to Ohio, so a reconciliation might not be possible.

"Well, ya won't know till ya try," Velma

muttered. She punched in her folk's number and held her breath.

"Hello."

"Mama, it's me, Velma."

Silence.

"Did ya hear what I said?"

"Yeah. Never thought I'd hear a peep outa you again."

Velma's left knee bounced uncontrollably. She placed her free hand on it and pressed hard. "I wanted to let you know that our place here in Walnut Creek caught fire, and it burned to the ground."

"Oh, my! Is everyone all right? Are you okay, Velma?"

"Yeah, I'm fine. Hank wasn't home when it happened, but thanks to the firemen, me and the kids got out okay. Except for breathin' in a lot of smoke, all three of us, and even our dog, were fine."

"That's a relief." Her mother paused. "By the way, how are those youngsters doing these days?"

"Eddie and Peggy Ann are good."

Velma explained about the cooking class and how she'd been doing some chores for Heidi to pay for Peggy Ann's lessons.

"If you need any help financially, all ya have to do is ask," her mom offered.

"I appreciate that, Mama, but thanks to the

help of some people in the area, we're managing. Losing everything in the fire was horrible, but some positive things happened because of it."

"Good to hear. So, where are ya staying?"

"Heidi, the Amish lady who teaches the cooking class, and her husband, Lyle, took us in. Some other Amish folks from the community are gonna help build us a new house. The community support's been amazing."

Velma went on to tell about the car they'd been given, and then brought up the subject of Bobbie Sue and Clem. "Have ya seen or heard anything from either of them?"

"As a matter of fact, Clem called a few months ago. He joined the army and is stationed at Fort Polk, Louisiana."

"Is he doin all right?" Velma's voice trembled a bit.

"Seems to be."

"What about Bobbie Sue? Do you know where she is?"

"Sure do. That girl's sittin' right here at my kitchen table." Another pause. "She and that creepy boyfriend broke up, so she came here, askin' if she could live with us."

"So they didn't get married?"

"Nope. Bobbie Sue got a job as a waitress at a place not far from here. Seems to like it there."

"Can I talk to her?"

"Sure, but first, there's somethin' I wanna say."

447

"What is it, Mama?"

"Just wanted to say I'm sorry for all the hurtful things me and your pa said about Hank before you all moved. It was wrong of us to drive a wedge between you and your man. Hank was your choice for a husband, and we should have accepted it and welcomed him into the family instead of pointing out his faults. Had we done right from the start, you'd still be livin' here and not in Ohio among strangers."

"Heidi and Lyle have become our friends, Mama. But you're correct. Had it not been for the things said about Hank, and even to his face, we'd most likely have stayed put." Velma opened the door of the phone shed a crack and drew a deep breath. "I'm sorry for my part in the blowup we had with you and Papa before we moved."

"All's forgiven. It's in the past. So, do ya think ya might ever come back? You'd be welcome."

"Maybe for a visit, but we like the area here, and we're settling in."

"That's important, Velma. I'm glad every-thing's workin' out for you." Velma heard her mother blow her nose. "We'll look forward to you comin' to see us, and hopefully that won't be too long."

"Maybe once we get the house built we can make the trip." Velma doodled on the writing tablet next to the phone as she thought about a verse her grandma had taught her when she was a girl. She couldn't remember where it was found in the Bible, but knew what it said: "Honour thy father and mother; which is the first commandment with promise." By making this phone call, and apologizing, Velma felt that she had honored her mother, even in some small way.

"I'm ready to talk to Bobbie Sue now," she said.

"Okay, sure. Take care now, ya hear?"

"You too, Mama."

Velma's knee started twitching again. She hoped she wouldn't mess up and say something to aggravate her daughter.

"Hi, Mama." Bobbie Sue's voice sounded far away—like she might be holding the receiver away from her ear.

"It's good to hear your voice, Daughter. I'm glad you're okay and are livin' with my folks. I've been worried about you."

"What about Dad? Has he been worried too?"

Velma shifted on the chair. "I'm sure he has. You know how things are. Your dad don't talk about things the way I do."

"Yeah, well I've been worried about you, too, but scared to reach out. Figured you'd be plenty miffed with me for leavin' like I did."

Velma was tempted to ask Bobbie Sue to come back to Ohio, but thought better of it. She was obviously content to live with her grandparents, and if she came back to Ohio, there might be conflict again. "Bobbie Sue, we all make mistakes. I sure know that. But the good part about mistakes is you can learn from 'em."

"I've had my eyes opened," Bobbie Sue admitted. Then she changed the subject. "How are things going there, Mama? Is everyone okay?"

"We are now, but . . . Well, your grandma can fill you in. I told her all the details of what's been happening with us."

"Okay."

They talked until Bobbie Sue said she had to hang up and get ready for work.

"All right then, I'll let ya go for now, but let's not be strangers. We need to talk now and then."

"I'm fine with that. Oh, before I go, would ya give my love to Papa, and also to my little brother and sister. I kinda miss them sassing me."

Velma chuckled. "I'll be sure and give 'em the message. They'll both be glad I talked to you. They miss their big sister too."

"I miss them too."

When she hung up the phone, Velma noticed the light blinking on the answering machine. No doubt, the Troyers had several messages. Since it wasn't her place to check them, she left the phone shed and headed for the house to tell Heidi about her call home, and also mention the blinking light.

Chapter 44

Heidi hummed as she dusted the living-room end tables. It was amazing how quickly a film of dirt could develop when the windows were open during the hot summer months. August would be over soon, though, and then fall would be on its way, with cooler days and chilly nights, which she found most welcome. It would certainly be a pleasant change from the sticky humidity that came after the summer rains.

Heidi thought about Randy, and how he would be starting first grade the week after next. For sure, it would be an adjustment for him. But he was a smart little boy, and Heidi felt confident he would do well in school.

She stopped humming and turned toward the door when Velma stepped in. "Did Hank bring all the groceries in?" Velma asked.

"Yes, and they're all put away."

Velma snapped her fingers. "Sorry, I shoulda been here to help with that. I went to the phone shed to call my mom."

Heidi nodded. "Hank mentioned it. How did things go? If you don't mind me asking, that is."

"Don't mind a bit."

Velma took a seat in the rocker, and Heidi seated herself on the couch across from her. She sat quietly, waiting for Velma to speak.

"It went better than I expected. Mama and I had a good talk. And guess what?" Velma grinned. "Bobbie Sue was there, and I got to talk to her too."

"I'm glad. Is she staying with your folks?"

"Yeah." Velma let her head fall against the back of the chair. "Bobbie Sue broke up with her good-for-nothing boyfriend, and she's got a job at a restaurant near my folks' house. I'm sure glad she's all right. Oh, and Mama said they've heard from our oldest boy. Guess Clem joined the army."

Heidi smiled. "It must be a relief to know your children are safe and doing okay."

"You got that right. After everything we went through with those two, it sounds like they are going down a better path in life—one they've chosen on their own. Guess it's good to let kids learn from their own mistakes rather than tryin' to make 'em do something you think they should do. That causes resentment and rebellion—at least in our case it did."

Velma closed her eyes and rocked silently for a few minutes, but then her eyes snapped open, and she sat up straight. "Whoa! I better not get too comfy here or I'll be out like a light."

"Maybe you should go up to the guest room and take a nap," Heidi suggested.

"No way." Velma stood. "I need to get busy doin' something. So what have ya got for me?"

Heidi straightened her headscarf, which she wore whenever she worked around the house and didn't want her white covering to get soiled. "Let's see now . . . You could go out to the garden and see if any of the produce needs to be picked. I'm fairly sure more string beans are ready. We got a lot the last time we picked them, and it looked like more were on the way."

"No problem. I'll get to it right now." Velma started for the door, but turned back around. "Oh, I almost forgot . . . When I was makin' the call to my mom, I noticed the light on your answering machine was blinking. Figured you'd probably like to know, so you can check the messages."

"Actually, Lyle checked early this morning, before he left for the auction he's in charge of today. There's probably no reason for me to check it again until sometime this evening."

"Okay." Velma turned and grasped the door handle. "I'm heading outside now. Give a holler if you need me for anything."

Dover

When Darren entered the house, carrying a black-and-white puppy, Jeremy jumped off the couch. "Wow, Dad, where'd ya get the mutt?"

"It's not a mutt." Darren stroked the dog's silky ears. "As near as I can tell, this is a cockapoo."

Jeremy tipped his head. "What's a cockapoo?"

"Part cocker spaniel, and part poodle."

"Oh." Jeremy didn't show much enthusiasm.

Darren lifted the whimpering pup and held it out to his son. "She's a cute little thing, isn't she?"

"I guess so, but why'd you bring the dog here?"

"I rescued her earlier this morning from an abandoned building close to one that had caught fire. Poor little thing was so scared she was shaking all over when I found her."

"Wonder what happened to its mommy." Jeremy stroked the dog's head.

"I'm not sure, but she was nowhere around, and this was the only puppy in the building. Now you understand why I couldn't leave it there." Darren rubbed the puppy's nose and it started chewing on his finger. "Looks like this little gal is hungry. How about we go warm up some milk?"

"Okay, but what are you gonna do with her?"

"Thought maybe we could give her a home here."

Jeremy held up his hand. "No way, Dad! Bacon would have a fit if we brought another dog into our home. He hid under my bed the night we brought Velma's dog home, and he didn't come out till we took the black Lab to Heidi's place the next day."

"True. Guess I'll take the pup with us to Heidi's next Saturday and see if any of the kids would like her."

"But that's a whole week away. What are we supposed to do with her till then?"

"Good question." Darren snickered when the puppy licked his ear. "Do you think Bacon could deal with the pup for a week? We could keep her in the utility room at night, and outside in our fenced yard during the day."

Jeremy shrugged. "It might be okay, but what happens if none of the kids from the cooking class want a puppy?"

"I'll deal with it then." Darren shifted the pup in his arms. "Where's Mrs. Larsen?"

Jeremy nodded with his head in the direction of the kitchen. "She's baking cookies again."

"I should have guessed." Darren sniffed the air. "I'll go show her the pup. Maybe she'd like a dog to take home."

Canton

Denise and Greg sat on chairs inside their screened-in patio, sipping lemonade. The overhead fan rotated on medium, keeping it comfortable, despite the outside heat.

"It was nice going for ice cream after lunch, Greg." Denise looked at her husband, feeling a tenderness she hadn't felt in a while. "I can't remember when we last did something fun as a family, or when an ice-cream cone tasted so good."

"It's my fault for not taking the time to be with you and Kassidy more." Greg rubbed his thumb over a brow. "We're going to do more of that from now on." He looked toward the door leading into the dining room. "By the way, where is our daughter?"

"She's on the phone, telling Hillary about our outing today." Denise shook her head. "I have to tell you, Greg, our daughter was more excited about spending time with us today, than about all those niceties we've given her over the years."

"Objects don't give or show your love, that's for sure." Greg took a deep breath. "I'll tell you something else. Last week, when the lightning struck close to that guy at the golf course, I had an epiphany."

"What do you mean?"

"I realized how quickly someone's life can change." Greg snapped his fingers. "Lightning could have struck me, and it may have turned out far worse than it did for that man. Imagining you and Kassidy having to fend for yourselves really put a scare into me."

"Last Saturday was an eye-opener." Denise inhaled sharply. "Even for Kassidy."

"Really?" Greg cocked his head. "But you're right. I have noticed a difference this week in our daughter's attitude. What has changed?"

"During the cooking class last Saturday, I overheard the kids talking in the kitchen while we parents waited in the dining room. And then later, Kassidy told me she heard one of the boys tell how his mother had died from cancer. Kassidy was quiet the whole time Jeremy told how he has to have a babysitter whenever his dad has to work. Jeremy also said he missed his mom, and it's hard for his dad to do everything."

"Wow, imagine our daughter learning a lesson from another kid."

"Yes, it certainly wasn't planned. And coming from someone who has had a huge loss in his life made her think what it would be like if something happened to one of us. In fact, when she heard about the lightning strike on the news, she was highly upset and feared it was you. You can only imagine how relieved we both were when I called and you answered the phone."

"I was a bit nervous myself," he said. "Just thinking about you driving home from class in that terrible weather had me on edge."

"Thank the Lord, we are all okay." Denise placed her hand on her husband's arm and gently squeezed it.

"You know, this is nice sitting out here, just the two of us, talking. I need to stay home more instead of playing golf so often. I still have my work, of course, and so do you, but when we have free time, we're going to spend it as a family. Besides, I have a lot of catching up to do around our property—especially taking care of those gutters."

Denise clinked her glass against Greg's before they took another sip of lemonade. She almost felt like a young woman again who'd been kissed for the first time.

Walnut Creek

Heidi put a kettle of freshly snapped beans on the stove. They would go well with the ham and potatoes baking in the oven for supper. Having the oven on had heated up the kitchen, so they would eat their meal outside this evening.

Heidi was about to light the gas burner but decided to hold off a bit, since Lyle wasn't home yet. After working in the garden several hours, Velma had gone to take a shower, and Hank was in the living room, keeping all four kids entertained. That was evidenced by the giggles coming from the other room.

Think I'll go out and check for phone messages. There might be something from our lawyer or the social worker about the adoption proceedings.

Heidi dried her damp hands on a paper towel and scooted out the back door. As she approached the phone shed, Rusty ran across the driveway in front of her. She jerked to one side, nearly losing her balance.

"Rusty, you scared me." She shook her finger at him.

Arf! Arf! The dog ran around her in circles, and then dropped at her feet, looking up at Heidi with his big brown eyes.

She paused and bent down to pet him. "So you need some attention, do you? Where's your new friend, Abner?"

Woof!

Heidi laughed and looked toward the shade tree in the backyard where Velma's dog was stretched out. "That's what I thought. You played him out, huh?" She gave Rusty a few more pats, then continued on her trek to the phone shed.

Once inside, she closed the door so her dog wouldn't follow. It was hot and stuffy inside, so she would hurry and jot down any messages she found.

Heidi took a seat and punched the button to retrieve the first message.

"Hello, Mr. and Mrs. Troyer. This is Gail Saunders, and I have some unexpected news to share with you."

Heidi leaned forward, eager to hear what the social worker had to say. *Please let it be about the adoption. It would be wonderful to have some good news to share with Lyle when he gets home.*

"I know this may come as a surprise, because it

did to me, but Randy and Marsha's grandfather has contacted the agency. Mr. Olsen wants to see the children as soon as possible, so . . ." Gail's voice was cut off. Apparently Lyle hadn't deleted enough messages this morning, and now their voice mail was full.

Heidi brought a shaky hand up to her head, where she felt the beat of her heart in her temples. *How could this be? We were told the children had no living relatives. Who is this man who says he's their grandfather, and why has he come forth now after all these months?*

Heidi released an uncontrollable whimper. *Oh, no . . . He's come to take the children away from us.* Tearfully, she bent into the excruciating pain. *Dear Lord, what are we going to do?*

Chapter 45

Heidi spent the next hour fixing supper and keeping her ear tuned for a car that might pull into their yard. She could only imagine what it would be like when the children's grandfather showed up and demanded that Randy and Marsha go with him. She hadn't returned the social worker's call, fearful of what she would say. But if he was coming to see the children, Heidi needed to know when it would be so she could prepare them.

Heidi looked up at the clock on the far wall. It was too late to call Gail now. She would have already left her office for the day.

She rubbed the bridge of her nose, trying to clear her thoughts. Since this was Saturday, Gail might not have been in her office at all when she made the call. Did she call yesterday, and somehow Lyle missed the message when he'd gone to the phone shed this morning? So many jumbled and conflicting thoughts raced through Heidi's mind. It was hard to concentrate on anything else.

She glanced out the kitchen window. *I hope Lyle gets here soon. I need to talk to him about this before we say anything to the children.* Heidi held her arms tightly against her sides. She feared that she and Lyle were about to suffer yet another shattering disappointment. *Why would God allow something like this? Doesn't He care how much we love Marsha and Randy?*

"Are you okay, Heidi?" Velma asked when she entered the kitchen. "Your face is the color of fresh-fallen snow."

"I . . . I . . ." Heidi stuttered. *Should I tell her, or wait until I know something more?*

Velma rushed forward and slipped her arm around Heidi's waist. "You look like you're about to pass out. Why don't ya sit down?" She pulled out a chair at the table and guided Heidi to the seat.

"Where are the children?" Heidi asked.

Velma took a peek into the living room, then quietly returned to the kitchen. "Hank must have played them out. All four kids are sound asleep, and Hank's snorin' away in the rocking chair." Velma rubbed Heidi's arm. "Now what has you so upset?"

A moan escaped Heidi's lips as she answered quietly. "We may lose Randy and Marsha."

Eyebrows raised, Velma took the chair beside Heidi. "What do you mean?"

With a desperate need to tell someone, Heidi told Velma about the social worker's message. She sniffed back tears threatening to spill over.

"I can't believe this is happening to us. We were told the children had no living relatives." Heidi paused to pick up a napkin and blow her nose. "If this man Gail Saunders spoke of is truly the children's grandfather, then where has he been all this time, and why did he wait till now to come forward?"

"I—I don't know. It makes no sense to me."

"I'm not sure what I'll do if we lose Randy and Marsha. I love them so much, and Lyle and I have been looking forward to adopting them." Heidi nearly choked on the sob rising in her throat.

Velma stroked Heidi's forearm with a gentle touch. "Maybe the man isn't really their grandpa. He could be an imposter tryin' to steal their inheritance."

"There is no inheritance." Heidi shook her head. "From what we were told, the children's parents barely had enough insurance for burial expenses. And the money they had in the bank was meager. Basically, they were living from paycheck to paycheck."

"Did they own a house and a car?"

"No house. They were renting. They did have a car, but it was totaled when they were hit by another vehicle." Heidi sat quietly for a few seconds, staring at the table. "If the man is really the children's grandfather, his interest in them would not be for any money he might receive."

She stood and moved over to the stove to check

on the ham. "Please don't say anything about this to Randy and Marsha, or even Lyle. I'll discuss this with him, of course, but not until after the children have gone to bed. Lyle and I need time to talk this through and decide the best way to tell them."

Velma's head moved back and forth. "Don't worry, Heidi. I won't say a word."

Millersburg

The doorbell rang, and Ellen took one last look in the hall mirror to make sure she looked okay. Opening the front door, she put on her best smile. Darren looked so handsome there on the porch, holding a bottle of sparkling cider. Jeremy stood beside his father, wearing a cheerful smile.

"It's nice to see you both. I'm glad you could come for supper this evening."

Darren grinned and handed her the bottle. "We're glad you invited us." He looked at Jeremy. "My son gets tired of his dad's bland cooking."

She laughed. "Come on in."

They followed Ellen into the living room. She smiled when Jeremy flopped down on the couch beside Becky. There had been a day when those two would never have sat beside each other.

"What's new with you?" Jeremy asked, looking at Becky.

"Nothing much. How 'bout you?"

"My dad brought home an abandoned pup, but we're not gonna keep the mutt, since we already have a dog." Jeremy bumped Becky's arm. "Say, how'd ya like to have a dog? You don't have any pets, right?"

"Actually, we do," Ellen spoke up. "We got a cat last week, and most cats and dogs don't get along very well, so we'll have to pass on the pup."

"We went to the pound and got a cat that needed a good home," Becky explained.

Just then the pretty calico entered the room and meowed.

"There she is now." Ellen pointed. "Guess she heard us talking about her."

"What did you name the cat?" Jeremy asked.

"We call her Callie." Becky giggled when the cat walked over and rubbed against her leg.

Jeremy looked up at his dad. "Guess there's not much point in takin' the cockapoo to the cooking class next week. Peggy Ann and Eddie already have a dog, and so do Randy and Marsha." Jeremy tapped his chin. "Come to think of it, Debbie and Kevin told me one time after class that they have a dog named Blondie."

"Theoretically, Rusty is the Troyers' dog, but since Marsha and Randy live with them, I guess they figure the dog is theirs too," Darren interjected. "Anyway, there's still Kassidy to ask. She might be happy to take the puppy."

Becky's nose scrunched up as she shook her head. "I wouldn't even bother asking her. She's too snooty and prissy to take care of a pet."

"Be nice, Becky," Ellen warned. "You don't know Kassidy well enough to make a judgment about what she would or would not do."

"Your mom's right," Darren put in. "So it won't hurt for me to ask." He leaned close to Ellen and stroked her arm, sending shivers up her neck. "Now lead the way to the kitchen, and I'll help you get supper on the table."

"Thank you." Ellen smiled. *What a thoughtful man. I'm glad you came into my life when you did.*

Berlin

"Sure am glad you and the kids were free this evening. I've wanted to take you all out for a picnic supper, and this is the perfect night." Trent looked over at Miranda and smiled.

"Yes, it's a beautiful evening." Miranda waited until the kids were in the back, along with their dog, and then she slid into the passenger's seat. Unconsciously, she reached over and took his hand. "I know I've said this before, but I'm so pleased that you gave the Kimballs a car they so desperately needed." She gently squeezed his fingers. "I'm proud to be your wife."

He leaned closer and whispered in Miranda's ear. "Does that mean what I hope it does?"

She nodded slowly. "I'd like you to move back in with us whenever you're ready."

"Is tonight too soon?" His eyes glistened.

"Tonight would be fine. When the picnic is over, we can stop by your apartment for a few of your things. The rest you can bring home at your convenience."

Trent turned and looked in the back seat. "Did ya hear that, kids? Your dad's coming home."

Debbie and Kevin clapped their hands and shouted, "Hooray!"

As though not wanting to be left out, Blondie joined in with a few excited barks.

Trent pulled Miranda into his arms and kissed her tenderly. When the kiss ended, he looked into her eyes and said, "I can't promise to be the perfect husband, but I will always try to do my best. And I'll go to church with you, and study the Bible on my own, because I want to be the kind of husband and father you and the kids deserve."

Walnut Creek

As Heidi sat at the picnic table during supper, she could barely eat anything. She stared at the slice of ham next to the few green beans she'd put on her plate, and as her thoughts took her to the message she'd listened to earlier today, her fear and insecurity increased.

Lyle must have sensed something, for he looked over at Heidi and pointed to her plate. "You've barely touched a thing. Aren't you *hungrich* this evening? Or is the oppressive heat we've had lately getting to you?"

"A little of both, I guess." She wanted to blurt out the real reason for her loss of appetite but was committed to waiting until the children were in bed before she told Lyle about Gail's message.

"Well, the heat hasn't hurt my appetite any. I'm hungry as a mule!" Hank reached for a second baked potato and slathered it with butter and plenty of sour cream. "You're married to one fine cook." He grinned at Lyle.

Lyle smiled back at him. "You're right. That's why Heidi's the perfect woman to teach others how to cook."

Normally, Heidi would have blushed at the compliment, but this evening she felt so flustered, all she could manage was a quick, "Danki."

She continued to pick at her food, only half listening to the conversation going on around her.

Everyone had finished eating, and Heidi was getting ready to clear the dishes, when a car pulled into the yard. Her mouth went dry. It was the same vehicle she'd seen parked across the road and again at the end of their driveway. When a short man with silver-gray hair got out and started walking toward them, her adrenaline spiked. Could it be him? Was this man Marsha and Randy's grandfather?

With fists clenched so hard her nails bit into her palms, Heidi sat rigidly waiting for him to approach.

"Good evening, folks. I'm sorry to barge in like this unannounced, but I'd like to talk to you." He walked up to Lyle and extended his hand. "I'm Gerald Olsen, and I understand that my grandchildren live with you."

Heidi's stomach clenched, and her mouth felt so dry she had trouble swallowing. This was like reliving the nightmare she'd had several weeks ago. Her precious foster children were about to be snatched away, and she was powerless to stop it from happening. *I should have told Lyle about the phone message when he first got home. We could have prepared Randy and Marsha for this.*

Gerald looked at each of the children who sat at the picnic table. Then his gaze came to rest on Marsha. "You have to be Judy's daughter. Same color hair . . . same blue eyes." He gestured toward Randy. "And you must be my son's boy. You look so much like Fred when he was about your age."

Randy and Marsha looked up at the stranger with fear in their eyes. If they'd ever met the man, they obviously didn't recognize him.

Lyle's eyes narrowed. "Is this some kind of

a joke? We were told that the children had no living relatives."

Gerald shook his head. "It's not a joke. My son was their father. When he ran off and married his high school sweetheart, my wife, Maggie, and I lost all contact with them." He paused and drew in a breath. "After Maggie died, I moved to Europe to pursue my desire to write."

Heidi glanced at Velma, needing some support. Velma reached over and touched Heidi's arm.

"I came back to the States a few months ago and decided to see if I could locate my son. When I hit a brick wall, I hired a detective, and he found out about the accident that killed Fred and Judy. He also found out they had a couple of kids and that they'd become wards of the state until an Amish couple took them in." Gerald looked at Heidi, then turned his gaze on Lyle again. "I'm guessing that'd be you and your wife."

With a pained expression, Lyle nodded. He, too, must be realizing what was about to happen. Heidi rose from the bench she sat upon and moved toward Gerald. "I listened to a phone message from our social worker this afternoon, saying that you wanted to see the children. But I had no idea it would be this soon or that you would come here without calling first."

He nodded. "Yes, I've spoken to her. I had to go through quite an ordeal to prove who I was."

"I can't believe any social worker worth her

salt would give out someone's address and let you come here unannounced." Hank eyed Gerald suspiciously. "Are you on the level?"

"I most certainly am." He focused on Lyle. "And the social worker did not give me this address. I got it from the detective I hired." Gerald stood with his arms folded, staring at the children with a look of longing.

Heidi's hands fluttered as she spoke in an emotion-choked voice. "Please don't take them from us, Mr. Olsen. My husband and I love Randy and Marsha so much, and we're on the verge of adopting them."

"You're gonna adopt us?" Randy leaped off his bench and ran up to Heidi.

She gently patted his head. "Yes, we have been trying to do that but didn't want to tell you until we got the word that it was about to become official."

Marsha left her seat too, and darted up to Lyle. Looking up at him, her chin trembled. "We don't know this man. Please, don't let him take us."

Before either Heidi or Lyle could say anything, Gerald spoke again. "You little ones have nothing to worry about. I'm not here to steal you away from people you obviously love." Gerald tweaked Marsha's nose. "And I can see they love you very much too. I just wanted to connect with my grandchildren, and if possible, have some sort of relationship with them." He stopped talking and swallowed so hard, Heidi saw his Adam's apple bob. "I won't stand in the way of the adoption. I'm just happy my son's children have found a good home and will be raised by nice people who will love them the way they deserve."

Struggling to find the right words, Heidi took hold of the man's hand and shook it. "Thank you, Mr. Olsen. Thank you, ever so much."

Bobbing his head, Lyle moved over to stand beside them. "Why don't you join us for dessert, Gerald? We'd like the opportunity to get acquainted, and I'm sure the children would too."

Tears welled in the older man's eyes. "I'd enjoy that very much."

Heidi looked upward and prayed silently, *Thank You, Lord, for answering my prayer.*

Chapter 46

As Heidi set out the ingredients for her final cooking class, she felt like she was walking on air. The past week had been so exciting. She was anxious to share it with her young students and their parents this morning. Heidi would be teaching them to make surprise muffins, and what she had to share was most certainly a surprise. "The Lord works in mysterious ways," Heidi murmured.

"Is that from the Bible?" Velma asked, joining Heidi at the table, where she'd placed the children's recipe cards.

"No, it's not; although folks often quote it as though it's a verse of scripture. Those words are actually from a hymn written in the nineteenth century by a man named William Cowper." Heidi smiled. "We often pray for things and then are surprised when God answers in ways we never expected."

"I know exactly what ya mean." Velma nodded enthusiastically. "Never in a million years did I expect someone would give us a new car or that so many people, including you and Lyle, would be so generous toward us. The fire was terrible, but so many positive deeds have come about because of it. And did I tell you? When Hank came back from our place the other day, he handed me my grandma's Bible. Said he found it lying on top of the chicken coop. How it got there I don't know. Maybe one of the construction workers found it in the rubble."

Heidi's smile widened. "You are so right. See what I mean about the Lord working in mysterious ways? I was beside myself with worry after I got the phone message from Gail. My mind went in a totally different direction than how it turned out. I certainly didn't expect Randy and Marsha's grandpa to show up and say he was happy the children were with us. And I'm sure you were equally surprised when your grandma's Bible was found."

"Yes, most definitely." Velma moved toward the window. "I hear a vehicle pulling in. Yep, it's Darren's rig. He just got out and he's holdin' a puppy, of all things."

Heidi joined Velma at the window. Sure enough, Darren held a black-and-white ball of fluff.

"I wonder why he brought a dog with him today." Velma grunted. "Thanks to Abner being here, you already have two mutts runnin' around your place."

"I'll go out and talk to him. There must be a good reason he brought the dog." Heidi opened the back door and stepped outside, then popped her head back in. "Velma, I hope you are going to join us today for class, since it's the last one."

"Yep, I'd love to."

When Darren saw Heidi coming toward him with eyebrows squished together, he began to have second thoughts. *Maybe I shouldn't have brought the pup here today. She might not appreciate having another dog running around the place. If it weren't so hot I'd leave the pup in my vehicle.*

Darren glanced over at Jeremy, who was kneeling on the ground, petting Heidi's dog, Rusty. Then Velma's black Lab showed up and pawed at Darren's leg. The pup got all excited and tried to wiggle out of his arms. *Oh, great. This probably was a mistake.*

"Good morning, Darren." Heidi tipped her head up to look at him. "Oh, how cute. Where did you get the puppy?"

As Heidi reached out to pet the dog's head, Darren explained how he'd found the pup, and then added, "I brought her with me today, hoping Kassidy or one of the other kids might want to adopt her." He looked at the other two dogs and shook his head. "But it wouldn't be good to let her run loose in your yard during the class."

"It could get a bit chaotic." Heidi pointed to the barn. "Why don't you put her in there for now? After class, you can bring the puppy out and see if anyone would like to take her home."

"Good idea. If you'd like to lead the way, you can show me where in the barn I should put her."

"Okay, but would you mind if I hold the puppy?"

"Course not." Darren could see Heidi had a soft spot for the cockapoo. He laughed along with her when the puppy licked her face.

"You're such a cute little thing. I wish I could keep you, but hopefully you will find a good home soon." Heidi repositioned the puppy in her arms and looked toward Jeremy, who now had the Lab and the Brittany spaniel vying for his attention. "When you've had enough of their friendly greetings, you can go on up to the house," she told him. "Randy, Marsha, and Peggy Ann are waiting inside."

"Where's Eddie? Will he be joining us today?" Jeremy asked.

"He went fishing with his dad early this morning."

Jeremy looked up at Darren. "When are we goin' fishing again, Dad? You can invite Becky and her mom if you want to."

Darren grinned. It was good to see his son had accepted them. If things should work out and Ellen was to become his wife, he felt sure Jeremy would be okay with it now. Becky, too, for that matter. It was too soon to bring up the subject of marriage to Ellen, but he'd sure be thinking about it.

Once all her students had arrived and everyone sat around the kitchen table, Heidi explained that they would be making surprise muffins. The children were all ears as they listened to her directions. There seemed to be excitement in the air this morning. What surprised her most was Kassidy. Instead of the defiant look she usually had, the girl looked happy. *I wonder what happened in the last two weeks to bring about this change.*

"What about the muffins are a surprise?" Debbie wanted to know.

"We will be putting a small amount of jelly in the center of them before they're baked," Heidi explained. "And when someone, like your parents—who are sitting in the dining room again—eat a muffin, they'll discover the little surprise."

Marsha grinned and bounced on her chair. "I like surprises!"

"Who doesn't?" Jeremy put in.

The other children nodded in agreement.

"I can't wait to make these for my dad," Kassidy said. "He loves most kinds of jelly, and will be surprised when he bites into a muffin."

Heidi smiled. "Well, that's good. After these muffins are baked, and we're all eating our treat, I'll share a surprise with you and your parents."

"Bet I know what it is," Randy spoke up.

Heidi put a finger to her lips. "Shh . . ."

"Don't worry. I won't say nothin'."

"Anything," she corrected, then patted his head. "Now, please get busy mixing your muffin batter."

When the muffins were done and had cooled sufficiently, everyone went outside to the picnic table to enjoy the treat.

"This is sure tasty," Denise commented after she'd taken her first bite. "Kassidy, you did a good job making your muffins."

The girl fairly beamed. "Thanks, but keep eating. There's a surprise inside."

Denise took another bite and smiled. "Oh, yum. There's strawberry jam inside."

The other parents enjoyed their treats, too, and everyone agreed that the surprise muffins were a hit.

"Can I say something?" Darren spoke up.

Heidi nodded. "Of course."

"I want you to know that both my son and I have enjoyed your classes. And even though I've neglected to say anything, the verses you included on the back of the recipe cards were an inspiration."

"I agree with Darren," Denise spoke up. "Those scriptures were most helpful."

The other parents nodded their heads as well.

Heidi's cheeks warmed. "Thank you. The idea came to me when I was preparing to teach my very first class, and I've been doing it ever since." She tapped her spoon against her glass of iced tea. "And now, I would like to share my own surprise with all of you."

All heads turned in her direction as she gathered Randy and Marsha to her side. Lyle was there, too, sitting next to Heidi. "My husband and I applied to adopt Marsha and Randy, and yesterday . . ." She paused and looked at Lyle. "Maybe you'd like to share our news."

He shook his head. "That's okay. You go ahead."

Heidi placed her hands on the children's shoulders. "Yesterday we signed the final papers, and the adoption became final. These two special children, whom we love dearly, are now officially Randy and Marsha Troyer."

A round of applause went up, and Miranda shouted, "Congratulations! Such wonderful news."

Randy and Marsha clapped the hardest and hugged their new parents.

Heidi noticed a few women wiping their eyes. The others congratulated them, as well, and when things settled down, Velma spoke up. "I think we should all get together sometime and have a real celebration."

"I'm all for a little celebrating too," a strange voice announced from behind.

Just as Heidi turned around to see who it was, she heard Velma's sharp intake of air.

"Clem! Oh, Clem, what a surprise! I can't believe you're really here."

Heidi's mouth opened as she watched Velma and Peggy Ann rush over to the young man in uniform with outstretched arms.

Heidi glanced around at the others who sat at the picnic table. Ellen held her hand in front of her mouth, and Denise swiped at a tear running down her cheek. Miranda reached in her purse and offered the women a tissue, then she dabbed at her own eyes.

After the emotional greeting, Velma and Peggy Ann returned to the table, clinging to the soldier as if he might disappear.

"This is my oldest son, Clem," Velma announced. "He's in the army, and he told me he came here to be with us while he's on leave."

More clapping transpired and even some stomping of feet. Then Lyle stood up. "Please join us, Clem. Oh, and we have room if you'd like to stay here while you're visiting your folks."

"Thank you, sir. I would be most appreciative of that. I have a lot of catching up to do with my family." Clem pulled his mother close and kissed her cheek.

Velma looked at Heidi and sniffed. "I can't remember when I've been this happy."

"I'm sure I speak for all of us when I say that we're happy for you too."

Everyone nodded in unison. Then Darren stood up. "I have a little surprise also. I'll be right back." He sprinted off toward the barn.

When Darren returned with a squirmy pup, he explained how he'd found her and asked if anyone wanted the dog.

"If it's okay with my mom, I'd like to take the puppy." Kassidy looked at her mother. "I promise to take good care of her."

Denise smiled and nodded. "I think it would be good for you to have a pet."

Kassidy reached for the pup. "Think I'm gonna call her Patches."

"I like that name." Becky moved closer to Kassidy. "Sorry about the fight we had. I lost my temper when you said mean things to Randy, but that was wrong."

"I'm sorry too." Kassidy lifted the pup. "Wanna hold her?"

"Sure." Becky took the puppy and stroked behind its ears. "She's so soft."

Heidi was surprised when Kassidy went over to Randy and apologized for making fun of his chickens.

"Kevin and I have something special to share that happened since we were last here too." Debbie looked over at her mother. "Is it okay if I tell 'em?"

Miranda nodded.

"Our dad's living with us again, and we all went on a picnic supper."

"Yeah, even our dog Blondie came along," Kevin added.

"That's wonderful." Heidi clasped her hands to her chest. It seemed that everyone had cause for celebration today. How thankful she was for the opportunity to teach cooking classes, where she'd met so many wonderful people. She didn't know what the future held, but one thing was for certain: she would thank and praise God on a daily basis, for He had brought her and Lyle so many good things.

Tenderly, she hugged Marsha and Randy. It didn't matter that she wasn't their biological mother. Heidi loved these two children as if they'd always been hers. Someday she might teach another cooking class, but for now, she would simply enjoy being a mother—something she'd been wanting for a long time.

Epilogue

One year later

Heidi laid down the announcement they'd received in today's mail on the table. Kendra and her husband, Brent, who'd gotten married last December, were expecting a baby this coming November. *My namesake, little Heidi, will have a new brother or sister by Christmas.*

Heidi smiled at her own sweet baby, nestled in her arms. One-month-old Laura had come to live with them a few weeks ago, and there was no chance of her being taken away. The adoption had been prearranged so that Heidi and Lyle would take the baby soon after she was born. Now they had three precious children to raise.

Randy had done well during his first year in school and looked forward to starting the second grade. Marsha seemed to enjoy Laura as much as Heidi did, for she hovered around the baby and sang her some silly songs.

Both Randy and Marsha had become fluent in the Pennsylvania Dutch language. *But then,* Heidi reasoned, *children learn more quickly than most adults.*

Laura's eyes fluttered open, then closed again. She was such a good baby—truly a blessing.

More good news had come a few days ago, when Darren, Ellen, Jeremy, and Becky stopped in for a surprise visit. Heidi was pleased when they asked if she and Lyle would attend their wedding in September. This news in itself was cause for a celebration.

Heidi felt certain the Lord had been with her through every cooking class she'd taught. Many people's lives had changed for the better, and she, as well as her students, had made some new friends.

Her gaze came to rest on the Bible, lying on the table beside the rocking chair where she sat. Heidi reflected on Psalm 6:9, the verse that she'd written on the recipe for surprise muffins: "The LORD hath heard my supplication; the LORD will receive my prayer."

Heidi's thumb caressed the baby's soft cheek. Even though she couldn't bear children of her own, God had given Heidi the desire of her heart by allowing her and Lyle to raise three precious children. *Thank You, Lord, for receiving my prayer. May every day with my friends and family feel like a celebration.*

Heidi's Recipes

Fresh Fruit Salad

Ingredients:
6 peaches, peeled, pitted, and chopped
1 pound fresh strawberries, rinsed, hulled, and sliced
½ pound seedless green grapes
½ pound seedless red grapes
3 bananas, peeled and sliced
Juice from one lime
½ cup pineapple juice
1 teaspoon ground ginger

In large serving bowl, combine cut-up fruit. Toss gently. In smaller bowl, whisk together lime and pineapple juices with ginger to make light dressing. Pour dressing over fruit. Toss gently to combine. Cover and chill fruit for half an hour or so before serving.

Mini Corn Dogs

Ingredients:
1⅓ cup flour
⅓ cup cornmeal
1 tablespoon baking powder
1 teaspoon salt
1 tablespoon shortening
3 tablespoons softened butter
¾ cup milk
1 package hot dogs, each hot dog cut in half

In medium bowl, mix dry ingredients with shortening, butter, and milk. Using rolling pin, roll out dough on greased cutting board or mat. Cut circles from the dough. A wide-mouth canning jar lid works fine for this. Place ½ of hot dog on each circle. Bring the sides of the dough up and pinch in the center. Place on greased cookie sheet. Bake at 350 degrees for 12 to 15 minutes.

Strawberry Shortcake

Ingredients:
½ cup sugar
4 tablespoons softened butter
1 egg, beaten
½ cup milk
½ teaspoon vanilla
1½ cups flour
2 teaspoons baking powder
Pinch of salt

In medium bowl, mix cream, sugar, and butter. Add egg, milk, and vanilla. Mix well. Add flour, baking powder, and salt. Mix well. Pour into greased 9-inch pie pan. Bake at 350 degrees for 25 to 30 minutes. Top with fresh strawberries and whipped cream.

Egg-Salad Sandwiches

Ingredients:
3 hard-boiled eggs, chopped
⅛ cup mayonnaise, or more if mixture is
  too dry
¼ teaspoon vinegar
⅛ teaspoon salt
⅛ teaspoon celery salt
1½ teaspoons yellow mustard
1½ teaspoons sugar
⅛ teaspoon onion salt

In medium bowl, mix chopped eggs with all other ingredients, stirring well. Serve on bed of lettuce or make sandwich using fresh bread. A leaf of lettuce, pickles, or sliced olives may be added.

Meatballs

Ingredients:
1 pound ground beef
1 large egg
¼ cup finely chopped onion
⅓ cup old-fashioned oats
¼ cup milk
1 teaspoon Worcestershire sauce
⅛ teaspoon salt
⅛ teaspoon pepper
1 cup tomato sauce or ketchup

Using shortening or coconut oil, grease 13x9x2-inch baking dish. Set aside. Mix ground beef, egg, onion, oats, milk, Worcestershire sauce, salt, and pepper in bowl. Use tablespoon to scoop mixture and shape into 1½-inch balls. Place meatballs in prepared baking dish. Pour tomato sauce or ketchup over meatballs. Bake at 400 degrees for 20 to 25 minutes. Makes about 25 meatballs, depending on size.

Surprise Muffins

Ingredients:
1 egg
1 cup milk
¼ cup cooking oil
2 cups flour
¼ cup sugar
3 teaspoons baking powder
1 teaspoon salt
Strawberry or blueberry jam

Grease bottom of 12 muffin cups or use paper baking cups. In medium bowl, beat egg with fork. Stir in milk and oil. Blend flour and other dry ingredients until mixture is moistened. Batter may be a bit lumpy. Do not overmix. Fill muffin cups half full of batter. Drop scant teaspoonful of jam in center of batter on each muffin cup. Add more batter to fill cup so it's two-thirds full. Bake at 400 degrees for 20 to 25 minutes or until golden brown. Muffins will have gently rounded and pebbled tops. Loosen from pan immediately and remove with spatula. Serve warm or cold. Makes 12 medium muffins. Discovering the jelly inside the baked muffin is the surprise.

Discussion Questions

1. As in the case of the Troyers helping the Kimballs, would you be able to open your home to a family in need without hesitation?

2. Do you think Hank was too harsh on Velma about the accident she'd caused that left them without a car? Why do some people react to bad news in a negative way?

3. Has a tragedy ever brought positive results into your life and made a bad situation better, like the fire did for Velma?

4. Do you think Velma should have neglected her parents because of the disagreement she and her husband had with them?

5. Do you agree with Velma that it's best to let our children learn life's lessons from their own mistakes?

6. Miranda gave Trent a second chance. Would you be willing to do the same when a person

you don't trust is trying to prove they can be trusted?

7. Do you think it is wrong for a couple who is going through an unsettled marriage to use their children as go-betweens or to ask questions about the other spouse the way Trent did?

8. Did Ellen wait too long to tell Becky she was adopted? When is the right time to tell a child about their adoption?

9. Should a parent let their children's influence get in the way of happiness as Darren and Ellen almost did? Would you find it difficult to love again after you've lost your soul mate?

10. How would you handle a child such as Kassidy? Do you think children today are being pacified with too many material objects? Does giving a child a lot of gifts cause them to take important things for granted?

11. Do you think Denise's husband put too much responsibility on her for raising Kassidy? Was it right for Greg to spend so little time with his wife and daughter while he worked long hours at his law firm?

12. How did you feel about Becky standing up for Randy when Kassidy made fun of his chickens? Is there ever a time when it's all right for a child to become physical? What kind of damage can bullying cause a child?

13. In a blazing fire or any situation where it means risking your own life, would you be able to save another person, or even their pet, the way Darren did?

14. After losing a loved one, have you kept a memento that reminds you of them, as Jeremy did with his mother's barrette? How would you feel if you lost that special item?

15. Do you think any of the children or their parents received help from the scriptures Heidi wrote on the back of the recipe cards? Were any of the Bible verses your favorite, and if so, which ones?

16. Which of the characters in this book do you feel changed the most by the end of the story? How did Heidi's influence affect any of these changes?

17. Was it good for the children's parents to attend the cooking class with them, or should

they have dropped their kids off and come back to pick them up after the class?

18. If you had the opportunity to take a cooking class hosted by an Amish woman, what questions might you ask her?

Books are produced in the United States using U.S.-based materials

Books are printed using a revolutionary new process called THINKtech™ that lowers energy usage by 70% and increases overall quality

Books are durable and flexible because of smythe-sewing

Paper is sourced using environmentally responsible foresting methods and the paper is acid-free

Center Point Large Print
600 Brooks Road / PO Box 1
Thorndike, ME 04986-0001 USA

(207) 568-3717

US & Canada:
1 800 929-9108
www.centerpointlargeprint.com